ONCE UPON A DREAM

A MYSTIC BEACH FANTASY ROCKSTAR ROMANCE PREQUEL

AISLINN ARCHER

MYSTIC BEACH PRESS

Paperback: ISBN 979-8-9862117-0-1

First paperback edition May 2022

Cover design by Mystic Beach Press
Front cover original photograph by Ronald Sumners
Back cover original image by Annet Stab

CONTENTS

For my muse.

Content Warning

(Spoilers Ahead!)

This book includes a brief depiction of an emotionally abusive relationship, severe depression and an "off-the-page" suicide; as well as sporadic incidents of bullying and body-shaming; religious discrimination; under-age drinking (sometimes to excess), mild drug use and sexual activities; recreational drinking; loss of a parent; and an incident of questionable consent to minor sexual foreplay (under the influence of alcohol). Scenes of a graphic sexual nature are present throughout, and this book is not recommended for anyone younger than 18.

If any of this content would be disturbing to you, please do not read.

Disclaimer

PROLOGUE

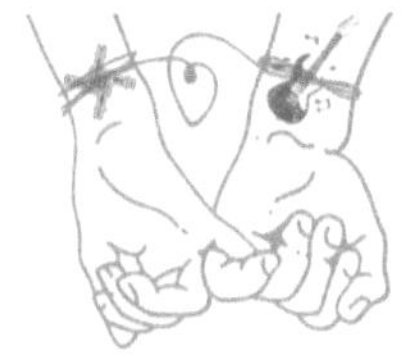

Brighid
Present

The thing about dreams is you rarely know they're just dreams until after you wake up. In the moment, you're there, living another life — maybe someone totally different from who you are when you're awake, maybe the person you really are inside but who you never let anyone else see. But in your dream, you *are* that person, and you live that life, no matter how mundane or how astonishing. Until you wake.

And even then, what your dreams show you doesn't always evaporate like fog on the beach after the sun rises. Sometimes, it leaves its mark on your waking life, whether that's the insight it gives you on your own subconscious or something... more.

I had a dream once. Well, more than one, obviously. But this particular dream — if that's even what it was — changed my life. My real life, and probably a few others. Technically, I guess, it changed millions of lives, because if I hadn't had that dream, hadn't confessed it to my best friend, chances are one of the most popular rock bands on the planet wouldn't even exist. And while that might seem like a trivial thing, I can tell you now that many more lives than mine would be very different if aMUSEd hadn't come together and made their mark on the world.

Music is the medium of dreams, and sometimes of nightmares, and the music of these six musicians tells tales of our collective dreams and nightmares alike. Thankfully, it even made some of those dreams come true.

This first part of our story — it begins with a nightmare. Not my nightmare, though in my heart it felt like it. And I had my own heartaches coming, though even I couldn't have predicted most of it. Some of our dreams came true. Others were dashed. And some that were dashed came true after all, in the end. Some of the things that happened because of my dream, and aMUSEd's music, were literally life-or-death. Others... simply beyond belief.

This is the story of what happened... once upon a dream.

CHAPTER 1

FATHER FIGURE

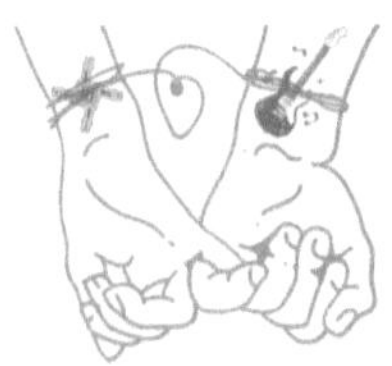

Hunter
Fifteen years ago

"I cannot believe you brought another of your 'girlfriends' back to our home! You promised! Isn't it enough that you can't stay faithful to your wife, but you have to bring your mistresses into our house, while our son is home?"

"I didn't realize Hunter was here! He's usually over at Ellie's house in the afternoons, or at his guitar lessons. I mean, I'm paying for those lessons, so I didn't expect him not to have gone to the one he had today!"

I cringe. It was bad enough walking in on... that... Realizing that Dad gives so little of a shit about me, or what's important to me, that he doesn't have a clue about what I'm doing in most of my spare time, it's just icing on the fecal cake that is today.

"That shows just how little you care about your family, Howard. Hunter switched from the kids' teacher to the one for advanced students. His lessons aren't on Wednesdays anymore — they've been on Thursdays for the last three months."

"Well, how was I supposed to know that? It's not like I can stand listening to that heavy-metal crap he's been playing lately, and he spends the little time he's at home shut up in his room with that guitar you gave him. Like mother, like son..." he adds derisively. And I flinch. Mom's been struggling on the good days lately, and this is clearly anything *but* a good day. She'll stay in bed for a week straight after this, if we're lucky.

"And, really? A two-thousand-dollar guitar for a 14-year-old? As if you haven't spoiled that boy enough with the lessons and the concerts and letting him run wild every summer with that chunky little friend of his when he should be getting a summer job, or at least going to the beach with the rest of his friends so he can see what a real girl looks like!"

My hands clench into fists so tight that even my short fingernails start to cut into my palms. No one talks about my Elle-belle like that. Especially not some smug asshole who can't keep it in his pants and hasn't managed to even stick with the same mistress longer than a few months at a time. Fuming, I head toward the locked door to my bedroom, ready to tell him just that.

"He's 15."

I stop in my tracks. She's right. I am.

"What?"

"He's 15, not 14," Mom says so quietly that I have to strain to hear. "I gave him that two-thousand-dollar Paul Reed Smith guitar for his 15th birthday, which was six months ago."

"Whatever... All the more reason for the boy to be getting a job. He'll be 16 soon. And I'm not spoiling him even more than you already do — I am not buying a 16-year-old a car, and neither are you. He's going to have to earn it on his own."

"He's still a child, Howard. He should be studying or having fun with his friends, or pursuing his music. And you may be able to get away with insulting me for my weight, but Ellie is a perfectly sweet, lovely girl with gorgeous bone structure. She'd be beautiful if she'd just lose ten or fifteen pounds."

I growl to myself. Mom looks great. And Ellie's beautiful right now, just like she is. I hate that even Mom won't treat her with the respect she deserves. She's been my best friend since we were 6, a part of the family, really, and not only does she do something special for me for all my birthdays — the ones Dad can't remember, apparently — but she remembers Mom's birthdays and makes her a handmade card every year.

She used to do the same for Dad, but the last five years or so, she's been avoiding him as much as possible. She won't tell me why, except she said he gives her the creeps sometimes. I've wondered whether five years ago was when he started sleeping around on Mom. Ellie's a good judge of character. Always has been. I hope that's all it was. I don't want to even think of her having walked in on him like I did tonight, especially not at 10.

"He spends too much time with her. At his age, he should be chasing cheerleaders and getting some experience under his belt."

"Howard! That's disgusting!"

I don't know why she expected anything different from him.

"It's the truth! That's what I was doing at his age. Granted, I was on the football team, so I didn't have to chase the cheerleaders — they chased me." He chuckles in a way that turns my stomach.

"But if he keeps spending all of his time with the fat girl, he'll never get cheerleaders chasing him, or any other girls. He'll end up with Ellen Langdon, and she'll spread her legs for him and 'accidentally' get pregnant by a guy who's out of her league, just to tie him down, and then his life will be over!"

It's embarrassment that's making my face red now, not anger. I've known for a while now that Ellie has a crush on me. And I can't deny that a few of the times we've crashed at each other's houses lately, sleeping in the same bed hasn't been entirely as innocent as it was when we were 6 or 8.

We haven't even kissed, which I know some of my guy friends did with girls years ago. But I've woken up hard more than a few times in the last year or so, pressed up against her back with my arms around her, my hand between her breasts, even though we'd fallen asleep innocently side by side. I don't think she noticed, but if she hadn't been fast asleep, I'm not sure how she could have missed that tree branch poking her in her curvy ass. And she smells so good sometimes — well, all the time, really, I just notice it more at some times than others — but I've been leery of damaging our friendship if we took things in that direction and it didn't work out.

I don't want to hurt her. She's had enough guys doing that without even trying to date them. Even the girls are mean to her sometimes. No one says anything mean to her twice, though, at least not when I'm around. I take care of my Elle-belle, and I'm nearing six feet tall, my arms and chest filling out not from time spent in the weight room, like the jocks, but from hours spent every day strumming a guitar, hoping I'll be good enough someday soon to be in a real band with other people who love making music as much as I do. Performing takes stamina, and I'm working on building up enough to do a three-hour set without breathing hard. In the meantime, if it means a look from me gets people to lay off messing with my best friend, all the better.

"Would him ending up with Ellie really be all that bad? She's a good girl. Smart. Loyal. She'll make a great wife and mother, even if she doesn't end up with Hunter."

"My parents told me *you'd* make a great wife and mother, and look where we are now," he says acidly. "If you hadn't had that trust fund, I'd have done the smart thing and played the field during college and bagged myself a cheerleader or a model to go with my varsity jersey and my MBA."

Things get very quiet. Too quiet. I'm suddenly worried about Mom. My hand is on the doorknob when I hear her bedroom door slam down the hall. A few seconds later, I can hear her sobbing.

"Stupid sad cow!" my dad says loudly enough that her sobbing gets even louder. I hear the front door slam shut and the engine of the Corvette that Mom got him for their 15th wedding anniversary revving before it peels out of the driveway.

My hand still sits on the doorknob. I'm torn between wanting to make sure Mom is OK, and wanting to run to Ellie's and climb in her bedroom window so I don't have to face her parents just to feel the comfort of having her arms around me on what is the worst day I can ever remember having.

I swallow and decide to do the right thing, opening the door and walking down the hallway to Mom's bedroom door. I knock lightly.

"Mom? Are you OK? Can I do anything for you?"

She stops sobbing for a moment.

"No, dear. Thank you for offering. I'll be fine," she says just loudly enough for me to hear her without putting my ear to the door. "I think I just need a bath and some rest. Your father won't come back tonight, so we'll have some time for things to cool down again. It'll be fine. Why don't you go spend the night at Ellie's? It'll do you some good to get out of the house. Take some cash out of my purse and order a pizza for the two of you. I'm sorry I'm not up to making dinner for you tonight."

"That's OK, Mom. I can make dinner for you, if you want. Or I can get pizza for us here."

"Oh, that's not necessary, dear. I really do want a bath and a good long rest. Take your guitar and your school things over to Ellie's with you so you don't have to get up early just to come back here and get ready for school. Get a good night's rest and don't let this whole thing bother you. Things will be better in the morning."

"OK. If you're really sure, Mom. I love you!"

"Love you, too, my beautiful boy!"

I throw a change of clothes into my backpack with my school stuff and grab my prized PRS with my other hand. Things are quiet in Mom's room as I pass by. I get her wallet out of her purse, pausing momentarily in grabbing pizza money as I see the family photo she has in there from when I was 10 or so. We looked happy. I'm not sure what went so wrong, but I suspect it has to do with my dad and not with either Mom or me.

I lock the front door behind me, wishing I could change the lock so Dad can't bother her, or me, ever again.

I walk the short distance to Ellie's house and knock on her bedroom window. She's surprised to see me, but her beaming smile instantly sets me at ease. There's no doubt that I'm welcome here, regardless of what brought me. She pulls open the window and helps me pull my guitar case and my backpack inside before I boost myself through. I sit down on her bed, unsure what to say... She looks at me, increasingly concerned when I don't say anything at all. She reaches for my face, and it's only then that I realize I'm crying, as she wipes a tear from my cheek.

"Oh, Hunter... Oh, my beautiful Hunter," she says, her expression collapsing into shared sorrow, as it always does when I'm hurting. She doesn't just sympathize, she empathizes, feeling my pain as if it was her own. She wipes a tear from my other cheek before sticking her thumb in her mouth. It's strikingly intimate, even as intimate as the two of us already are, and my eyes are frozen on her lips as she licks the transferred salt from them.

She brushes the hair away from my eyes in another tender gesture that has my eyes welling again. She frowns and then gives me a soft smile before turning around and going out into the hallway.

"Mom — Hunter's spending the night again. Can we order a pizza to eat while we watch some TV?"

"Sure, honey." I hear her mom reply. "Your dad won't be home until late. Order me a small cheese pizza. I'm not very hungry, but I know you two will devour a large between you. Teenage boys and their appetites and all..."

I nearly chuckle at her unintended double entendre. She's totally comfortable with a teenage boy sleeping in the same bed as her daughter. This teenage boy, anyway. As she should be. Having Ellie offer me sanctuary like this reminds me that I can't afford to fuck things up with our friendship. She and my mom, and my music, are all I really have. She's sacred to me, and I'll do whatever I have to to protect her. Even from myself.

Ellie comes back into her room with gentle scrutiny focused on me now. She doesn't ask what's wrong or why I'm here. She just climbs into the bed beside me and pulls me down next to her, wrapping her arms around me and laying her head on my chest, where she fits perfectly.

"It'll be alright, Hunter. I'm here. I'll always be here. Besides — in 30 minutes we'll have a large meat-lover's pizza, three-quarters of which has your name on it. Literally — I asked them to write out 'Hunter' in pepperoni."

She chuckles, and I join her this time. A little of the cloud lifts, and as she starts the next episode of her favorite Robin Hood series, right where we left off, I feel like maybe everything will be OK.

Full of pizza, I drift off with her head back on my chest and her arm around my waist. I wake up just a little when she gets up to throw the pizza box away and turn off the light. She snuggles back in with me, and we sleep straight through until just after sunrise, when the phone rings down the hall and her father stomps heavily to the kitchen to answer it, clearly not thrilled at being awakened so early after his late night at work.

I look down at Ellie, still asleep and still in my arms — no morning wood poking her in the ass this time, thankfully — and marvel at her sweet expression. Innocent, like a child, but still full of her warmth and caring. She doesn't even have to be conscious for you to see it. My hand is inches from her cheek, ready to stroke it as she did mine last night, that horrible, horrible night I don't even want to remember now as I watch her sleep so peacefully.

There's a light knock at the door and Ellie stirs as her dad opens the door without waiting for a reply. I'm glad we're positioned so innocently. I really don't want him deciding I pose a threat to his little girl's innocence.

"Hunter, son... Can you come out in the living room, please? I... We have something we need to talk to you about. And it can't wait."

I wonder if maybe he's decided I shouldn't sleep over anymore, no matter how we were positioned in the bed just now.

"What's going on, Dad?" Ellie asks groggily next to me.

His expression sends chills down my spine. Ellie sits bolt upright, instantly wide awake, for no perceivable reason other than that I'm suddenly alarmed by what's happening here and she can feel that.

"I think both of you had better come out in the living room," he says. He pauses and swallows. "It's about your mother, Hunter."

CHAPTER 2

MOTHERLODE

Hunter
Almost a week later

Much of that day passed in a blur. My mother is dead. I know that. They've told me that. They haven't told me exactly what happened to her, but I have an idea.

I know now that I should have stayed with her, should have ordered a pizza for the two of us and hugged her and told her I loved her, even if my dad is a cheating bastard, and that I'd take care of her. He could leave and go off with his girlfriends, and we'd be fine, just the two of us.

But it's not two of us anymore. Mom's gone, and she's not coming back.

I should be able to count on my father to console me, help me mourn her, and handle the very adult tasks of organizing a funeral befitting her and dealing with her legal matters, like any normal father would. Instead, I'm staying with the Langdons while my mother's attorney handles all of that other stuff. Dad's home, but he's shown no interest in getting involved with the funeral arrangements, just in getting the funeral over, the legal issues resolved. Only a handful of people other than my dad, me and the Langdons attend the service. Ellie clings to me the whole time, as if she thinks she's the only thing keeping me from collapsing. She's probably right about that. I've been sleeping in her bed with her all week. It's the only way I've gotten any sleep at all.

We stay up late at night, watching my favorite shows — mine, never hers; she won't even turn them on, especially her Robin Hood show, which we last watched that horrible night — and conspicuously not talking. I just don't know what to say, and she's fine with that, though I catch her looking at me at times with deep concern on her face. Even when I'm not looking at her, I can feel her worrying over me. I want to tell her not to worry, but I'm so lost right now...

She's my rock through all of this, making sure I eat something, even if I'm not hungry; bringing me my favorite foods in hopes that chocolate really can make me feel better, if just for a moment; forcing me to take a shower by telling me I'm getting too ripe to sleep next to her. (I laughed at that one, even though she was probably telling me the truth.)

She's the one — not my dad — who informed my teachers I'd be out for at least a week. I'm not sure how that measures up in terms of an official absence excuse, since she's only 15 and not a relative, but it's a small town, and nearly everyone has heard that my mom is dead. I've been avoiding going out, taking refuge from phone calls and unexpected visitors by staying at Ellie's. Her parents have been kind to me, and her mom's been giving me so many random hugs that it's starting to make me uncomfortable, because I want my mom to be the one giving me hugs.

Ellie's wrapped herself around me like she wants to become a layer of armor protecting me against the world. She wants me to talk to her about what happened, how I'm feeling, but she's respected my silence on the subject, even though I know she doesn't think it's healthy. Maybe someday, but right now, I suspect if I start talking about it I'll break into a million little pieces and won't be able to pull myself back together again. So she holds me together from the outside, by sheer force of will.

I haven't talked to my dad. At all. I've listened to him talk, mostly about how Mom had been sick for a long time and it had always been just a matter of time before something like this happened. He's asked me to come home — ordered me, really — saying it looks bad that I'm staying with the Langdons at a time like this. I couldn't give a fuck what it looks like or whether people are blaming him — for her being gone or for me not being home. They're both his fault, as far as I'm concerned. Except for the part that's my fault. He's pissed off that I won't stop "being dramatic." About my mother being dead.

Yeah. He's an asshole.

He's so pissed at me, in fact, that he's decided to stop paying for my guitar lessons. That's not as devastating as it would be if I was still playing. But I haven't been able to bring myself to open up my guitar case since that night. Every time I look at it, I remember the day Mom gave it to me — how happy I was to get a locally-made pro-level instrument, and how proud I was that she believed in me enough to make that kind of investment, how happy she was seeing how happy it made me. The last birthday present she'll ever give me. It's too painful to even think about taking it out of the case, let alone playing it.

Ellie asked if I wanted her to put it away in her closet until I was ready. She's seen the haunted look on my face when my gaze falls on it there in her room. I told her I don't want to forget that it's there. That would mean forgetting my mom's gift to me, and I don't want to do that. If I keep it out where I see it every day, I can think every day about taking it out again. When I'm ready. It keeps me moving forward.

So, Dad can keep his guitar-lesson money. He wants me to get a job? As soon as it warms up again, I'll take my guitar out on the boardwalk and throw open the case for tips. I'm good enough already that people will pay to hear me play. Or so Mike said when I told him I couldn't do lessons for a while. He's been playing in the area for 20 years, in a couple different bands, so he knows what he's talking about. I appreciated the vote of confidence. Next to my mom's belief in me and Ellie's unwavering support for my music, it's been the most important factor in my decision to try to make a living with my guitar. He's keeping an eye out for possible guitarist slots for me.

In the meantime, I'll see how well I do busking. Ellie offered to pay for my lessons out of her birthday savings, but I kind of want to do this on my own. It's the first hurdle in proving I can make a living doing music. If I can't make enough to keep up with my lessons, I'll never make enough to live off playing guitar. So this is a test I've set for myself going forward. My first step toward independence.

But first I have to start playing again.

CHAPTER 3

BREAK ON THROUGH

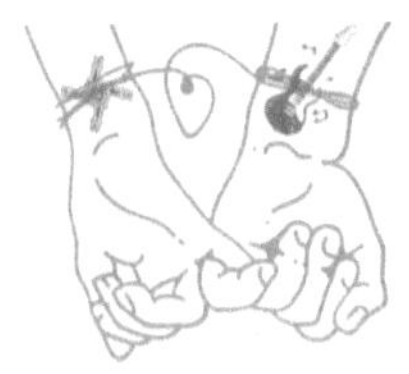

Ellie
A week later

I'm terrified for Hunter.

First to lose his mom in such a horrible way, then to have his father act like such a selfish bastard when he should be putting Hunter first above everything...

I wish I could say I was surprised, but something has always set my teeth on edge with that man, ever since I was little. That feeling has only gotten worse over the years, and I have to say I wasn't the least bit surprised when Hunter confessed to me that his dad was sleeping around on his mom.

As if that wasn't all bad enough, Mrs. Graves' attorney just stopped by to tell Hunter that he's too young to receive the trust fund his mother left to him. Until he's 25, it's under his father's control, and I don't think any of us — not even my parents, who used to be friends with Hunters' — trust Howard Graves to not dip liberally into that trust fund until then, at Hunter's expense.

The lawyer apologized to Hunter, said he felt horrible about it, but that a junior clerk had drawn up Mrs. Graves' will before he'd even been at the firm and hadn't done a very good job of protecting her or Hunter's interests, even with the trust.

Maybe she didn't know back then how much of a nightmare her husband was, including marrying her for her own hefty trust fund, as Hunter eventually admitted to me about that night. She'd always used the money she'd inherited just to do nice things for Hunter and for his dad, who seems now like he never deserved either of them, let alone the big payday for himself that he seems to think Hunter's trust fund is.

He keeps insisting that Hunter come home. At first, that seemed like he might actually be trying to look out for his son and rebuild their relationship. But he was so aggressively insistent that it made me wonder. Dad — who's a real estate attorney, so he knows a little about such things — just told me that Mr. Graves accessing Hunter's trust before he's 25 is much easier to justify if Hunter is living at home with him. And now it starts to make sense.

I don't want Hunter to go home. That house isn't comfortable for him anymore, and that's without his dad breathing down his neck and trying to suck every penny he can out of Hunter's inheritance. But I'm not sure how much longer we're going to have any choice.

Mr. Graves is already pissed off at my parents for letting Hunter stay this long, and his behavior hasn't endeared him to either my mom or my dad, who've always treated Hunter like part of the family. Mom is talking about challenging his father's control over the trust. Dad doesn't want to get involved, other than being willing to let Hunter continue staying with us. And now the two of *them* have started fighting about *that*.

I crank up the sound on the TV during these little spats while Hunter and I watch whatever I think will take his mind off things. You'd be astonished how often it happens that the plotline on your favorite show turns out to invoke a dead parent when you're trying to keep your mind off your own recently deceased parent. Ugh.

I've been trying to get Hunter playing his guitar again. It's not healthy for him to bottle up his feelings like this. He won't even talk to *me* about his mom most of the time. And the one thing that might give him an outlet — he can't bear to do it because it reminds him too much of his mom. I offered to pay for the lessons out of my savings, just to get him out of the house and doing something he loves. But he's determined to do things for himself. He doesn't want to rely on his dad, or my parents, or even me.

I get it. He's lost his entire foundation, and he wants to get his footing back where he knows he can count on it — by being the only one he's relying on. But he doesn't have to make it so hard on himself. Not right now. Not yet, anyway.

He's gotten contrary since his mom died. I don't know if it's fighting against his father's demands or if he's acting out against what other people want for him as a way of ensuring that he's constructing his own life going forward. I try to be the one person who's not telling him what to do. But sometimes I have to do it anyway. For his own good.

Thankfully, he's eating and showering regularly again. I mean, I said it to get him motivated, but he really was getting a little ripe when we're sharing a bed every night. Don't get me wrong — I love the way Hunter smells. Kind of like pine needles, with a hint of sunshine and something warm and spicy. I even got him a fresh bottle of his favorite shampoo to use while he's staying with us, so he didn't have to even go back into that house — and the bathroom, where they found his mom in the tub. Poor Mrs. Graves...

So I snuggle with Hunter every night, with my arms wrapped around him so he knows someone is there to protect him from the nightmares. I don't think he realizes how often he has them, and I don't want to make him aware of it, because if he knows he had one, it's more likely that he'll remember it, and I don't want him remembering whatever he's dreaming that gets him jerking and moaning and sometimes even crying like some of these nightmares do.

I'm a light sleeper, and I don't ever sleep through his nightmares. So I wrap my arms around him tighter, rub his back gently and tell him I love him and I'm here to keep him safe. It really feels sometimes like that's my main purpose in life — taking care of Hunter. I've been doing it forever, just like he's been taking care of me.

Sleepovers have gotten a little more... interesting in the last few years, even before all of this happened. More than once, I've been awakened by Hunter's erection poking me in the butt. (I know — it's just biology. I got an A-plus in biology. At school. Keep your mind out of the gutter!) When that happens, I usually just pretend that I'm still asleep, but like I said — light sleeper. There's also nothing that smells so good to me as Hunter does, and I admit, if only to myself, that I enjoy being surrounded by his scent, on my pillow and my sheets and wrapped around me as we doze. And that seems to be mutual, since I've caught him inhaling my scent more than once when he thought I was asleep or not paying attention.

I'm pretty sure he knows I have a massive crush on him. I have for as long as I can remember. I tried to kiss him once when we were younger — just a peck on the cheek, since we were only like 6 or 7 at the time — but he saw it coming a mile away and did that "Yuck! Girl! Cooties!" thing that boys do when they're younger, and took off running.

I thought I was going to die of embarrassment, right on the spot. But Hunter came right back, gave me a hug and told me, "I love you, Ellie-bellie. You're my bestest friend ever! Just don't kiss me again. Yuck!"

And we both cracked up and giggled until he said, "Race you to the slide!" (He won. He always won.)

I could have lived the last eight-plus years mortified by that one moment. But even though I remember it vividly, like the most embarrassing moments of my life, it's actually a memory I cherish, because when a lot of boys would have just run right out of my life, and probably made fun of me with their friends for the rest of eternity, Hunter, even at 6, loved me enough to tell me he did and let me off the hook.

As his best friend, it's kind of on me to get him playing his guitar again. He's too good not to keep playing, and it's part of who he is, his solace. And if he needs anything right now, it's solace.

Well, maybe that and a boot to his butt to get him playing again. Sometimes taking care of Hunter means tough love.

So, I've got a plan. He may get mad at me, but I hope against hope that it'll let him move on and get back to being himself again.

CHAPTER 4

WAITING FOR A STAR TO FALL

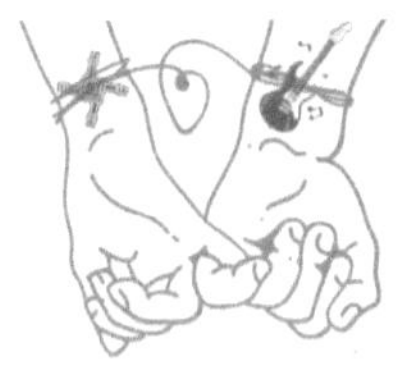

Hunter
Two weeks later

Mom's been gone more than a month now. And it's been that long since I played my guitar. Ellie's parents finally convinced me to go back to school. I squeaked by, but only because Ellie helped me get a few big projects done at the last minute.

The work wasn't hard. I just wasn't feeling motivated, about much of anything, until Ellie's mom reminded me that Ellie would end up graduating a year ahead of me if I didn't pass my classes. So Ellie and I spent the last few weeks getting me caught up with classwork and finishing our projects. Mine, really. She had hers mostly done, despite spending so much of her time and energy on me the last couple of months. But without her, I would have failed at least two classes.

She left my guitar case sitting in front of her closet door, where I had to step over it every day to get to the basket where we'd been keeping my clothes since I basically moved in. I moved it out of the way once, and she just moved it right back. I got the hint, but I just wasn't ready to face it. So, every morning, I step over the case, get dressed and then sit on the bed, staring at it, until Ellie's mom calls us for breakfast.

I'm getting fewer hugs these days from Mrs. Langdon, which has probably at least as much to do with my obvious discomfort with it as it does with the fact that my mom's been gone for more than a month. She means well. And while it's not the same, if I had to pick anyone to be a mom substitute, it would be Ellie's mom.

Her dad... He's ready for me to go home. He hasn't said anything, but I've overheard him arguing with Mrs. Langdon a couple times a week. My dad's name comes up a lot during these arguments, and I suspect Dad has been ramping up the pressure to send me home.

Mrs. Langdon is adamant that I stay. And I've heard Ellie get into it with her dad over the issue a few times. He thinks I'm a distraction for her, which is probably true. But she got all A's and B's in her classes, despite helping me get caught up, so he doesn't have much to complain about there.

I know I'm going to have to go home sometime soon. I just can't deal with my dad right now, and I can't face being in that house, especially with him there and Mom... not. I kind of feel like whenever I'm ready to play again, maybe I'll be ready to go home. But I don't tell Ellie that. She wants me feeling better and playing again, but she won't hear of me going home.

Summer's here, and I'm going to have to start busking on the boardwalk soon if I want to save up some money of my own and get back to lessons. I just can't quite bring myself to take out my guitar. I've reached for it a couple times this week, but I just couldn't do it.

So, when I got up this morning and went to get dressed, I didn't even make it to the closet door before my heart stopped. Because it wasn't there. I looked inside the closet, in case Ellie had finally had enough and stuck it in there. No guitar.

Ellie hadn't been there when I woke up, and I expected to find her in the kitchen, eating breakfast. She wasn't there either.

"Good morning, Mrs. Langdon. Have you seen Ellie this morning?"

"I think she went out a while ago, Hunter. She said she had a project she was working on. Did you want your eggs scrambled or in an omelet?"

"Uhh... scrambled is fine. Thank you."

"You should really get out and get some air, Hunter. It's nice out today. You've been cooped up too much since school let out."

"Sure, Mrs. Langdon..." I reply absently, too distracted to give my eggs much attention when she hands me my plate. Where is Ellie, and where is my guitar?

"Have you seen my guitar, Mrs. L?"

"Not today. Is it not in Ellie's room somewhere?"

"No. I looked."

"Hmm... Maybe Ellie took it to get new strings for you. She said something about stopping at the music store the other day."

"OK..."

I'm not wild about Ellie taking my guitar out for someone else to work on. But maybe she thought new strings would motivate me to play? If she took it to the music shop, she's probably downtown. Mrs. L is right — I need to get out of the house for a change. After breakfast, I'll head down there to find her. And my guitar.

The fax machine goes off.

"Hunter — this appears to be for you," she says.

"What?"

"This fax — it's for you."

Sure enough, my name is handwritten across the top of the page, in what looks like Ellie's handwriting. There's also a Polaroid of my guitar. Sitting on a bench that looks like one of the ones in the park downtown.

"Wish you were here!" is written below the photo.

"Is that a ransom note?" Mrs. L asks with a note of humor.

"I think it's more of a postcard."

"Oh. So the guitar went on vacation without you?"

"Apparently."

"Are you going to join it?"

"Yeah," I decide. "See you later, Mrs. L."

I want to be irritated that Ellie's taken my guitar, but I know she'll take good care of it. She knows better than anyone what it means to me. It's pretty clear she wants me to go find it, and her. The sun's out. It's warm. And my best friend is out there somewhere with my guitar.

I politely return a wave or two as I pass by neighbors in their yards but don't stop, lest it turn into a parade of condolences. There's a bustle of activity — tourists headed to the beach, a family on their bikes, some joggers, a couple rollerblading and three younger guys on skateboards. As I near the park, I see what looks like the bench in the photo. A young couple is lying on the grass nearby, the girl reading a book while the guy listens. I can see that my guitar is no longer on the bench, and for half a second I panic. But Ellie wouldn't have left it unattended.

Instead, I find another photo. Of my guitar. In front of the popcorn shop downtown. "Enjoying some pop music!" is scrawled across the top of the photo.

I'm sensing a trend here.

I stick the photo in a pocket and head off toward the popcorn place.

No guitar. And no Ellie.

I walk inside.

"Umm... Strange question... But have you seen this guitar?" I ask the clerk, showing her the photo.

"Oh! You want the special!" she replies with a knowing smile.

"Uh... I guess..."

She hands me a small bag of my favorite white cheddar popcorn. There's the corner of another photo sticking up out of it.

"Cool and sweet, come get a treat!" is written atop another Polaroid, this time showing my guitar in front of the frozen custard stand the next block over.

"We're not open yet," the guy behind the counter says when I get there, without even looking at me.

"I was... uh... sent here? By a guitar?"

"Oh! Have a sample, then!"

He hands me a napkin with a tiny sample cup with my favorite Dutch chocolate flavor inside.

"Thanks."

The napkin is too stiff. I pop the spoonful of custard in my mouth and unwrap the napkin. Another photo.

"You're my hero!" this one says, showing my guitar in the comics shop a few doors down.

Off I go.

"Are you looking for anything in particular?" the clerk asks when I get inside.

"A guitar?"

He chuckles.

"The music shop is on the other side of the street."

"I know. But I was sent here... by a guitar..." I feel pretty silly right now.

"Jerry!" he bellows across the shop. "Did we have any guitars?"

"Yup. It took off a bit ago. Needed new strings or something, I think. Here," Jerry says, handing me a Wonder Woman comic. "Maybe this will give you some inspiration. On the house."

Ellie loves Wonder Woman. Especially that golden lasso. She says it's the notion of people having to be honest, to admit to their deep truths. Seems a little kinky to me, but she's fierce. And hot. Wonder Woman, I mean... I think.

I open up the comic as soon as I get out on the sidewalk. The third page in, there's another photo.

"I'm really amped about this!" is written above a photo of my guitar in front of — you guessed it — the music store.

"Hey — Hunter! Long time no see!" Mike says when I walk inside. "Hope you're coming back soon. You're too good to quit."

"Yeah, man. I'm doing OK. It's been a rough month. But I'm going to come down and busk on the boardwalk sometime soon."

"Awesome! When you do, swing by and see me, and I'll come jam with you if I can get free."

"That would be great!"

"You know — I have just the thing if you're looking to busk."

He hands me a small Marshall amp from behind the counter.

"Battery-powered. Good sound quality. Loud enough to be heard by a small crowd, but no need to find an outlet."

"Nice! I'll have to put some money aside."

"Why don't you take this one out for a test drive? If you don't like it, I can find you something else."

I look at him, questioning.

"You sure? I can take it outside?"

"Yeah. I mean, it's yours. You can do what you want with it. Fresh batteries in it and everything."

"Wait... What?"

"It's yours. This cute blonde Amp Fairy stopped by earlier." Ellie!

"But you'll need a guitar to try it out."

"I'm hunting for one right now."

"In that case, don't forget your accessories!"

He hands me a manual for the amp. It flaps open to reveal another Polaroid.

"Mother of Pearls! Who would have thought you'd find such treasure here?" is written across the top. "X marks the spot!" is written below. The photo shows my guitar on a beach blanket on the sand, a big X traced in front of it.

"Thanks again, Mike. I can't tell you how much I appreciate this."

"Don't thank me — thank that fairy of yours." He clears his throat. "If I was 25 years younger..." he shakes his head. I'm not sure I like hearing him say that, even if he doesn't mean anything by it... "But if you still want to thank me, you can get out there and get playing. You can't deprive the world of your music. Go get on that!"

I load my pockets up with all of today's loot, and grab my — *my!* — new amp, and head for the beach.

I spot the bright blue beach blanket and the familiar emerald green of my Custom 24 sitting in the sundress-covered lap of my favorite Amp Fairy, her windblown ash-blonde hair covering part of the fretboard as she leans down and aims for what looks like a C-major chord — one of three I've managed to (almost) teach her.

Just then, she looks up, beaming at me, as if she knew I was there. Which she probably did. I head down to her.

"Your ring finger needs to move one fret over," I tell her. "Good thing you weren't plugged into an amp, or they'd have driven you off the beach with pitchforks and torches."

She throws her head back and laughs freely, the sound rippling through the air between us, and my heart clenches. I'm not sure I've ever felt so loved, or if I ever could again. Mom was the only one who has ever come close.

I shake off a wave of sadness, concentrating instead on Ellie's shining violet eyes, so full of delight. Sometimes, like now, it seems that light inside her shines just for me. The sudden need to protect it strikes me, like shielding a candle flame from the wind, and I kneel down beside her on the blanket, placing the amp next to the open guitar case before taking the guitar from her and putting it inside.

I pause, marveling at this amazing creature who is my best friend, and perhaps the biggest treasure I found on this little journey today. I grab her arms and pull her to me, squeezing her within an inch of her life.

"Hunmurr," she mumbles against my chest. "Oo cenn lemmeh guh nuh."

"Nope. Not gonna. You're mine. Not letting you go. Ever."

I place a kiss on the top of her head before pulling back to look at her again.

"I can't believe you did all this for me! The hunt, all those clues — and the amp! You really shouldn't have done that."

"Well, you wouldn't let me pay for your lessons. And you said you wanted to busk for the money. You need an amp you don't have to plug in if you're going to do that. Now you have one."

"I can't thank you enough for doing this...." My emotions swell to overflowing, all over the place — sorrow, joy, love, longing, delight... I look down for a moment, trying to pull myself together.

"I can't even tell you what this means to me, Ellie. I'm not sure what I'd do without you..."

"Well, you'll never have to." She grabs my hand and gives it a squeeze, her expression warming me from the inside out. "Now, why don't you show me how it's done."

I take a deep breath. With all I went through to get here, even with her overwhelming love and support, I'm still not sure I can bring myself to play again. She takes my hand and places it on the neck of the guitar.

"It's time, Hunter. You need this. And your mom would want you to have it again. She'd love hearing you play, seeing how you become one with the music. She always did. That's why she got this guitar for you. She wouldn't want you to just stick it in the case and mourn her. She'd want you to live your life with all the joy music brings you, and to the people who hear you. That's what you have to hold on to — that joy. It's a gift she gave you, and one you give to others in turn. Let it ring."

My eyes well with the image of Mom's smile as she watched me play just a few weeks ago. It's an image that will stick with me for the rest of my life. Right alongside this moment, with Ellie lighting the way for me, out of the darkness and back into the sun. And now I know the perfect song to play.

I pick up the guitar, settle it into my lap and plug in. Ellie is looking at me expectantly, her hand on the power switch of the amp. I give her a nod. I make a tentative strum, and then I begin playing.

It was Mom's favorite song, the Beatles classic whose bright tones perfectly suit its lyrics and this moment, as the clouds lift away from me and the sun comes out to shine. It's a light reflected in my best friend's eyes, full to overflowing with belief in me and joy in my music.

A crowd begins to gather, and before I get to the chorus, a few dollars have been dropped into my guitar case.

Two guys about my age — brothers, based on their resemblance — approach and listen intently for a minute. One begins to sing along, quietly and tentatively, and quirks an eyebrow at me, asking without words for my approval. I give him a nod, and he starts singing loud enough to be heard over my guitar.

He's good. Like, really good. And no sooner than he's joined in than his brother does likewise, providing harmonies like only brothers can do. The bills continue to accumulate in my guitar case, people tapping their feet and swaying, mouthing the words as they follow along. I've never had this many people listening to me play at once, and I like it, I like that they're so clearly enjoying it. And now I'm not just playing for myself or my mom, or even Ellie, but for the sheer joy that is spreading to everyone around me.

I glance over at Ellie, her gentle smile reinforcing that feeling. She's always believed in me, and I'm here now because of her. It's an incalculable gift. One I'll never be able to repay in full. But darned if I'm not going to try.

CHAPTER 5

INTO THE FIRE

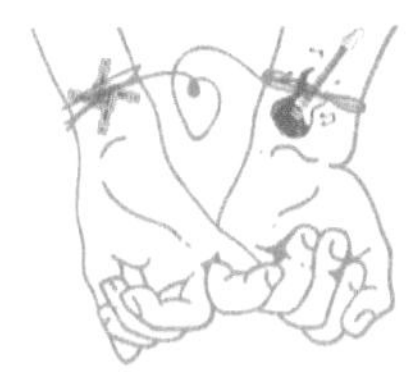

Ellie
Later that day

Hunter spent all afternoon busking on the beach. Even sharing part of his haul with the Carter brothers — Declan, the cocky singer, and David, his quieter brother — he accumulated nearly what I paid for the amp. Enough to afford his next guitar lesson, and then some.

But, vastly more importantly — he's playing. He's found his joy in music once again, and he's finally begun healing the wounds of his inconceivable loss. I'd be stupid to think he doesn't have a long way to go with that, but watching him play today, I could practically see the glow hovering over his skin, like broken bones being knit back together before my eyes by some sparkly magic. The feeling of watching that, of knowing I played some small part in it — it's pretty much the best thing I've ever felt.

Hunter even bought us both dinner after agreeing to meet up with the Carter brothers tomorrow. They're not local kids — just summertime visitors — but they're down the whole summer with their mom while their dad comes down on weekends from his job near D.C., and the two of them and Hunter are going to keep playing together while they're here. David's actually learning to play the bass guitar and already plays guitar pretty well. Declan mostly sings, but he can play guitar, too.

I'm glad Hunter has finally made some friends our age who share his passion for music, and at least some of his talent. I felt a little like a third (fourth?) wheel when they were deep in their musical discussion, but seeing Hunter light up like that, the contagious energy as they talked about what they should play — that was almost as good as seeing him pick up his guitar again today.

That breakthrough seems to have stuck. He's sitting next to me on the bed now, playing quietly. I did a lot of running around this morning with all those clues, and I'm already nodding off. The peaceful feeling he exudes now from behind his guitar is also contagious, and I don't think I'm going to be able to stay awake much longer, though I'm soaking up every note like a cactus in a summer rainstorm. He was silenced by his grief for much too long. The warm feeling he exudes now lures me into slumber.

My eyes pop open again, and I stretch and yawn. It's warm and cozy in here, listening to Hunter play by the fire, the light of the flames flickering across his dark gold hair and shining in those deep green eyes. The sound of the penny whistle is bright and sweet, like Hunter himself, and I smile warmly at him, though he's too engrossed in his tune to see it.

I lean down to give Crógan a pat on his shaggy head where he sits by Hunter's feet. He's my husband's constant companion in the fields all day, keeping the sheep from straying too far. At night, he keeps us company while I spin their wool into yarn and weave it into cloth. We make enough selling my yarn and cloth to live comfortably here, just inland from the coast of Donegal, near the town where Hunter and I were both born.

He's been my lifelong companion, my beloved partner and my daily joy. Evenings spent listening to him play are the highlight of my day. He comes home with new melodies most days, and I marvel at his gift of creativity. I can play the bodhrán a bit, but my fingers can't keep up with the intricate patterns he weaves with his whistle.

When the men in the village get together to play, he's at the core of every song. He enjoys his nights spent playing with them, but he appreciates the quiet comfort of our evenings together by the fire. I look over at him now, the final notes of today's tune drifting away. He feels my eyes on him and looks up, his smile behind several days' growth of beard shifting from distant and engrossed to intense, heated. And my blood warms instantly.

I set aside my spinning and reach for his hand. He's out of his seat before my fingers can reach him, grabbing me up out of my own chair and pulling me tightly against him, his lips smashing into mine, hard enough to bruise.

I moan into his mouth, and his hand drops to my hip, sliding up the layers of skirts separating his skin from mine. His mouth moves to my neck, and he licks a path from my collarbone to my ear. We're both breathing hard now as he massages my flank before pulling my leg up to wrap around his hip.

My arms wrap around his back, under his arms and grasping for purchase on those shoulders made strong by hard work on the farm. I pull at his shirt, freeing it from his pants, and he pushes me away just long enough to pull it off over his head.

My mouth falls to his chest, licking a trail of my own along his breastbone down to the flat brown coins of his nipples. He hisses when I bite lightly down with my teeth before laving the flesh with my tongue, teasing it to a hard peak.

Not to be outdone, he pulls open the ties of my chemise, lifting up one heavy breast before sucking it into his mouth and squeezing the other firmly with his other hand, almost painfully. My fingers contract, clawing into his back. He slams his hips into my own, rocking like hardened steel against the parts of me that have gone molten at his fervent touch.

He lifts my thighs to frame his on either side, sliding his hands under my rear and carrying me, my arms twined around his neck, the few feet to the alcove where our bed lies. He drops me there, just an instant before he follows. pressing himself into me and me into the bed.

There's too much fabric between us still, and I fumble with his pants, palming the hard length of him through his fly before unfastening them. He scrambles to pull my skirts above my waist, running his hands up and down the outsides of my thighs before pulling them roughly apart.

He gazes down at me like a starving man before a feast, dropping his trousers and stepping clear. My eyes fall to his cock as he takes himself in hand, stroking along his length, the head glistening and bobbling against his stomach as he lets go, walking toward me as I lay splayed out for his view.

I can barely breathe, caught up in anticipation as our eyes meet. I lick my lips, my mouth having somehow simultaneously gone dry and salivating at the sight before me. He looks down at the downy copper curls between my legs, glancing up at me again before licking his own lips, and I moan again. The sound elicits a growl from Hunter, who falls instantly upon me, mouth first, gathering my legs up over his shoulders and burying his face in my sex.

A single swipe of his tongue has me writhing beneath him. Then he pulls my clit into his mouth, sucking on it and then flicking his tongue back and forth across it. I'm already dripping under his intimate touch when he slides a finger through my folds, circling my opening before slipping inside. His finger curls upwards, pressing against the soft pad of flesh there, and I'm thrashing beneath him as he presses me down into the bed with his other hand.

He circles my clit with his tongue, adding a second finger before continuing the rhythmic pressure inside me. Again he looks up at me, smiling with lustful pride when our eyes meet and I begin whimpering, bucking my hips up against his mouth and fingers.

There's a slow, intense pressure building inside my core, and my muscles clasp at his fingers, begging for more, for release from this exquisite torture. I reach down and pull his head hard against my mound, and I can feel him smiling against me this time before he speeds up the movements of his tongue and fingers, pushing me to a crescendo with my mouth falling open but producing not a sound.

My pussy clenches around his fingers, pulsing rhythmically as he continues to slowly lick that now exquisitely sensitive spot between my lower lips and plunge his fingers in and out of me, milking every last delicious contraction from my body.

When my spasms have faded and I'm a puddle of pleasure lying boneless beneath him, he slides his fingers from inside me and, making sure to hold eye contact with me, puts them into his own mouth, sensuously licking them clean. I'm left moaning once again as he raises himself up, smiling that same self-satisfied smile, before fitting himself into me and slowly, tortuously sliding home.

When he's finally fully seated inside me, he pauses just a moment, resting with his elbows on either side of me, before rocking his hips back and then slamming home once again. We both grunt with the impact. I mewl as he withdraws again, only to slam back inside me, making the most deliciously sensual sound as our flesh meets in earnest now.

The sounds we produce between us become their own sweet symphony, an ever-increasing core rhythm accented by soft moans, gasps and grunts, building in intensity and complexity as he continues to pound into me and I oh-so-willingly accept the invasion, his movements rubbing across that sensitive bundle of nerves just above where we are joined, stirring another rising tide of tightness coiling inside me.

Again my mouth moves soundlessly, grasping for sense and meaning when all rational thought has been driven from my mind. I reach down and grasp his rear, pulling him harder into me with each thrust.

Grunts of increasing volume and pace issue from Hunter-'s mouth, and I find myself mimicking them, no longer mute but no more in control of my utterances than I was when rendered silent. The primal dance continues, working to a peak as our sensual symphony rises to meet it, finally crashing with cacophony as Hunter shouts my name, "Brighid!" and I scream my pleasure as he fills my core with his essence.

He collapses on top of me, the heavy comfort of his solid, masculine weight grounding me and keeping my body and mind from flying off into the ethers, where they're wont to go, borne aloft on a raft of pleasure.

He lifts his head from my chest long enough to dart his tongue inside my mouth, where it again tangles with my own, mirroring the erotic dance we just brought to a glorious finale. He pulls back, smoothing my copper-washed waves from my damp forehead before pressing a sweet kiss there.

He drops his head back onto my chest, pressing another kiss atop my breast before settling into my arms.

"I love you endlessly, my sweet Lady," he murmurs.

"And I you, my beautiful love. Always," I reply softly into his hair as we both close our eyes in the peace of each other's presence. A tune floats through my mind as I drift to sleep, the remembered tones of his penny whistle carrying me off into my dreams.

I wake feeling satisfied and at peace, as if hours have passed in blissful slumber, and my ears again follow the beautiful melody Hunter weaves as easily as I spin fibers into yarn.

I go to reach for him and pull his face to me for another kiss, and then I stop mid-movement. He plays his melody not on a penny whistle but upon a guitar resting on his lap as he hums along, lost in his own creative stream as he sits next to me in my bed.

Confused, I look at the clock on my dresser, baffled to see that only a few minutes have passed since I drifted off to sleep while listening to him play this green guitar his mother gave him. There's no fire, no spinning wheel, no penny whistle, no shaggy dog and no heavy wooden bed smelling delightfully of us and of sex. And this Hunter — younger by a good 10 years and still beardless — is not my husband, but my best friend, clad in a T-shirt and cargo shorts.

Feeling my scrutiny upon him, he stops playing and turns to look back at me.

"You OK, Elle-belle?" he asks.

I have no idea what to say. I have no idea if I'm OK. It was so real, so tangible and complete — not a detail absent, from the textures of the dog's fur, my yarn and Hunter's skin to the sounds of our lovemaking and the scent and sensation of our arousal spilling down my thighs as he lay between them.

It was Hunter. I know to the core of my being that it was, despite the fact that he looked a bit different. I pull a strand of my own hair in front of my eyes, surprised to find it blonde, with not a hint of warm copper.

Hunter is now staring at me, staring at me staring at my own hair, which now only seems distantly my own.

"Elle?"

"Yeah... Yeah — I'm fine. Just a weird dream, I guess..."

He looks less than convinced and reaches toward me to smooth my hair out of my face.

My eyes go big. The memory is so vivid. Or the dream... I'm lost in some kind of limbo between waking and sleeping, dreaming and knowing.

I shake my head, trying to get it clear, to find a tangible thread to follow back to reality, whatever reality actually is.

"Thank you for today," Hunter says, leaning over to kiss my forehead. Dream vision overlays the reality in front of me.

"You're welcome, Hunter," I reply absently. "Love you," I add, glancing up at him in surprise when I realize I said that aloud. "Always," echoes inside my head, thankfully unspoken.

"Love you, too, Ellie-bellie," he replies, invoking the earliest version of his childhood nickname for me.

He lays his guitar down inside the case and lies down next to me, snuggling up with his arm around me, his nose in my hair and his mouth by my ear. He heaves a deep, satisfied sigh, and I can hear him breathing quietly, his breath rustling in my hair and each of us inhaling the other's scent.

"What was that you were playing?" I ask, suddenly remembering that melody that crossed from wakening to dream and back again.

"Oh, nothing... Just a little melody I've been hearing in my head. The beginning of a song, I think... I want to start writing my own songs, and that just popped into my head just now."

"It's beautiful."

"Thanks. Not sure where it came from. Maybe I've got a muse speaking to me," he jokes mildly.

"Yeah, maybe..."

We go quiet again, just breathing and enjoying the physical contact that's come to mean so much to both of us.

Only now, every touch of his skin on mine stirs memories — because that's what they feel like, memories — of deep erotic intimacy. My nipples harden beneath my tank top and I pray that he doesn't notice, though he's got a perfect view of my chest.

I try to put the vision out of my mind, focusing on our breathing, which has synchronized as we lie intertwined on the bed.

Tonight's revelation, whatever it was, whatever it meant, is too much for me to process right now, especially with Hunter so close. Maybe tomorrow — after some real sleep this time — I'll be able to make more sense of it all. And, for right now, I just want to enjoy the simple peace of Hunter's arms around me and his soft breathing in my ear.

I hope he's finding some of that peace for himself. I really wanted to give him that. Really, I want to give him the world.

Chapter 6

In for a Penny

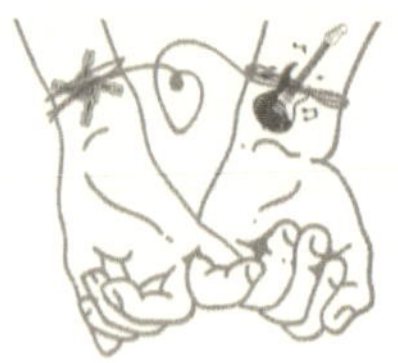

Ellie

I feel like I'm split in pieces. Part of me is thrilled that Hunter is playing again. Another part of me is worried that he's still avoiding talking about his mom — even if he seems to be putting those feelings into his music — and about how his dad treats him. Still another part of me can't forget what I saw in that dream... vision... whatever it was. And I want to tell Hunter about it, but another part of me is terrified of what his reaction would be.

And, weirdly — maybe? — while I still have stuck in my head images of older past-Hunter and older past-me having some amazingly hot sex, I'm also remembering all too well how it felt for that little girl on the playground to have that little boy run away from her after she tried to kiss him. That feeling is etched on my soul, no matter how much water has gone under the bridge of our friendship since then.

This feels *really, really* important. And I can't imagine *not* telling my best friend, not telling the man who was featured so prominently in that... whatever it was... about what I saw. Even if it was just a dream, it feels like I need to tell him. Honestly, it's pushing me to tell him how I feel about him, period, whether I take what I saw seriously or not.

We're almost 16, and it's hard to believe neither one of us has started dating or having sex yet. OK — I'm having a hard time believing *Hunter* hasn't started dating or having sex yet. I've overheard enough comments in the halls to know some of the other girls think I'm too chubby for anyone to want to date. I don't doubt that the guys are saying the same thing, though that's probably happening in the locker room. The girls seem to talk about me in the hallways just so I can overhear what they're saying.

There's a tiny little part of me that has hoped maybe Hunter would have at least kissed me by now. I can't tell if our sleeping together every night is having the same kind of effect on him as it is on me. Probably not. If it was, I don't think I'd still be wondering how he felt. Guys seem to make it pretty clear if they want you. At least it seems that way from the outside.

I do know that since I had that dream, every single moment our skin touches or our eyes meet or we lean close to each other, I'm drawn to him — like, literally, physically. Like a magnet. And it's almost possible to resist, while at the same time, it's impossible to do anything about it — like there's a brick wall keeping me from doing it, while a strong hand keeps pushing me toward him, and toward that. I feel like toothpaste in a tube, with the cap on and someone squeezing it. Something's got to give. But it never does.

Sometimes, I look in his eyes and I see the other Hunter looking back at me. In those moments... I can almost see myself leaning forward to kiss him. It happens sometimes, too, when he's playing that little melody — the one I heard in the dream and then woke to find him playing on the guitar. Instinct makes it feel right to reach out and touch him as my husband, but I stop every time, filled with terror over what this Hunter will do when this Ellie kisses him or touches him like that.

I really don't want to cause him more stress than he's already under right now. If this didn't feel so urgent, so important, so right, I wouldn't even consider it. But it does. It's so frustrating, I feel like screaming.

And one day I do — sitting next to him on my bed as he's playing that melody again, hearing both the guitar and the penny whistle in my head, I look over at him and feel like I'm being torn in two, between then and now. And I scream.

"You don't like it?" Hunter asks, taken aback.

I'm at a loss as to what to tell him, but he's clearly thinking that I've had more than enough of his little tune, when I really can't get enough at all. It's part of me.

"It's not that... I..." I hesitate, which seems to be my default state of being where he's concerned these days.

"What? You can tell me, Elle. Whatever it is you're feeling, I can take it."

I swallow. Hard.

"OK — now I'm getting really worried. What's up, Elle?" he asks, putting aside the guitar and rubbing my upper arm supportively. "Just tell me."

I take a deep breath and desperately hope this doesn't go as badly wrong as it seems like it could.

"That dream I had the other day — the one I said was weird?"

"Yeah, I remember. You seemed really out-of-it when you woke up. What about it?"

"It was about you. And me."

"Oh." He seems not to know what to say, and I immediately re-think saying any more. "What about us? It seems like it's bothering you. So just tell me."

"It was us, but it wasn't us. I mean — I knew it was us, but we both looked different. Older. My hair was a little different. You had a beard."

"Well, we know that was a dream. I'm still battling peachfuzz on my upper lip, and even if I don't shave for a week, I've barely got a five-o'clock shadow," he says with a laugh.

"I know — like I said, it wasn't us now. It was us... a long time ago."

"OK... Now I'm confused. We were older but it was a long time ago?"

"Yeah. It looked like it was a couple centuries ago, actually."

"You've been watching too much 'Robin of Sherwood.' *We've* been watching too much 'Robin of Sherwood," he joked. "I know you like that Michael Praed guy. I mean, your dad has been pushing me to get a haircut lately because it's gotten so long, and his hair looks kind of like mine, just darker. Plus, Herne the *Hunter*? Maybe things just got cross-wired and that was who you were dreaming about."

"No. It was you. I know it was you."

"OK... Well, what happened in the dream?"

"I was spinning wool into yarn."

"Well, also not something you can do. So — dream. Has to be."

"It felt real, Hunter. Like, I thought I was there, and it all felt normal and right and like that was where I belonged, where I was comfortable. We had a dog, and sheep. And you played music on a penny whistle."

"Well, I was playing when you fell asleep. I'm sure it just carried over into your dream. That's all."

"No, Hunter — that wasn't all..."

Now I'm stuck again. This is almost as hard as breaking through that wall that's kept me from kissing him.

"What? Just spit it out, Elle. It was just a dream. It can't be that big of a deal."

"We were married. In the dream, or whatever it was, we were married. And we were *together*."

"Oh... Wait — you mean *together* together? Like *sex* together?"

"Yes, 'like sex together.' Like unbelievably hot, erotic, sexy sex, together. Like a married couple... only actually sexy."

"So you had a sex dream about me."

"No! I mean, *yes*, but it wasn't us. And it was us. And... I don't know. It's all very confusing."

"Yeah. I can see why it would be."

He seems to be thinking pretty hard. And I can only imagine what's going through his mind.

"We haven't... I mean, we've been *sleeping* together a lot, but not like that."

"I know."

"Does that... do you... Do you think of me like that?"

Yet again, stuck! I want to tell him yes, that I did before, and I do even more so now, and I want to kiss him to show him that's how I feel and maybe he'll admit he feels the same... Or he'll take off running like he did when we were six. And that would crush me. Just flat. Like a pancake under a steamroller.

But he's waiting for an answer now. And I regret I even said anything, while a tiny ribbon of hope unreels in my mind. Maybe...

"I think I do, Hunter," I say, leaning in close. We're locked onto each other's eyes again, like we do sometimes, only this time, neither of us seems to be able to break the eye contact. It's like an electromagnet has kicked in and we're just locked together, soul to soul. *This* is what it was like in that dream. And *this* is why I can't dismiss it as just a dream. This connection is real, and it feels just as real as it did in that vision from the past.

I reach up and touch his cheek, and then, suddenly, I break through that wall. I lean into his lips, ready to touch them with my own...

"Stop, Ellie," he says quietly, pulling my hand away and leaning back. "Don't."

He's having a hard time meeting my gaze now. And I close my eyes, feeling utterly humiliated. I'd wanted to do that for so long, and I finally got up the courage to try, to admit to him how I felt, and he pulled away from me. Not only does he not feel the same, in an instant it's cost us that sense of comfort we always had with each other. I've actually made him uncomfortable.

"I'm sorry. I shouldn't have..." I can't even look at him now. I'm looking everywhere *but* at him right now. "It was just so *real*, Hunter — that... dream. It felt right. But, I'm sorry. I should have known better. *Please* tell me I haven't messed this up, messed up our friendship."

The seconds that pass while I wait for him to answer stretch out to an eternity. There's a pit opening up in my stomach, and it's swallowing my heart like the sarlacc in Star Wars — digesting it so slowly and painfully that it feels like it'll take a thousand years to die. I have a momentary urge to flee... somewhere — anywhere. I must make a movement, because Hunter grabs my arm and holds me in place. I stare at his hand where it grasps my forearm.

"No, Elle... You haven't messed up our friendship."

I look up at him, wanting to be relieved, but not trusting it.

"I just... I can't. I can't be like that with you. Not with you," he says.

"Oh. OK. Well, I'm sorry I... did that. I didn't mean to make you uncomfortable. It's just been eating at me... and..."

"I could tell something has been bothering you for a while now. I'm glad you told me, actually, so we could get things cleared up between us."

Yeah. Glad... All clear. Somehow, I think he's feeling at least a little better about this outcome than I am. Because part of me is so hurt that I want to burst into tears, and part of me is so relieved that I didn't destroy our friendship that it wants to cry, too. Either way, crying seems to be the appropriate response to this.

And I don't. I feel like that ready-to-explode tube of toothpaste has been shoved into a freezer full of dry ice. I can't react. I can't just let it go, either. It's like something is stuck in my throat and no amount of swallowing, no amount of water can fix it.

He's looking away from me now, like he's trying to figure out what to do now that this conversation has stuttered to an awkward halt. His eyes rest on his guitar, and I think he's going to start playing again, and I'm once again divided — I can't bear the thought of him playing that melody from my dream again, and I also can't bear the thought of him not playing it.

He sighs heavily. And I feel even worse. But he lies back on the bed next to where I'm sitting and holds his arm out, inviting me to snuggle in with him again. And, after a second, I do, because I can't imagine anything that would make things better between us right now unless it's this. I just have to hope that we can find our equilibrium again, after the giant boulder I dropped into our tranquil little pond. If we can't, I'll have spoiled that refuge for both of us. And I couldn't stand to have that happen. I can't let that happen.

CHAPTER 7

HOME IS WHERE THE HEART IS

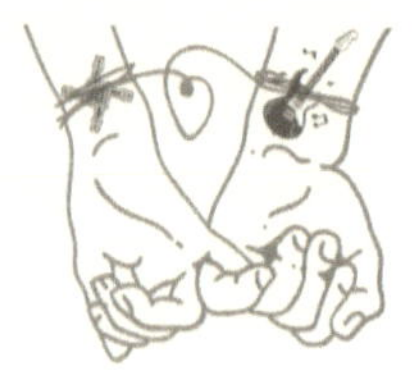

Hunter
A month later

Things between Ellie and me are... tense.

Not like angry-with-each-other tense, but like the weight of her hopes... the weight of that dream-vision-whatever, has settled on top of us both, weighing us down. I feel heavy, like I'm being pressed down into soft, wet grass — swallowed up, but only enough to feel constrained, rather than like I'm dying.

The ease with which we slept in each other's arms lately — for basically our entire lives, really — has been lost. I know she wants more, and she knows she can't ask me for it, because I can't give it to her. And every time I wake up with my arms around her waist, my hands tantalizingly close to her breasts, my dick hard and threatening yet again to poke her in the ass, I pull myself back, put space between us, turn over, turn away from her.

And sometimes that feels symbolic, like I have to pull away from her if I'm going to do the right thing here. Because I can't be with Ellie. I just can't. I'm looking at the life I have ahead of me, what I've had behind me, what I have now, and I know I just can't do it.

Because after all these years of being best friends, all these years of knowing her so well, there's one thing I know about Ellie: She's not a girl you just have sex with, or even just date. She's the one you end up with. And I know I can't be the one she ends up with. I couldn't do that to her. So I just won't. Any of it. No matter how much she wants me to. No matter how much I want to. No matter what that dream of hers showed her.

I know I hurt her. But hurting her a little in the short run seems way better than hurting her a lot in the long run. And the one thing I've learned this year is that making a lifelong commitment to a woman isn't a guarantee that you won't hurt her. It isn't a guarantee you won't ever sleep with someone else. It isn't a guarantee that you'll love her and treat her with love and respect. And I've had a terrible role model on that front.

Even worse — I left my mom alone that night and took care of myself, hid out with Ellie. And if I couldn't put my mom ahead of myself that one night, when I knew things were so bad, how could I promise to put Ellie first in any kind of relationship? I couldn't take care of Mom. I can't be trusted to take care of Ellie.

She might be feeling like I'm that guy, the guy who would do that, but someday she'll find someone who could really do it, and I can't let what she feels for me stand in the way of that for her. So, I told her no.

She's hurt. I'm doing what I can to comfort her, but I can't see how the person who hurt her can be the one to help her heal. It's like peeling off the scab just to put ointment on the fresh wound. It might eventually heal, but it's going to be a mess getting it there, and it would always be an emotional scar. I'm trying, but I just can't figure out how to be there for her as her best friend, consoling her over the rejection, when I was the one who rejected her.

So, yeah — it's weird, it's tense.

Still, I have to admit that I can't really imagine not sleeping next to her these days. We've been doing it since we were little, and we've been together every night since that night. She's my comfort and my solace. The smell of her hair alone gives me peace and helps me get to sleep, even when my mind won't stop running in circles and my heart feels torn in two. I'm going to have to buy a fuck-ton of that shampoo of hers and wash my pillowcases in it for the rest of my life, just to ensure I can sleep.

That thought makes me smile. And that's just one more piece of evidence that I am between a rock and a hard place, and I don't mean my dick. Which needs to learn to behave itself. Because now that Ellie told me she wants me like that, that she's "seen" us having "hot, erotic, sexy sex," I can't stop thinking about it. I'm sure my extra-long showers are raising suspicions with her parents, and maybe with her, but I don't know what else to do.

And I'm already getting the feeling that Mr. Langdon wants me to go home, even though Ellie and Mrs. Langdon are adamant that I stay and not return to living with my dad, who's still cranking up the pressure on the Langdons to send me home. The perceptible tension between Ellie and me seems to have made Mr. Langdon feel even more strongly that I should leave, and I suspect I'm not going to be welcome here much longer.

Falling asleep in Ellie's bed is one of only two sources of peace that I have these days. The other is my music. I'm either busking or practicing with the Carter brothers nearly every day now, and we've started writing some originals together.

I still haven't shared with them that little melody that keeps coming into my head at odd moments — usually when I'm trying to take my mind off the stressful shit in my life. I'm not ready to share it with anyone yet. Well, except Ellie, but she's heard me playing it a lot already. It really does seem sometimes like it was just handed to me. Who knows — maybe I'll turn it into a Top 40 hit someday. But, regardless, it's going to be something special. I just know it.

I'm dreading the end of the summer, because the Carters will head home to D.C. and I'll lose that outlet and the chance to collaborate with them. I really feel like we've gelled these last few weeks. We've already talked about next summer, maybe even trying to book some gigs locally. It'll be a challenge, at 17, since so many of the venues are for people 21 and up, but we might be able to get a spot at a restaurant that offers live entertainment on a Thursday night or something. I feel like we're good enough for that.

Declan *knows* we're good enough for that. But that's Declan — nothing if not confident in himself and determined to make things play out just how he wants them to go. He's a born lead singer. He's lucky his brother is so easygoing. It seems more like Declan just runs roughshod over David sometimes, but they seem to be used to the dynamic, so I'm not going to get in the middle of it.

David and I have gone skimboarding a few mornings here and there. You can tell he loves it here, in the water especially. He's a decent surfer, too. We don't have enough surfable waves that I ever learned, but David's mom takes him out to Assateague or up to the Indian River Inlet when there's a decent break.

Those are the days I busk on the boardwalk by myself or stay at Ellie's and work on writing some songs. I'm making enough busking that I've gone back to weekly lessons. Mike's teaching me some advanced techniques that have helped me smooth out my chord changes and play some of the faster lead parts that he loved during the heyday of metal.

I lean more hard rock than metal, but it's excellent practice for whatever I might want to play now, or in the future. He says there's not much left to teach me, that it'll be all practice from this point on, maybe picking up some pointers from top pros when I run into them, which he assures me will happen.

We'll see. I know it's what I want to do for my career, but it takes more than talent and practice to really make it as a musician. It takes a lot of luck, and not a little bit of charisma. Declan has it — "the thing," as Ellie calls it. She says I have it, too, when I lose myself in what I'm doing and just become one with the music. I think she's biased. But I think I might just be able to do this.

CHAPTER 8

MAMA I'M COMING HOME

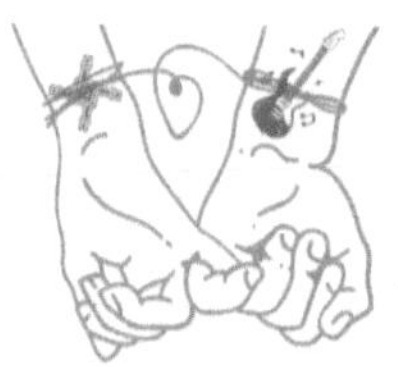

Ellie

"No! You are not sending Hunter home! You can't! His father is horrible, and he's already dealing with losing his mom, and his father just makes it all worse! You can't possibly think this is OK."

"He's Hunter's father, his only living parent. If he wants Hunter to move back home, then there's nothing I can do to stop him. I've held him off this long, but we've reached the end of the road, Ellen," my father says.

I don't believe that's true. I think he's decided he wants Hunter out and he's using this as an excuse to overrule my mother and me on what I think are very good reasons to keep Hunter with us.

"We've indulged your caretaking where Hunter is concerned, Ellen, but it's not appropriate to have him living with us, with no legal authority, a teenage boy sharing a bedroom with a teenage girl."

"We're just friends! We've been like this since we were little. That's no reason to force him to leave and go back with that horrible man! I can't believe you're this heartless. After all he's been through!"

"The boy's going to have to learn to stand on his own two feet sometime soon, Ellen. He can't have you taking care of him for the rest of his life. You need to be focused on your grades so that your college applications are top-notch. And you've been talking about getting a job, which will look great on those applications. You can't be splitting your focus at a crucial time like this!"

"Ellie has been a consistent straight-A student, Thomas. She can't get her GPA much higher, and I have to agree with her — Hunter's been through enough these last few months. He doesn't need to be forced to go back into that house, where his mother died..."

"Killed herself, Mom. Let's be honest about this. She killed herself. After arguing with his dad, who you now want to send Hunter home to live with, against his will."

"I agree with you, Ellie. But there's no need to be insensitive about the issue."

"Thomas, Ellie is correct," she continues. "Hunter has been traumatized by this whole thing. Sending him back there, where it happened, is unnecessarily cruel. I think we should look into getting him a guardian ad litem, who could maybe file a petition for emancipation..."

"And then who is he living with, this emancipated minor, with no job, who spends all his time playing guitar, some rockstar wannabe..."

"Dad! I'm not going to listen to you tear down Hunter like that. He's good. He's beyond good — he's already a pro-level player. If you knew anything about music, you'd realize that he's going to make it. He's going to be a star. He just needs a place to stay where he can feel safe, just until he can get the band going."

"And when is that, Ellen? In a year? Three years? Ten years? Music is a notoriously bad investment as a career. Very few people make a living at it. And there's no guaranteed paycheck coming in, no guarantee of forty hours a week of responsible work, no insurance or paid vacation. And all for the dream of a fast life full of fast women, parties, booze, drugs... Is that the kind of life you think you should support? That we should support in a boy who'd be living in our house until he's at least 18, and probably longer?"

"The boy is quite talented..." Mom interjects.

"It's not like that, Dad. Hunter is a serious musician. He's already got two band members he's working with. They could be playing regularly, with paid gigs, next summer! The people on the boardwalk love him!"

"I'm sure they do, playing that noise for tourists who stop to listen for two minutes and toss a dollar in a cup like he was some kind of homeless man, begging for change!"

"Thomas!" Mom says, outraged.

I am, too.

"I can't believe you! This is Hunter we're talking about! He's been my best friend since we were 6. You've watched him grow up! You know he's not this person you're describing. You know he's a caring, responsible person, and you know he's had a hard time lately. I can't believe you're turning all of this around on him as an excuse to throw him out!"

"I don't *need* an excuse, Ellen! This is my house. The house I pay the mortgage on. The house where I pay for the electricity, for the water — all these things you need a solid, reliable job for. Which he does not have, and will not ever have if he sticks with these silly dreams of stardom. He'll drag you down with him, Ellen, and I can't allow that to happen. I won't allow that to happen. So, yes, Hunter is going to have to go home, whether you agree with that or not, whether your mother agrees with that or not!"

Mom glares at him but doesn't object.

"It's my decision and I've made it!"

And that's the day I found out we were sending Hunter home, to hell.

And the most astonishing — and infuriating — thing was that Hunter didn't argue. He didn't fight it. He didn't try to tell my dad how horrible his father was. He didn't tell him what he'd done to his mother, how he'd been treating Hunter himself. He didn't stand up for himself at all.

And that worries me more than anything about this whole situation. I can't tell if he wants to go home to put some distance between us, or because he thinks he deserves to be treated how his dad has treated him.

Either way, he's wrong. We'd be fine if he stayed. Things are weird now, strained, maybe, but I don't care about that. I know we'll get past it. And it's my fault, anyway. I'm determined we'll get things back to normal, regardless of how I feel, regardless of what I've seen. And I can't make that happen if Hunter isn't here to work through it with me. It would just cement the strain in our relationship if he leaves now.

But I can't stop Dad from kicking him out, and I can't stop Hunter from letting him.

I can, however, take some steps for the future, for *our* future. And if Hunter is going to insist on going back there, I'm going to do what I can to ensure that I'm there for him going forward. And I'm going to take a page from our past to make it happen.

Three weeks later

I've just finished my shift at the yarn shop. I've been working there eight hours a day, five days a week, for the last two weeks, selling yarn, knitting needles, crochet hooks, patterns, canvas, thread... You name it — if it's used for needlecrafts, we sell it.

I'm saving up for a car. Something modest, used, reliable. With enough room to haul an amplifier and guitar, or two, because I already know that Hunter's dad won't help him get a car, and Hunter needs to save up whatever he can for college, which I also know his dad won't help him with. A penny spent on Hunter is a penny less that's there for his dad to spend. And Hunter's talking about going to college near D.C., where the Carter brothers live and are probably going to be going to college, too. So, that's out-of-state tuition.

My parents will cover my tuition and board, pretty much wherever I decide to go to college. And I could even end up with some scholarship money, if I'm lucky. So, the priority is on getting a car, so that wherever I end up — wherever *we* end up —we'll have transportation.

The only thing I'm spending my pay on other than savings is to learn how to spin my own yarn and weave. I may have had to let go of my vision of Hunter and me together — *together* together — but the spinning wheel from my vision has put me under its spell as surely as that other one did Sleeping Beauty. Just with a way more positive result.

Actually, I'm kind of obsessed with the whole thing. Which is a good thing, since I'm not spending nearly as much time with

Hunter as I was. Learning to spin yarn keeps my mind off that. As much as possible, anyway.

Lindsey, the shop owner, ordered all the necessities for me when I mentioned I was interested in learning. She couldn't offer me much in the way of instruction, since she only knew the basics herself, but she encouraged me pick up some books and look online for more information, and she offered to break the cost up into small payments taken out of my paycheck each week, since I told her I'd keep working part-time once school starts.

So now I have my own spinning wheel, spindle and all the other tools I need to learn, and plenty of roving to make my own yarn. I find it very relaxing, putting all my focus on the process, which is rhythmic and immersive, almost hypnotic. Actually, it kind of reminds me of Hunter practicing his guitar, especially early on.

That's the other thing that's changed in these last few weeks. Hunter went... I hesitate to call it "home," because neither of us considers it a safe and comfortable environment. But he's staying there at night, not in my bed anymore, and he's leaving there each morning to go hang out with the Carters and work on their music.

We haven't talked a lot since he left. We've both been busy, for sure, but I no longer go down to the boardwalk with them when they're busking. Most of the time, I'm working while they're down there. And Hunter still seems slightly uncomfortable being alone with me, like he expects me to try to kiss him again or make declarations of everlasting love. Believe me — I had enough humiliation the first time. I'm not doing it again. Ever.

He seems to want some space right now, so I've been giving it to him. Actually, he asked for it.

"I think we need to take some time," he said before he moved out. "I think things have gotten weird between us because we've been spending almost all of our time together. We're not little kids anymore. We can't be together 24/7 and not have things go pear-shaped."

"I'm already pretty pear-shaped," I joked.

He laughed and gave me a quick hug.

"You're hourglass-shaped. Marilyn Monroe would be jealous."

I snort at that.

"Thank you for trying to make me feel better. But I think you need your eyes examined. You should get on that."

"My vision is 20/20," he says. "I think your mirror needs cleaning."

The word "vision" hits me, reminding me momentarily and uncomfortably of that dream of mine. But I don't say anything.

"I just think some time apart will help us reset things, get them back to normal, back in balance again," he adds. "I know I've got some thinking to do after everything that's happened this year," he says, with a distant and pained look flashing across his face that makes me want to just fix things for him. But I can't fix it, and he doesn't seem to want me to try. "We've both got things we need to be doing, and we can do them separately and then catch up later, like normal friends."

But we're *not* "normal" friends, I think to myself. We weren't normal *before* I had that dream, and I can't honestly say I think we're supposed to *be* "normal." Normal is overrated.

"I get it," I tell him. "I'll give you some space. Just don't disappear on me."

"I could never disappear on you, Elle-belle. You're my bestest friend!" he jokes with me. I can hear his 6-year-old voice telling six-year-old me that. And it warms my heart. It gives me confidence that we can get through this, even if we have to do part of it separately.

That's why I'm standing behind a post right now, watching him busk with Declan and David. They're good. I mean, really, *really* good. And they're being rewarded for it, with applause and with tips. Even if I wasn't inclined to check in and see how Hunter is doing, I wouldn't want to miss this, because they're that good, and because I love the music they're making. I'm officially a fan.

But a secret one. Because if he knew how often I was standing here to listen, it might seem like more than it is. And I think Declan, and maybe David, would tease him about it.

It's weird being a girl with a guy best friend and vice-versa, and more so the older we've gotten. I've heard enough comments at school about the two of us being inseparable to know it's misconstrued. And that I'm apparently pretty transparent to anyone who sees how I look at him. Except Hunter himself, I guess, since that confession of mine seemed to take him by surprise.

I can safely guess that the Carters would make the same assumptions and the same jokes. At Hunter's expense and mine, if mostly at mine. And I won't do that to him. I *can't* do that to him if we're going to get back on solid ground.

So I'm standing behind a post, for the fourth time this week, watching them perform and loving every minute of it. I mean, *I'm* loving every minute of it, but they are, too, clearly. Hunter lights up when he's playing in front of an audience. There's a thing that some people just inherently have — it's not quite charisma so much as it is a light inside them that turns on when they're doing something they're passionate about that draws people right to them. And all three of these guys have that.

Declan has it in spades, and he knows it. The self-confidence he exudes is almost to the point of arrogance, but it makes him magnetic, and that's a useful quality in a lead singer/frontman. So I can forgive it. David isn't so much flashy as intense. He's clearly immersed in the music and making his bass speak for him, with his vocal harmonies perfectly matching his brother's lead vocals.

Hunter... He's the perfect third voice to add to the brothers' performance, and his guitar playing just continues to get better and better. Like staggeringly better. I'm guessing he's spending a lot of his time at home practicing, too. But whatever is going on there under that roof is a mystery to me, because Hunter has avoided answering the question every time I've asked.

"I'm doing OK," he says. "Just putting one foot in front of the other."

That doesn't sound like he's doing OK to me. Surviving isn't OK, it's just surviving.

And that's the biggest reason I've been coming down to the boardwalk to watch him play. I need to see that light inside him still shines, that it hasn't been extinguished by how his father treats him or the pressure of being back in that environment, that he hasn't been lost to grief once again. It tells me everything can really be OK, as long as he has his music.

So I watch him light up, from a distance, and take what comfort I can from that distant beacon. And, every once in a while, he looks over in my direction, and it's like he can feel that I'm here with him, even if he can't see me. That connection is still there, through all of this tension, through all the drama and change. I'm holding onto that like a lifeline, because I have a feeling that one day we're both going to need it.

CHAPTER 9

HOME ON THE RANGE

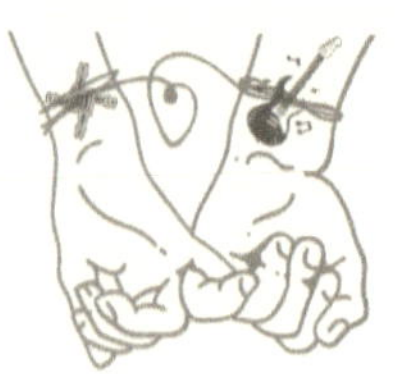

Ellie
Several weeks later

The summer is nearly over. We start our junior years of high school in just a few days.

I'm both excited and stressed. So much of our future will be mapped out this year as we get in another semester or two of grades for our college applications, take the tests that will mean almost as much as our entire academic careers added together and make a decision on where to go to college.

That's a big reason why it worries me that Hunter remains distant. We'd always assumed we'd go off to college together, and now I have to wonder if that's still what he wants. I haven't broached the subject with him yet. I was kind of hoping he'd have had enough space by now that we'd be thick as thieves once again. But not yet.

He's pulled away. I'm giving him space. One of those. Or both. And it feels like part of me is missing. Excised. Cut away.

I have had the chance to talk to him a couple times a week these last few weeks, though. And he, too, is both excited and stressed, though for different reasons. The Carters have headed home, so he's lost his musical partners. But they've promised to come back next summer so the three of them can work on finding some paying gigs, and not just busking.

"We said we'd each try writing some originals before June, so we can have some ready to go when we get a paying gig," he says. "Whoever has the best collection of original material when they get back here, he gets to name the band," he adds with a laugh. "I'll believe that when I see it. Declan runs the show. He's never going to let someone else name the band. But it'll be fun to see what they come up with, and I'm going to do my best to win, even if I don't actually get the prize."

Hunter said he's also decided for sure that he wants to go to college in the D.C. area, probably in Northern Virginia, where the Carters live, so they can all go to the same school, play frat parties and college clubs, pull together enough equipment to play out on their own.

I'm looking at D.C.-area colleges, too. And I've decided to pursue a bachelor's degree in art, somewhere that offers fiber arts as a focus. I haven't told my parents about any of that yet. I already know what Dad will say. And I'm sure Mom expects me to pick a more academic major, but I've discovered my passion, just like Hunter has his, and I'm going to pursue mine, too, no matter what their opinion on the matter is. If I have to go in as an English major and then change to an art major as soon as I get there, that's what I'll do. My grades are good enough, any major I pick will likely snap me up.

I've got a little savings built up from my summer job, and I'm going to keep working at the yarn shop about 10 hours a week during the school year. That, I *have* told my parents about, and while they weren't thrilled that I wasn't going to be focused solely on my academics, they both thought it was a responsible and practical decision, and since my grades are good, they figured I could handle balancing school and work.

Hunter's been coming over once or twice a week for a few hours now that the Carters have left. It's nothing like it was at the beginning of the summer, and I'm starting to wonder if we'll ever get things back to normal between us. I'm still feeling horrible about that. I don't think he's holding it against me so much as he's still looking for a "reset" to give us a clean slate. I'm not sure what that's going to take. But there's no question that I have to remain silent about the other visions of the past I've had these last few weeks.

The one thing Hunter is really looking forward to this school year is the annual talent show, which is the one chance the students get to perform outside the scope of the more staid and restrictive venues of the band, chorus and drama productions. He's been working on a solo version of Nirvana's "Heart-Shaped Box," and he's let me hear what he has so far.

I was floored. He's just indescribably good. He's going to blow them away.

Three weeks later

"Are you nervous?"

"Kind of," Hunter admits as he paces around the band room where the talent show performers are gathered. They've got less than an hour before it starts. I snuck in by carrying Hunter's amp for him. He seemed to welcome the company, and I was glad of that.

"You've got the song down. I've heard you do it a dozen times without a single mistake. And it sounds great! You're going to be amazing. Just trust in that. Relax. Engage with the music and bring the audience with you. I've seen you do it a hundred times. Pretend it's the boardwalk. It's your domain. Own it."

He smiles nervously, giving me a quick hug.

"Thanks, Elle. I always know you'll be in my corner."

"Darn right! And that's not because you need me there. You've got this."

"All non-performers need to leave the room now! If you're staying for the show, you can proceed into the auditorium!" the band teacher instructs.

"That's me," I tell Hunter.

Without thinking, I give him a quick peck on the cheek.

"For luck," I add, lest he think it means anything more.

"Thanks. I'll need it," he replies ruefully.

"No, you don't. But I'll always offer it anyway. I'd say 'Break a leg,' but you're not an actor and this isn't a theater, so instead I'll say, 'Have a good gig' to the pro you are, and you will."

I give him a quick wave as I dart out the door and head off to find my seat for the show. I aim for front and center, so he can see a friendly face in the audience, just in case. And within fifteen minutes, the seats are nearly all full.

We sit through a clarinet performance, a song from a Broadway show, a tap-dance routine, a pop song from a group of girls in costumes I'm surprised passed muster with the administration, a classical piano piece and a group that seems more rubber band than rock band.

By the time we get to Hunter's slot in the show, I've started to think of the lineup as a roll of the dice. We could get nearly any type of performer, and the quality could vary between abysmal and extremely good. I don't think anyone's really won over the audience, except maybe the guy who recited sections of the Constitution in rap form. He could be a hit if somebody ever takes hip-hop to Broadway with a historical theme.

And now it's Hunter's turn. I can tell he's still nervous as he steps out on stage and plugs in his guitar, looping his cable through the guitar strap. I give him a bright smile and a thumbs-up, even though I'm not sure he can see me past the stage lights. The audience settles into silence, waiting.

What Hunter gives them is an almost bluesy rendition of the Nirvana classic, which most of the audience knows, even though it's more than a decade old. He's worked it up into a percussive rhythm with a plaintive slide that conveys the tone and drive of the original vocal but does so without words or drums.

Any nervousness has left him as he finishes the first phrase of the song, and to my eyes, it's like someone flipped a switch and turned on the sun. He just shines. Every bit of passion, the love of the music, his soul engaged with the meaning behind the song — it all beams out of him directly to the audience, which has dropped into dead silence after an initial few moments of wondrous murmuring when they first realized what he was doing.

The song drifts from sensuous and almost slow to aggressive and electrifying, and it takes the audience with it. I can hear the woman behind me mouthing the lyrics that aren't being sung but that she's still hearing in her head. I look to each side and see a few jaws dropped and people poking the people sitting next to them, as if to say, "This — this here is amazing. Listen and remember."

I smile to myself, knowing he's done it. He's finally shown all of these people who he is, what he can do, what he *will* do with his career, his life, in the not-too-distant future. It doesn't matter what his father thinks, what *my* father thinks — he's just shown an audience of several hundred people that he's going to be a star. No — that he *is* a star.

There are no prizes to be awarded in this show, but Hunter has won. He's won the audience. He's won their admiration. He's won their favor, perhaps even their love. And his life will never be the same. I know it as surely as I know that melody I first heard played on a penny whistle and now will never forget. The music is in his soul, and he has just bared his soul to everyone in this room. It's not the first time, and it, by far, won't be the last, but it will be the one that changes everything. For both of us.

A half-hour later

The emcee has to ask people to hold their applause after about five straight minutes of adulation directed at Hunter's performance. He'd left the stage after about three minutes and several bows, and I'd thought they were going to demand an encore before the administration said it was time to move on to the next act. (I feel a little sorry for the guy with the accordion. But only a little.)

I play the good little audience member and don't abandon my seat to go find Hunter backstage. I applaud politely for each subsequent act, even though I'm ready to chew my fingers off in anxiousness to celebrate with him. After the last act takes their bows, the assembled group of performers comes back onto the stage for a final bow, which yields a riotous response when Hunter comes out from behind the curtain.

He looks a little uncertain at first, but there it comes — that Hunter Graves beaming smile that almost replicates the light shining from inside him when he was playing. And the audience eats it up. It looks to become another lengthy round of applause until the administration again calls an end to things.

As soon as the curtain drops, I'm out of my seat and up the aisle, racing back into the band room, past the teacher set to control access, who is too surprised by my previously unheard-of speed to keep me out and shrugs once I clear the doorway.

I barrel straight at Hunter, throwing my arms around him in a tight hug before jubilantly jumping up and down in front of him.

"You were brilliant! You killed it! I think half the audience is now in love with you, and the other half is just too jealous to admit they're in love with you, too!"

"Oh, come on, Elle — it was good, but it wasn't angels beaming down with harps good."

"I think you'll find that a number of the people in that audience saw a halo over your head, and I'm not sure it's not still there, you rockstar, you!"

I smile delightedly at him, and he returns a rather bemused smile that almost looks like embarrassment.

"Hunter Graves! You've got a large number of people out here requesting to see you. You want to join your fans out in the hallway? Because I can't let them all in here, even if one slipped through." The band teacher smiles indulgently at me, and I smile back. She clearly knows she's got a star in her classroom, even if he's not one of her actual students.

"Well, go on!" I encourage him. "Go meet your adoring public!" I add with a laugh.

But once we're out in the hallway, I realize that the overblown description of the number of people waiting to see him, talk to him, touch him, actually wasn't overblown. There's dozens of people clustered around, waiting to shake his hand, chat him up and more.

I stand proudly beside him as they rush to surround him, but as the handshakes become pats on the back and hugs, high-fives and even some girls trying to cling to him, I get shunted aside. I find myself standing on the outside of a wide circle of admirers, marveling at what a scene this has become. I try to make my way back in to tell him I'll talk to him when he's done, but I can't get anywhere near him.

I wait for five minutes, then ten, with no sign of the crowd thinning, and I realize my mom will be waiting outside. I sigh in disappointment. There's no way I'm getting back to him tonight. I'll have to talk to him tomorrow and do a recap of the night. I wave to get his attention and only just manage it, nodding my head to the exit doors and waving goodbye to let him know I'm leaving. He nods and waves back, excitedly engaging with his newly acquired gaggle of fans.

Mom drives me home, asking me how the show was, how Hunter was, and I effusively tell her how he stole the show. She looks almost as proud of him as I feel, and I'm glad at least one of my parents seems to understand that Hunter is going to make something of himself with his music. I knew this was coming, of course, but I'm not sure I understood in that moment exactly how big things might get or how much they would impact Hunter's life, and mine.

Chapter 10

Home Sweet Home

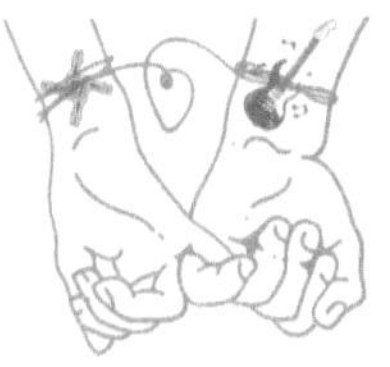

Ellie
Several weeks later

Things have changed since Hunter played his cover of "Heart-Shaped Box" for the talent show. I've hardly had a chance to talk to him, let alone see him. He's swamped every time I see him in the hallways. He's still got guys patting him on the back, yelling, "Hunter!" down the halls, even though these same guys wouldn't have given him the time of day a month ago. The same is true for the girls, only there's a lot of clinging happening. Any time I make an effort to walk from one class to another with him, he's intercepted by a cheerleader or one of the school glamour-girls, and after the first ten or twelve times, I just give up.

He wanted space. I gave him space. And now I've got no choice but to keep giving him space, because I can't get within 10 feet of him anymore. If I'm going to spend any time with my best friend, it's clear now that he's going to have to come to me, which he doesn't do. And now I realize that the wedge that's driving us further apart was set there by my confession, and I'm to blame for this. Even my efforts to get Hunter back to playing music have helped lead us to this. And there's nothing I can do about it.

It's been a little over a week since the talent show, and I spotted one of the cheerleaders ringing the doorbell at Hunter's house last night. Her car was still there at nearly midnight. A pair of girls in short skirts and tube tops arrived around 10 tonight and haven't left yet, and it's one in the morning.

I wasn't so much checking to see what was going on at his house as I was unable to sleep and idly looking out the window when I saw them arrive. (Really, I promise!) I'd been wistfully wishing he'd show up and knock on my window like he used to, only to realize that he certainly wasn't coming over here to see me and sleep innocently in my bed the way we used to, because he was apparently seeing plenty of girls in his own bed, and not so innocently. I couldn't think what would draw this particular selection of girls into his house late at night unless he was having sex with them. All of them.

On some level, I'm still hurting over his rejection. And on another I'm hurt because he's so quickly taken up not just a single girlfriend, but many of them, it seems. And then, on top of it, my best friend has apparently lost his virginity — with considerable enthusiasm — and we haven't even talked to each other, at all, let alone about that.

And it isn't just the girls coming and going late at night. He's been out late himself several times this week — which I only know because whoever's been dropping him off, even though it's never the same people twice, is always noisy and giddy, which I assume to mean fellow passengers, if not the drivers themselves, have been drinking. And then I'm worried both that he's going to end up getting himself killed by riding with a drunk driver, and also that his life has changed tremendously and I've been left entirely behind.

Can I really have lost Hunter to this teenage version of rock stardom? Is this a preview of what his life will be like in five years or ten years or twenty? All sex, booze and rock-and-roll? Will he even have time for a friend who's not part of that world? Will he even remember me by then? Or will I be some lost remnant of his childhood, like a broken toy that got tossed aside and never reclaimed?

The change in him reminds me far too much of how his father acts, and what he told me his father said to him and his mother on that horrible night this past spring. And I start to wonder whether this was what he saw coming when he said he couldn't be with me, if he knew that he had a life of casual sex ahead of him, just like his father before him, and doesn't want to be tied to someone who would expect a commitment from him, like his mother had from his father, to her eventual demise. Maybe he wants the freedom to screw whoever he wants, whenever he wants, without consequence or care.

And if all this unwelcome change and concern wasn't enough, today I got called into the guidance counselor's office to pick up the schedule for my behind-the-wheel driving class, which Hunter and I had signed up to do together when scheduling opened up last spring. Back when we were inseparable. And now we are very separable. Very.

I'm tempted to ask Mrs. Dorman if I can switch partners at this late date, but this may be the only time I actually get to spend with Hunter this year, if not for the rest of our lives, and I just can't bring myself to give that up.

Two months later

I'm waiting outside the gym after school. Most of the students have left. In fact, most of the teachers have left, too. But this is my assigned time for driving lessons, and I'm waiting for the teacher.

"Hey, Elle."

Hunter.

I smile wanly at him.

"How's it going?"

"Well enough. You?"

"Yeah... Um... I know I haven't been around in a while."

"No, you haven't."

"I'm sorry about that. Things have been crazy."

"I noticed. I pretty much haven't seen you since the night of the talent show."

"Yeah. Like I said, it's been crazy. My dad's been on my back, and I've just been trying to stay out of his way or just get along when I can't do that."

And now I feel like a bitch. The fact that Hunter's basically ignored me for three months hurts. A lot. But I also know what he was facing when he moved back home, and I can't blame him for wanting to escape.

"Are you OK? Really?"

"It hasn't been easy. But I'm doing OK. Really. I'll make it through."

"Making it through isn't doing OK. It's surviving, and you should be doing much more than that."

"Thanks."

"For what?"

"For still caring."

"Of course I still care."

I love you, you idiot.

"I'm actually having some problems keeping up in my classes these days. I'm kind of glad this class came up when it did, because I could really use some help getting my grades back up before the end of the semester so I can have a better shot with the college applications."

"Are you still going to a D.C.-area school?"

"If I can get in. That's the big question mark right now. If I can't get in someplace I can afford, I may just have to move there and get a day job while we sort out the band."

I sigh.

"Did you want to come over and study with me until you get things back on track?"

"That would be awesome, Elle. Thanks. And, hey — I'm sorry about how things have been. I kind of got lost in it all. I didn't mean to stay away like that. It just kind of happened."

Just kind of happened? You abandoned your lifelong best friend for months, and that "just happened"?

"Shit happens."

"Yeah, it does. But don't let Mr. Reynolds hear you say that. You'll end up in detention instead of behind the wheel," he teases me. I almost smile.

"I hope my little revelation this summer didn't push you to do that. I know things had been weird even before the talent show, but I thought we'd started to get back where we'd been."

"Yeah, we had. I think I'm just still coming to terms with losing my mom, and then the conflict with my dad. It all snowballed on me, and then the talent show just kind of set off an avalanche."

There's a desperation in him, on top of the grief, and every bit of my protective instincts kick in. "I've been trying to ride it out to the bottom of the mountain, I guess, just trying to keep ahead of it before it crushes me."

"Are you in danger of being crushed now?"

"Not if I can get my grades up."

"Then we'll make that happen. Can't have my best friend crushed under a giant snowball of lousy circumstances, lousy father, lousy rockstar lifestyle and shitty grades," I reply with a chuckle.

He grabs me in a bear hug, seeming almost desperate for the contact.

"I missed you, Elle-belle. I really did. I'll do better." He kisses the top of my head.

"I missed you, too, Hunter. We'll do better together."

We'll have to, because we don't seem to do too well apart.

"I don't see how someone who is so good at making three-point turns can forget something as vital as not taking her foot off the brake when she's stopped on a hill!"

"It was a trap!"

"You are not Admiral Ackbar!" he reminds me. As if I missed the memo on that one.

"I'm serious — Mr. Reynolds set me up by telling me to parallel park on top of that hill, which has to be the only one in the entire state of Delaware, but not telling me I should be sure to watch out for the inevitable effect of gravity on a multi-ton vehicle when I shifted into reverse."

"But it worked, didn't it? You won't forget ever again, will you?" Now he's just laughing at me, and I can't help but join in.

"I won't. I'll be telling that story until I'm 80."

"Meanwhile, *my* parallel parking on *flat ground* could use some serious work."

"No kidding. It's not supposed to take you eight tries to get into the space."

"It was a small space. And a big car."

"It's a standard space, and it's a mid-sized sedan. My mom said she took her driver's test in a station wagon, on a frozen parking lot, and still managed to parallel park on the first try. Your spacial skills just suck."

"Sad, but true."

"And *you* are not Metallica."

"Thank god, because Lars is a dick."

"Yes. Yes, he is."

"And they screwed over Jason Newsted."

"Yes. Yes, they did." I agree. "Too bad you're minus a drummer and not a bass player."

"He would make an awesome member of the Carter Brothers Band."

"Is that really what you're going to call it?"

"For now, yeah, I think so. Declan's being his usual dick-ish self whenever I bring it up. He's almost as big of a dick as Lars is."

"Yes. Yes, he is."

"Hey! That's my bandmate you're talking about!"

"Yes, but he has LSS. He's earned the criticism."

"Lead-singer syndrome is real. And incurable."

"Sad, but true. Ask Hetfield."

Now we're both laughing. It feels good to just chat and laugh with Hunter again. I was starting to think we'd never get this back again.

We're hanging out in my room after driver's ed, with plans to work on Hunter's essay for English and prep for a biology test. Hunter's finally started coming over regularly again, though he never sleeps over anymore and I'm still seeing girls coming in and out of his house at all hours. I find myself hoping they're coming to see Hunter and not his dad. Because, eww. But it's a close call.

I've told him I love him a couple of times, kind of trying it out after both of us being hypersensitive about it since the summer. He hasn't flinched or anything, but he hasn't said it back. He's said, "I know" a couple of times, and it's becoming a bittersweet joke between us.

We watched "Princess Bride" together again last week, for the first time in a while, and I managed to get an "As you wish" out of him. I haven't had the heart to ask him to watch "Some Kind of Wonderful" with me again yet. It used to be one of our things, but it hits too close to home these days, and I don't want to mess things up again. Even if I think Hunter is just as stupid about me as Keith is about Watts.

And we don't watch "Robin of Sherwood" anymore either. Between the fact that we were watching it the night his mom died and his pointing out the period nature of my first vision — and I'm calling it a vision now, if just to myself — watching it just doesn't feel right. Maybe someday.

On the vision front... I've had more of them. The spinning wheel seems to put my mind in a state where it's open to them. Not many super-sexy erotic other-Hunter dreams. Instead, I've been wide awake when I suddenly find myself elsewhere, elsewhen... I've arrived to find I'm at the spinning wheel in my vision. And I've arrived to find I'm snuggled in other-Hunter's arms in a heavy wooden bed covered with warm wool bedding. And I've arrived to find myself sitting on a beach I don't recognize, with rolling emerald-green hills behind me, with a small cottage and a pen full of sheep snuggled in between them.

They're trying to tell me something, though I can't think what that would be except to keep spinning — and weaving, which I've started learning, too — because if Hunter and I had a past, it sure doesn't seem to be playing out along those lines in the present. That way lies madness, and I can't afford to let wishful thinking turn visions into something that will drive Hunter and me apart in *this* time and place. Not again.

Hunter is still super-popular at school, commandeered by the jocks and the cheerleaders and the rest of the upper-echelon of the high-school societal structure when he's anywhere that's not class. I'm helping him study for classes that I rarely see him outside of, unless it's in driver's ed or in my own bedroom, and the latter not in the fun way he seems to be using his own for.

I've found myself the target of more comments from the other girls at school, and I've overheard a few of the guys talking about me and Hunter, too, mostly teasing him about me being his groupie — one who they think is too far beneath him to be getting any of his time at all. I've heard Hunter shut that kind of stuff down a few times before, and they seem to mostly do it when he's not there to defend me.

I try not to let it bother me. I know Hunter's star is on the rise. He's going to be a rockstar. I have no doubt. It's probably better if I just accept that I'm going to be labeled a hanger-on as far as his friends, fans and bandmates are concerned. Or worse.

But I'm determined to make a life for myself that doesn't rely on him and his career. I want my own business, making yarn and weavings, maybe a few gallery shows for fiber arts? It's all just in the earliest stages of planning, but I feel like I can do this. Almost as strongly as I feel Hunter's going to really make it as a musician.

CHAPTER 11

MOVE IT ON OVER

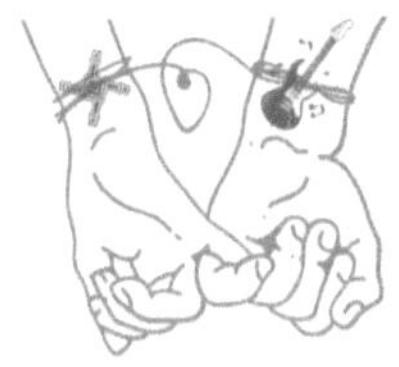

Hunter

I didn't object when Margot and Sarah both showed up on my doorstep tonight.

Dad didn't blink. In fact, he gave me a very enthusiastic thumbs-up as I led the girls to my room. I've still got a big box of condoms from what seemed like a lifetime supply when he gave them to me after the first time Margot arrived at our house, asking to see me. It's kind of creepy, really. But then my dad isn't exactly known for his propriety where sex is concerned. He wants me to be a chip off the old block, and since I moved back in with him and found myself the established rockstar at school, it's the one spot in our relationship that isn't a source of conflict.

What he really wants me to do is follow in his footsteps and join the football team, then go on to college to get an MBA and marry a co-ed with lots of money and very big boobs. He did all of that in his youth, except the big boobs part, which he continues to remind me whenever the issue of my career comes up. Instead, he married my mom, who was an attractive girl with a really big trust fund, who he then insulted pretty much every day of her life for being overweight and not a cheerleader.

Margot and Sarah are cheerleaders, so them being here gives him hope.

Since I first let Margot in my bedroom, I've been on a tear through the cheerleaders and party girls from school who swarm to me in the hallways and at every party I get invited to. Which is a lot these days. I hadn't even kissed a girl until six months ago. Then there was the talent show, and that was all she wrote. A few beers, a little weed and a short skirt are now my favorite party favors. And I get to do that a few times a week.

It sure beats sitting home, listing to the moaning and screaming as Dad fucks his latest girlfriend.

And when I'm out at a party or in my bedroom with a girl, Dad leaves off, if briefly, from nagging me about "getting a job." But I finally managed to get him to shut up about it the other day after the two-hundredth fight we had about the issue.

"Hunter — I'm not funding your college education for you! Your mother wasted countless dollars on coddling you and buying that guitar." My fists clench. He shouldn't even mention her, when he's the one who killed her, if indirectly. "You need to find a job and save up for tuition, dorm, food. I'm not spending another needless penny on you. It's time for you to pull yourself up by your bootstraps."

I've learned its best to let him monologue at me, like a cartoon villain, and just pretend to listen.

"You're old enough to drive, and if you want a car and the gas to put in it, you'd better find something that'll bring in some serious money. Cars don't come cheap." This from the guy whose wife bought him a Corvette for their anniversary and who drove away in it the night she died. "I'm glad you've seen the light with the girls, dropped that pudgy Ellie and gotten your dick wet in someone who's actually in our — your — league. But you need to start thinking about your financial future, too."

Now I'm pissed. Not because he wants me thinking about money and my future — because I've already been doing that — but because he's putting down Elle and acting like she's not good enough for me, when it's the other way around. He was a dick to my mother, and I refuse to do the same to Elle. So, I distract myself with the cheerleaders and party girls, and I dodge Ellie when things get uncomfortable after her confession about that "vision." But that's a decision I made to protect her, and if he's going to start insulting her, he's going to learn very quickly that that's not acceptable.

"Any guy would be lucky to have Ellie, and you can shut the fuck up about her. You're not good enough to speak her name! And I *have* a job. I'm a professional musician."

"Getting a couple bucks dropped in a guitar case during the summer isn't being a professional, Hunter. It's begging for change, with music."

He's pushing all my buttons tonight.

"A couple bucks? Begging for change? Do you have any idea how popular the Carters and I are on the boardwalk during the summer? How many people hang out down there, waiting for me to play on the weekends in the fall and spring?"

I'm going to shut him up about this, once and for all. I walk into my room and dig into the planter I made for Mom in fourth grade — the one that has her photo on it — and I come back out with the proof of how successful I've been.

"There — does that give you any idea?" I hurl the words at him, tossing a thick wad of bills on the coffee table in front of him. All told, it's about three thousand dollars, even after paying for my own guitar lessons and taxes. I got Mike to trade up the smaller bills we got as tips for larger ones, so I didn't have to worry about hiding a giant stack of cash that was mostly ones. Even then, it's the better part of an inch thick, unfolded.

His jaw drops. I'm momentarily concerned he'll make a grab for it and take it for himself, so I snatch it back up and start planning a new hiding place, because now that he knows I have it, chances are he'll go looking.

"And that's just from busking. The Carters are due back in a few weeks, and we're lining up full-on gigs. This is going to be chump change next to what we're bringing in by the end of the summer. So, you can take your fixation on an MBA and shove it. I don't even need to go to college to be successful. I've got enough to buy a cheap car right now, if I wanted to."

Well, that seems to have done the job. Because he still hasn't found any words to respond. I stalk back into my room and lock the door, trying to decide if I can even safely leave the cash in the house when I'm not here. Probably not. But Elle will hold onto it for me.

Two months later

"Great work, boys! Just great!"

That's Phil, the local promoter who's booked us at our last few gigs, including tonight's big gig at the bar in an Ocean City hotel. None of the four of us is old enough to be in the bar unless we're playing, except for Matt, our drummer, who's 22 and already pretty jaded. Which is weird for a guy who's just a decent drummer. We really need to get somebody better.

"Head on up to the hospitality suite. I've got some clients and their friends coming by, and they want to meet you. Help yourself to the goodies!" Phil says, handing us a key card with the room number on it.

The suite's on the top floor of the hotel, and judging by how few doors there are on this floor, it looks like it's huge, just from outside. Declan takes the key and unlocks the door, and I realize that the room is pretty well sound-proofed, because there's a whole separate party going on inside, and no one is carding us at the door.

"Whoo! The boys are here!" a very busty bottle-blonde announces to the room, and I recognize her from earlier in the bar. She's the one who kept pushing her tits into Declan's face while we were playing. She seemed like she was pretty tipsy then, and she's clearly sloshed now. She clamps onto Declan's arm and drags him over to a sofa

I wonder if she's what Phil meant by "goodies." Or maybe it's the large quantity of alcohol, which seems to be well broken-in by the couple dozen people of various ages who got here before we did. There's a lot of clapping of backs and shaking of hands as they realize the band has arrived, and I don't make it across the room before a svelte little brunette in a skintight dress attaches herself to my side.

"I just *loved* your performance tonight," she tells me. "You were just so sexy up there with that guitar, running your fingers up and down..." she demonstrates on my arm, "touching it all over..." And I see where this is heading. There's a few states where she'd be in legal jeopardy if she took me to bed, but Delaware and Maryland aren't among them.

On the other hand, Declan's lady might need a lawyer in a few hours, judging by how things are looking over there. Correction — Declan's *actual* lady isn't here, because she's not old enough to get into the bar. But as she's not here, that seems to have given the blonde a green light. On the other hand, I'm single, and this one... looks like fun.

Five hours later

"Fucking shit!"

That's Declan. Who appears to be unhappy. I sit up and realize I am also unhappy. My head is pounding like it's stuck inside Matt's kick drum. I'm also not thrilled to find last night's brunette lying naked on top of the sheets next to me — passed out, rather than sleeping, based on the fact that Declan's outburst didn't rouse her. I check to make sure she's breathing, which isn't too hard since she's got no clothes on. Check.

I head out into the center room of the suite to see what bug has crawled up our diva's butt. Did he run out of champagne? Was room service unwilling to bring him breakfast at... seven? Seems unlikely. Probably a champagne problem.

"Fuck! Fuck! Fuck! Fuck! Fuck! Fuckity fuck!"

Declan appears to be writing a song based entirely on alliteration using the letter F. He missed an S there at the start. But it's early. Give him time.

Dave has emerged from one of the other bedrooms down the hall and is rubbing his hand over his face, clearly just as freshly awakened as I am. He stands there, staring at his brother, who's pacing frantically back and forth across the room. Naked.

"Dude — put some clothes on! I haven't had to see that since we were kids. I have no desire to see it again now. Or ever."

I grab a blanket off the sofa, which is blessedly empty, and throw it at Declan, who catches it and wraps it around his waist, glaring at his brother.

"What's up, Dec?" I ask, at this point curious as to what's got him so riled so early in the morning.

"There's a blonde in my bed."

"There's a brunette in mine. Wanna trade?" I ask with a smile.

Now he's glaring at me, and I get the impression he's way more pissed about my joke than he was about David making him get dressed.

"You cheated on her?" David asks him, and all of a sudden I realize why Declan's bent out of shape. Unlike the two of us, he's got a steady girl. She's been working during every one of our other gigs this summer, and he'd wanted to sneak her backstage last night just so she could see us perform once, but she had a last-minute job interview and couldn't do it. With the blonde having waylaid him last night, I figured they weren't actually exclusive, but apparently they had been. Until now. Ouch.

See — this is why I won't do this to Ellie. One night in a hospitality suite with booze and a bevy of partying people of all ages, and Declan had fallen off the fidelity wagon. The rockstar lifestyle is not conducive to committed relationships, and we aren't even 18 yet. Dave will be soon. But my point stands.

"Where the fuck is Phil?"

"No idea, dude."

"Did I hear my name?"

Phil comes down the hall, wearing boxers, an undershirt and dress socks, his balding head crowned by a tracing of hair that's currently standing straight up.

"You sure as fuck did, Phil!" Declan confirms. "What the hell was this scene here last night? You brought a bunch of minors back to a room full of liquor and groupies?"

"Hey, hold on a minute now," Phil says, holding up his hands. "The people who attended your post-performance party were clients and friends, not groupies. If some of them happened to be very big fans who wanted to wish you well as your career takes off under my tutelage and offered toasts involving alcoholic beverages, I can't be held responsible for that."

"You sure as fuck can, Phil," David points out, uncharacteristically confrontational. "Providing alcohol to minors is a crime, in Maryland or Delaware."

"Oh, like you all have never gotten wasted at a party before..."

"I haven't. I didn't last night," Dave says. "Slept alone, sober, and was doing just fine until my brother started screaming his head off. Naked."

"So what's the big deal? You all aren't exactly teetotaling virgins here. You're objecting to booze and some pussy?"

"Declan's got a girl." Dave explains.

"Hey — not my fault you can't keep your dick in your pants after a few beers..."

Declan lunges for him, while I'm uncomfortably reminded of my father's — and now my — inability to keep it in *our* pants, before *or* after a few beers. Dave grabs Declan around the neck, holding him back from Phil, who's now backpedaling down the hallway.

"You're fired, Phil!" Declan yells at him.

"And you all are done here! You won't book another gig on the peninsula once I get done with you!" he yells back.

"Dec — you realize Phil doesn't actually work for us, right? He's a promoter, not our manager."

"Oh. Yeah. Right."

Declan goes from fighting mad to deflated in about three seconds.

"I can't believe I fucking did that," he says. "I don't even remember touching that woman, other than her grabbing onto my arm when we got here. I was drunk, but I'd remember that, wouldn't I?"

"Depends, man," I tell him. "I've had nights I got home from a party and didn't remember whether it had been two girls or three."

David and Declan are both staring at me.

"What? I got very popular last year after the talent show at school. I've been busy making up for lost time."

Dave just shakes his head.

"I want to tell you to just be honest with her, Dec," he says. "But I don't think that's going to cut it here. We're on the verge of breaking through, and we don't live here and she does, and you're going to have a lot more nights like this one from now on. If you can't be faithful to the girl now, what's it going to be like when we're on the road for four months at a time?"

Dave's straight-talk doesn't seem to have given Declan any peace of mind.

"Well, are we actually breaking through anywhere now that Phil's decided to ruin us?" I ask.

"He won't do a thing, Hunter. We're under-age, and he supplied alcohol to a party he encouraged us to attend, and which he attended, fully aware we were drinking. He's got nothing to leverage against us that won't end up with him in jail. And I'm going to remind him of that right now."

Dave heads down the hall.

"Well, at least we still have a career ahead of us," I tell Declan.

"Yeah. That's going to have to happen, since the rest of my life just imploded."

I pat him on the back, because I can't think of anything else to do.

CHAPTER 12

MOVIN' OUT

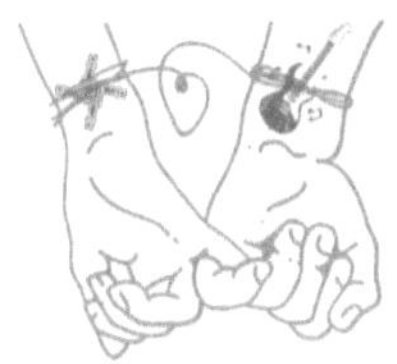

Hunter
Three months later

"**H**unter! Get your ass out here!"

Oh, boy. Dad's back on my case again. It's only gotten worse since school started, and I suspect that has to do with what he hasn't been able to find, even with me gone all day.

"Did you request a college application from George Mason University?"

"Yes. Ellie and I have been talking about going to school in Virginia."

"And do you think you're going to be able to get a scholarship to cover out-of-state tuition and all your room, board, books?"

"I don't know, Dad. I'm going to see what they offer. That's just one of the schools we were going to apply to."

"Well, your little bookworm may plan on getting some scholarship money, or maybe her parents are willing to pay out-of-state tuition, but I'm not."

"Mom left me my trust fund. I'll use that."

"You can't touch that money until you're 25. *I* can't touch that money until you're 18."

"And that's the real problem here, isn't it?"

"What are you implying?"

"That you'd very much like to dip into my trust fund to support your habits, including all your girlfriends."

"Where'd you get an idea like that?"

"Watching you. I know you've been looking for my savings, Dad. You should be more careful about putting things back where they were when you found them."

He's gone from slightly pale to livid red.

"I'm a grown man with a successful real estate career. I don't need your piddling little handful of bills from sweaty tourists."

"Then why have you been looking through my room for it? Or were you in sudden desperate need of more condoms and couldn't locate them in the well-hidden spot in the big drawer in my bedside table?"

He looks like he's ready to explode. I'm tempted to stand back a few feet just to avoid the mess that would make.

What he doesn't know is that, thanks to full summer of gigs — not just busking — my savings has ballooned up from the roughly three thousand I had back in spring to nearly seven thousand, once I'd set aside money for taxes. Ellie didn't just stick it in a ceramic planter in her bedroom. She put it in her savings account, where it's been collecting a tiny bit of interest and is safely out of the reach of my dad.

It's not the kind of money that's in my trust fund, but I could use it to buy a car, or to get an apartment if the college thing doesn't work out. Which suddenly feels more likely than it did yesterday.

"You can't go to college at 17 without a parent or guardian's approval. Especially not out of state. And I'm not signing anything that's going to send you off playing house with that girl, or pursuing your rockstar delusions with those Carter kids. You can stay home, attend community college and get a job — learn to really work for your money."

"I *do* work for my money, Dad. How do you think I saved all that money you've been trying to find in my room? I worked a ten-hour day two or three days a week, and you never even noticed, did you?"

"Music isn't work. And you've been going to a lot of parties, coming back late at night, bringing home girls — don't think I haven't noticed that."

"I could say the same about you, Dad," I point out. Yeah, there's an explosion on the horizon.

"Hunter! You are not going anywhere but community college in Georgetown. I'm not giving my permission, and I'm not paying for it. Your grades aren't good enough for a full-ride scholarship, and there's no way you've saved enough to pay all your own expenses once you turn 18. So, get your head out of the clouds and prepare to get to know what the real world is like. Because it's not going to coddle you like your mother did."

He stomps off. Which is a good thing, because I was just about to punch someone for the first time in my life.

Two weeks later

"I've got to get out of there, Elle. I can't stand it anymore. He's finding ways to drive me nuts, even when I'm not home. He's still looking for the money. He's nagging me about getting 'a real job.' I can't even get homework done at home, because he's always interrupting me to complain about the fact that I don't have a job and am playing music. I'm not sure I can even leave my guitar at home now, because I don't trust him to pawn it or just destroy it out of spite. And if I lose that guitar... I can't just replace it. Mom gave it to me."

"Bring it over here. You can come get it whenever you need it. Practice here if you want. Mom won't mind, and Dad'll get over it," she says, giving me a hug and leaning her head against my shoulder. "I can talk to them again about letting you move back in. Mom wanted to look into making you an emancipated minor. She'll be on board with one or the other."

"That would be great, Elle, but your dad already doesn't like me. He's not going to let me move back in just because my dad is making life uncomfortable for me. And my dad isn't going to let me do that when he can use me to keep control over my trust fund."

"I'll talk to Dad. I'll make him understand! We can fight your dad for control of your trust fund and guardianship."

"Thanks for wanting to do that, Elle. But I don't see how. Dad's really determined. Maybe I can stick it out until I'm 18 and then find somewhere to live in Virginia. We were making good money gigging here. We should be able to do it there, too. He's right that I can't afford to pay for college on my own, and my grades aren't good enough to get as big a scholarship as I'd need."

"But we were going to go to college together! I've got applications in at George Mason and GWU, and I'm in the process of finishing the one for American and a couple others."

"It's not in the cards for me, Elle. You've got the grades to get in all those schools and probably even get some scholarship money. And your parents will pay for the rest. He's not giving me a penny, and what I have saved up just won't cut it. But, more importantly, he won't let me go, so I'm stuck here until I'm 18 anyway."

She sighs, seeming to have reached the same conclusion I have.

"Have you talked to Dave and Declan?"

"Yeah. I told them I'm likely going to be stuck here another year. They're willing to come here to gig again next summer, even after Declan's big blow-up with his girlfriend, but we'd been wanting to get an early start on booking gigs in Virginia and D.C., and we need to find a drummer there to do that. This isn't just causing problems for me. It's causing problems for them, too."

"We need to find a way to persuade your dad to let you go, to either give over guardianship to my parents or just let you live here until you're 18."

"That's not going to happen, Elle. He's fixated on that money. Right now, I'd almost rather Mom hadn't left it to me, because Dad's using it as a ball and chain to keep me stuck here with him until he can figure out how to get it. Then he's got seven years to spend it on gifts for his girlfriends and a new Corvette for him. It doesn't matter that it's not aboveboard to do that. He'll do it anyway. And I can't do anything about that until I'm 25. There'll be nothing left by then anyway."

"This just isn't fair. At all. He's going to end up with your money one way or another. There's got to be a way to convince him to let you go to Virginia, whether it's to college or to start performing with the Carters."

"At this point, if I didn't have to worry about living on nothing, I'd happily give him my savings just to get him to let me go. But I don't have enough to make it worthwhile for him to let me go and my trust fund with me." I'm wracking my brain for anything that might get my father out of my life— "Wait... If all he cares about is getting the money... Why don't I offer him money?"

"What? You just said you don't think your savings is enough."

"No — I mean give him the trust fund. Or access to it, anyway. If there won't be any left with him in charge of it, then why not just hand it over to him?"

"Or you could tell him you'll do that, and then once you're 18, we can find you an estate lawyer who'll fight him for control of it."

"I really don't care about the money, Elle. I just can't stay under his thumb much longer. At this point, I'm almost tempted to just run away and try to make it on my own as a musician."

"No! You can't do that. You wouldn't be safe out there on your own."

I don't think Elle thinks I'd be OK anywhere without her to take care of me. She might be right about that, to some degree, but if it meant getting away from my dad, I'm willing to sleep on sofas and work multiple jobs until the Carters and I can get our careers on track.

"The Carters!"

"What?"

"I need to get to Virginia so we can get the band going there. I need Dad to let me go so I can do that. He wants the trust fund. I can agree to let him have it, not fight him over it — if he'll let me go to Virginia. Where, maybe, I could stay with the Carters — in their garage, with the band equipment or something. I can get a job, take the GED once I turn 18."

"You'd drop out of school?"

"I'd need to have a job to support myself, Elle. I can't expect Declan and Dave's parents to support me, even if they're willing to let me live in their garage. And I'm happy to do that, if it means I can play with the guys and start building up the band."

"You think your dad will go for it? You think the Carters' parents will?"

"I think he will. I think they might. This could be the solution, Elle. All I'm losing is the trust fund I won't be seeing any of anyway."

"And the chance to finish high school and graduate with me..."

She's devastated by this, I can tell. And probably by the fact that I'd be leaving her here, for the better part of a year, until she could come to Virginia for college. I give her a tight hug.

"I'm sorry, Elle. I really am. I just can't do this much longer. I've got to get out from under my dad's thumb, get started on my career. And I'm willing to do just about anything to make that happen. The hardest part of this isn't giving up the trust fund my mom left me — it's leaving you here. But you'll be able to come after graduation. It's not that long. We can do this. Both of us."

She's crying silently now, and I wipe her tears from her cheeks. I press a kiss to the top of her head. I don't do that much anymore, but it's comforting for both of us, and facing this separation after basically spending our entire lives together, I think we both need that. We can do this. I can do this. I have a plan, and it's time to put it in motion.

CHAPTER 13

CHANGES

Hunter
Two months later

It's a new life for me. I've had to leave behind my home, my school, a thriving social life, any hope of a normal high-school graduation, the nominal security I thought I'd had with at least one parent still living, a substantial trust fund and my best friend — the only family I felt like I really had left. That last one is the one that hurt the most. But it will all be worthwhile. I'm sure of it.

The Carters — Bob and Carolyn — agreed to let me move in with them. David and Declan were thrilled because we'd finally be able to get the band moving onward and upward, especially once we found a drummer.

Demonstrating exactly how greedy he is, my father refused to transfer guardianship to the Carters, worried they could wrest the trust away from him. I signed papers that I knew would never hold up in court, releasing my trust fund entirely to him. The Carters had him sign papers giving them legal authority for my medical care and other emergency needs. They refused my offer of rent or money for food but agreed that I could get a full-time job and study for the GED in my free time. I can take it next fall, as soon as I'm 18.

I decided to go around the Carters and ensure that I had some additional freedom and security — especially if I was going to be trying to book us gigs. I took some of my savings and bought a fake I.D. that says I'm 21. I look old enough that I can pass. As soon as I let it slip to David and Declan, they wanted their own — not to drink, but so we could all perform in bars without having to worry about any age restrictions. I dumped most of the remaining money I brought with me into in-ear monitors, new effects pedals and a new vocal mic, so we'll be ready to play out as soon as we find a drummer.

I figured I'd spend my days working whatever jobs I could find, and we'd be rehearsing and gigging a few nights a week, at least until David and Declan finished college. We could get an apartment together near campus, and I could chip in on rent while the Carters cover their portion. And that's where we hit a snag.

It was college application season, and while Elle had sent in a handful of applications to schools in the D.C. area, Declan had refused outright to even apply anywhere.

"There is no good reason for me to attend college, Mom," he says one night as I sit in my borrowed bedroom down the hall. I'm not liking where this is headed. "We were making enough gigging last summer that Dave and I can basically support ourselves once we get the band going full-time, with a new drummer. Why would you want to waste tuition money?"

"You need a college education, Declan. This is a non-starter. You need to pick a school and apply. It doesn't have to be the same one as your brother. But you can't just opt out of going to college. We won't let you."

"I'm almost 18! I'll be 18 before classes would start in the fall. This is my choice to make."

"It's a decision you would regret, Declan," Bob says, his voice grave. "You can't make anything of yourself in this world without a college degree!"

"I'm going to be a music legend, Dad. This is where I'm headed, where this band is headed. We've already started making our mark. It only goes up from here."

"It's a pipe-dream, Declan. We were happy to support you boys using your talents when it was just playing at the beach, but it's time for you all to buckle down and get serious about your lives, your careers going forward. You need a college education," his dad says.

"Moreover, your brother is already set to go to college," Carolyn points out. "You can't expect to spend all your time on the band, because he's going to have other priorities. Sure, keep practicing, build the band, play out once a month or something. But you need to put the band on the back burner and finish college first."

"Why should we wait? Hunter's already done with school, except for one stupid test. I'm not going to spend all my time in a classroom or with my nose in a book when I could be out making a name for myself! If Hunter can skip his last year of high school, why is it so important that I go to college for four years?"

"Carolyn — see, I told you this was a bad idea. It's set a bad example for the boys, helping Hunter get out of the normal obligations of a boy their age."

I assume they don't realize I can hear this. They're nice people. They wouldn't talk like this about me if they thought I could hear them. But I can. And I feel bad knowing they think I've caused this. I would happily have gone to college if things had been different. I don't want Declan to lose his chance at a normal life that I, frankly, envy.

"After his thing with that girl ended, Declan going to college wasn't even in question anymore, until Hunter moved in with us," Bob continued. "We've put him on a path that our boys now want to go down, and that path doesn't lead to college. I knew we'd end up regretting this."

"Bob, shhh… That's unfair to Hunter. He's been put in a terrible position. Honestly, the boy should have been emancipated, or better yet, actually protected by his mother's will."

"I don't disagree, Carolyn, but we're still dealing with a situation with Declan that we wouldn't be dealing with if Hunter had stayed in Delaware. We've got to get both boys through college, even if Declan has an overambitious sense of his own talent."

"Uhh… Standing right here!" Declan reminds them.

"If you're going to act like a prima donna, you're going to have to learn to take criticism," Bob tells him. I admit it. I smiled a little.

Two months later

"Are you kidding me? Seriously, how did we get here?" Bob asks, making no effort to keep his voice down this time. "We went from two sons going to college to one refusing so they can go chase this ridiculous dream of theirs, and now *both* want to skip college so they can be in a rock band. Where did we go wrong?"

"You could argue that it was the moment we gave the boys guitar lessons. If we hadn't done that, we wouldn't be in this predicament," Carolyn suggests.

"I still think it's the example Hunter's given them. They weren't refusing to go until he decided *he* couldn't go and then came here, giving them ideas of chasing this dream of stardom. Having him come live with us was a mistake."

This is, by far, not the only time this has come up since I moved in with the Carters. It's been a semi-regular refrain since Declan informed them he would not be going to college. But things have ramped up today, after David told his parents that — despite having been accepted at three different colleges, with a partial scholarship — he was not going to college either.

I'm not sure David would have made the same choice if Declan hadn't made it first. But once that was done, David had a choice between going to college and trying to do the band part-time for four years, or skipping college and doing the band full-time.

We'd already proven we could potentially make a living doing this if we did it full-time. And we'd started to build a reputation at the beach that we could parlay into bookings here. That wasn't going to hold through four years of part-time gigs. If we wanted to make a real go of things, it was going to be as soon as we'd all turned 18 and the Carters finished high school, in eight months.

I'm set to take my GED next month. Ellie's been quizzing me over the phone. She says I'm a cinch to pass.

"You've aced every practice test I could dig up, Hunt. I'm not sure you could be more prepared. It's hard to believe you're going to be done with school so soon," she said.

"You don't have that much longer. You're nearly there. Do you have everything lined up for college?"

"Yeah. The formalities are all done. It's just a matter of registering for classes, arranging for the dorm, having my parents pay the tuition." She sighs. "I tried, Hunt — I crammed as many classes as I could into my schedule, and I'm still two credits short of being able to graduate early. I could have been there in January instead of August."

"Why would you do that, Elle? You deserve to enjoy a normal senior year, prom, graduation..."

"School is torture without you here, Hunt. I don't even want to be in the building except to take my classes. Prom? I didn't go last year. I haven't been to a school dance since before you left. What point is there? I'd just be sitting by myself. Or, worse, getting picked on by all the people there with their dates. I'm just counting down the days until graduation, and my parents are more excited about that than I am. I'm just ready to get out of here."

"You can make it. It's not that much longer."

"How's everything else going?"

"I got a second job — it's just another restaurant job, but the people are nice and the hours fit with the diner, since they only do breakfast and lunch. Still leaves me time to practice and gig, as long as I plan ahead."

"And how are things with the Carters?"

"Tense. David deciding not to go to college has put them in a tailspin. I'm going to start looking for another place to live, now that I'm almost 18."

"I wish things had gone better with them. I don't like that you feel like you have to leave. And I don't like missing your birthday, either. It's the first time since we met that we haven't had our birthdays together."

"We'll make up for it next year. I promise. We'll do two birthday celebrations for each of us — two cakes, two presents..."

"I miss your silly face."

"I miss yours, too."

Eight months later

Elle looks so grown-up in her cap and gown. I'm glad I didn't miss this. I had to beg for a day off from both of my jobs and for a ride from David in order to get here. I'm just lucky her graduation wasn't on the same weekend as his and Declan's, which I did not go to. Because I wouldn't have been welcome.

I'm standing next to a tree at the back of the crowd, hoping she doesn't spot me, because if she knows I'm here, she'll want to spend the night with me instead of celebrating with her parents, and I can't handle another hostile parent right now. And because I'm a lousy liar. I'd never be able to lie to her face when she asks how I'm doing. Because I never told her I moved out of the Carters' house without having anywhere else to go.

The day I turned 18, I went to work as usual. Only I stashed literally everything I owned in the break room at the diner. OK — everything except my guitar and other gear, which remain safely in the Carters' garage.

Jerry, my boss, noticed the big bag of clothes and took pity on me. He set up a cot in the storeroom, which is where I've been sleeping ever since. Declan and David both told me I didn't need to leave, but it was pretty obvious that their parents were relieved, even if it hadn't changed the guys' minds about college. Dave insisted I at least shower at their house after rehearsals.

I'm in Mystic Beach just long enough to watch Ellie graduate. I just had to see her complete this one ritual of a normal senior year. I could have been up there with her, but it would have been hollow, because Mom wouldn't have been there, and my dad probably wouldn't have either. I'm an official high school graduate now anyway. I took the GED a week after I moved out of the Carters' and, as she predicted, aced it.

Watching her cross the stage now to accept her diploma, I take in her radiant smile and I love seeing how proud of herself she is. I wonder how much bigger that smile would be if I was crossing that stage ahead of her. But that wasn't to be. And that's OK. I just miss her.

At that exact moment, she turns to look out at the audience, her eyes sliding in my direction. I duck back farther behind the tree, giving it a beat before I peek back out and make sure she didn't see me. She's got an odd look on her face — confused, questioning, concerned. But then she moves back to her seat, and it seems like I managed to avoid her seeing me after all.

I stay long enough to see the tassel thing with the caps and then all of them tossed up in the air, despite a warning from the administrators. Ellie finds her parents and gets a big hug from her mom, while her dad stands proudly behind her. There's a pang in my gut, knowing that I could have had that moment, too, but that fate had decided it wasn't for me. I'm happy she gets it, though. I wanted that for her.

I blow her a kiss she can't see, and I head out toward Dave's car, ready for the ride back to my life, as crappy as that seems sometimes these days. But now that the Carter brothers have graduated, the Carter Brothers Band can graduate to the next level, too. And if I have to work two jobs and sleep on a cot to help us get there, I'm totally willing to do it. And once August arrives, I'll be able to do it with my best friend by my side.

CHAPTER 14

LITTLE LIES

Ellie
Two months later

"**E**llie! How wonderful to see you!"

I'm immediately suspicious. This is not how Declan usually greets me, which is with eye-rolls and annoyance.

"Look who's here, Davey! It's Ellie!"

The brothers exchange a look that tells me something is going on and that I'm probably not going to like it.

"How's it going, Elle?" David asks.

"Good. Just got my stuff unpacked at my dorm. Decided to surprise Hunter by taking him out to dinner, since I came in a day early."

"Ah! A surprise! How wonderful!" Declan comments, still in that strangely ...elated tone.

"OK, guys... I know we haven't seen each other in like a year, but what's going on here?"

"Hunter isn't here, Elle," Dave says in a refreshingly normal voice. "He's at work."

"Oh. His hours changed?"

"There *have* been some changes," Declan says, acting nervous.

"Come on, guys. What is this? You're acting really strangely."

Dave frowns at Declan, clearly laying the blame for whatever this weirdness is at his feet.

"What? Spit it out! Did he get fired? Is he out on a date? Knee-deep in groupies?"

"No, but that sounds like fun!" Declan says with genuine enthusiasm.

"He really is at work, Elle," David says. "You should call him, let him know you're here early. I'm not sure what time he might be free."

"OK. Thanks." I sit behind the wheel of my car for a minute, trying to figure out what might be going on that the Carter brothers are acting so strangely just because I showed up a little early, hoping to find Hunter at home. That sense of something being off isn't reduced by the fact that the brothers haven't returned to the garage now that I'm leaving, but are instead arguing animatedly right where I left them.

I give Hunter a call, but it goes to voicemail. And now I'm worried. I'm sure whatever is going on has to be something considerably less worrisome than my imagination, but I've been getting an odd feeling from Hunter lately, and it's better than I figure it out now than keep worrying. So I head off to the first of Hunter's two jobs, where he should already have been off. He should have been off from his second job today entirely, but I'm no longer sure of that.

The little diner serves breakfast and lunch, and they should have been closed two hours ago. But Hunter had stayed late before. I head to the back door off the alley, which seems the most likely place for an employee to answer the door.

I can't see any lights on inside. I knock loudly anyway. When there's no answer, I dial Hunter again, once again getting voicemail. Part of me is sure he's here, but...

One more time, then I'm going to go try the other place.

I pound hard on the door, going on longer than I normally would, just in case they're up front or something. Still no answer. Just as I turn to go, the door opens behind me.

"Sorry — we're clos..."

It's not unexpected that Hunter would answer the door, since David had said he was at work. What's unexpected — in addition to me, clearly — is that Hunter is not dressed for work. He's barely dressed at all, in fact. No shirt. No shoes. Just socks and a pair of cargo shorts.

"Elle! What are you... What are you doing here? I thought you weren't getting here until tomorrow."

"I decided to leave early. I was hoping to surprise you and take you out to dinner tonight. David and Declan said you were at work, after acting really weird about me being there. Hunter — what's going on?"

He sighs.

"Come in. I'll explain," he says, clearly not happy to see me under whatever circumstances these are.

He disappears into a storeroom the moment he shuts the door behind me, coming back out with a shirt on. I'm suspicious about that but opt not to say anything as he leads me into an employee breakroom nearby. He gestures for me to sit down and pulls up a chair right next to me, turning me so that our knees are bumping and we're facing each other.

"Hunter? What is going on? You're worrying me."

"That's what I was trying to *avoid*," he says, looking downcast. "I moved out of the Carters' house."

"When was this?"

"On my 18th birthday."

"Hunter! That was almost a year ago! Why didn't you tell me?"

All of a sudden, I know why something had seemed off for months now...

"You're sleeping here. You're *living* here. In the storeroom."

He nods solemnly.

"And you didn't want me to worry that you were essentially homeless. Because you knew I'd have moved heaven and earth to fix that."

"You couldn't have done anything, Elle. If I'd been truly desperate, I would have asked you to send me some money from my savings, even though I was hoping to save it until I had an apartment lined up. But the day I moved out, my boss here, Jerry, offered to let me crash on a cot in the storeroom. I haven't been sleeping on the streets."

"And showers? Washing your clothes? Have you had enough to eat?"

"I shower at the Carters' when I go over for rehearsals. Same with clothes. Dave insisted and his parents seem to be OK with it. And I've never gone hungry. I work at two restaurants, Elle," he says with a sheepish grin, "and people like me. Just gotta turn on the charm."

I'm taking deep breaths now to keep myself calm. Because if I don't, I'm not sure Hunter will have to worry about having a place to live. Because you have to be alive in order to need one.

"You're pissed," he concludes.

"Fuck, yes, I'm pissed!" He flinches. "You lied to me! For nearly a year! And if I wasn't furious at you for having done it, for not letting me do whatever I could to help, for now giving me retroactive nightmares about how things have been for you here, for not feeling like you could be honest with me... I'd be furious at myself for not having realized that there was something going so wrong in your life. I knew something was off, but..."

I put my hand on the side of his jaw, stroking the stubble there with my thumb, and I hazard a look into his eyes — something that has been so fraught these last couple of years. And I'm just stunned by what I see. Physically, he seems fine — no evidence he's lost any significant amount of weight, clean, relatively recently shaved, clothes in good shape.

But his eyes are... haunted, like he's gone through a lot. Stronger for it, perhaps, but marked by it. Embarrassed, certainly. Regretful, I suspect for having lied to me. And, somehow, for some reason, guilt, self-punishment. With an undercurrent of vulnerability that I haven't seen in him since just after his mother died. And my anger dies with that thought.

I grab him into a tight hug, pulling him into my shoulder.

"Don't you ever do that to me ever again! Don't lie to me. Don't pretend things are OK when they're not. Don't feel like you have to rely on yourself when I'm always going to be there to help, even if I'm hours away. Do you understand me?"

"Mmmkyy, melle. Moo cn lemma guh nowm," he mumbles into my skin.

"Sorry... It's just..."

"I made you worry, after the fact."

"You *scared the living crap out of me*, after the fact."

I take a deep breath.

"I set up a bank account when I did all the school registration stuff. I'll transfer all your savings in there, and you can start putting your paychecks in there, too. Here's the debit card," I tell him, digging in my purse. "You know the PIN already," I tell him with a wink.

"Jerry's been paying me in cash. I didn't want to risk using my fake I.D. for a bank account," he says. "This will help."

"You have a fake I.D.?"

"I wanted to be sure I never got into a position where being younger would cause problems. I'm officially 21, almost 22, if you believe my I.D. It's a good one. I paid for quality. And now we can play in bars without having to worry about the age thing."

"Take some of my money and get me one, too," I tell him. "If you're playing in bars, I'm going to need to be able to get in, too."

He gives me a look up and down, as if weighing whether he should abet my first criminal act.

"You'll pass," he says, giving me a wry smile. "I'll get it set up and let you know."

"Go get a change or two of clothes, and anything you want me to hold for safekeeping."

"Why?"

"I'm taking you out to dinner. And then you're coming back to the dorm with me, where we will stash anything you don't want to keep here, and where you will sleep in a real bed in a room with its own shower and all the fluffy towels you could want, courtesy of Mom."

"You're not going to get in trouble for that? Your roommate won't mind?"

"I'm an early arrival," I point out, giving him heavy side-eye. "Hardly anyone is in the dorm yet. Roommate isn't due in until next week, right before classes start. And, if need be, we can sneak you in and out of the window. I'm on the ground floor. It's not so high up you can't boost yourself up or drop down safely to the ground."

"I wouldn't mind a good night's sleep on a bed that's meant to hold someone more my size."

"Don't get overambitious — it's my bed, too, and I will not tolerate bed-hogging."

"I promise — no bed-hogging. And it's not like we haven't shared before, Elle-belle," he says, giving me a hug. "I'm kind of used to it."

"Me, too, Hunt. Me, too."

CHAPTER 15

MAD WORLD

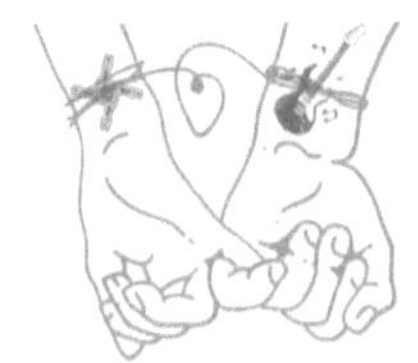

Hunter
Three weeks later

Being able to get some solid sleep, in a real bed, has been a real boost. I slept in Elle's dorm room for a week. When her roommate arrived, I told her I was going back to my cot, where I stayed for three days, until Elle informed me that the roommate was spending most nights with her boyfriend and that the coast was clear. When the roommate comes back, I make myself scarce.

"Hunter, have you considered looking for a job in a music store? Maybe giving lessons? Seems like that would be a better fit for you than washing dishes and busing tables," she points out one night as we share a sub and a huge pile of fries in the campus cafeteria. "Might even pay better."

"I looked when I first got here, but the Carters' house was too far from anywhere that had an opening. Too many wannabe professional musicians who need to make ends meet."

"Have you looked around *here*?"

"I haven't looked around *here* because I was living *there*, and I don't have a car. Can't rely on being able to get to a job I can't walk to."

"Then use my car."

"I can't do that. How are you going to get around?"

"I brought it with me so that I could be sure to be able to see you, even if you didn't have one. But I'm taking a full slate of classes. How often am I going to need to go out anywhere that needs a car unless I'm going there with you?"

I'm not entirely comfortable with this idea. But I do like the idea of swapping out one or both restaurant jobs for something more in my wheelhouse.

"It might also help with making contacts, getting gigs booked, finding a drummer."

"Yeah, it might. If you're really sure..."

"Hunter — what did I say about feeling like you have to rely on yourself when I'm always going to be there to help?"

"Not to." She gives me a meaningful look. "O.K. — I'll start looking tomorrow."

The next day

"I don't have anything right now, but we usually lose a guitar teacher or two every year, with graduation, people taking off for L.A. or New York to try their luck at going pro... I can keep you in mind. But that all depends on whether you've got the chops," says Eddie, the manager of the music store closest to the campus.

I unpack my PRS and plug in to one of the amps in the guitar room.

I start the signature opening to Led Zeppelin's "Stairway to Heaven." After three bars, I look over at Eddie, who has an expression of deep suffering on his face. "Just kidding!" I tell him with a wink, sliding straight into Eric Johnson's "Cliffs of Dover."

"Stairway" is a gorgeous song, but almost literally everyone plays it when they're in a guitar shop, and the staff comes to hate it with a passion. "Cliffs of Dover," on the other hand, is considered to be one of the most technically challenging songs to learn, but especially to learn to perform it well and cleanly, with its fast runs and hybrid picking techniques. Almost no one plays it in a guitar shop.

If Eddie was pissed off at me for yanking his chain with "Stairway," he wasn't by the time I glanced back up at him. His eyes said "kid in a candy store," and his slack jaw said, "We're not worthy." There's a reason I had practiced the shit out of this song. And he wasn't alone. When I looked up at the end of the last run, it looked like everyone in the store had gathered behind him. There was a moment of dead silence and a few heads being shaken, and then I had half a dozen musicians clapping me on the back.

When I put my guitar back in the case, Eddie's still shaking his head.

"You're at the top of my list if anyone leaves. Hunter, was it?"

"Yeah, man. I appreciate it. My band's working on booking some more gigs locally," I tell him, "and until we get a new drummer, I'll happily pick up some hours in the shop or teaching."

"I'll be in touch. Stop by anytime if you want to give the stock a workout."

I finish latching up the case and get ready to hit the next shop on my list.

"You said you're looking for a drummer?"

A tall guy with wavy bright-red hair down to his shoulders walks up to me and extends his hand.

"My band is, yeah," I tell him, shaking his hand. "You a drummer?"

"Among other things. Music major, junior year. Name's Rhys Madigan — that's R-H-Y-S, like the candy."

"Isn't the candy spelled R-E-E-S-E?"

"I've heard it both ways."

O... K...

"Anyway — my bandmates graduated last semester, so I'm actually available right now. And if the rest of your band is as good as you are, you can sign me up!"

"Well, I'd have to talk to the other guys. But, yeah, they're good."

"You got a rehearsal space?"

"Yeah. Their garage. It isn't far."

"Can it be reached by boat?"

"Uh... No. It's a garage. On land." *What is this guy on?*

"I'll make do."

"Thursday afternoon work OK? Around four?"

"Are there any tall trees or power lines nearby?"

"Well, yeah, a few... What does that..."

"No open fields?"

"Nothing closer than a couple blocks. Why?"

"I can do 4:02 on Thursday, but I'll need a landing zone nearby."

"Landing zone?"

"Yeah. At 4:01, I'll be around 4,000 feet overhead."

"You're a pilot?"

"No. I'll be jumping out of the plane at four. The pilot's staying on board."

"I would hope so." *This is not looking very promising.* "How about we say 5:30 on Thursday? Would that work?"

"Yeah. That'll give me time to get my kit. Otherwise, I'd have to jump with it, and kick drums aren't very aerodynamic."

Oh, boy...

"No offense, man, but do you... uh... do any recreational drugs?"

"Don't touch the stuff. Mom warned me not to when I was younger. 'Just say no, Rhys!' she'd say. 'Unless it's your Adderall. Take that. *Please.*'"

"I see... You've got ADHD?"

"I just have a hard time staying focused, unless I'm on my kit. Or plummeting 10,000 feet a minute."

"O.K. I see." *I really, really hope this guy can focus long enough to unload his kit. Otherwise, Dave and Declan are going to be ribbing me for the next year.*

"What's the band's name?"

"For right now, we're the Carter Brothers Band."

"My mom won't let me change my name. And I'm already adopted, so I'm not sure this will work out."

What?

"Uh... No need to change your name or become a Carter brother. It's just that the other two guys are brothers. The Carter brothers, Dave and Declan."

"So you're not their brother?"

"No, man. I used to live with them, though."

"Where do you live now?"

"I'm camping out with a friend on campus."

"You want to come crash on my couch?"

"Umm... Why don't we start with an audition for the band?"

"Sounds like a plan, man."

Thursday, 5:29 p.m.

"Guys... I gotta warn you... This guy is a little... odd."

I figure it's best to come clean about this before they see for themselves.

"Like what? He's got a weird sense of humor and thinks geeky jokes are funny?" Declan asks.

I roll my eyes at him.

"He thinks he's been kidnapped by aliens?" David suggests.

"He has an unnatural relationship with his pet hamster?" Declan offers.

I'm starting to think Rhys is going to fit in just fine.

"No. He's got ADHD, I think, and his thinking seems to be a little... erratic."

"Can he play?"

"No idea."

"If he kicks ass on a kit, I don't care if he runs off chasing squirrels between sets," Declan declares.

"I'm not sure I'd rule that out."

Well, at least I warned them.

Rhys arrives at 5:30 on the dot. With the largest drum kit I have ever seen up close and personal.

"Wow, man... How'd you even fit this in your car?" Dave asks.

Rhys is driving a very large SUV. And still it's clearly taken a master at Tetris to have loaded up this kit.

"Madigan magic," Rhys says, wiggling his nose like he's Samantha on "Bewitched." I can't tell if he's serious. But I'm not going to ask. He seems a little more focused today, and I'm not going to be the guy drawing his attention to the squirrel.

We pitch in unloading everything into the garage and when Rhys declines the offer of help setting up, we go ahead and start warming up, just the three of us jamming. But "Madigan magic" apparently also includes the ability to set up said massive drum kit at record speed, and before we know it, Rhys is on his throne, thumping his kick pedal and checking the tuning on his toms.

"O.K. — what do you want to start with?" he asks.

"Why don't you just show us what you can do, and we'll go from there."

And Rhys Madigan launches straight into Dream Theater's "The Dance of Eternity."

Six minutes later, the three of us exchange a look and shake our heads in wonder.

I jump into Soundgarden's "Spoonman," which Declan loves to sing but which really needs a drummer for the drum break. It also gives the bass player and drummer a chance to play off each other as the drum break slides back into the main riff. And Dave really seems to enjoy that.

"Dude! You are a madman on that kit!" Dave enthuses. And I take that as a benediction, because it's coming from the other half of our new rhythm section.

"I like the sound of that," Rhys says. "Madman — it rhymes with Madigan."

Thus, Rhys "The Madman" Madigan becomes part of the Carter Brothers Band.

CHAPTER 16

WE WILL ROCK YOU

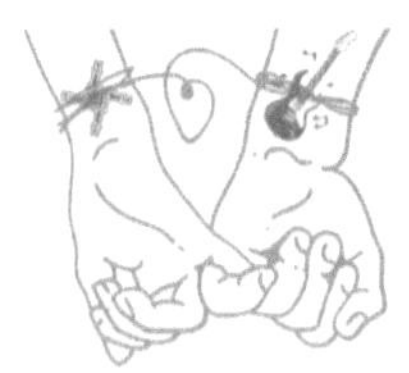

Ellie
Six weeks later

"No, Mom, I really can't come home. I missed Hunter's birthday last year, and we agreed to do a double celebration this year. It's only a few days anyway. I'll come home over the winter break for sure."

"Ellie, your dad would like you to come back sooner. He's very concerned that you're spending too much time with Hunter instead of on your classes, and he really wants to discuss you changing your major."

"I'm not changing my major. I've already told him that a dozen times. And I'm doing fine in all of my classes, thank you. The fiber-arts teacher even has me working at an expedited pace."

"Well, that's nice to hear. I'm glad she's got such confidence in you."

I wish Dad had that, too.

"I'm doing just fine, Mom. Tell Dad that. He doesn't seem to hear me when I say it. He's so fixated on blaming Hunter for everything, even when there's nothing to blame anyone for."

"I know, dear. He's been very unreasonable about this. I'll keep trying. Just make sure you keep your grades up in your academic classes, and come home for the winter break. Please. I'm not sure what he'd do if you stayed there over Christmas."

"I'm not planning on it, Mom. I miss you, too. And I'll have plenty of time to get home in December."

"Alright, Ellie. Keep that good head on your shoulders and let us know how things are going."

"I will, Mom. Love you! Bye!"

Well, that was no fun. I really do think it's silly for my dad to get bent out of shape over my not coming home for a break that doesn't even last a whole week. But there's no way I'm leaving here when it's both Hunter's birthday and the debut gig for the new lineup of the Carter Brothers Band! Hunter, as promised, hooked me up with a fake I.D. that declares me to be 21, so I can attend the gig.

For his part, Hunter's been a little more scarce the last few weeks. He's actually crashing on the couch at their drummer's apartment these days. He still comes over to hang out with me a couple nights a week and usually sleeps over when he does. But I've gone to a few of their rehearsals, and they sound awesome!

Rhys is... Well, he's a lot like an overenthusiastic large-breed puppy. I think people may assume he's not very smart, just because his thinking is kind of disjointed at times and his attention span isn't great. But we've spent a little time talking about the anthropological and psychological underpinnings of Star Trek and Star Wars, so I know better. I've only ever been able to talk to Hunter about that stuff.

I actually think Hunter's a little worried about how well Rhys and I get along. He's mentioned my thing for redheads a couple of times, and I've had a little fun at his expense by playing that up. Rhys' hair is lovely, with those loose copper ringlets cascading down to his collarbone. And I like a tall guy, so Rhys' 6-foot-4 is very much in my wheelhouse. But there's really no room in my heart for anyone else, and I've got no designs on Rhys, even if it amuses me to have Hunter think I do.

"You ready to go, Elle? My gear's all packed up," Hunter says.

"Yup! Just got off the phone with Mom. You ready for this? You nervous?"

"Me? Nah. We've done all of this before. It's just a new drummer, a new setlist, a new venue..."

I chuckle, because I can feel Hunter's nerves on high alert already, and we haven't even gotten to the venue yet.

"You'll do fine, rockstar. Settle in. You're going to be doing this for a long while to come."

I help Hunter load in his gear and pitch in with Rhys’ drum kit, too. None of the venue staff give me a second look. I didn’t even have to show my I.D. I’m almost disappointed.

It’s hours before the guys will go on stage, but they’ll be spending that time setting up and doing their soundcheck. I get myself a soda and just try to stay out of the way.

Pretty soon, Hunter is pacing backstage, which seems to be his coping mechanism for his nerves. They’ve played for a crowd this size before, about 350 people maximum, so it’s just a question of how many people will turn out and how they’ll respond to the Carter Brothers Band. But I know these guys — they’re rockstars. It’s just that not everyone has figured that out yet. But they will. The hundreds of people here tonight will know before they leave. This is just the beginning.

I give Hunter a quick hug for luck before I go back out front, trying to find a spot to watch where I can see him without feeling like I’m drowning in people. Ideally, he’d be able to see me, too, just to give him a friendly face in the crowd, but it looks like the venue is near capacity tonight, so I’m not counting on it. I steel myself against the press of humanity around me and wait for the guys to make their debut.

“Have you seen these guys before?” I turn to see if someone is asking me, accidentally elbowing the cap-wearing guy pressed up right behind me. I mutter an apology, only to realize the person who asked the question is facing the other way anyway.

“I caught them a couple times in O.C.,” a guy replies. “They were awesome. Their drummer wasn’t anything special, but I heard they’d replaced him. Hopefully, this guy is as good as the rest of them, because they kicked ass.”

“My sister said she’d seen them at a private party. She couldn’t stop talking about the lead singer, said he was *so* hot!”

“I care a lot more about whether he can sing than what he looks like,” another girl replies. “Someone said he’s better than Mace Mason. I’ll believe that when I hear it. Telltale Signs is the best band out there right now, and he’d have to be amazing to even come close to Mace.”

Hunter and I had seen Telltale Signs on their last tour. Mom took us, trying to keep up the tradition Hunter’s mom had set with taking us to some amazing shows over the years. It had meant a lot to me, but Hunter had been beyond appreciative.

He'd lost so much when his mom died. It was nice that Mom was willing to step up and help give some of that back to him.

To hear Declan now being compared to Telltale Signs' lead singer is amazing. If the comparisons hold for the band, even if the Carter Brothers Band has years to go to get to that level... This is very exciting.

The house lights drop down and the stage lights come on. I hear the familiar tones of Hunter's guitar before I see anything. The next thing I know, Rhys is crashing through the room with a wall of percussion. Hunter strolls out on one side of the stage, and David on the other, laying down a base of sound that holds an expectant note...

Until Declan prowls out onto the stage and lets loose a wail that draws every eye in the house straight to him. From there, they're putty in his hands. He entrances, ensnares and entices them into his world, where they find themselves part of the story of this magnetic man who tells these strangers his innermost secrets, his deepest desires, his secret pains and his greatest joys.

He shares himself with them, and they offer themselves up to him in return, moving in time with the soundtrack to which his collaborators in creativity set his story, hips and shoulders and heads shaking and swaying, eyes closed in immersion in the sound and open with avarice for every glimpse they can get as he transits from one side of the stage to the other, leaning back to back with his brother, whose low bass beats join Hunter's soaring guitar riffs to Rhys' primal rhythms, and then leaning out over the front of the stage to collect the adoration of the crowd he has made his own.

A low growl ushers them into the next song, accented by a bass line David uses to take control of their feet and a crashing, driving rush from Rhys, which then pulls back just slightly to boost Hunter on top of their sonic shoulders, a literal and figurative spotlight on him as he tears through a guitar solo that has Declan gesturing to him with respect and encouraging the audience to give their own accolades to the golden-haired guitar god who has deigned to deliver himself and his muse into their presence.

And they're as transfixed upon him as they had been upon the man who opened the door to this magical realm of music for them. They reach for him as he, too, leans out over them, a glorious presence almost within their grasp, until he pulls himself back to approach Rhys' throne, where the copper-haired percussionist is demonstrating how strongly a beloved and beneficent monarch can rule from his own seat of power.

Hunter's riffs drift away, leaving Rhys to take center stage in the soundscape and prove to everyone in the room that he is, indeed, a madman on the drums, a pied piper of percussion who'll take them along on a ride where their feet will dance until they beg for mercy, before being compelled to turn around and do it all over again, carried along on the engrossing backbeat of David's bass guitar.

It's then that the four of them, the sole focus of the audience's attention, join together as one, creating a wave of sound that grabs every limb, every heart, every mind and eye in the building and joins them, too, as one, a writhing mass of movement that itself becomes part of the music that fills the entire space to overflowing.

I find myself carried along with the current, no longer the girl who'd been there with Hunter after his first guitar lesson or sitting alongside him when the Carter brothers joined in an impromptu beachside show, nor even the woman who had sat in on so many rehearsals and helped them haul their gear. Instead, I'm one of the mass, worshiping at the altar of the stage these men now own, as surely as they own the hearts, bodies and minds of every single person in this building.

Hunter is a bright, blinding light rising to the surface atop this sea of humanity, and I can see in him both that other-Hunter who'd been joined to that other me, body and soul, and the rock god who is emerging before our very eyes on that dais, a miracle of the muses who offer them up to us for adoration in a manner that offers no alternative. We would fall on our knees before them or perish for the loss of them.

And when the wall of sound finally dwindles to silence, every living being in that room is frozen, waiting for the world to crack in two with the vacuum it creates. Until it does crack open, and a deafening chorus of screams, sighs, whistles and applause replaces the silence. And the four men on the stage are themselves stunned into silence, just then realizing that they have conquered hundreds tonight, in just the smallest taste of the triumphs to come.

Chapter 17

Oran Sniomh (Spinning Song)

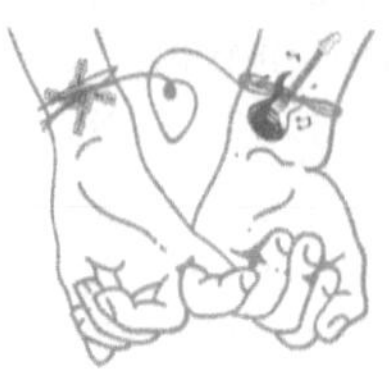

Ellie
A few months later

The movement of my feet on the treadles is hypnotic... Left, right, left, right... The gentle pull of the bobbin on the loose wool roving in my hands, my fingers shifting back and forth as I feed the strands evenly into the twisted string that forms...

I could do this forever. Part of me feels like I *have* been doing this forever. It's a part of me, as sure as my violet eyes and wavy blonde hair, my round earlobes and... Hunter.

I always lose myself in my work, making yarn from wool and weavings from yarn, the rhythmic movement of wheel and loom taking me away, letting my mind run free and aimless. It's meditative. It feels good to empty my mind and just *be* for a while. My brain is too busy most of the time, and it could use the vacation.

So, I press on... Left, right, left, right... the wheel spins on... the wool twists and spins onto the bobbin, which rotates smoothly between the maidens, across the flyer, filling up the bobbin bit by bit... Left, right, left, right... on and on... spinning and spinning... twisting and rolling... Left, right, left, right...

My knee gets nudged from the side. I stop and look down, pausing to scratch Crógan's shaggy head.

"He'll be in shortly, you great lazy lump," I tell him. "You should be out there with him in the rain, you big baby, you."

He has the grace to look a little abashed about it. Strange dog. He loves swimming in the sea, but he dislikes getting soaked with rain. So the dog is inside, drying near the fire, while my husband is outside, settling the sheep in their pen for the night before he comes in to join us for dinner. Myself and the dog.

I chuckle.

Roused from my work, I get up and go to the big pot hanging over the fire, giving the stew a stir, then dipping out a spoonful and blowing on it to cool it before I give it a taste. It's savory and thick, full of potatoes, parsnips and mutton — a good meal for a wet night when the chill has started to come on and the wind is blowing in off the ocean.

I put out a plate of oatcakes and a crock of fresh dillisk butter, dropping a bit of butter on the floor in front of Crógan, who forgives my "clumsiness" and kindly cleans up after me. Whatever would I do without him? A pitcher of buttermilk joins them on the table, along with some fire-crisped dillisk, and I get bowls out to dish up the stew as soon as Hunter comes in out of the rain.

It seems like just moments later when the door swings open, bringing with it the scent of the rain and sea, and my bedraggled husband, who quickly shucks off his coat and shoes, picking up the piece of toweling I've left for him nearby.

"Let me. You've done enough for the day," I tell him, snatching it from his hand and moving to dry his dripping hair, no longer golden but drenched to several shades darker. He grabs my wrist before I get towel to head, pulling me hard against him.

"Wet isn't inherently a bad thing," he drawls lazily, sliding his other hand up my thigh toward my center. The rain continues to drip off his hair and down his nose and cheeks. I step up on my toes and lick away one trail as it heads toward his jaw.

"On that we agree," I reply.

Behind me, Crógan sighs and settles in a corner near the fire. He's a smart hound, if perhaps too coddled by his master.

Hunter drags me up against his chest, dampening my top with the rain soaked into his own shirt. The thin fabric goes translucent as my nipples bead beneath it. He bends down, taking one into his mouth through the fabric and wetting it further, sucking it sharply and making my back bow as I push toward him.

He grasps my other nipple between his fingers and twists it tightly, on the cusp of causing pain. I hiss with the sensation, my head falling back and inviting him to drag his lips from nipple to throat before he licks from my chin, up my jaw and to my earlobe, which he takes between his teeth and nips lightly.

I growl, begging him for more. He swipes his thumbs across my lips, center to sides, staring intently into my eyes, smiling before the expression shifts to pure lust and he takes my lips with his own, demanding entrance and receiving it just as quickly. He licks inside my mouth, tasting me, being tasted in return.

My hand reaches down, tracing up the now-hard length of him, and it's his turn to growl. He nips at my throat, and I know it will leave a bruise, one he'll trace with his fingers in the morning and smile again, proudly, having marked me once more as his own.

He grabs my hand again, pressing my palm against his cock and dragging it up and down, taking control of the rhythm as I caress him firmly through the fabric. He swells under our combined touch and rocks into my hand, his breath becoming shallow and fast.

His other hand grabs me from behind and presses me against him with the same rhythm, and my hand and his together press into my core, causing my breath, too, to speed up, my pulse to race. The dampness between my thighs mirrors the rain on his hair, and the entire world feels like it has gone liquid... rain drops, tongues, a light sheen of sweat erupting around my neck and across my chest, the dampness of his shirt...

Suddenly, he spins me around, pressing my backside up against his front, and I shudder as my desire ramps up once again. He grasps my breasts through my top, squeezing, kneading, pinching my nipples between his fingers, until I moan.

The next thing I know, I'm pressed up against the table, Hunter's hand probing through the fabric around my mound, making me pant, before he roughly shoves the empty bowls aside and I find my face pressed down next to the butter, close enough to see in detail the flecks of seaweed running through it.

Hunter grabs at my skirts, lifting them up above my waist. He finds my slit and runs his fingers through the moisture there, caressing and cajoling even more from inside me as my body prepares itself for him. His touch is possessive, and why shouldn't it be, because I'm his as surely as he's mine.

His hands pull mine behind me, settling my wrists in the curve of my back and pressing them there, making it clear that I'm not to move them until he says so. He releases them, and I follow the silent instruction, shivering in anticipation. With his hands free, he opens up his pants, laying his cock in the crevice between my cheeks, making a promise to us both of what is to come.

He rubs his length along my slit, slathering my juices over him and tantalizing me with the sensations. He slides home inside me, and we both gasp. He rotates his hips against me, pulling back slightly before shoving back in to the hilt. He begins a slow dance, rocking, plunging, withdrawing, over and over again, with ever-increasing speed.

As my center begins to tighten, fluttering against him from inside, he pulls back once more, leaving just the tip of himself inside me. He pauses as we both pant wildly. I turn my head to look behind me, and his eyes are closed, jaw fixed in concentration.

"Please, Hunter! Move. Move, please. Don't leave me stuck here on the precipice!"

His eyes blink open, and he smiles lasciviously at me, running his hands along my thighs, no sense of urgency or mercy about him. He reaches around to run his fingers lightly between my lips, giving the smallest of glancing touches to my clit. My hips roll involuntarily and my back spasms, pressing my rear hard against his thighs.

"That's my hungry girl... All this wonderful food you've laid out. And the only thing you're truly hungry for is my cock in that ravenous pussy of yours..." He chuckles, caressing my ass before smacking his hand sharply against the flesh there. He rubs the spot gently before pinching it. I squeal and moan and writhe against him, seeking to impale myself upon him. He smacks my rear again. I'm panting, right on the cusp, and he's not even inside me.

Then, suddenly he is. He swoops back inside, poking that sensitive spot that he knows so well. There's no pause, no slowness, no technique to what he's doing to me now. He's just pounding into me, over and over again, hard enough to shake the dishes on the table and, like them, my arousal jumps higher with each thrust. There doesn't seem to be any room for it to go higher, become more intense. I'm full of him, filled with lust and sensation and the rising tide that I know will claim me any moment.

We're both grunting with the force of him pounding into me, the table stuttering across the floor, my hands trapped between us, his clasped tightly around my waist to try to anchor me, and the table, in place. It's a losing battle, as his hips piston into me, slapping against me, until I'm in fear that both the table and I will shatter.

And that's the moment when he loses all control, slamming inside me so perfectly that I roll right over that precipice, dangling, hanging by my toes into a bottomless crevasse, weightless, limitless, eternal. My muscles grasp hard at him inside me, over and over again, and I can feel him erupt as he shouts senseless syllables into the air while his hips press a final few times against my rear.

I'm boneless, splayed across the table, the butter crock overturned, oatcakes having escaped the confines of their plate, buttermilk spilled, though the pitcher has somehow remained upright.

Hunter pulls slowly from inside me, and I want to weep for the loss. And my body seems to agree, dripping our combined fluids down my thighs. Hunter slides his fingers between them, pinching my clit and causing my hips to slam against the table one more time. I look back at him again, not yet able to pull myself upright, and the mischievous smile on his face sets my heart alight.

So domineering and rough when he wants to be, when I want him to be... and so playful and gentle when it suits us. He pulls me up against his chest, his arms lifting my breasts and brushing the fabric of my top against the sensitive nipples. My head is so heavy from the exertion that my chin remains tucked into my chest.

My knee bumps against the table as my right foot slips from the treadle and my forehead rests against the drive wheel. My eyes blink open as I register the fact that I've dropped the wool roving and the partly spun yarn.

There's a knock at the door.

"Ellie — it's getting late. You should let the spinning go for the night and get ready for bed. Don't forget that we have that Christmas party at your dad's office tomorrow afternoon..."

I would rather not go to this party. I've never enjoyed them, with all the stodgy business associates trying to network rather than celebrate. And Dad and I are getting along so badly these days that I know he'll be scrutinizing every interaction I have. He's still hoping I'll switch to a business major or pre-law — anything more practical than art. Too bad.

"Wear your nicest dress — something conservative, please. Your father is trying to make a good impression on the new partners. There are clean towels in the bathroom for your shower."

Shower? Suddenly, all l can feel and hear is the rain, pouring down on Hunter... then-Hunter... dripping onto my breasts, down his cheeks, through his hair, which drapes around my neck and blends with my own, golden and copper-yellow strands intertwined like the fibers of the yarn now filling the bobbin on my wheel.

It's clear to me now that this is something — both the memory of that time before, and my remembering it again now — that I'm going to have to tuck away and never tell anyone else. Because if Hunter won't believe me, then no one ever will.

But it's a memory I already treasure, cataloging this and others as I continue to piece together that life before. There is a world of experience for me to access, some of it offering insight in a sensual world I'm eager to explore, and it all lies within my mind — not on the pages of a book or a video of strangers having anonymous sex for others' pleasure. Instead, it is an encyclopedia of highly erotic sexual experience of the most personal sort, with my body, and that of my husband, as the tools of advanced learning, and his mind and my own as my teachers. It's a precious gift.

CHAPTER 18

MOTHERS TALK

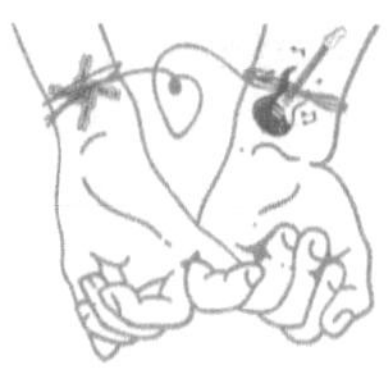

Ellie
A year later

"Ellen, you can't continue on like this. I've already talked to you until I'm blue in the face about how hard it is to have a successful career as a musician. A career as an artist? Making yarn and tapestries of all things? We'd be better off spending your tuition money on lottery tickets."

"Can we do that? The big prize is up over a hundred million..."

He glowers at me.

"This is serious, Ellen!"

"So is a hundred million dollars!"

"Enough!" he shouts.

"I agree, Thomas — that is quite enough," Mom interjects, cutting him off right as his face goes purple — well on his way to blue again.

"Ellie is getting excellent grades, especially with harder classes in her sophomore year. Even if she remains an art major, she won't have graduated without a basic education to carry her into the future. A lot of college graduates end up in careers outside their majors."

My father harrumphs.

"I see no reason why she can't continue as an art major. If she decides to change later, she can do that. We can afford an extra semester or two if she needs other classes later on," she says. "The girl has a good head on her shoulders, Thomas. And she's 19 — old enough to make this kind of decision for herself."

"Even if she's making a huge mistake?"

"You don't know this is mistake, Dad! You can't predict the future. And, frankly, your lack of faith in my abilities and your lack of respect for me as a person are very disappointing. I've earned the right to make this decision for myself. And I've made it."

"We don't have to keep paying your tuition, Ellen. It may be you taking the classes, but this is an education I'm paying for. That gives me every right to encourage you to make better decisions. That Hunter has been a terrible influence on you, with all the time you spent on him in high school, and then luring you off to Virginia for college..."

"Hunter hasn't 'lured' me anywhere! I found an excellent school, in a safe area, with well-accredited teachers in my area of focus. That's the same kind of criteria most people use to select a college. And so what if Hunter happens to be living nearby? If Mr. Graves had let him go to college instead of effectively forcing him to go straight into the workforce, Hunter would have been there anyway. This has nothing to do with Hunter, and you need to get over your irrational need to blame him for everything in my life that's not exactly how you'd like it to be!"

"Playing music doesn't make him part of the 'workforce,' Ellen. I'm talking about a real job."

"Hunter has a *real* job, Dad. He's got *three* of them, in fact."

He blinks, waiting.

"He's doing two restaurant jobs, plus his music, which is also a *real* job." He rolls his eyes at me. "He's working harder every day than you do!"

Dad looks like he's ready to explode.

"Thomas, it's time to drop this. At least for now. It's Christmas! Ellie's going to be going back to school next week, and we don't need hard feelings between us when she leaves. So, please — for me — just let this go."

"Fine, Rebecca. I'll let it go — for now. But Ellen is going to have to make some tough decisions going forward, and keep in mind who's paying for her classes, dorm, food..."

"Thomas, please!"

Dad sighs and heads into his office — where he's been spending most of his time since I got home a couple weeks ago — and firmly shuts the door behind him.

Mom and I exchange looks of helplessness. He won't listen to either of us, the same as he did when we'd disagreed with him about sending Hunter back to his dad.

The key difference now being that I can leave and go back home. To Virginia, where Hunter is waiting.

"I'm sorry, Ellie. He's gotten pigheaded in his old age," she adds with a chuckle.

"You're not old, Mom."

"You'd be surprised how fast it catches up with you, Ellie. That's one reason your father is so determined to ensure you have the best start in life that you can. He's not going about it in the best way, but he means well."

"Mom — I can't be who he wants me to be. I know who I am, and that's not it — a business major or a doctor or lawyer. I'm never more myself than when I'm working with my yarn. And I'm good at it! I could really make a living at it, even without gallery shows for my weavings. I've even been thinking about eventually opening my own shop, so maybe I come back here and take over the needlework shop once Lindsey retires, make it my own!"

"I think that sounds like a wonderful idea, Ellie. It would be nice to have you closer to home." She gives me a hug. "I've been missing you while you've been gone."

"I've missed you, too, Mom. But I have to get out on my own, and the time for that is now. I appreciate you all covering my school expenses. I just can't let Dad leverage that against my choice of career."

"And you shouldn't, honey. I'll talk to him. He'll see reason eventually. Just give him some time."

"I hope you're right, Mom." I sigh again, not really holding out hope after seeing Dad's ongoing issue with Hunter rear its ugly head again. "All the same — I think I'll head back to school tomorrow instead of next week. I'd like to talk to Kara about getting more hours at the shop. She could really use the help this week, since Maire's off skiing with her boyfriend."

"I understand, dear. Maybe if we give your dad some space he'll realize he can't just dictate everything be how he wants it.

And you're being very responsible taking on some extra work while you have time. Just don't let it interfere with your classes."

"I won't, Mom. I haven't been."

"I know, Ellie. We're really both very proud of you. Your dad will see that it'll all work out."

She kisses me on the forehead.

"Go ahead and pack, get your spinning wheel loaded in the car, and get some good sleep tonight. I'll get you a nice breakfast in the morning, and you can get an early start."

"Thanks, Mom. I love you."

"Love you, too, Ellie. Get some rest."

Three days later

"Thanks so much for pitching in this week, Ellie," Kara tells me as she wraps up yet another large yarn purchase for one of our regular customers, Dottie. "Everyone is stocking up for this coming year's projects. I'll start giving you a few more hours per week after New Year's, if that works. You're so much more interested in the shop than Maire is. I expect I'll lose her to her paper business after graduation, which is a shame. But she's so good at it, I can't really begrudge her following her own path."

"I should have you talk to my dad," I tell her with a wry laugh. "He's still pressuring me to change my major."

"I'm sorry to hear that, dear. You've really got a talent for that handspun. Dottie and the girls can't get enough of it. You could start making it full-time tomorrow and I'd buy up every skein and have it sold within days."

"Thanks. That's great to hear. Mrs. Pomeroy keeps giving me the advanced assignments. She's going to use the 302 curriculum with me this semester, since I've already worked my way through the ones for 201, 202 and 301."

"I can tell the difference in your work already, Ellie. You've gone from very good to near master-level with just three semesters of classes. It's like you were born to do this!"

"It feels like it sometimes," I admit, omitting, as usual, any mention of my visions.

"Maire said you might be interested in joining our circle..." Kara says, seeming to read my mind.

This is the first time I've talked to Kara about her religious practices. But Maire and I have spent hours talking about spirituality, philosophy, cosmology, mythology since we met in our 101-level fiber-arts class. I'd confided in her that I felt like I had a connection to Ireland, and she suggested I talk to her mom about her religious group.

"I'm definitely intrigued by what she told me. It feels like it fits me, the Irish mythology and stuff."

"We're kind of an eclectic group," Kara says. "Some of us have a Wiccan background, some a more generalized Pagan practice, some reconstructionists, a couple Druids... The common thread is the Irish and larger 'Celtic' connection." She takes a deep breath and fixes me with a cautioning look. "You understand we're not talking about Satanism or anything like that — no devils, no evil spells, no green-skinned witches, no 'The Craft' levitation, no lighting candles with our minds... For one — it would take way more energy to even try that than it would to pull out a pack of matches. And we're kind of practical folks, underneath it all," she adds with a laugh.

"I've read a couple books," I admit. "I think I get what you're talking about, though it seems like there are as many variations as there are people."

"Pretty much." She laughs. "We often joke that these groups are like herding cats, though personally I sometimes think herding cats would be easier," she adds. "We tend to be very independent people, and there is no one book or belief system that everyone follows, unlike the dominant faiths of today."

"I went to church when I was younger," I tell her. "It was interesting, but I never felt like I made a personal connection with it. Something about this feels almost like it's calling me."

Kara gives me a long look.

"Usually, if you're feeling that, it is," she says. "Could be it's the practice calling you because you need it. Or it could be the cultural connection is forging a link to something in you. It's also possible that you're being called to priesthood. The gods have a tendency to let people know when they claim them."

"Claim them?"

Kara smiles warmly.

"If they want you as a priestess, you'll feel at some point like you belong to them," she says. "For me, it came in my meditations... a sense of a hand on my shoulder, a benediction... sometimes my dreams suggested a special task I was being given to work on. The Welsh goddess I serve — her stories are in the Mabinogion, which dates back to the Middle Ages and whose stories are set as far back as five hundred years before Christ. But some of the others in the group serve other gods or goddesses. Éiru, Banba, Ogma, Brighid — they're all in the Irish mythology."

Brighid — I remember that name. Vivid memories of then-Hunter calling me that... Are my visions trying to tell me something again? Suggesting a path?

"And some of us just practice, without being called to priesthood."

"It sounds interesting. I definitely want to know more."

"Well, you can come over to our house before the next gathering and ask all the questions you like. No obligation. You're not signing a deal for your soul or anything," she adds with a laugh. "But I have a feeling you're right about being called. And if that's the case, you'll know soon enough."

"It definitely feels like I'm being pulled in that direction."

Kara smiles. "Then you probably are. Follow your intuition, and in more than just this one thing. It will rarely steer you wrong."

CHAPTER 19

BREATHE (2AM)

Ellie
The next day

My phone is ringing. At two-something a.m. When this happens, it's often Hunter. Or one of the guys in the band who's "acquired" Hunter's phone. Often drunk. Most often Rhys. Their hours are a little different from mine to start with, and I was supposed to be sleeping in today, working the late shift. But I'm also their designated driver.

So, dutifully, I answer the phone, still in bed, groggy and with my eyes still mostly closed. My roommate hasn't returned from the break yet, so I don't have to worry about waking her, thankfully.

"Guys — this hadn't better be a prank call... I was asleep."

"I'm sorry to wake you, Ellen. But it's about your mother..."

Suddenly, I'm thrown back two years.

I know what he's going to say. And my mother's face appears instantly in my mind's eye, smiling warmly at me as she did only a few days ago, only to be replaced with the image of Hunter's stricken face on that horrible morning, and then flashing back and forth between them like an old piece of film in an endless loop.

"I'm sorry to have to call with bad news, but I wanted you to know — your mother, she had a heart attack tonight. She didn't make it."

My brain freezes and races at a hundred miles an hour, all at the same time. I'm not sure what to say. Nothing you say in that moment will change anything that has happened. You are rendered utterly helpless in an instant. There's no way to help the person you've lost, no way to save them. And the only thing you can do is deal with those who are left behind.

"Ellen? Are you there? Did you hear me? Your mother has died."

Those words will be the ones that stick with me. It's a permanent state. Past tense. Done.

"Yes. I hear you. I'm sorry. What can I do?"

It's the only reasonable response, even if the answer is usually "nothing."

"It looks like the funeral could be as soon as Saturday. You'll need to be there, of course."

"Of course... Is there anything I can do to help with... arrangements?"

"No. Your mother and I had most of that pre-planned. Honestly, you probably will just be in the way at this point..."

My heart clenches. In the way?

"...since I'm going to have to meet with the lawyers and finalize everything in the next day or two, before the holiday. But you need to be here by Friday."

"I can do that. Are you sure you don't want me to come sooner? I can help with the house... be there—"

"That's not necessary, Ellen. Stay where you are. Just come back on Friday."

"OK... I'm really sorry, Dad. Let me know if there's anything I can do."

"I'll see you on Friday," he says.

The line clicks as the call ends..

My mother. I just saw her a few days ago. She made me breakfast. Told me she loved me. Told me to drive safe, that everything would work out...

This doesn't feel like things working out.

I find myself staring at my hand. The phone is still in it. And I'm not entirely sure why... I'm trying to think... what am I doing?

My mother's dead.

Oh.

A 15-year-old Hunter's grief-stricken face comes back to me again.

I need to call Hunter!

And I need him to hold me like I did then for him.

I dial the phone. It rings and rings and then cuts to voicemail. And I really have no idea what to say. Can you leave someone a message telling them your mother died and you need them to come hold you? Is that approved etiquette?

I hang up.

I dial again.

One ring, two rings, three rings, four rings...

I prepare to hang up.

"Hello?" an even groggier Hunter says. "Elle? What are you doing up at... two-thirty? Man... I only went to bed — well, Rhys' sofa, anyway — half an hour ago..."

I fail to hold up my end of the conversation. Not good etiquette.

"Ellie? Elle? Are you there? Is something wrong?"

My throat has frozen up just as solidly as my brain. It feels like I've swallowed a tennis ball covered in cactus spines.

"Ellie!" Hunter shouts, concern carrying clearly in his tone, and it's, finally, enough to jumpstart my brain and tear my vocal cords loose from their restraints.

"Hunter!" I call, my voice a quiet wail that seems to take every ounce of energy I possess just to get past my lips.

"Elle — tell me what's wrong... Are you hurt? Are you safe?" The panic he's feeling carries across in every syllable, instantly crossing that connection between us, even miles away.

"I need you," is all I can think to say. "Come help me, please."

"Elle — are you in your dorm?"

"Yes," I manage to get out before my throat freezes again and the tears finally start running down my cheeks.

"I'll get Rhys to bring me over. I'll be there in ten minutes. Tell me you'll be OK until I get there."

I nod, before I realize that he can't see me.

"Yes," I whisper.

"I'll be right there."

Ten minutes later

There's a tapping at my window. Not rap-tap-tapping at my door, thankfully. In my current state, I find that amusing and almost laugh.

I take a deep breath and sit up, my head swimming.

"Elle! Open up!" Hunter stage-whispers, aiming not to wake up whoever else might be here during the break.

I walk to the window, unlatching it and pulling it up a few inches. Hunter pulls his long-practiced maneuver, boosting himself up enough from the ground below the first-floor window to push it open another eight inches and then pulling himself through the gap, onto my desk.

I'm just standing there, hesitant and aimless, unsure what to do now.

Hunter takes one look at me and crushes me into a tight hug. It feels like he's trying to mash my broken bits back together, and maybe it would even work if he could keep doing it for the rest of our lives...

He releases me just long enough to guide me over to my bed, sitting down with me before wrapping his arm around my shoulders and pulling my head to his chest.

"What's up, Elle-belle?" he asks softly. "What's happened?"

"Mom..." is all I can manage to say before my brain goes blank again and I'm on the verge of sobbing.

He lifts my head up to look in my eyes, and I break the eye contact again a moment later. But it's long enough...

"Gone?" he asks simply.

I nod.

He pulls my head back down and kisses the top of my head.

"I'm sorry, Elle. Come here."

He pulls us both down onto my bed, his head on my pillow, my head on his chest and the rest of me tucked alongside him, my arm wrapped around his waist like he's the only thing keeping me above water.

Tears are running silently down my cheeks now, already making a wet spot on his T-shirt, right over his heart. My brain breaks free of shock's stranglehold long enough to utter a single sob. Hunter starts rubbing my back soothingly, peppering my head with kisses that help me survive the moments that pass, tiny distractions and reminders that I am still loved, even if my mother isn't here to do that anymore.

"It'll be OK, Elle. I'm here. I'm not going anywhere. We're going to get through this the same way we did before."

The waterworks start running full-steam. And I just lie there, held tightly in the arms of my best friend, the only person on the planet who can really understand.

CHAPTER 20

HUNDREDS OF TEARS

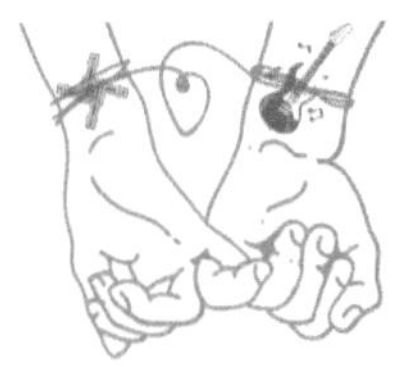

Ellie
Later that morning

"Yes, ma'am. She's going to need some time off. She's very distraught. This has been a shock. ... Yes. Thank you. I'm glad you understand. ... Of course. I'll tell her. ... I'll be sure to do that. Thank you, again. Goodbye."

I can't quite put together what's happening. I roll over in my bed, away from the wall I'd been sleeping up against. Hunter's leaning against my desk, my phone in his hand, looking worriedly at me.

And then I remember. Mom's gone. I need to go home Friday, but not before, so I'm not in the way, Dad said. OK. I can do that. Clear instructions. No problem. One foot in front of the other... *"soon you'll be walking..."*

"How ya doin', Elle?"

"Not great."

"I'd be worried if you were," he says, sitting down next to me on the bed. "Can you tell me what happened? What's going on? Do we need to head back home?"

Home? It's not home if Mom isn't there...

"Elle?"

"She had a heart attack," I reply, suddenly ready to dump what little I know on the one person who will understand. "Dad called right before I called you. He said she had a heart attack last night, and she didn't make it. He said to come Friday, not before, so I wasn't 'in the way.'"

I go from dispassionate to sobbing in a single moment. He grabs me around the shoulders again, pressing his lips into my hair, which appears to have gone from tame waves to bird's nest while I was sleeping. He doesn't seem to mind.

"I'm sorry," he repeats. "You're going to get really tired of hearing those two words," he adds with a touch of black humor. "They're nice to hear, but they're not any easier to accept than it is for people to know what to say."

"How did you even do this, Hunter? I can't even function right now. I keep starting to think about something else, and then it snaps right back again. How did you survive it?"

"I had my best friend to keep me together when I was ready to fall apart. To soothe me to sleep and chase the nightmares away. To remind me to eat and sleep, and even take a shower," he says with a gentle smile. "And to remind me that while I lost one person who loved me, someone else was still here who loved me, too."

"Oh, Hunter..." I wail, bursting into tears.

"I'm here, Elle. Not going anywhere. I called in sick to work and told them I didn't expect to feel well enough to come in on Thursday either. And they're closed Friday and Saturday. I'm going to take care of you just like you did me."

"You don't have to do that, Hunter. I'm not 15, and you have to work. You can't afford to lose two days' pay."

"A day and a half. They were already closing early on New Year's Eve."

"Oh my god — it's New Year's! Kara needs me at the shop!"

"I was just talking to her. Called her on your phone and told her you'd need some time off. She said to take all the time you need and let them know if there was anything they could do to help. She said you're 'still invited to circle' if you want to come. Whatever that means..." He shrugs, looking a little baffled. "But she'll be fine through the end of the holiday. She was very adamant about that."

"She's got the post-Christmas rush. And Maire's gone. I have to go in."

"She said she won't let you in the door if you show up. She seems to know you well. She doesn't want to see you — for work, anyway — until after New Year's, she said."

"New Year's!" I cry again. "You can't miss your gigs! They're the biggest ones you've got all year, right?"

"I'll have the guys cancel. Somebody will be able to fill the slots. There's lots of bands that would kill for those gigs."

"Yours being one of them! You can't do that!"

"I can and I will. Declan can play a little. They can switch up the set and make it work that way."

"Declan can play. But he doesn't play nearly as well as you do, and he can't play the combined rhythm and lead parts to save his life!"

"Don't let him hear you say that," he warns with a chuckle. "He thinks he's god's gift to music."

I roll my eyes.

"Bottom line — you cannot miss your gigs. I forbid it!"

"Oh, you forbid it, do you?" He laughs, apparently completely unbothered by my ultimatum. "What are you going to do to enforce your edict? Hmm?"

I see it coming, but I'm too slow...

"Are you going to tickle me out on stage?" He dives for my ribs, setting off a tirade of giggles until I beg for mercy. We're both lying there, panting, and our gazes collide, and there's a feeling of tension, sweet and warm and soft, but starting to pull sharply at us both. He breaks the eye contact, and I swallow, trying to regain some sense of footing.

And then the wave rises up again... Mom.

He's holding me tightly before the tears have dripped from my eyes, murmuring words of comfort in my ear that don't make sense to my grief-stricken brain but whose tone is so soothing that they work anyway.

A minute later, things are back under control, and I tell him flatly, "You cannot miss those gigs. I couldn't handle the guilt of knowing you'd thrown your career off-track just to keep me company. And the guys would never forgive me. You know that."

"They'd be fine with it. They'd understand. At least, Dave and Rhys would. Declan..."

"Is a dick. Yes, I know. But that doesn't change the fact that you can't do that to them or yourself or the venues. I'll be fine.

I'll go over to Kara and Maire's and let them keep me company. You do your gigs. Do them *for me*, please."

Hunter hesitates, clearly weighing the impacts of a decision that he and I both know could severely impact his career. Which he cannot afford — monetarily or otherwise — to have happen.

"OK. Fine. I'll do the gigs as planned. But I don't have to like it."

He sticks his tongue out at me, and I find myself chuckling.

"Are you going back on Friday? I'm sure your dad didn't mean you'd be in the way. I'm sure it's just that he didn't want to leave you alone at the house while he's dealing with the arrangements."

"I'm not so sure he didn't mean it... but to answer your question — yeah, I guess I'll head back Friday morning. He said the funeral would probably be Saturday."

"OK."

We're both silent now.

Hunter doesn't have a car. If I leave Friday morning and he has a gig Friday night, he won't be able to get there for the funeral. And that fact has just hit us both.

"I'll be fine. Don't worry. You're already doing so much. Even coming over this morning... that was way beyond what you had to do."

"What I *wanted* to do. What I *needed* to do. Even if I didn't owe you the same kind of care gave me when I lost *my* mom, I'd still be here for you, just like this. Because you're my best friend, and I love you. And I'm going to take care of you as best I can."

"Thank you. I love you. You're so good to me. Mom would be so relieved to know I had you here for me. She always loved you."

Hunter is quiet for a minute, and it's only then that I realize that Mom had been the closest thing to a mother — to a parent — that he'd had after his own mother died. He's lost one of the most important people in his life today, too.

I reach up to smooth his hair out of his eyes, which have gone liquid and shiny. Again our gazes meet, but it's not that heated tension of before. Instead, it's shared sorrow and loss. I run my hand down his jawline and press a kiss to his temple. We hug each other and lie back down, resting quietly until we both fall asleep.

CHAPTER 21

FELL ON BLACK DAYS

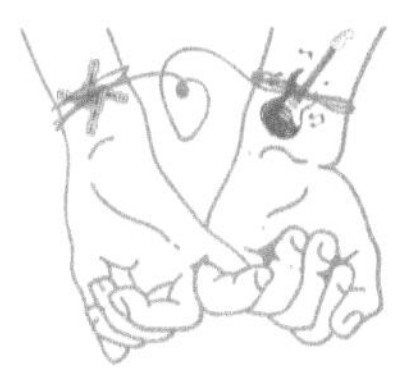

Ellie
Two days later

Hunter didn't leave my side for two days, except to go to the bathroom and to grab pizza from the delivery guy so he could ensure I was fed. That and the gig I insisted he do on New Year's Eve.

He asked me if I wanted to go with him, but he knew a New Year's Eve party wouldn't be a good place for me. Instead, he dropped me off at Kara's, took my car to the gig and came back to get me as soon as they were done playing. David even packed his gear up for him and took it with him for Friday's gig.

Would I rather he'd stayed with me? Honestly, yes. But would I have been able to look at myself in the mirror afterward? No. So I insisted, and, for once, he did what he was told.

I'd spent last night talking to Kara and some of her circle ladies about their beliefs and practices, and I felt so at home amongst them that I hardly noticed Hunter was gone. At least until I crashed on Kara's sofa to wait for him to come back and pick me up.

I think I'm going to keep going, explore what I feel called to do. Kara said not everyone particularly enjoys group practice, and I'm thinking that might be true for me. But she said they're happy to have me participate when I like, and I can continue to explore on my own and ask them whatever questions I want.

So, now I'm making the drive back to Mystic Beach, where we're scheduled to bury my mother tomorrow. That thought is unreal...

I've called Dad a couple times since he first let me know what happened. He's been stiff, even terse. Kara said I need to keep in mind that everyone grieves differently, and give him some time and space to deal with things how he needs to deal with them.

No one seems to be monitoring the dorm population over the holiday break, so Hunter's been able to come and go without any hassle, and I've been able to fall asleep in his arms each night. He's dried my tears and held me when I started to fall apart, and even stuffed me in the shower this morning. He did everything but hand me a brown-bag lunch before waving goodbye from the curb.

Three hours and change later, I'm pulling up in the driveway at my parents' — wow, that feels weird to say now — house. My mom's car is the only one in the driveway, so I guess Dad is out, even though it's New Year's Day and pretty much everything is closed. I drop my bag in my bedroom and sit on the bed, unsure what to do next.

After fifteen minutes of sitting, I decide to go in my parents' room, just to get as close to Mom as I can get now. I walk past her low dresser, with its big mirror on the back, stopping to look at the family photos, mementos and pieces of jewelry that are just sitting there, as if she'll be home any minute to wear them.

There's a drawing I did in eighth grade that got a second-place award in the art show, one of my handmade birthday cards from a few years ago, a picture of me and Hunter at the beach when we were 10, my graduation photo, their wedding photo, pictures of her parents. One of my first woven pieces cushions the top of the dresser. It's rough, but I used her favorite colors and she was so delighted with it that she rejected my offer to replace it once I got better at my craft.

I pick up her wedding photo, with her wearing the dress her grandmother had worn, with a few updates, and I sit down on the bed with it. There are so many moments I remember, from playtime as a little kid to my first day of school, being home sick with the flu and Mom bringing me flat ginger ale and saltines, laughing over her favorite comedy, helping her make cookies for Christmas... And I won't ever be able to do that again.

I'm tearing up again when I hear a noise down the hall. Dad walks into the bedroom.

"Ellen! You shouldn't be in here! Go wait for me out in the living room, and we can discuss the plans for tomorrow."

I'm wounded by the subtle rejection, being told that I shouldn't be in her room with the things that prove she was here and had lived a full, if too brief, life. But I do as I'm told rather than starting an argument. Dad is brusque, telling me the funeral is all arranged, with my mother's friends notified, the local minister asked to speak and then to move to the cemetery for the burial. He said he doesn't plan to speak and doesn't feel I need to either.

Again, I'm tempted to argue. Maybe *I* feel like I need to speak! But I doubt I'll win that debate, unless I just stand up during the service and start talking. And, in the end, it feels more important to me that Mom knew how I felt about her, that she was loved, than that I say it in front of a handful of other people.

We eat dinner in silence — a casserole one of the neighbors dropped off that I popped in the oven to reheat — and Dad heads into his home office, where he remains until I'm ready to go to bed. I walk up to the door to tell him goodnight and raise my hand to knock, but it just doesn't feel right, so I walk quietly back to my bedroom, shut the door, put on my tank top and yoga pants and climb into bed.

I stare at the ceiling for a long while, realizing that I haven't slept alone since I found out Mom was gone, and I miss having Hunter's arms around me, soothing me to sleep. I turn on the TV and watch whatever's on, eventually nodding off.

I'm awakened by a knocking sound, and I start to head for the bedroom door before I realize the sound is coming from behind me, at the window...

Not possible.

I lift up the shade, and Hunter's beaming face is right there, waiting for me to open the window to let him in, just like the old days.

So I do.

Once he's climbed inside, I stand back and marvel that he's actually here! Somehow, I'm not imagining this!

"How? How did you get here? Did you threaten Rhys' life? Steal his drum key?"

Hunter laughs.

"Nope. Caught a ride on a broom!"

My eyebrows reach for my hairline.

He gestures back out the window, and I peer out into the darkness, now noticing the small sedan parked on the street, with Maire smiling excitedly back at me. I wave. She waves back and then drives off.

"What? How? When?"

"Keep going — you'll eventually get all of them!" Hunter teases. I give him an exasperated look in return.

"I called your boss while you were in the shower. I told her you had ordered me to do tonight's gig and I was concerned you wouldn't have anyone here with you tomorrow. She said Maire had wanted to come but wasn't sure about making the drive for the first time by herself, and she suggested I ride out with her. She's going to the hotel down the road for the night. I told her I wanted to stay here with you."

"Oh, Hunter... I can't tell you how much it means to me that you did a gig, then drove three hours, just to come sleep with me!"

He gives me a curious look.

"I mean... Oh, you know what I mean!" I smack him lightly on the arm.

"I told you I'd be here for you, Elle. I meant it. I may not be perfect, but I try."

"You're pretty darn perfect as far as I'm concerned," I tell him, cradling his face in my hand. "Thank you for being such a good friend. Thank you for being you."

I give him a hug.

"Any time, Elle-belle," he whispers in my ear. "Always."

A shiver runs down my spine.

He notices and seems ready to ask me something, but a yawn catches him first.

"O.K., Mister Rockstar — bedtime for you! You've had a busy day!"

He smiles.

"Happy New Year, Ellie."

"We can only hope."

He strips down to his underwear, with me trying to behave myself and not ogle, and we slide under the covers together, as we've done so many times in this bed. Somehow, tonight, with one pillar of my world conspicuously absent, it means everything.

The next morning

"Ellen, can I speak with you for a moment?" Dad asks as I exit the bathroom, headed back to my bedroom to get ready for the funeral.

"Sure. What's up?"

"I know that Hunter's here, and that he slept in your bed last night."

"Yes, the way he's done a few thousand times since we were 6, including for a couple of months after *his* mother died."

"It's inappropriate."

"How so?"

"Are you having sex with that boy, Ellen?"

"Dad! Not that it's any of your business, since we're both 19, but, no, we are not having sex."

"This is my house, Ellen, so it's very much my business. I won't have it under my roof!"

"What? Sleeping? Or sex?"

"Either. It's not suitable behavior for you."

"*I* decide what is suitable behavior for myself, Dad. I'm an adult now. That's my right."

"And it's my right to stop paying for your college."

"You wouldn't!"

"I most certainly would! You're going to start behaving like a responsible adult, or you're going to have to deal with the very adult consequences of your bad decisions."

"If that's the way you want it, Dad. Hunter and I will leave straight after the burial, and you won't have to deal with the two of us under your roof anymore. Do what you want to about my tuition. I won't have you holding it over my head."

I head back into my bedroom, locking the door behind me. I'd hoped Hunter might have slept through that, but he's sitting on the edge of the bed, looking troubled, and like he might have been in the process of trying to come to my rescue. Again.

"Ignore him. He's out-of-sorts and wanting to spread misery whenever he goes," I tell him. "Mom said to give him some time and space, and he'd realize it was all going to be OK..."

Hunter's face conveys sympathy so deep that I almost stagger upon seeing it.

"It's hard to believe that was only a week ago..."

"She was right, Elle," he tells me, grabbing hold of my hand and rubbing it in small circles with his thumb. "It's all going to be OK."

He pulls me to him, resting his head on my chest and wrapping his arms around me. It fortifies me for the day ahead, and I can't express how much that means to me.

Hunter and I drive to the funeral home in my car, our overnight bags and a few remaining precious possessions from my room already loaded up in the trunk. Hunter looks years older in his suit and tie, like a real adult. He keeps hold of my hand from the moment we exit the car, releasing it only briefly when Maire approaches to give me a hug.

The three of us go into the little chapel and sit together, each of them now holding one of my hands, except when someone approaches to offer their sympathies.

Soon, my father arrives, taking brief but clear note of the handholding, though I have no idea what he thinks of Maire's presence.

The rest is a blur, until the moment when my mother's casket is being lowered into the cold ground, when I turn into Hunter's chest and cling to him like I'll fall apart if I have to let him go for even a moment. He holds me tight until we're the only ones left by the grave except the cemetery staff. He kisses my head and then leads me back to the car.

My father is standing with a cluster of other mourners, shaking hands and accepting sympathetic pats on the back. He looks over at me and nods, which is as much of a goodbye or expression of sympathy as he can give me, apparently.

Maire stops to give me another hug and then heads out in her own car.

Hunter settles me in the passenger seat of my car, taking responsibility for driving us both back home...

There's that word again... and I realize that home is no longer where it was a week or so ago. Home is where I am with Hunter nearby and good friends like Kara and Maire, and even the ladies of the circle.

Hunter picks up my hand from my lap, squeezing it in his own and raising it to his lips for a kiss. I smile wanly, exhausted.

"Get some sleep, Elle-belle," he says. "I've got you."

It's the first time I can remember sleeping in a car being as restful as sleeping in a bed, and the common thread seems to be that Hunter is right by my side.

CHAPTER 22

SPINNING

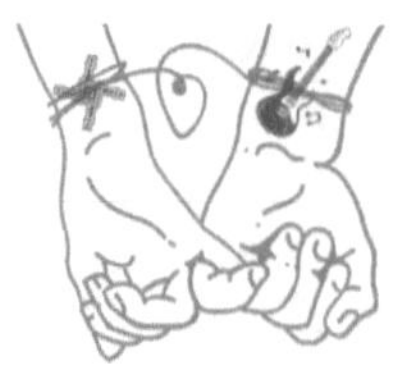

Hunter
A few weeks later

Ellie is spiraling out of control. I can feel it, like the worn fibers of a rope pulling apart under tension. It was subtle at first. She seems to still be going to her classes and she hasn't mentioned failing any tests or anything, but I can tell that the only things she's putting any real effort into are her fiber-arts class, working at the shop and spending time with me. Which isn't as easy as either of us might like.

I'm still working two jobs, trying to save up enough to get an apartment of my own and help get some better gear for the band. And then there's practice and gigs. I barely have time to breathe, let alone take care of her like I'd like to, like she did for me three years ago. My stuff is still stashed at Rhys' apartment, but I'm not sleeping on his couch anymore. When I get off my second job, I head straight to Ellie's dorm, make sure no one is watching and boost myself through the window.

The first couple times I did it when her roommate was home, I was sure the roommate was going to scream and call security. But when I waved and flashed her a smile before crawling into bed with Ellie, who immediately snuggled up against me, she shrugged and went back to sleep. Just like the last one. And, just like the last one, she's been a little more scarce since that happened. I think we weirded them out. This one apparently took it as a good reason to start sleeping over with her boyfriend at his place.

Either that or Ellie's growing collection of books on Paganism and the big goddess statue on her bookshelf caused some concerns.

Regardless, I'm worried about Ellie. She seems to only be truly peaceful when she's sleeping or spinning, and no one can go on like that indefinitely. Coming with me to rehearsals seems to be a good distraction for her, but the guys don't always give her a warm welcome, and I'm worried she's sinking into a depression, feeling rejected — I know. I know. I bear some responsibility there, too.

I'm hoping that coming to this Friday's gig will take her mind off things. We've been hired to play a big party at a frat house just off campus. It's one of the biggest private gigs we've had here, though calling a frat party "private" is kind of an oxymoron. Ellie's never been big on parties, but I figure getting a few beers in her, letting her dance and enjoy the band with a bunch of other people could be just the recipe.

After we set up on the makeshift stage in the frat's back yard, I borrow Rhys' car and go pick Ellie up from work. She's fidgety, keeps smoothing down her sundress and messing with her hair, like she's unsure of herself. I don't like seeing that, but I'm hoping that getting some experience attending a party like this will help her settle in to college life the way most of these people seem to experience it. Maybe a handful of parties with me there as her security blanket will help her feel more like she belongs there.

"Hey, Mike — what's up man?" I ask the host when we get back. He's an acquaintance of Rhys' from one of his classes and the reason we got this gig. Keeping things friendly is part of the job now.

"Looking like a great party tonight! Glad you all were free. And who's this lovely lady?"

Ellie is looking down at her feet, avoiding eye contact with everyone, and I'm briefly tempted to ask her if she wants me to take her home. But she really needs to get out and meet some people, so I plunge on.

"This is Ellie, a friend of mine. She's a little shy, and she's had kind of a rough time recently, so I wanted to get her out to have some fun. It's OK that she's here, right?" I ask even though I know they never make invitation lists for these things, which how they get out of control so often.

"Sure! Nice to meet you, Ellie. Let me know if you need anything while you're here — me or my buddy Kyle. That's him over there," he says, pointing at a guy with short blonde hair and a T-shirt with a bunch of Greek letters on it that I assume are the frat's name. "Do you want a drink? Kyle and the guys are setting things up right now." He doesn't wait for her reply. "I'll go grab you one. Be right back!"

This seems like a positive start to the night. I get her a chair and set it near my side of the stage, where she can see me. She's fiddling nervously with her new pendant, and I sit her down in the chair and kneel down in front of her.

"It's going to be OK, Elle. Just have a drink, relax. I'll be right nearby if you need me."

"Sure, Hunter. It looks like a fun time. I think I just need to get out of my head for a while." She gives me a tentative smile.

"That's exactly why I brought you." I give her a quick hug and jump up on stage to finish the final setup for my rig before we do our soundcheck.

A few minutes later, I see her chatting with Mike, who's brought her a red plastic cup I'm pretty sure contains beer. She seems to be feeling more comfortable now. She's always taken a while to warm up to people, so I'm glad to see she's found a friendly face in what is soon to be a crowd of mostly strangers. I keep an eye on her during soundcheck, teasing her a little over the mic when it's my turn to do vocal levels. She smiles back and seems to be having a decent time as the yard starts to fill up with people.

I can't say I'm not feeling a little relieved. I can't draw her out of her pit of grief by holding her spinning wheel hostage, like she did with my guitar. The only thing I can think to do is encourage her to come out and get her mind off things using myself and our music as a lure. And it seems like that's working tonight.

Pretty soon, it's time to start the first set, and I make sure to catch her eye, exchange a smile with her before we kick off the first song. From there, I lose myself in the music, as I always do. But I look over every once in a while to make sure she's still doing OK, and she seems fine. She's got a few more people gathered around her now, chatting, and she seems to be taking part in the conversation. Awesome! Mission accomplished! I dive into the next song on our setlist feeling pretty good.

An hour or so later, we're winding up that first set, and it's been great. Everyone seems to be having a good time, dancing, singing along to the covers, listening with interest to the few originals interspersed between them. I put my guitar back on the stand, pull out my in-ear monitors and hop off the stage, heading for Ellie. I get stopped by a couple people along the way, and I pause to chat — gotta be friendly with the audience — slowly making my way over to where she's sitting.

"How're you doin', Elle?"

"I'm doing pretty good, Hunter. Thanks for bringing me out. This is more fun than I thought it would be. Now I see why you enjoyed all those parties back in high school. Lots of people to talk to, good music—"

"Only good?" I tease her.

"You know what I mean," she replies, smacking me on the shoulder a little haphazardly, and I realize she's tipsy.

"You doing OK with the beer? I know you're not used to it..." I venture.

"No — no beer!" she says, smiling, despite that lack. I raise an eyebrow at her.

"Mike brought me a lovely fruity drink. Beer tastes horrible!" she adds with a hearty laugh. She shows me her cup, which has a decidedly fruit-punch Kool-Aid color and fragrance to it. I take it and give it a sniff. Just fruit-punch scent. I take a sip.

"Hey — that's mine! Get your own," she teases me, grabbing for the cup.

"That's got alcohol in it, Elle. Be careful! It's stronger than beer."

"Oh, I know. Mike said it'd help me relax, get over my shyness. It actually tastes pretty good. But I'm being careful, Mom!" she adds with a chuckle before her face goes blank and her eyes fill with pain.

I bend down and give her a hug, putting my forehead against hers and looking her in the eyes.

"It'll be OK, Elle. Just keep putting one foot in front of the other. Give yourself a break. I'm right here. I'm not going anywhere. ... Except back on stage," I add with a groan when I hear David turn up his amp and start tuning his bass. I give her a kiss on the forehead and a quick wave and hop back up on stage.

Ninety minutes later, we're nearing the end of our second and final set. I'm high off the energy of the crowd, with just a hint of a buzz from a couple bottles of beer while we played. Ellie's still over where I left her, now standing and chatting with Mike, Kyle and a couple of girls, who I assume are their girlfriends. Maybe Ellie could even make some new girlfriends here.

Speaking of which... I'm waylaid about three seconds after I jump down from the stage, a cute brunette with a nice rack grabbing hold of my arm and shouting to be heard over the music from the DJ who just took over entertainment duties. I pull her back behind the stage, where the mains aren't blasting in our ears, and we get to talking.

"I'm a *huge* fan of yours," she tells me, running her fingers up and down my upper arm.

"Mine or the band?" I ask, half joking.

"The band, but mostly yours," she replies, flirting pretty flagrantly with me now.

"Well, that's nice to hear. Let's go get you a fresh drink. I could use another beer."

I put my hand on the small of her back and guide her back over to the makeshift bar. She tucks herself right under my arm, her head barely reaching my chest. She's cute. And that low-cut top frames a pretty attractive picture, so when she pops up on her tiptoes to kiss me, I'm happy to bend down the extra couple inches to meet her.

"Hey! Hunter! Great show, man!" Mike says, clapping me on the back. "I see you've met Missy," he adds, giving me a thumbs-up that the girl can't see because she's still stuck to my chest, apparently waiting for the making-out to resume.

"Yeah, man. Nice party. Thanks for taking care of my friend. She's not used to drinking like the guys and I are, so I'm not surprised she didn't like the beer."

"No problem! She seems like a nice girl, once she's relaxed a little. Kyle seemed to be taking a shine to her. He likes his girls a little thicker..." he adds with a smirk.

And alarm bells start sounding in my head. How long had I been talking to Missy? How long has it been since I've seen Ellie? Where is she now?

Fuck!

CHAPTER 23

CHERRY PIE

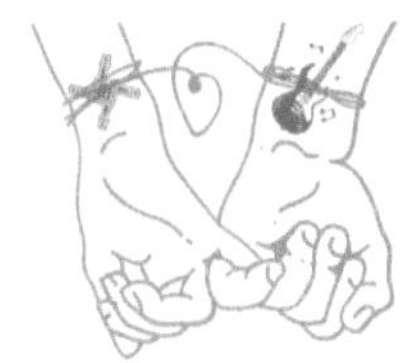

Ellie

"Mmmm... You taste delicious, Ellie. Has anybody ever told you that?"

"No," I admit with a giggle. "You're the first."

"You taste like fruit punch and sex..." Kyle says.

I'm not sure what sex tastes like, but the fruit punch tasted pretty good. And Kyle doesn't taste bad himself, though I think his fruit-punch taste is partly from my own mouth. He's certainly sweet enough, regardless. He gave me a tour of the house, showing me where the bathroom was when I asked, getting me another cup of that fruity drink, telling me he liked my dress, that my long hair is sexy.

We're sitting on the bed in his room now. He brought me upstairs to show me the view of the party from the back deck. Everyone seemed to be having a lot of fun. I'm glad I came out with Hunter tonight. The band was awesome, and Mike and Kyle and the girls we were talking to seemed really nice. It's nice to talk to other girls in a setting like this and not have them making insulting comments.

I'm not sure I like that other girl... the brown-haired one who dragged Hunter back behind the stage. But, hey — he's not my boyfriend. He's been very, very clear about that. So, more power to her, I guess.

And with Kyle's lips drifting down into my cleavage, I'm not sure I really have much of a problem with that anymore. Hunter can have his girl. I'm busy right now.

Kyle's hands are running up and down my sides, and it feels delightful, sending my senses reeling. I lose myself in the sensation, dropping my head back. Kyle latches on to my throat with his lips, sharp little kisses that make my skin burn ever so slightly where he touches me. He works his way back up to my lips, his kisses turning demanding, and I open my mouth to allow his tongue inside. Ooh... That's nice. I like that. Whoever invented this should get a medal... French, right? A croix de guerre...

The thought makes me giggle, and Kyle pulls back to look at me for a moment before diving back in. His hands run up my sides and around my back, wrapping around my shoulders from underneath and pulling my chest tight against him. I wiggle a little bit, enjoying the sensation of my dress brushing across the fabric of his T-shirt, over my nipples, which I can feel tightening.

I let out a little moan, and Kyle's mouth drops back down, licking at the tops of my breasts, down deeper into my cleavage. I look down at him, and his eyes are big, taking in the view and seeming to delight in it. It makes me feel wanted, desirable, and I can't say that doesn't enhance the experience. Hunter has rejected me so many times that I was starting to wonder if there was something fundamentally wrong with me.

Kyle doesn't seem to think so. His hands are skating across my shoulders, down my shoulder blades, caressing the top of my spine above my dress.

"These are some spectacular breasts, Ellie. Has anyone ever told you that?"

"Hmm..." I say, lost in the feel of his jaw brushing along them. "No. No one. You're the first."

"Am I the first in any other way?" he asks, his voice a slow, sensual drawl, implying what he's really asking me.

"Did you want to be?" I reply, feeling bold but not bold enough to answer him directly.

"Fuck yeah!" he enthuses. "That fruit punch flavor of yours is great, but cherry's my favorite," he adds, his words heavy with meaning. I kind of like it. His hand caresses my back while his lips resume their gradual invasion of my cleavage, teasing the flesh out from under the sweetheart neckline of my dress. I'm kind of curious how long it will take him to get to my nipples at this pace. I'm not sure I want to wait long enough to find out.

His other hand has dropped down to my hip, tracing its way up and down the outside of my thigh. The full skirt of the knee-length sundress starts to gradually travel upwards with his hand, and the feel of his fingers on the bare skin of my thigh adds exponentially to the sensory input that I'm already all but lost to.

"Oh, Kyle — that feels nice."

"Yes, it does... You want me to make you feel even better?"

"That sounds wonderful," I reply absently.

His hand on my spine slides to the zipper on the back of my dress, slowly easing it down, his mouth drifting farther down, closer to my nipples, as the dress begins to loosen around my chest. He stops to slide the straps off my shoulders and down my arms, his fingers tracing along the skin of my outer arm. I gasp as the feeling takes root in my mind, one more on a pile of sensations I'm collecting tonight. Such a delightful little collection...

Kyle takes one of my nipples in his mouth, sucking on it tightly. I moan, loudly. He bites down lightly, and I'm panting, unable to process all of what's happening. How many hands does the man have? The image of a Hindu god comes to mind, and I have to open my eyes to confirm Kyle hasn't grown any extra limbs in the last few minutes. He hasn't, but one of his hands is now pushing up my skirt from the center, tracing the tender flesh of my inner thighs, which start to open for his exploration.

When he reaches the apex of my thighs, he cups my mound, sliding his finger into the depression between my lips. I cry out and grab his head, pulling him up to my mouth, where our tongues wrestle and we both begin to moan. His fingers move to the side, reaching underneath the edge of my panties, and I can feel him making his way to my center, where I'm desperate to feel him touch me, already drenched.

"This is going to feel so good," Kyle warns me, and I'm looking forward to it, pushing my hips up against him, feeling an answering hardness through his pants where he brushes against my leg.

There's a loud noise in the hallway, but I'm too far lost in what he's doing to me to make sense of it. But Kyle's lips are no longer on mine, his head swiveling toward the door... Which is no longer closed. Because Hunter is standing in the doorway, panting from exertion of his own, bits of wood landing at his feet, broken out of the wooden door frame where the door lock had been engaged.

"Hey, man! Why'd you do that? She your girlfriend or something?" Kyle demands, his hands having withdrawn from my panties and now raised up in surrender, as if he expects Hunter to get violent with *him* now that the door has been rendered a non-obstacle.

Hunter is looking at us, at me, looking somewhere between stunned, terrified and livid. There has to be a Venn diagram for that, with Hunter's pretty face right in the middle. I giggle. That seems to snap Hunter out of his reverie.

"Ellie! Are you OK? This asshole hurt you?"

"What? What are you talking about? Kyle's been *very nice* to me," I purr, kind of wanting Kyle to get back to what he was doing. "*Very* nice... He says I taste good."

"I bet he does," Hunter answers with derision.

"You're being a party-pooper, Hunter! I was having fun! Weren't you having fun, too? Pretty little brown-haired girl..." I muse.

"She's nobody. Just like this asshole," Hunter growls.

The sound wakes me up just a bit from my brain's vacation to a super-soft happy place. I look down and realize the bodice of my dress is still pulled part of the way down. Hunter's eyes follow mine and get just far enough down that I know he's seeing the top of my nipples. I pull the bodice back up against me, giving him a resentful glare.

Kyle's jumped up off the bed, leaving my skirt pushed up around my hips, so Hunter's now getting at least as much of a look at my lower body as he's had since the last time we went swimming together. But the context is so thoroughly different, and so is his expression. Almost... hungry... And then angry.

"Get your clothes on, Elle — we're leaving. Now!" he barks at me.

"You don't tell me what to do! I'm an adult. You are not my father," I tell him angrily. "Even if you're acting a lot like him right now," I add derisively. "And you're not my boyfriend. You've made that abundantly clear to everyone for years now, except Kyle here, apparently," I note, since Kyle had to ask the question. "And clearer to no one more than me."

I was feeling so good, so nice and warm and wanted, and everything was soft and pretty and good, and now it's feeling harsh and unfriendly and... embarrassing...

Because I've just now noticed that Hunter's not the only one standing in the doorway. We have an audience. Thankfully, Hunter's broad shoulders and height seem to have blocked most of their view of my semi-unclothed self. I push my skirt back down to my knees and reach behind me to zip the top of the dress back up, but my fingers won't work.

"Out!" Hunter barks. And at first I think he's talking to me. But then Kyle scrambles past him, trying to keep as much distance between them as he can while Hunter still looms in the doorway. Hunter glares at his retreating back before turning that glare on the bystanders, who, I note, include Rhys, Declan and David. Awesome. I'm never going to live this down... They all begin to disperse under the weight of his disapproval. He closes the door, glaring at it, too, as if to inform it that it had better stay closed, despite the broken latch, or it will see even more of his wrath. It, wisely, seems to shudder in fear of the threat.

Hunter crosses the room to me, grasping my jaw in one hand and pushing up one of my straps with the other. His gaze is full of concern now, while mine returns anger, mixed with mortification.

"Why did you do that? Why did you make that scene?"

"Because you're drunk, and nothing you were doing with that guy was being done with your reasoned consent," he tells me quietly, plainly.

He reaches around my back, setting the dress to rights but not zipping it up.

"I'm not *that* drunk," I retort, trying to zip the zipper up on my own again and failing utterly as my fingers refuse to grasp the zipper pull solidly enough to pull it upward, even now that Hunter has pushed the back back into place.

"But you recognize that you *are* drunk, right?"

I take a deep breath.

"I was. A bit."

"A lot," he corrects. "Especially when you aren't used to drinking. Have you ever had any alcohol before? At all?"

"I dipped a finger in some wine one time. I didn't like it."

He chuckles.

"So innocent," he says, seemingly to himself, caressing my cheek. He shakes himself out of his musing.

"I'm sorry, Elle — this was all my fault. I brought you here when I knew you were still upset, and I let a stranger give you a drink, and then I left you alone with a bunch of other strangers, who brought you more drinks, while I was off chatting up a groupie. Any one of them could have slipped you something — you realize that? And I didn't even think..." He shudders.

He stands up and walks behind me, tugging my zipper back up to the top and sliding the other strap back into place. He runs his hand over my hair before holding out his hand for me to take.

I frown at him.

"Let's go, Elle," he says gently. "Please. I need to get you home safe."

"I can get home on my own."

"I know you can. But you shouldn't have to, because I'm the one who brought you here and got you into this. So I'm going to take you home myself. That's my job."

"Your job is to be a rockstar."

"Yeah, well... This rockstar was a rockstar of an asshole tonight, and I'm going to have to undo the asshole part before I can just be a rockstar again. OK?"

"Are the guys going to be pissed?"

"At me? For making a scene? Probably not. That guy earned it when he brought a drunk girl up to his room to seduce her. I'll pay for the damage to the door. It'll be fine."

"I mean at *me*..."

"Why would they be pissed at you?" he asks, apparently mystified.

"I'm the reason there was a scene." I'm already cringing at how they must be thinking of me now.

He pulls me up by my hand, wrapping me in his arms.

"You're the reason for a lot of things, but there being a scene at a frat party isn't one of them," he replies cryptically. My brain isn't working well enough yet to puzzle out what he might mean by that.

"Let's go."

I wobble a little, only then accepting that I am, indeed, more drunk than I'd realized. I'm not sure it merited breaking down a door to preserve my innocence, but I'm definitely not sober, even now. I grab Hunter's arm to steady myself. He smiles slightly and tucks me under his arm, walking me back downstairs and out to David's car, where he leaves me — admonishing me not to move from that spot until he gets back — before bringing back the keys and his gear. He tucks me in the car, buckles me in and takes me home.

I'm half asleep when he unbuckles me and leads me to my room. He sticks his hand in my pocket, and it tickles. I can't help but giggle.

"Whatcha doin', Hunter?" I drawl. "I've already been felt up once tonight, and I don't think that's how you're s'pose to do it..."

"I'm getting your key so I can get you in bed..."

"Ooh... is that a threat or a promise?" I ask with a little waggle of my shoulders. His eyes follow the movement to my cleavage. Then he takes a deep breath, closes his eyes for a minute and resumes looking for the key. Which he eventually finds in the other pocket. I could have told him it was there, but he didn't ask, and I was having too much fun letting him look.

He leads me to my bed and sits me down there, giving me a concerned look as I stare up at him, just marveling at how pretty he is...

"Get some sleep, Elle," he orders me gruffly.

"Don' wanna go to sleep. Not tired," I tell him, even though my eyes are sliding closed as I say it. "Don' like sleeping alone... feels lonely..."

He sighs and pushes me back toward the wall, guiding me down with my head on my pillow. I pout right at him.

"Oh, stop it," he says. "It's not working. And I'm already coming in, so turn over."

I do as ordered, facing the wall on my side, and he climbs onto the bed beside me, spooning up against my back. It makes me picture him as a talking, dancing, guitar-playing spoon, and I laugh.

"What's so funny?"

"You'd make an excellent animated ad for dishwasher detergent, all golden and shiny and spoonlike, playing your spoon guitar with your big, bright spoony eyes telling people they should buy Hunter brand dishwasher detergent. For their dishwashers. And their dishes. Spoons..."

"Go to sleep, Elle," he tells me firmly wrapping his arm around me and smoothing my hair down before placing a little kiss on the side of my head.

"I love you, Hunter..." I murmur. "I really, really love you..."

"I know."

"Stop doing that!" I tell him, suddenly slightly more awake than I had been. "It makes me sad every time I watch Star Wars."

"Apologies, Your Highnessness," he says with a sigh, pressing another kiss onto my hair. "But you like me because I'm a scoundrel."

"I like nice men," I tell him sleepily, the dialogue settling in my remaining consciousness.

"I *am* a nice man."

"No, you're not... You're a rockstar." And I snuggle into his arms and fall right asleep.

CHAPTER 24

THE FAB FIVE

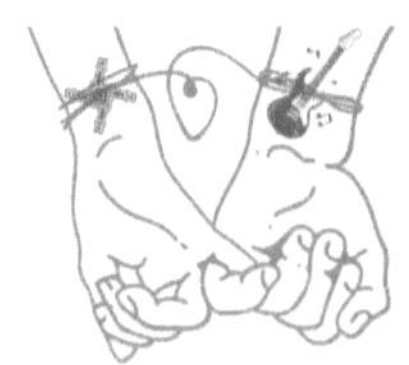

Hunter
The next day

I'm not entirely sure what got into me last night. I may have used my size and a pointed glare to get some of our high school classmates to stop teasing Ellie, but I've never laid a finger on anyone in anger. And I still haven't, thank god, or I might be in a world of trouble right about now. But Ellie in danger kicks all my protective instincts into high gear.

"Hunt..." David ventures. "You can't be breaking down doors at private parties that we're performing at. You know that, right?"

"Yeah. Sorry about that, guys. I told them I'd pay for the damage. Mike was actually kind of apologetic. I think he was just glad I didn't call the cops and report Kyle. That would have brought the party to a crashing halt, with most of the people there under-age and drinking."

"What the hell were you thinking!" Declan demands, his tone the polar opposite of his brother's calm and measured one.

"I was thinking that my best friend — whose mother just died and who I'm not sure has ever *been* to a party, let alone gotten drunk or felt up at one — was just about to have some douche with a cup of Kool-Aid take her virginity. That's what I was thinking, Declan," I reply derisively.

"She's still a virgin?" Rhys asks. "How in the hell did that happen? Are you sure?"

"Don't even think about it, Rhys..."

"You said she likes redheads, right?"

"She likes Eric Stoltz from 1987. You are not Eric Stoltz, and 1987 was a long time ago. And, no, I'm not sure. Not entirely. But in all the time I've known her, she's never had a boyfriend or gone on a date that I was aware of. She's super-shy until she gets to know people. I mean — you've seen how she is, and she's known most of you guys for years. And the guys in high school were kind of mean to her. So were the girls, for that matter."

"That sucks," David empathizes. "I get why she'd avoid parties and guys in general. So why'd you even take her with you?"

"She's struggling, man," I admit. "She hasn't been the same since her mom died. I was hoping getting out and meeting some new people would pull her back out of her shell again."

"Well, it did," Declan points out. "And nearly out of her dress, too. Actually, about halfway out of it..." he adds with a smirk.

"Don't even," I warn him. "You saw what I did to that door."

He raises his hands in surrender, stepping away.

"Anyway — between the hangover and the embarrassment, I don't think she's going to be drinking again anytime soon. So, it shouldn't be an issue. I handed Mike back most of my pay for the gig to cover the damage. He said things were cool and not to worry about it. He even offered to have Kyle apologize for his 'misstep.' But I don't want that guy anywhere near Ellie."

"He was open to us playing there again?" Declan asks, ever the booking agent.

"Yeah. He said so. He seemed to mean it."

"Good. It was a good-paying gig, even if you didn't get to keep your portion of it. And word will get around from those who were there and liked the music. Assuming they aren't concerned about their doors staying intact," he adds.

"Let it go, Declan," David urges.

"So you really never tapped that?" Declan asks.

"Be respectful, man. Come on," I plead. "She's my best friend. We've never been like that."

"Hunter, I hate to break it to you — but that girl has got it for you, bad. Really bad. Have you seen how she looks at you? I've never had *any* girl look at me like that," Rhys says. "I'd have been on that like sticks on a snare. How the fuck have you managed to stay just friends?"

"I'm just not into her that way, guys. We've been best friends since we were 6."

"So, she's like a little sister to you, then…" David suggests.

"Yeah. Kind of. I guess," I reply, not wanting to get into the details of why I've kept Ellie at a distance in that respect.

"So she's off-limits?" Declan asks.

"Fuck yes, she's off-limits. Especially to you."

"I take offense at that. Well… No, not really. If I had a sister, I wouldn't want her around me, either."

"That makes no sense, Declan. Unless you're into things I really hope you're not into," David adds.

"You know what I mean," he replies, rolling his eyes.

"You're kind of adamant about that off-limits thing. And the 'not into her that way' thing. Are you sure that's not a 'protests too much' kind of deal?" David asks.

"No! I'm not sure how else to say it, guys. I mean, with all the groupies we've got these days, why the heck would I be looking to screw my best friend? Those girls are much more suitable for a backstage quickie. No expectations, no phone numbers, no emotional baggage, eager to please…"

"I'm not sure you can get more eager to please than Ellie is with you, man," Declan jokes.

If I had eye-lasers, Declan could pick up a second job as bookends right about now.

"Be straight with us, Hunt… Is it her weight? She's not exactly a girl you throw over your shoulder and carry her to your bed," David says. "As much as those curves suggest trying it."

"And those eyes," Rhys says. I try to ignore the wistful tone in his voice.

David's waiting for an answer, and I'm torn between being angry and being honest but tactful.

"I'm just not attracted to her like that, guys. Can we drop it? I took care of the door situation, and I swear, it won't happen again."

"Got it. Done," David declares.

"On to the next item on our agenda for today, gents!" Rhys announces. "I've found us a keyboard player!"

"Really? Is he? she? any good?" David asks.

"He — the guy's name is Alex, and he's a music major, like me. I ran into him when he was leaving one of the practice rooms. Killer on the keys, man. Just killer. He had some old pro teaching him when he was younger, and the guy wanted him to go to college, and he's just got this last semester left."

"Is he cool? We've got to work with this guy," I ask, mindful of how challenging Declan is to work with sometimes. The last thing we need is *two* divas in one band.

"The coolest. I mean, I only spent a couple hours talking to him, but he seems kind of low-key and practical, mature. He's already 21. Very intense about his music. Kind of into the glam-rock/metal scene, and he's got that kind of look, with the dark hair, eyeliner, jewelry, tats and stuff. But he's also into hard rock, so he's a perfect fit for us. And he's got a girlfriend, so no competition for pussy!" Rhys crows, as if that's the biggest checkbox on his list for a great keyboard player.

The other guys and I exchange a look.

"And he wants to join us? Has he seen us perform?" I ask.

"He caught the last show we did at that place down on 13th," Rhys says. "The one where we had to do a third encore?"

"That was a great gig," David agrees.

"And he said he's got some contacts in the local clubs, so he can help with booking. This could put us over the top, guys! I know it!"

Rhys is known for his... enthusiasm? But also for his impulsiveness. He could think this guy is the greatest thing since the double kick pedal today and decide he's meh tomorrow. So, I'm going to stick with cautious optimism for now.

The next evening

"That fucking rocked, man!"

When Dave is that enthusiastic, it's reason to think things are on an upturn.

"Whooo!" yells Rhys. "See — I told you! This is going to be it, guys. The perfect setup for the Carter Brothers Band to really make it."

"You need to re-think that name."

That's Alex. And, as I could have predicted, that suggestion goes over like a lead balloon with Declan.

"What's wrong with the name?" he asks Alex, his tone hostile.

"Well, for one, there's now five of us, and only two of us are Carter brothers." He's got Declan there.

"And, second, it's a mouthful, which makes it harder to spread word-of-mouth, harder to get the clubs' bookers remembering us. Heck — harder to create merch. And we're going to need merch if this is going to be a serious band. We need something short and sweet — preferably just one word."

"Rhys!" Rhys calls out enthusiastically. We all stare at him.

"Dude — why are you calling your own name?" David asks.

"I mean we should call ourselves 'Rhys'! It's got name recognition. People will associate us with peanutbutter cups!"

"For the tenth time, Rhys, that's Reese — R-E-E-S-E — not 'Rhys,' like your name," David explains.

"And?"

"And it will confuse people. Not to mention that, again, there are more people in this band than just you."

"But I'm *awesome!*" Rhys advises.

"Yes, you are," Alex agrees with a chuckle. "But I'm not naming our band after you."

"Well, that's disappointing," Rhys says, sitting down heavily on his throne and tapping his kick pedal idly a couple times.

"How about Thump?" he suggests.

"No!" we all shout.

"Styx?"

"No!"

"Not the least of reasons being that there's already a band named that," Alex points out.

"No, I meant Sticks, like drumsticks!"

"And how are you going to tell people we're not the classic rock band without spelling it every time?"

"Oh. Yeah."

"OK, guys — let's put the name change on hold. Keep thinking about it. If you come up with something, we'll discuss it again," I say, not wanting to invite more crazy suggestions from the mind of Rhys Madigan. I mean, I love the guy like a brother, but sometimes he's just plain odd.

"I still like Carter Brothers Band," Declan puts in. The rest of us ignore him.

"Alright — rehearsal tomorrow? We've got another gig on Friday, and we're going to need to work out the arrangements if Alex is going to join us for that one," David says.

"Tomorrow's good for me," I say, getting agreement all around. I'll have to get someone to cover me at day-job number two, but if things are as promising as they seem to be right now, I'm not going to need that job for long.

CHAPTER 25

A MUSE BY ANY OTHER NAME

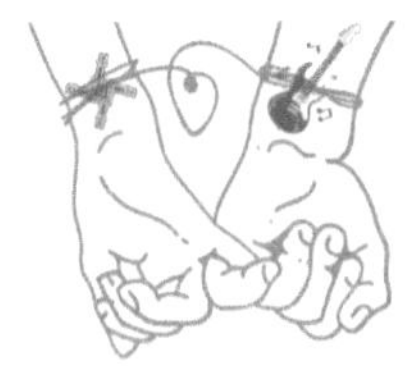

Hunter
Later that night

Honestly, I was ready to drag Ellie to rehearsal today, just to keep an eye on her, make sure she didn't sink any lower. But she ended up taking an extra shift at the shop, and I was glad she was at least not sitting at home, stewing over this week's sexual debacle.

When Rhys drops me off at her work, she's just coming out the front door. I walk up behind her and grab her in a hug from behind. She freezes for a moment, then relaxes against me as she realizes it's just me.

"Hunter! You startled me!" she admonishes. But she's smiling gently, and I know she appreciates the hug. "How'd the tryout go? Is the new keyboard player going to work out?"

"Oh, yeah — I think this is a game-changer. He's pretty much a virtuoso, and he seems like he's really got his shit together. No diva attitude, even though he's good enough he could get away with it. Ready to pitch in with bookings. And he — get this — he immediately told us we need to change the name of the band."

I can't help but smile from ear to ear about this turn of events.

"You've been wanting to change the name of the band for two years now!"

"Exactly!"

"Did you come up with a new name?"

"Not yet," I shudder thinking of Rhys' suggestions. "Rhys had some ideas."

"Oh, I bet he did," she replies with a laugh. She's spent enough time around Rhys now that she knows exactly what I'm talking about. "Do I want to know?"

"Nope. Categorically not."

"Thank you."

"You're very welcome," I reply with a chuckle.

"You coming back with me?" she asks.

"I thought I would."

"I'm fine. Really, Hunter. I've sworn off parties and ever drinking anything ever again, so I'm not going to go get myself into trouble. Really, I'm fine," she insists.

"We both know you're not. And until you are, I'm taking care of you, just like you did for me," I tell her firmly. "So, did you want to come to rehearsal with me tomorrow? See the new lineup in action?"

"I think I have to work," she says, refusing to meet my eyes. She knows I'd see the lie in them if she did. But I know it even without her looking at me.

"You don't. I know you don't, Elle. You already told me you were off tomorrow."

"Maybe I picked up some hours while I was here today..."

"Maybe. But you didn't, did you?"

She sighs with a tone of resignation.

"No."

I lift her chin so she has to meet my eyes.

"Come with me. It'll be fun. You'll get to meet Alex. He's cool!"

"Maybe. But the others... after the other night... I just don't think I can face them."

"It's fine. I talked to them today about it, and it's fine. They were a little pissed at me losing my temper like that, but we all agreed that what happened to you shouldn't have happened, and I've already sorted things out with the frat president. So there's no reason for you to be embarrassed and no reason why you can't come and hang out with us for a few hours."

"They really didn't see anything?"

"Hey — I'm a big guy. I mean, I'm not built like a football player, but I'm tall. I can fill out a doorway pretty well. Short of covering you with a blanket, you were kept as modest as could be. No reason to be self-conscious about it."

She's staring at her feet again, and I can feel her thinking.

"I'm not taking no for an answer."

"Fine. Whatever," she replies, rolling her eyes at me. "But if any of them say one word about what happened, I'm leaving. And you'll have to get your own ride home."

"Deal." I give her another hug, and we hop in the car.

The next day

"There she is! Our little sultry little minx!" Rhys announces the moment we walk into the Carters' garage.

Ellie instantly turns on her heel and walks back out.

"Elle! Wait! Come on. It's just Rhys being Rhys," I call out, chasing behind her. I grab her arm so she has to stop. "The other guys will behave, I promise. You know you can't rely on Rhys to follow any rules of etiquette. So, come back in. Come on!" I plead.

She sighs heavily and lets me lead her back inside.

"Hey there, Ellie! How's it hanging?" David asks. "Can I get you a drink? We're all out of Kool-Aid, I'm afraid, but I can get you a soda."

Ellie grimaces and looks down at her feet, her head bowed in resignation. But David actually does bring her a soda, giving her a pat on the back and adding a wink for me.

She looks at Declan expectantly, waiting for his root note in this chorus of ribbing.

"Nice nips there, Elle. You should wear that dress more often."

Her head drops down again, her palms going to her forehead and fingers wrapping over her hair.

I glare at Declan, but he appears to be glare-proof. I again wish for laser-beam eyes.

"Elle..." I start, knowing I'm going to have to talk her into staying.

"Thanks, Declan. I'd be happy to loan it to you. Rose really is your color! Sets off those blue eyes so nicely! I've even got a pair of matching heels that would fit you, if the ones in your diva closet don't match!"

All of us are staring at her now. Did she just do what I think she did?

"Whoa. Burn! She got you there, Dec," Rhys trumpets.

"I can confirm there are heels in his closet," David adds, trying to keep a straight face.

"What's this about heels in Declan's closet?" Alex adds, walking up behind us. "Is this a new part of the stage performance? Have you added a drag segment?"

"We'd have to start with you and the eyeliner, glam-boy," Declan retorts.

"I can give you some tips if you like, Declan. It takes a bit of practice not to come off like a third-grader who got in her mother's makeup bag."

Declan sighs, walking up to Ellie. We're all holding our breath.

He extends his hand out to her. She takes it.

"Nicely done, my lady," he acknowledges with a nod. "Touché. Good to see that feisty inner Ellie show up for our rehearsal. I'm expecting constructive criticism! Can't let these assholes get lazy just because they've got the glamour-girl there covering their butts with fancy keyboard tricks..."

"Those are the only tricks I turn, Dick-lan, so don't get your hopes up for anything else."

Declan's jaw drops. David's, Rhys' and mine, too. Ellie is just standing back and appreciating someone taking Declan down a peg for once. Well, twice, since she just did it herself.

Declan recovers himself.

"I've got plenty of ladies eager to visit Dick-land already, so you'll just have to wait your turn, Alexandra."

"That's Alexis to you, Dick," Alex retorts.

And now we're all laughing, Ellie included. The puzzle pieces feel like they're falling into place.

An hour later

We've gone through about half our setlist, all covers so far, and Alex is jumping in like he's always been part of the band. He knows every single song we cover, and it's just a matter of massaging the keyboard parts into our existing arrangements. In some cases, they were part of the original and we'd been doing a stripped-down version. In others, Alex adds extra layers to the song, enriching the end result.

It's really, really good. If I do say so myself.

We're taking a break before we start on the handful of originals we've been working into our sets. This will be the real test of whether we can make this work, but with what Alex has shown us so far, I have no doubt that he will not only be able to handle what we've written, he'll make it better.

In the meantime, the topic has turned back to the new name for the band. Rhys came prepared with a laundry list of the worst names I think I've ever heard people suggest for a band.

"Columbaria," he suggests.

"Why?"

"We're a D.C.-area band. You know — District of Columbia-area. But we can't be called Columbia, because we're not from the actual Columbia, and people will think we speak Spanish."

"I actually had three years of Spanish in high school," David volunteers.

"Columbaria is what you call the little niches you stick dead people's ashes in at a cemetery," Ellie points out.

"What is 'I got an A-plus in English and I need to show off my vocabulary' for a thousand, Alex?" I snipe at her. She sticks her tongue out at me.

"OK — no Columbaria. How about Headstock?" Rhys suggests, moving on.

"Like on a guitar?"

"Yeah, but it's also like Woodstock and Headshop had a baby."

Crickets. We're just exchanging side-eye with each other while Rhys waits for a response.

"Moving on..." he says with a sigh. "Knights in White Satin. With a K."

"Sounds like a Moody Blues cover band."

"The Ungrateful Dead."

Dead silence.

"OK — you wanted a one-word name. I think I've got it."

We're all waiting, expectantly. Well, some of us (me) are dreading whatever he's going to say. But still, expectant.

"Supercalifragilisticexpialidocious."

He's waiting for a response, rapt on our faces.

"I think that's a great one," Declan says.

Rhys is smiling even bigger than before.

"If we want to get our asses sued by Walt Disney."

The corners of Rhys' mouth turn down as fast as they went up.

"Anybody *else* have a suggestion?" I ask, trying to head off whatever else is on Rhys' list. He's waving his hand wildly at me, like the kid in class who has an answer but the teacher won't call on him because she knows she'll have to send him to the principal's office.

In the silence, scrounging for ideas, I start whistling that little melody that came to me a couple years ago, which I still haven't worked into a song.

"What about aMuse?" Ellie suddenly suggests. "Hunter — you remember what you said to me that day you started playing again? The day you met Declan and David, and played together for the first time?"

"I remember that day... but what—?"

"You were in my room, and I'd fallen asleep while you were playing. When I woke up, I asked you about that melody you were playing, the one you were just now whistling. You said, 'Maybe I've got a muse speaking to me. — 'A muse,' like the inspiration...'"

"And 'amuse,' like we're entertaining," I continue, catching on to where she's headed with this.

"What about aMUSEd?" Declan suggests. "With the 'muse' in capital letters to emphasize it. It's just enough different to be unique, and can you imagine how fun it's going to be to tell the audiences, 'We are aMUSEd'?"

"That's clever!" David assesses.

"Personally, I've always been easily aMUSEd, so I'm all for it!" Alex adds with a laugh.

"The *only* reason I *ever* need to do something is that it keeps me 'aMUSEd'!" Rhys puts in, making it both unanimous and final.

We have a name!

If rehearsal is any indicator of our future success, today was an omen of epically awesome proportions.

Ellie got over her embarrassment and seemed to settle into the band dynamic like she never has before. Declan got his ego checked — not once, but twice. (And seemed not to mind terribly much. Though, that might have been since it was only coming from Ellie and the new guy. But, still...) We had a great rehearsal, covering our entire setlist, with only a couple false starts, all of which we got ironed out before we were done. Alex is just as talented as Rhys suggested he was and, moreover, he seems willing to put in the work to make this band a success, including helping us get bookings.

He's also amazingly laid-back. Firm, responsible, mature, but eminently chill. A good antidote to Rhys' impulsiveness and Declan's diva behavior, with a drive that provokes more enthusiasm in David than I've ever seen him show. And he's willing to step up and take on battles that I've always tried to duck. In short, a perfect fit for the band. We got really lucky there.

Alex's girlfriend, Megan, showed up to pick him up when we were done. I'm not quite sure how he managed to load up his keyboards with her hanging from his arm the entire time, but he refuses to leave them in the Carters' garage. I think he's even more attached to them than he is to her. And she's more attached to him than any girl I've ever seen attached to her guy. It's a little disturbing, actually, and I say that as a guy with his own built-in one-woman fan club.

Bizarrely, she's not living with him. Well, that could be purely a defensive measure on his part. I'm not sure I could handle someone that possessive hanging on me 24/7. She finally lets go of him when she gets back in the car and he comes back in the garage to say a final goodbye to the rest of us.

"You need a ride, man?" Rhys asks me. "Are you going back to Ellie's or are you coming back with me tonight?"

"Ellie's. For now," I tell him, still concerned about how she's dealing with her loss, even though she's perked up a good bit while hanging out with the band today. "Thanks again for letting me keep my stuff there, even though I'm not crashing on your couch at the moment."

"You're crashing with Rhys?" Alex asks.

"Yeah — I've kind of been couch-surfing since I moved out of here," I explain, gesturing over at the Carters' house. "A few nights on a cot at work, a couple on Rhys' sofa, a few at Ellie's dorm — until the last few weeks, anyway."

"So, she's your girlfriend?"

"No. No — just friends," I clarify, hoping Ellie is too engaged in her conversation with David to hear. "We've been best friends since we were kids. So a lot of people make that assumption. But I'm a free agent," I add with a grin. "Too many lovely ladies to choose from to pick just one."

"Rockstar attitude — I like it," Alex says with a smile.

"But, yeah — I've been staying with Ellie since she lost her mom, trying to keep her spirits up. As soon as she's feeling more steady, I'll probably be back on Rhys' couch again. He's got his drums set up in the second bedroom there, so I'm a semi-permanent resident of his living room."

"You looking for a place of your own? I know someone who's looking for a roommate."

"Yeah, actually. I've been waiting until things were a little more stable financially, and that's basically now, but I haven't had a chance to look for anything yet, with job, rehearsal, gigs... and Ellie."

"Well, if you can handle sharing space with about five keyboards, you're welcome to take the second bedroom in my apartment. Actually," he adds with a laugh, "you can have the bedroom to yourself. I'll move the keyboards in with me. Gotta keep my girls close by."

"Megan isn't moving in with you?"

"She's got her own place with one of her girlfriends, and frankly," he says, looking behind him to make sure she's not within earshot, "I'm not ready for that yet. I need at least a few minutes a day to myself, and I'd never be able to even take a piss by myself if she was living with me."

"She seems a little..."

"Irrationally possessive and clingy?"

"I was going to say 'attached,' but I was trying to be polite," I reply, chuckling.

"Yeah. I'm aware of the fact that she's a little overboard in that department. I'm trying to convince her she can take her claws out of my arm without losing me to another woman. But she's... very determined. You'd actually be doing me a favor by moving in, because then it's less likely she'll decide to show up on my doorstep one day with all her shit in boxes."

The three of us laugh.

"Well, if you're serious, I'd love to let Rhys have his couch back. You need a deposit or anything?"

"No — it was paid when we moved in, and my old roommate graduated last year, so all I need to do is move my keys back in my bedroom and it's ready for you to move in. He didn't even take the bed with him, since he moved to L.A."

"Sounds perfect! Thanks, man."

And so, this wonderfully auspicious day ended even better than I could have dreamed. As soon as Ellie's back on solid ground again, I'll have my own bed, my own room and, at least from what I've seen so far, a pretty cool roommate who'll have no problems understanding my passion for my music or my musician's hours, because he'll be keeping them right along with me.

Puzzle pieces, man. Just raining right down and snapping into place.

CHAPTER 26

WITCHY WOMAN

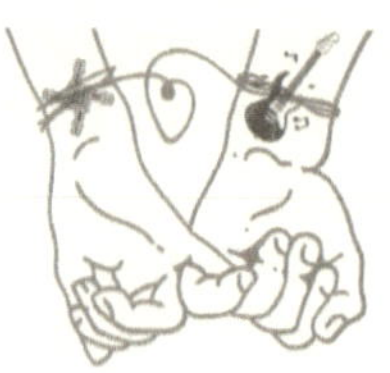

Ellie
A couple weeks later

"So she's not coming back?"

Hunter's asking about my nominal roommate, Zoe, who hasn't slept in our dorm room in weeks. She's moved all her stuff out, too.

"No. She's basically living with her boyfriend at this point."

"So, they're going to assign you a new roommate?"

"No. She doesn't want her parents knowing she's living with the boyfriend — so, officially, she's still living here."

"And she just suddenly decided to move in with the boyfriend? Or was it me spending so many nights sleeping over?"

"I think it was both, probably. But I suspect it had more to do with my books and stuff."

Hunter glances over at my bookshelf, where I've got a statue of the Irish goddess Brighid, a woven reed cross, some candles and an assortment of books on mythology and Paganism.

"People are going to be weird about that stuff, Elle. It isn't something they're going to even have on their radar, let alone accept without question."

"And they won't ask the questions, either," I point out. "They just make assumptions and act on them. It's hard to explain to people that you aren't part of the vast majority in being at least nominally Christian. So many people never go to church, let alone practice their faith in their daily lives. And yet here I am — deeply, positively religious — and I'm perceived as weird and dangerous."

"They don't really have a frame of reference," he says. "Especially when what you're talking about instead isn't being Jewish or Muslim or even Buddhist. I mean, I know you, have known you forever, and I'm still wrapping my brain around this stuff."

"Hunter — you know better than anyone how lost I've been since Mom died. No anchor, no rudder. Home isn't home. Dad has done everything but step up and be a supportive parent." He reaches over and gives me a hug.

Hunter has been and remains my touchstone, but I keep telling him that he doesn't have to stick so close to me. And I mean it. I'm glad he's found an apartment, and especially glad it's with Alex, who seems like he'll be a great roommate for Hunter. Things are really falling into place for him, and the band, and I couldn't be happier about that. But if I'm honest, I've kind of gotten used to sleeping in his arms every night. I totally get now why he stayed with us so long after his mom died. Even when things were at their worst, tucked into his side, I felt grounded, loved and whole, when otherwise I still felt broken and cut adrift. And now I've found something that fixes that, too.

"My whole world has changed, been turned upside down. Even before Mom died, I was looking for that place within me where my sense of self resides. Mom dying just shook everything up, like getting knocked off my feet by a wave and trying to find my way back to the surface."

"Not knowing which way is up," he says, as familiar with that feeling as any beach kid.

"Not knowing where the air is. I may be half mermaid." Hunter smiles at the joke. "But I still need air to breathe. I've gone from being tossed in the surf to wondering if I'm going to drown before I find which way is up. But now — She..." I tell him, gesturing at the statue. "She's what feels right to me, where I belong. It's like She's been there all along, keeping watch over me, and She just waited until I needed Her and looked for Her, and She was right there."

"Tell me about her, then. Tell me why, how... what this all means to you. I want to understand."

"Brighid — she's also known as Bridget, Bride or Bríd — she's the Irish goddess of healing, poetry and smithcraft. Kara said that I'd know soon if I was being called. And she was right. As soon as I started reading the Irish mythology, spending time in meditation, I knew I was being called. It felt like home, Hunter. But not just replacing what fell apart in my life. It felt like a home I had never known, and yet always known, like being welcomed warmly into a space that perfectly suits you and knowing you never had to leave, that you could carry that with you as easily as breathing."

"It sounds amazing. Kind of like music is for me."

"Exactly! That's why I pushed you to start playing again. It's at your core. You're not you without it."

"And thank god — goddess? gods?" he tells me with a chuckle, "that you did. Now, I have my guitar and the melodies in my head that get me there. So how does this work with you?"

"A lot of people do rituals — kind of like church services, I guess — the practice of creating what they call 'sacred space.' It creates a place where the divine comes to visit, where you can focus yourself on worship, put yourself in the frame of mind where you're in tune with what's beyond the physical world around us. From what Kara says and my reading, it seems like everyone has a different ritual, but I'm finding my favorite sacred space is actually in my own head."

"Explain, please."

"A physical ritual can be useful for a number of things, but on a day-to-day basis, all I need to do to commune with Herself is turn my focus inward and think of Her."

"And, what — she pops up in front of you and you talk to her? Or is it like people praying?"

"I'm not sure these older gods are any more tangible to most people who worship them than the Christian god is to Christians. I've never perceived Her as an entity I could reach out and touch, but I know when She's present." I groan. This is the hard part — explaining to people what it's like to have the divine speak to you. "I know this sounds nuts, but it's not a 'voices in your head' kind of experience." He's listening patiently, not acting like he thinks I've lost my mind. So far, so good.

"I mean — you tell me... Other than some pretty normal grieving, my mental health is quite good, right? You're not planning on having me admitted to a hospital, are you?" I chuckle, but I have to admit, I'm a little nervous spilling all this stuff on my best friend. Having him declare me in need of professional help would be pretty devastating. You want the best friend who'll tell you when you need help, but you also don't want them thinking you're mentally ill when you're just being spiritual.

"No, Elle. You're fine," he says, giving me a kiss on my temple to reassure me. "If people can go to church to talk to god or pray for a good parking space, you're very normal."

"People have gotten so jaded about religious belief these days," I reply. "Even when they're going to church every week and aim to follow what their faith tells them is moral and right, people tend not to think in terms of communing with the divine in a tangible way. They send their prayers out to some far-off god they just hope is listening and don't expect to hear god answer back, unless it's in granting what they wished for, like tossing a coin in a fountain. It seems a little sad to me.

"And god forbid someone says, 'God talked to me' — people immediately go with side-eye and mental health concerns and worry about religious fanaticism, or they think it's something that's restricted to saints and popes. And that's the religious people." Hunter nods in agreement. "The average person on the street crosses to the other side when you say things like that. It seems the days of people spending time in prayer and coming away with a sense that they'd been given direction are largely gone. But why?"

"I don't know. Maybe we lost faith as we began the pursuit of science. Maybe we stopped believing in things we can't see when we became able to see things down to the micron," he suggests.

"'Any sufficiently advanced technology is indistinguishable from magic.' That's Arthur C. Clarke's Third Law."

"More practical than Asimov's laws, at least until we've made some more progress in artificial intelligence," he jokes.

"You are such a geek."

"Says the woman who's quoting Arthur C. Clarke at me." He nudges me with his elbow.

"Point taken," I reply with a laugh. "But I'm not sure it doesn't also work in reverse, where magic starts to merge with tech. In an age of technology, I seem to be one of the few who doesn't think the two are divided along concrete lines."

"So, is this stuff you're doing magic? Is it — here's a loaded word — witchcraft?"

"The kind of magic I'm talking about is like particularly emphatic prayer. Prayer that has passion and need, determination and will, organized intent and, often, a connection bridging the physical world with the spiritual one, which is where ritual comes in. The witches I've met and read about don't twitch their noses and have books fly across the room into their hand. They don't wave their arms or perform a chant and have fairytale creatures scurry to clean their homes."

"That would be handy, especially in an apartment with a bunch of guys. You'd need a large contingent of squirrels to take out the pizza boxes and beer bottles," Hunter notes with a grin.

"Is that what you're having these days when you're not with me? Pizza and beer?"

"Often enough," he admits. "Why do you think I spend so much time here with you and your goddess?" He laughs.

"You really do need to get a life, Mr. Rockstar. Maybe we should magic one up for you," I say with a grin.

"So, if we're not talking about house-cleaning squirrels, what is this magic stuff, then?"

"Most people do stuff like walk in a circle, light a candle and ask the divine, or nature, to provide opportunities for a better job, or to meet someone who will be their best partner, or to protect a loved-one serving in the military. The trappings, the ritual, are like a megaphone, concentrating their effort and amplifying their voice. So, magic is basically really loud prayer. And like prayer, it doesn't always work, and it doesn't always work instantly. Sometimes you have to wait and watch the things you've ask for come to pass over time. And lots of Pagans practice magic, though not all. And not all practitioners of magic are Pagan."

"So, you're Pagan now?"

"Pagan just means a follower of a polytheistic religion. So, all those old Greeks, Romans and Norse people whose myths we read even as little kids? Pagans. They had gods and goddesses and believed that there was more than one face of the divine. They were real people with real faiths, and people think of it as some kind of quaint, backwards belief system, but it's really not that much different from more modern religions."

"Why do you think we have so many religions then? If it's all kind of the same?"

"For me, it boils down to god being too big, too complex, too all-encompassing to fit into the little boxes humans try to stick Him/Her/It/Them in. Why wouldn't the divine show itself to different people in ways that best suit them? And why should humans limit the divine by insisting it stay in those little boxes, especially when so many of those boxes look so much alike? It's disrespectful to god, to how the divine chooses to appear to others. If there really was only one interpretation of the divine that was right and true, we'd be lucky if even one person on the planet had it exactly right."

"Makes sense. We can't even get people to let the bigger boxes coexist, let alone the small ones."

"The cool thing, I think, is that even the faiths that were lost to Christianity's rise are finding new life these days, with the lingering folk rituals and mythology that came from them now leading people back to the faiths that birthed them. The old gods don't cease to exist just because a new one becomes dominant. And those who are called to serve them are called even when they don't yet know who's calling."

"Like you."

"Yeah. Like me." I smile at that, because it tells me Hunter gets it. He may not believe the same things I do, may not believe in my visions, but he doesn't think I'm crazy and he understands why it's important to me. "When you're called and you find your way to where you're supposed to be, there is no other feeling like it. The only thing approximating the acceptance and love I feel from Herself is how I remember feeling as a little girl, when Mom was my world and I was the center of hers."

And a lot of the time, it's pretty close to how I feel in Hunter's arms. And it's how I remember feeling in those dreams — visions — of Hunter and me in the past. It's natural and easy and right. And I may not be able to persuade him they're real and true, but I know that he does feel a degree of comfort with me that stems from that same place.

I did break down and tell Kara about my visions. I didn't give her the details, but she put her priestess hat on and told me that weaving and spinning have long been associated with magic, with the fates of man and even with psychic vision. Its meditative qualities focus the mind and can open it up to new perceptions or to connections to other times and places.

"Kara said weaving and spinning with intention works along the lines of any ritual, including complex magical practices or simple prayer."

Without even realizing it, I've been immersing myself in the environment of visions and magic and fate, and I've been doing that since I first started spinning, at 15. No wonder I've been having visions so often when at the wheel.

"I also discovered that Brighid's not just known for her connection to smiths, healers and poets, but to practitioners of other 'womanly arts' — including midwifery, brewing, dyeing *and weaving.*"

"So, you've been headed in this direction all along."

Kara had told me to trust my intuition, and I've been doing that since that first vision, and probably before. And it seems like it's all been leading me to the same path. Hunter may not want to explore how my visions relate to him, to us, but that's his right. It's frustrating, but it's his right. Regardless, my soul-deep connection with my spinning and weaving have never been stronger.

"The work I've done the last few weeks is some of the best I've ever done. There's an energy — warm, serene, bright — to them for which I can't take full credit," I admit to Hunter. "Mrs. Pomeroy is even talking about submitting some of my weavings to area galleries for a possible show. She thinks I could be selling pieces for hundreds of dollars or more by the time I graduate, if not sooner."

"That's amazing, Elle! Wow. You'll be a famous weaver before I make good on that rockstar dream of mine." He gives me a hug.

"I don't know about that. I feel like you're on the cusp of breaking through, and Kara keeps telling me to trust my instincts. Which seems especially important when we're talking about a goddess of poets and your success in music."

And my connection to Herself only continues to grow. It's been a blessing. She's come at a time when I have sorely needed Her, needed the direction She provides, and I feel like my path from here is clearer than ever before: my faith, my work, my shop. I can only hope that fate will weave a fate in which Hunter's path runs alongside my own, whatever that may mean.

CHAPTER 27

NERF-HERDER

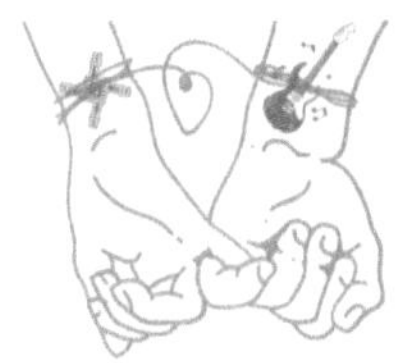

Ellie

“Ellie! Elle!” Hunter all but yells as he bursts into my room from the window. It’s dark out and I’ve been asleep for a while, I think... I sit up and blink, just in time to see his face about two inches from mine as he sits next to me on the bed.

“What’s up?” Because clearly, something is up. Besides me.

“The gig tonight — there was a guy backstage when we got off after the encores.”

“A guy?”

“A label guy. Not a big-label guy, but a label guy.”

“And...?”

“Sorry — this is just too exciting.”

“Then spit it out. You’re leaving me groggy and in suspense here.”

“They want us to open for a national tour.”

“You’re going on tour?”

“It’s just a regional opening slot, eight dates in about a month, starting in less than two weeks. The other act had to drop out at the last minute — they kind of imploded and there was an assault charge and a restraining order... something about an alligator... I don’t know — but their label picked aMUSEd to replace them!”

“Wow! That’s amazing! I’m so happy for you. This is a big deal, isn’t it?”

"Huge! But it gets better."

"Yes? And? Come on, Hunt!"

"They're offering us a deal for an EP. Four or five songs. All originals."

"Oh, my gods!"

"I like the S there, Bridge."

"I'm a polytheist now, Hunter. Gotta use the S."

He's beaming at me, and I can't tell if it's because he loves that quirky S so much or if it's still the tour and EP news. Probably the latter.

"Normally, we'd do the EP first and then tour, but they're strapped for an opening act since it's short notice. They liked our originals and live act enough that they wanted us, specifically, for the slot... And we've got enough originals to do a full set. So we can go right into the studio when we get back. Elle, aMUSEd is going to have its own professionally produced and recorded album! A short one. But still! I can't believe it — we're going to have an EP, and we're going on tour — with a national act!"

"Who?"

"No, the Who isn't touring right now."

I'm seeing where this is going, and I'm nipping it in the bud.

"I'm not doing Abbott & Costello-meets-classic-rock. Not when I'm still half-asleep."

"Party-pooper."

"Guilty. So, spill — who are you opening for?"

"Get this: Telltale Signs!"

"'Sleeping with the Sharks' Telltale Signs?"

"Yup!"

"Sleeping-outside-overnight-for-tickets Telltale Signs?"

"Yup!"

"Sleeping-for-a-week-straight-afterward-because-that-show-was-so-amazing Telltale Signs?"

"No — the *other* Telltale Signs..." he says, rolling his eyes at me. "Of course that Telltale Signs!"

"That's incredible! So you're not talking about an audience of two thousand people."

"More like eight, ten, twenty thousand!"

"Hunter — this is it! This is where your career goes from playing bars on Friday nights to touring for months, from trying to write songs to Top 40 singles! You're going to be a rockstar!"

"I love your faith in me, Elle — but don't get ahead of things. We've got to do tour prep basically overnight, and we've got to get the rest of our originals ready to perform *and* record. And then we have to get the EP done and see how it does, plus even more gigs to support it. And it all relies on audiences really loving us."

"They already do, Hunter! You see that at every gig!"

"It's different when you're talking about an audience who's paid money to see a national act, and you're just the guys who are filling the time before the people they really want to see go on stage."

"I get that. But this is it, Hunter — I'm telling you. From here, your star is on the rise!"

"Well, if nothing else, I know I've got one fan I can always count on."

"Always," I tell him gently. I'm ready to bounce up and down on the bed, I'm so excited for him! This is what I always knew he'd be doing.

"Elle..." he says slowly.

"What?" I'm concerned now.

"We're going on tour for a month."

"Yes, you told me that."

"We're going to be on tour for a month."

"Yes. I know."

"We're going to be driving from New York to Philly, Pittsburgh to Baltimore, D.C., to Virginia Beach to Richmond, and I don't know where else. And we're leaving in less than two weeks. We'll be gone for most of a month."

"Yeah — I got it. It's going to be awesome! Do I get a ticket and backstage pass for the D.C. show? Baltimore, too? I can drive to Virginia Beach, easy. Heck — I'll drive you from here to Virginia Beach myself, so we you can have one less day you have to worry about me, and then I can see you three gigs in a row!"

He laughs.

"I love your enthusiasm. And I'll see about getting you tickets and backstage passes for at least one show."

"Awesome!"

"Elle..."

"What, Hunter? What is the problem?"

"I'm going to be gone. I won't be here. I won't be sleeping here. With you."

"I didn't expect they'd fly you home every night to sleep in a twin bed in a dorm room with your best friend. Wow — that sounds weird even saying it. You're an adult, Hunter. You've been out on your own for a while — longer than you should have been. And you've got your own apartment. You don't have to keep sleeping here. I'm fine."

"I kind of want to. Sometimes, anyway."

"Is this 'I enjoy sharing a bed with you because you give excellent cuddles' or is this 'I feel better sleeping here because I think you need me, and I can't bear to think you'll need me and I won't be here'?"

He thinks about it for a minute.

"Be honest, Hunter."

He sighs.

"Mostly the latter. But definitely some of the former," he adds with a smile.

"I love you, you nut."

"I know," he replies with a grin.

"Come here, you scruffy-faced nerf-herder..." I tell him, settling back down in bed to log some more quality cuddle time.

"I *am* kind of scruffy," he admits, lying down next to me.

"I'll be fine Hunter. You'll be gone a month, and not even that, since you'll be here for the D.C. and Baltimore gigs, and you can come check on me then. I can take care of myself for a month. And if I can't, She will. So go, be a rockstar. And then come home and tell me all about it."

"As you wish..."

CHAPTER 28

MY GIRL

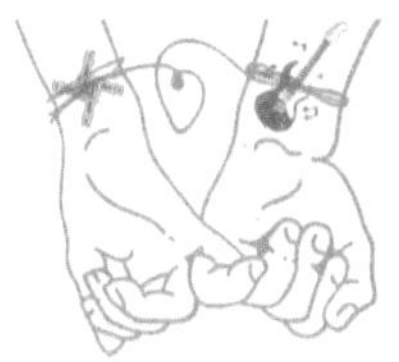

Hunter
Six weeks later

I thought performing in front of a crowd of 500 was intimidating. I had no idea how it would be to perform in front of an arena full of people — thousands and thousands of them. Before every show, I start off pacing frantically backstage and then grab life by the balls and drag my ass out on stage, taking on the persona of Hunter Graves, Rockstar(TM).

But every time I do it, it gets a little easier. There's a little less pacing, a little less ball-grabbing (life's — not mine, or anyone else's) and a little less dragging, and the rockstar persona comes on just a little quicker and easier. By the time we're taking the stage at the last of the eight opening gigs we had signed on to do, it almost feels normal to just step out there in front of that mass of people and flip the switch to performer mode.

The audiences are awesome. That was the scary part. But there's no booing, no heckling and only a minimal amount of bored chatting amongst some of the more diehard Telltale Signs fans, and by the time we're into our second song, even they are into the performance. It's a scaled-up version of our regular Friday-night gigs, with a receptive audience dancing and enjoying themselves, even if these audiences don't know our songs and can't sing the words back to us like the bar crowd does.

The first time we walked off stage from that, the guys and I just stood there, staring at each other, because we couldn't believe how well it had gone, how well we'd been received. Declan had toured the entire stage during the course of five songs, stopping by each of us at one point or another, singing back-to-back with Dave, jumping off Rhys' drum riser, standing back to watch me pull off a challenging riff and doing an "I'm not worthy" bow during Alex's most dramatic keyboard part.

The crowd was loving it, and that was before he even got to them, because get to them he did, leaning out over the crowd, making big gestures that could be seen from the back row, making eye contact, winking at the girls and blowing everyone's minds with his vocal range.

We were just enough different from Telltale Signs that the audience was predisposed to enjoy the music but didn't feel like they were hearing the same old stuff. We were something new. And they liked us.

The downside was that, with no EP, all we could tell the few well-wishers who stayed after to meet us was that we'd have something available next year and to sign up for our email lists and follow us on social media to hear where we'd be performing live in the meantime. But the fact that anyone stayed after to meet us was amazing in and of itself.

We even got along well with the headliners, which had apparently been a problem for the band we'd replaced. Declan was on his best behavior, with only a minimum of diva attitude. He recognized, at least, that he wasn't the top dog here. He didn't roll over and play dead, either, throwing down with Telltale Signs' lead singer, Aedan "Mace" Mason, when Mace spontaneously joined in on Declan's vocal warm-ups, until the two of them had drawn a crowd that had to have amounted to pretty much every person who was backstage at that point. They walked away patting each other on the back, mutual respect established.

From that moment on, we were welcome at every after-party Telltale Signs had during the tour, hanging out in their luxury hotel suite, chatting up the VIPs, helping ourselves to food and drinks, and girls... aMUSEd might have been sleeping on our tour bus between most of our gigs, but we enjoyed those after-parties quite a lot.

I did *not* indulge in any of the after-party perks the night we played D.C., because I'd gotten Ellie a ticket and backstage pass. She spent most of our set standing off to the side of the stage by me, her smile so wide and her eyes so bright that I thought the lighting techs would have to turn down the spots to compensate. She mouthed the words to every song, not quite dancing but moving along with the music, seeming to take in everything, but especially me.

Megan came back about halfway through the set, stepping right in front of Ellie to get closer to Alex. I saw Ellie frown, but I caught her eye over Megan's head and smiled, and I think both of us were glad that Ellie had a good three inches and change on Alex's brunette barnacle, because she smiled back. When we finished our last song, Ellie looked out over the audience and shook her head, seeming to marvel at it all.

I stay close during the after-party, wanting to make sure she feels comfortable. I get her a soda, and we sit on one end of the leather sofa along one wall of the suite's living room. There are a couple girls watching me from across the room, but when they seem like they might come over to talk, I take Ellie's hand in mine and lean in close to talk to her over the noise. They seem to get the hint.

I point her to the bathroom when she asks, waiting for her back on the sofa. When she hasn't returned after ten minutes, I go to check on her, surprised to find her standing in the hallway talking to Mace, seemingly comfortable chatting with this major celebrity and well-established heartthrob, who's about ten years older than us. Ellie doesn't warm up to anyone quickly, but maybe Mace's legendary disarming personality has broken through her shyness.

"Hey, Elle — how're you doing? Everything going OK?"

"Yeah, Hunter. I was just talking to Mace about Ireland. He spotted my Brighid's cross and asked me about it."

"I'm planning to spend some time there when the tour's over," Mace explains. "Your girlfriend's got some great background information on the language and mythology — the exact kind of thing I'm hoping will bring me some inspiration for our next album."

"Oh, Ellie and I are just friends," I clarify. Ellie flinches slightly. Maybe I shouldn't have said anything.

"Well, lucky me," Mace says. "I won't have to feel too guilty about monopolizing Ellie here while I pick her brain about some of the historical spots I might want to go."

"Well, as I said, I haven't been myself, yet," Ellie admits. "But I've done a lot of reading. And it's definitely on my bucket list to go. Sooner, rather than later," she adds with a smile.

"Don't tempt me," Mace offers, chuckling, and I'm not quite sure how to take that. Ellie is blushing, the warmth in her cheeks picking up the violet of her eyes. "With your permission then, Hunter, I'm going to borrow your *friend* for a little while. I'd like to hear more about this duality of Brighid as a goddess and as a saint."

I can't think of any way to respond except to nod, and Mace leads Elle off down the hallway.

Well... huh...

"You're not allowed to bust through *his* door," Declan says from behind me, smirking. "We'd get tossed off the tour."

"I know that," I reply, tersely.

"Why's he taking *her* back to his bedroom?" the blonde holding on to Declan's arm asks. "There are a ton of *pretty* girls here..."

I can hear the jealousy in her voice, and I realize then that Mace could have spent this time with anyone in the audience, backstage or at the hotel, and he'd chosen Ellie.

"Because she's a wonderful, interesting, intelligent, beautiful person, and he's a very lucky guy," I reply.

"Come on, Deckie — I'm getting bored... Let's go!" the girl whines.

"I think we can find a way to relieve your boredom, Mary," Declan purrs at her before smacking her on the ass.

"It's Carrie!"

"Sure it is," he replies absently, running his hands down her sides. "You want to join in, Hunt? I'm sure Mary here can handle both of us... And it looks like your girl has her hands full at the moment..."

"She's not my girl."

"No, I guess she's not," he agrees, lifting Carrie/Mary up by her arms. She wraps her legs around him and he immediately presses her into the wall.

CHAPTER 29

AS YOU WISH

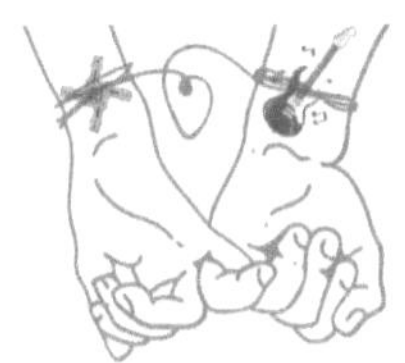

Hunter

I admit it. I sulked for a good hour, nursing a beer while I sat on that same sofa and waited for Ellie to emerge from Mace's room.

I finally hear a familiar laugh and look to find Elle emerging from the hallway, looking back over her shoulder at Mace, who's smiling down at her, sharing in whatever had made her laugh. He has his hand on her hip and is just way too close. I'm not used to Elle letting anyone get that close, except me. And I'm really not used to feeling jealous. And I am. She'd come to spend time with me at our big show on our own stomping grounds, and instead she's spending her time with Aedan fucking Mason and his megawatt smile and luxurious auburn hair... not that I'd noticed...

"Down boy," Alex suddenly says from behind me, having apparently momentarily freed himself from Megan's clutches.

"What?"

"If you had eye-lasers, Mace would be capable of doing duets with himself right about now."

"I guess it's a good thing I don't have eye-lasers, then. Not the least because Declan would have become bookends months ago."

Alex snickers.

"That girl's got you wound up kinda tight, doesn't she? Why don't you go reclaim her? I'm sure she wouldn't mind, even if it looks like Mace might."

"She's not my girlfriend. She's free to spend all night with Mace if she likes."

"Do you think she wants to do that?"

"I don't know..." I admit.

"Hunter, you are either the dumbest smart person I've ever met or the smartest dumb person. I'm not sure which." He shakes his head and heads back to get another beer.

An hour later, I spot Ellie yawn behind her hand as she perches on the arm of the chair in which Mace is sitting. I'm up in an instant.

"You ready to call it a night, Elle?"

"Not quite yet, Hunter. I'm having a good time. It's been a long time since I've had this good of a time."

I don't have a good reason to explain why hearing that hurts. But maybe I earned it.

"I haven't had this good of a time with someone in quite a while either, Ellie," Mace says, putting his hand on the back of Elle's neck, under her hair. "Thanks for bringing her tonight, Hunter. She's one of the most interesting people in the room, for sure."

"Why, thank you!" Ellie chirps, looking genuinely pleased.

"Can I borrow you for a minute, Elle?"

She looks surprised but nods, taking the hand I offer to her as she slides off the arm of Mace's chair. I lead her out onto the balcony so we can talk.

"Hi," she says, shyly. I'm not sure I like her acting shy with me. I can't remember her ever doing that before, unless it was during the time after she first told me about that dream...

"Hi."

We're silent for a minute.

"Uh... Hunter? Did you want to talk to me about something?"

"Yeah... Um... How are you doing?"

"I'm fine. Why wouldn't I be?"

"I don't know... You were in Mace's room for a long time... alone... with him... together."

A single eyebrow rises toward her hairline.

"I was," she confirms.

"And you're OK?"

"Of course I am. Why wouldn't I be?"

"I didn't bust the door down this time."

She starts, as if she's only now realizing what I'm talking about.

"You're... You... I... We... You're asking me..."

She's blushing from her forehead to her cleavage now. Not that I'm looking.

"I really don't know what to say to that."

"Are you saying you didn't?"

"Didn't what, Hunter?"

"You know..."

"I think you'd better spell it out for me."

"You know — with him. Together. *Together* together."

"More words, Hunter. Preferably with a verb."

"*Sex*, Elle. Did you have sex with him? With Mace?"

"I don't think that's any of your business, Hunter."

"But... I... But..."

"But what?"

I sigh in frustration.

She takes a little pity on me, sighing herself.

"Hunter — I wasn't drunk. I haven't had anything to drink tonight except soda. I didn't do anything I didn't want to. No one forced me to do anything. No one seduced me into doing anything I didn't want. I'm 19, almost 20 — well past the age of consent — and I've had my full faculties about me all night."

"That's not an answer, Elle."

"No. It's not. And as I said, it's none of your business. You're not my boyfriend. You made that very clear again tonight, to Aedan and to me. And if I want to spend some time with an attractive—"

I flinch.

"— intelligent, creative man who happens to find me interesting and wants to spend time with me, behind closed doors or not... then that is none of your business."

I frown. Because she's right.

"I never asked you about you losing your virginity, Hunter. Even though you're my best friend and even though you and I at this point have probably shared a bed more nights of our lives than ones we haven't. And even though I freely admitted the content of that vision I had when we were 15. I never asked, and you never opted to tell me, even though I assumed — safely, I think — that you have slept with someone in the last three years. And probably a lot of someones at this point.

"I can't keep doing this, Hunter. *You* can't keep doing this. You can't keep trying to leap to my defense every time a guy looks at me with something other than platonic interest. I'm not your sister. I've got a platonic guy friend — what I don't have is anyone who looks at me like *that*. For whatever reason. Whether that's because you're running interference or because they think I'm too fat to be worth fucking."

"Elle!" I object.

"Don't think I'm naive, Hunter. I may not have had the degree of experience you have. I probably never will. But that's fine with me. I know a lot of guys don't find me attractive because of my size. But if someone looks at me and actually finds me attractive, and I'm so inclined, I'm going to have sex with him. You can't factor into that decision. And you've got to find a way to be OK with that, because I've broken my heart a million times on the rocks of your rejections, and I can't do that for the rest of my life. Someday, someone will want to be with me. And whether that's for an hour or a lifetime, it's my decision to make."

"This isn't easy for me, Ellie. I don't really know what I'm supposed to do here."

"It isn't easy for *you?*" she says, clearly irate now. "Mother of twelve gods, Hunter! You have no *idea* how hard this can be, how hard it is on the other side of the equation. None at all. You think I don't see all those girls in there, hanging on the other guys? The short skirts, the barely-there tops, the fuck-me heels and the blow-you lips? You think I don't know that happens every night on a tour? You think I don't have it stuck in my head how many of these girls, or whatever selection is available that night, you've fucked, screwed, eaten... whatever? And you have the unmitigated gall, the *balls*, to tell me this isn't easy for *you?*"

I'm speechless hearing this come from Ellie. As well as we usually read each other, I wasn't sure she even knew half those words, let alone had some idea I might be doing them, some nights just hours before I crawled through her window and fell asleep with her in my arms. I feel a little slimy. And, for a moment, I question the decision I made not to ever get into a committed relationship, and especially not one with Elle herself. Is this the life I want, full of quickies and anonymous women?

And I look at her now, with the pain in her eyes tearing me apart, and I realize this was exactly why I made that choice. Because I can't be trusted to be the good guy, can't be trusted to turn down easy sex with someone whose name I probably won't remember an hour later, can't be trusted to commit myself to one woman and treat her with love, care and respect. I'm no better than my father. And Ellie deserves better than that guy. Way better. And that means I have to get out of her way and let her find someone who *is* better than that.

"I'm sorry, Elle. You're right. I'm not your boyfriend." I don't miss the secondary flare of pain in her eyes. But better to say it now than let her continue hoping. "And it's not my business who you sleep with. Even if it's Mace Mason. So, I'm sorry. I won't interfere anymore. But I want you to understand one thing: You are my best friend — one of the most important people I've ever had in my life. And I want the best for my best friend. So I hope whoever you decide to sleep with, now or ten years from now, will be as good for you as you deserve, which is the best. You deserve someone who will treat you well and love you with at least as much love as you offer him, which is pretty much limitless, as I know very well."

A tear trickles down her cheek, and I can't tell if it's because she's touched that I want so much for her or if it's because she's sad that I'm telling her that guy won't be me. I swipe the tear away with my thumb, and the image flashes into my head, of how she did the same to me the night my mother died. And I stick my thumb between my lips, just as she did then.

I lower my forehead to touch hers, holding her gaze with mine before wrapping my arms around her and holding her tight against me. As always, she relaxes into me, and I take comfort that she still considers me a safe place for her heart to rest, because even though I don't deserve her, I'm not sure what I'd do without her.

After a minute, we release each other, and I turn to bring her back into the living room so she can get back to Mace, if that's what she wants to do. We instantly spot Mace and Alex, both standing in the doorway, pretty clearly having observed at least some of that conversation. Alex's eyes are full of sympathy, and I can't tell which one of us it's for — or maybe it's both for both of us. Mace gives me a sharp nod, which I take as a sign of respect, as well as dismissal. He'll take it from here.

"My lady, I would like very much to continue our earlier conversation, if you're so inclined," he says to Ellie with distinctive formality. Her expression goes from downcast to expectant in an instant.

"I'd like that very much," she replies, taking the hand he proffers and following him back inside, clearly headed back to his room. She pauses before they reach the hallway, turning back to me.

"Hunter, I'll let you know when I'm ready to leave," she says gently. "I can play designated driver if you'd like to sleep somewhere other than a tour bus before the next gig, and then I'll drive you to Virginia Beach tomorrow afternoon, as planned."

I smile back at her.

"As you wish..."

Given her full permission, I proceeded to get rip-roaring drunk. To the point where I don't clearly remember a lot of what happened after Elle went off with Mace again.

At some point, she fished me out of the living room and led me to her car, buckling me in and then driving me back to her dorm. She left me sitting outside briefly and then snuck me in a side door and into her room, before sliding off my shoes, and then my shirt, too, when she deemed it too steeped in alcohol to be tolerable to sleep with.

"You throw up on me and I'm going to be pissed, Hunter. I've still got to get you to Virginia Beach in like twelve hours. And I need some sleep."

"Not gonna throw up. Come. Sleep," I command, holding my arms out to her from where I'm already lying down in her bed.

She sighs and grabs some clothes before heading into the bathroom. I hear the water turn on, and then off again, before she comes back out wearing her usual tank top and yoga pants. She lies down next to me and I pull her back up against my chest, snuggling in, like usual.

"Did you use a different soap than usual?" I ask, half asleep.

"No. Actually didn't wash up at all. Too tired. I'll shower in the morning."

"You smell different. I don't like it."

She's quiet, and I decide she's fallen asleep, so I do the same.

Later that day

"Up, Hunt! Get up!"

Ellie is pulling me up to sitting by yanking on my arms. She's a strong girl, but I'm pretty solid now, so it takes some effort, and she seems annoyed.

"Here — take these," she adds, handing me some ibuprofen and a cup of water. I comply. A cold, wet washcloth lands on my face.

"Wake yourself up. We've got to go."

"Where are we going?"

"Virginia Beach."

"Weird time to go to the beach, Elle."

She rolls her eyes at me.

"You have a gig — remember, rockstar? You're opening for Telltale Signs in about eight hours."

"Oh. Right. My head hurts."

"Which is why you just took some ibuprofen."

"Ah. Yup. It's all coming back to me now!"

She gives me an odd look.

"Don't worry. I'll be fine."

She looks a little remorseful now.

"The ibuprofen will kick in soon, and as soon as this headache wears off, I'll be good to go. Maybe after another couple hours of sleep..." I lie back down on the pillow and close my eyes.

"Hunter! Wake up!" she all but yells next to my ear. A cold, wet washcloth drops onto my face.

"I'm up! I'm up!" I say, sitting bolt upright.

"Here — put this on," she tells me, tossing a T-shirt at me.

"Is this your favorite Fleetwood Mac concert T-shirt? From the show my mom took us to in Hershey in...?"

"It was 2004."

"Good times... a day at the amusement park and a concert by one of the best bands of all time."

"With no Christine McVie. But Lindsey kicked ass."

"Yes, he did. Made me want to buckle down and get better."

"And you did. And look at where you are now... Which is three hours from where you need to be in about four hours. Mace said your soundcheck is at 6. Put that on and let's get moving! Your limo awaits, rockstar."

I slip on the shirt.

"Fits like it was made for me."

"Oh, I don't think so, mister!"

"What?"

"Just because your best friend isn't so petite you can't wear her concert tees doesn't mean you get to appropriate them! I want that back. Washed. Or there will be retribution."

"Sounds like fun!"

I get smacked in the face with the wet washcloth again.

"Get your shoes on. We need to go."

I wake up in the outskirts of Virginia Beach, with Ellie behind the wheel and Lindsey Buckingham's live fingerstyle version of "Go Insane" playing over the stereo.

"I love this song."

"I know. It's probably one of my favorite songs of all time. If it was just the guitar playing, it would be incredible. But the vocal performance... Just riveting, devastating. One of the best things they ever recorded, and it's purely him."

"People always assume you love Stevie, with that long blonde hair and the witchy style..."

"I like her. The vibe between them is odd, though. You can tell there's something there that comes before..."

"Before?"

She glances over and gives me a meaningful look.

"Oh."

"Anyway — we're nearly there, and it's perfect timing, because you're going to go wow them on that stage yourself in a couple hours."

"That I am. I hope."

"Head OK?"

"Better. The sleep helped. Thanks."

"It's not that long of a drive. About the same as back home, but with a concert at the end instead of a cranky parent."

"You're staying, aren't you? I got your backstage pass and everything."

"Mace gave me a tour lanyard last night."

"Oh?"

"Yeah. He wanted to make sure you hadn't forgotten me."

"I'll never forget you, Elle," I tell her, squeezing her hand where it lies on the armrest between us. She smiles but it doesn't quite reach her eyes.

"We OK?"

"Yeah, Hunt. We're OK. I've just got some things I need to adjust to."

"You and Mace had a good talk, then?"

"Yeah. We did. He's a very spiritual guy, it turns out. We kind of clicked over that."

"Well, that's cool. I'm glad to see someone appreciating you in the way you deserve."

She smiles at that.

We arrive at the venue, and Elle flashes her lanyard at the security guy, who points us to a gated parking area just off the performers' entrance. She pulls up alongside the tour buses and parks.

"You, sir, need to go get showered and ready for soundcheck. Mace said yours is right after theirs, which is in less than an hour."

"You coming?"

"I thought I'd look around the venue a little, grab something to eat. I'll meet you backstage after soundcheck."

"Sure. Have fun!"

I give her a hug, only now taking notice of a couple small bruises at the edge of the cutout neckline of her shirt. She fiddles with it, adjusting how it lies, and I wonder if she noticed me noticing. Because I know what those bruises look like, and I think I may just have to kill Mace Mason.

"Elle?"

"Hmm?"

"Uh. You and Mace..."

"We had a nice philosophical conversation last night. Yes."

The look in her eyes is so innocent and earnest that I don't know what to believe.

"Hunt — you need to go get ready. I'm going ahead in. I kind of want to get a look at the stage from the audience."

"Oh. OK. Well, come find me if you get bored."

"I don't think I could get bored here."

I give her a smile and a pat on the arm, and we go our separate ways.

No. There's no way. She couldn't have. No. I'll have to threaten some other guy someday, but thankfully, it won't be Mace Mason and it won't be today.

CHAPTER 30

SOUL OF IRELAND

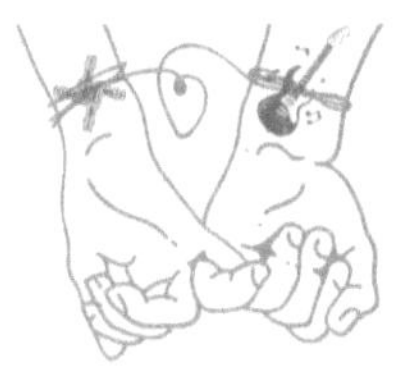

Ellie

After that night, that whole weekend full of epic surprises and turmoil and drama, I had made a decision. I was going to seize control over my own life and make it what I wanted it to be. My life could not revolve around Hunter; my plans could no longer hinge on where he was or where he was going.

Maybe I needed the confidence boost that came from someone like Telltale Signs' frontman paying attention to me to the exclusion of all others. Maybe the conversation between Hunter and me had clarified things for me by all but extinguishing the hope I'd held onto for so long.

Regardless, the next couple months were a time of self-contemplation for me. Losing Mom had changed my life in so many ways, directly and indirectly, big and small. Things would never be the same. The question was what did I want them to be?

My sophomore year of college was over. I'd gotten all A's and B's in my classes, which would have been a foregone conclusion six months prior, but had been harder to accomplish than I'd ever thought good grades would be for me. But I'd done it.

September was going to mark the start of a new school year, a new way of being, and I wanted — no, *needed* — to have a plan for my life that was concrete, directed at where I wanted to go and able to be put into motion immediately.

And then I immediately set that plan aside to do things I'd never thought I'd be doing.

I told Lindsey at the yarn shop in Mystic Beach that I'd be leaving to go back to college early this summer. I told Dad I was headed back early to stay with Kara and learn some of the business aspects of running her shop. (He was actually pleased by this, since it somehow gave him hope I might become a business major after all...)

I told Hunter that I was working crazy hours all summer and that Lindsey had pitched a fit about one of the new hires being on her cell phone all day and banned them during work hours. So he didn't really expect to hear from me, except by email, and he was so busy himself in the wake of the tour that I don't think he really minded.

I told Kara, and Kara alone, that I was going to be traveling for a month and not to worry unless I didn't make my regular check-ins via email. She was excited for me and ready to run interference if Dad called.

And, finally, I got my birth certificate and other documentation together and applied for a passport. I dipped into my savings and made a plane reservation for August 1, Dulles to Dublin, with a short stay booked at a little hotel overlooking the Liffey.

Talking to Aedan Mason in May had been inspiring, in more ways than one. I felt energized not just to take control of my life but to deep-dive into my faith.

I spent nearly a month traveling around Ireland, practicing my smattering of Irish in the Gaeltacht, where it is still the primary language, visiting areas along the northwest coast with a history and feel that was totally new and utterly familiar all at the same time, and I took in every musical performance I could, from traditional sessions in little country pubs to Irish rock in Dublin, and even one international act kicking off its European tour there. And I went to Kildare, soaking up an atmosphere of quiet contemplation and devotion that centered me like nothing ever had before, including Hunter, and getting some direction for my life going forward.

And when it came time to go back to Virginia, back to school and the dorm, part of me wanted to stay. It felt like home. The whole country did, really. But I missed my other home. Not home with dad. Not the dorm. Hunter. Emails a couple times a week kept me updated on what he was up to; though, in return, he got fictitious tales of difficult customers, summer parking hassles and arguments with Dad. Well, not entirety fictitious — just recycled from the prior two months I had actually spent in Mystic Beach. I wasn't ready to share this experience with anyone. How could they understand it unless they'd been there? Maybe someday Hunter and I would go there together, see if it finally jogged a memory in him. Barring that, I didn't really expect him to come around.

But all of that aside, I just plain missed him, hearing his voice, hanging out together, and, yes, falling asleep together. I told myself to get used to it, because it had gone on longer than should have been expected and would very much be a thing of the past once he was touring. But I still missed it. And him.

So, as August wound down, I found myself on a plane, headed back to D.C., with Maire waiting to pick me up and help me move my stuff from her house back into the dorm. It was cool for late summer and I opened the window to catch the breeze while we worked, missing both the salt air of Mystic Beach and the cool, dewy quality of the air in Ireland amidst the baked-concrete smell of the Virginia suburbs in the summer.

When we were done and Maire had headed home, I looked around the room — now half-filled with yet another stranger's stuff — and found just three things that I'd grab if I had to leave with no notice: my spinning wheel, my statue of Brighid and a photo of Hunter and me at the beach that last summer before he moved. We were splashing in the waves, both of us smiling from ear to ear, with the summer sunshine reflecting off the gold of his hair and the flaxen strands of mine.

It was precious enough of a memory just for that frozen moment in time with my best friend, but the third person who-'d been there wasn't in the image — they'd been behind the camera.

Mom.

And looking at the photo now, preparing to go into another year of college, I know Mom would have been proud of me. Not just for my grades and my skill in my profession, but for finally taking charge of my life, for steering my own ship. She'd have been just as proud of Hunter, who was all but a son to her. He had persevered through tremendous loss and challenges no teenager should face and was on the cusp of a career whose success would soon eclipse those of our fathers.

I email him to tell him I'm back. And then I email Mrs. Pomeroy to ask her about submissions for the holiday art showcase. It's almost unheard of for a junior to have work selected, and it was generally the bastion of seniors preparing for graduation and hoping to add some honors to their résumés ahead of graduation. It could make the difference between landing solo shows and grants straight out of college and facing a future where an arts degree set you up for teaching kids' classes at the local craft store.

I want to own my own store, featuring my own work. And I'm going to do everything I can to ensure that happens. Taking inspiration from my faith and my trip, while it's still fresh in my mind, I start spinning a new skein of Irish wool. I'm going to let instinct guide me, just as Kara had once advised, and I'm going to create from scratch a weaving that will tell a story that I hope will inspire everyone who sees it.

I wake with a start, not used to having a roommate anymore, to having other people making noise after I'd gone to bed. I look over at Julie's bed, finding it empty. And then I realize the sound is coming from the still-open window, where a hand is now grasping the inside of the sill. Instinctively, I tense up, ready to scream for help, before I lunge for the top of the window and pull it closed.

"Fucking hell, Elle!" I hear from below the window, belatedly realizing that the hand now pinned between the sill and sash is familiar. I grab for the window again, this time to pull it back open.

The hand is withdrawn briefly, before the matching part of the pair takes its place.

"Give a guy a hand, here, will you?"

The first hand comes back through, and I grab it by the wrist this time, levering an unhappy Hunter inside and onto my desk. Oops.

"What the fuck, Elle?" he demands, shaking his right hand, which I'm desperately hoping is only bruised.

"I am *so* sorry! Are you OK?"

"Got any ice?"

"If it's frozen. Let me check."

Luckily for Hunter, the water in the mini-fridge has successfully transmuted from liquid to solid. I grab a couple cubes and drop them into a towel, handing the bundle to him where he's now sitting on my bed. I pull the blessed cloth from around the shoulders of my Brighid statue and wrap his hand with it, too.

"Anything broken?"

"I don't think so," he says, moving his hand experimentally. "Hurts like hell, but feels like it'll just be a bruise. I hope. I've got a gig on Friday," he adds with a reproving glance at me.

"Sorry. Really sorry. You woke me up, and I wasn't expecting anyone coming through the window... I thought Julie would come in through the door, like a normal human."

"One who lives here. Officially. At least nominally, since she appears to not be here."

"She's not. She... well, she came back for an hour and introduced herself, and then she looked at my bookshelf and told me she was meeting her parents for dinner... ten hours ago..."

"Not again!"

"That would be my guess."

"Hey — less of a chance she'll report some guy breaking in at two in the morning. Though that might have been preferable to having my hand smashed in a window."

"I said I'm sorry. You woke me up out of a dead sleep. I reacted instinctively."

"Your instincts tell you to smash your best friend's hand in a window?"

"Only when you've pissed me off. Or woken me out of a dead sleep."

"I'll keep that in mind for future," he says, rolling his eyes at me before cracking a smile.

"So — how'd your summer go, Elle?"

"Busy. Lots of people coming and going, looking at new wool sources, research... You still working on songs for the EP?"

"Yeah. It's been slow progress. David and Declan aren't on the same page with trying to finalize a track list. I'm still working sixty hours a week on top of rehearsals and gigs, so I've had no time to write..."

"How's living with Alex going?"

"Great. I got lucky there. He's a great guy. Low-key. Insightful..."

"How so?"

Hunter seems disconcerted at the question.

"Oh, you know... Booking gigs, promotional stuff..." he says, but I suspect that wasn't what he had been thinking of when he said it.

I take the ice-filled towel away from him and examine his hand.

"How's it feeling?"

"It hurts."

"Not broken?

"Nope."

"You're lucky I didn't slam it down hard. I could have ended your career. All because you didn't give me a heads up you were coming over..." I tease. "You must really have needed a place to crash tonight. Megan screaming at Alex about his keyboards taking up too much room again?"

"Ha. Ha ha. Ha," he replies before getting serious. "I *needed* some Ellie-and-Hunter time. I missed you. Haven't seen you since after we got back from the tour."

"I was here when you got back."

"For like three days. I haven't seen you since then. Barely talked to you. Haven't heard your voice in a month."

"Oh, what a hardship..."

"It was," he says, doing a pouty face and making puppy-dog eyes at me.

"Oh, stop it!" I tell him, laughing and giving him a playful smack on the shoulder.

"Hey — I'm already injured. Stop attacking the wounded!"

Despite the protest, he grabs me around my shoulders and pulls me in for a hug before setting his forehead against mine.

"Missed you, Elle. Glad you're back."

"Me, too. I missed you, too."

He drops a kiss on my forehead.

"Roommate not coming back?"

"I suspect not tonight, if ever," I reply wryly.

"Then scoot over. You need to get some rest after all that driving and unpacking, and I have the perfect sleep aid for you."

"Oh?"

"Yeah. Me." He smiles and lies down next to me, pulling my head over to rest on his chest.

I snuggle in.

"You're too exciting to make a good sleep aid," I confess.

"Oh?" he says, seeming a little worried.

"Yeah. Not exactly conducive to sleep when you crawl in my room at two and make me defend myself with a window."

"Against little old me?"

"Have you looked in the mirror lately? You are anything but little."

There's a pause as both of us appear to notice the unintended double entendre and decide to ignore it.

"How tall are you now? Six-two?"

"Almost six-three. Think I've stopped growing, though."

"Finally! I was getting concerned that I'd be stuck looking up at you for the rest of my life with my head so far back that I'll need a chiropractor."

"Ha. Be glad you're tall. A lot of the girls looking up at me are having to look up much higher."

I'm silent. Picturing all those girls he's got looking up at him after every gig. Picturing them looking up even farther when they're down on their knees. Well, it seems hope wasn't quite as gone from my heart as I had thought. Apparently, spending time as the focus of one rock superstar's attention isn't enough to get me to move on completely from this one.

"I'm glad you're home, Elle," he says, kissing my forehead again. "It feels weird when you're not around."

"You're going to be out on tour half the time after that EP is out, Hunter. You'll have to get used to life on the road and on your own."

"I can't imagine getting used to being without you, Elle. Even on tour, you're always right here with me," he says, patting his chest over his heart.

"Same here. Same here," I tell him before we both nod off.

CHAPTER 31

MOVES LIKE JAGGER

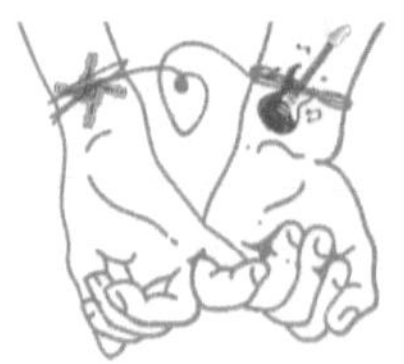

Ellie

I wake up before sunrise with Hunter getting up and heading to the bathroom. I turn back over and close my eyes, hoping to grab another hour or so of sleep.

"Elle? You awake?"

"Yeah," I say, without opening my eyes.

"Hand's still sore. Where's another towel?"

"Closet, on the shelf above my suitcase and the loom."

It's quiet.

"Did you find them? They're right on the front of the shelf."

"Yeah. Got it," he says, closing the closet door and getting some ice out of the mini-fridge.

Suddenly, I realize that my suitcase still has the airline tags on it. If he saw it, he's going to know I left the country... and that I lied to him about it.

I wait for the inevitable question.

He comes back to the bed and lies down with me, the ice once again on the back of his right hand.

"How's it feeling?"

"Hurts," he says. And I find myself hoping he's talking about his hand and not my deception. He doesn't say anything about the suitcase. Maybe I got lucky.

"It's a minor wound. It'll heal," I promise him, wrapping his hand in the bratach Bhríde again. "I signed up to take a reiki healing class, so I can offer that at my shop when I finally get it open, though that won't help you with this, unfortunately. I can ask Herself directly, if you'd like."

"So, she really talks to you? Your goddess?"

"Yeah. The time away seems to have really cemented that. Another reason I want to take the hands-on healing class. It really feels like things have been coming together for me these last few months."

"That's great, Elle. What's next?"

"Classes. Preparing an entry for the holiday art showcase. Chances are I won't get in, but if I do... Maybe a gallery show in the near future?"

"So you're getting ready to break out just like aMUSEd! Perfect timing!"

"When are you going into the studio for the EP?"

"The producer and studio are both booked until May. So, sometime after that. If we can get the songs together."

"Solid gigs until then?"

"Pretty much. Christmas week is insane, through New Year's Eve. Are you coming?"

"I didn't know I was invited."

"Of course you are! They gave each of us an extra ticket. You're my plus-one!"

"You sure you don't want to take one of your many admirers, Mr. Rockstar?"

"No. No one I'd rather ring in the new year with than my best friend."

I smile at that. He may not want to be my boyfriend, but at least I'm still good enough for a girlfriend substitute at a big event.

We're tangled up with each other in sleep when I hear the door open a couple hours later. Hunter's ice-filled towel is now a damp spot between us, and I grab it up and drop behind me so I can sit up.

Julie is standing in the doorway, staring. I'm guessing she wasn't expecting to come home and find a man in my bed, even if we've still got our clothes on.

Her gaze is fixed on my stomach, and I look down to realize that the towel has left a noticeable wet spot on the bottom of my tank top. I look over at Hunter and see a matching one on his T-shirt.

"I know how this looks—"

"No explanation needed," Julie says, clearly not believing, or caring, what I might have to say. Her eyes rove over past my spinning wheel to my bookshelf, and her frown deepens.

"I actually just came back to pack up some of my stuff. My parents decided they missed me too much to let me live on-campus this year... and they need the help at home anyway. I should be out by the end of the day."

"Oh. OK."

And another one bites the dust.

"Let me make sure the coast is clear. Stay right here," I tell Hunter, padding quietly down the hallway toward the foyer. I don't see anyone coming, so I head back down the hallway to get him.

"A witch! Can you believe it? Books out in the open like that! That statue — *not* the Virgin Mary! Devil-worship if I've ever heard of it! Julie said she had some guy in her bed, too, with cum all over both of them. What a slut."

That's coming from one of the other rooms on the hall. And my heart sinks.

Nevermind that Satan is a Judeo-Christian concept, and I'm neither of those things. I don't really even consider myself a witch. I just happen to be a priestess for a goddess...

One day into the school year and I've lost any chance I had of making friends in this dorm. And maybe the entire campus, knowing how the gossip mill runs, how it ran in high school.

I sigh, walking back down the hallway to my room, and open the door quietly before leaning back against it from the inside.

"Elle? What's wrong? Coast not clear? Did somebody report us?"

"Worse. The mean-girl gossip squad is fully engaged. You may want to rethink your New Year's plus-one, unless you're wanting to be known as the guy who spent the night with the devil-worshiping witch-slut. Actually, I guess you already are," I correct myself, "since Julie apparently told them not just about my books and statue, but that you and I were in bed together with 'cum all over' us."

"Wow. That went downhill fast."

"No kidding."

I sigh again.

"Anything I can do to make it better?"

"Nope. Black cat is out of the witchy bag."

"Sorry, Elle. We'll get through this. If you need a place to hide from the torch-bearing mob and their pitchforks, you know where I live," he adds with a smile.

I give him a repressive look.

"Too soon?" he asks with s chuckle.

I roll my eyes.

"I need to get going. Rehearsal."

"I'm not sure there's a lot of point in trying to be sneaky getting you out of here."

"Maybe not. But come with me," he says, grabbing me by my hand and pulling me down the hallway to the foyer, which, unlike my hall, has a steady stream of people walking through. He leads me to the front doors, stopping right off to the side, where he wraps me in his arms, then looks me intensely in the eyes and tucks a strand of my hair behind my ear.

"What are you doing?" I whisper urgently.

"Making them wish they were you."

"Ego much, rockstar?"

"Just the reality now, Elle," he admits.

Speaking more loudly, he says, "We just finished touring with Telltale Signs, and after seeing Mace Mason paying all that attention to you and then being away from you for weeks, I'm not missing a single moment I can get with you, my sweet Elle."

I know my eyes have to be wide with surprise at this turn of events, and my heart is pounding in my chest, for reasons I'd rather pretend didn't exist. Nonetheless, I'm not sure anyone is buying this little performance.

He wraps his arm all the way around around my neck, leaning in close, and instinct tells me to meet the kiss he appears ready to give me, whatever the reason may be.

He dots a kiss on the end of my nose, and I only barely avoid humiliating myself with him yet again.

"They can't see past my arm, Elle. They'll draw their own conclusions."

"Of course."

Our eyes are still connected, and his hand rises to trace down my cheek. I want to think this is something more than just subterfuge, but I know better.

He finally breaks the eye contact, and we both swallow, hard. He picks up my hand as he releases me from his arm, pressing a kiss to the back of my hand.

"Can't let Mace Mason show me up," he says, and his smile is full of humor.

He turns and walks away, only to stop in the doorway, so no one can miss him.

"Friday, Elle. Eight o'clock at the Orpheum. They've already got 'aMUSEd rocks!' on the marquee. They'll have a backstage pass for you at the door. Tell them you're Hunter's *special guest*. Don't be late! It's already sold out!"

He blows me a kiss and then walks away. For real this time.

Everyone in the lobby and gathered outside is standing there with their mouths agape. Including me. And I know that was all a setup.

Wow. The man is a rockstar. For real.

I spend the rest of the afternoon spinning that Irish wool. I've got a dozen skeins in various shades of green, blue, white and ivory, plus a little in heather purple and bright yellow.

I stand up and stretch, and I decide to head over to the cafeteria for some food. I slip on a sundress, lock the door behind me and head out for the three-block walk.

"Hunter Graves! Right here! Can you believe it?"

"Actually, I don't. He was here with her? The witch? And he kissed her? Sounds to me like she's put a spell on him."

My face turns red as I enter the lobby, where the voices are coming from. But I hold my head high and move briskly outside and over to the cafeteria.

I get in line at the salad bar, which *isn't* moving briskly. A group of girls a few people ahead of me is using the loose definition of a line, five of them standing in a semi-circle, waiting for the lettuce to get free.

"Guitar player..."

"aMUSEd..."

"Sex in her room!"

What I'm able to hear is disjointed, but I am getting the sense, somehow, that tales of Hunter's little performance have already spread to the general populace of the campus.

"I know! He's *so* hot! Lucky girl!"

Wait. No insult? No implication that I have used "black magic" to ensorcel the hot rockstar?

"They were great at the show in D.C. in May. Nearly as good as Telltale Signs."

That's the guy in line behind them, and his voice isn't pitched low, so I hear every word.

I *am* a lucky girl. I had two highly desirable men who were both focused on me that night, if for different reasons.

And then I shake myself free of the thought, because I can't let my life be about Hunter anymore, and definitely not about Aedan Mason.

"I can't believe Hunter Graves was right here a couple hours ago!" one of the other girls says, with no effort to keep her voice down.

"What?"

"Did you hear that? aMUSEd's guitar player was right here."

And now it seems like half the people in the cafeteria are talking about Hunter. After having been gone all summer, I'm just now realizing how much the band's popularity has soared since the tour. And they don't even have an album yet.

"I had to pay three times the face value to get tickets for Friday. But it's *so* going to be worth it. Declan's voice! Crazy. Reminds me of Chris Cornell."

"No. More Scott Weiland, mixed with a little Freddie Mercury and a dash of Robert Plant."

"The keyboard player is hot."

"You *would* say that..." There's a chuckle. "But the guy's one of the best I've ever heard. So few bands with a keyboard player these days. He kicks ass!"

"I heard his girlfriend goes here," I hear someone say. "The guitar player's."

"Oh?

"Yeah — someone said they'd seen him at her dorm earlier, making out with her in the lobby. All the girls were drooling over him. Totally jealous. Bitchy comments and all."

Someone clears their throat behind me, and I realize the line has moved on without me. I start putting together my salad, my mind awash with so many varied emotions that I have to keep reminding myself what I'm supposed to be doing.

I decide to take my food back to the dorm, see if I can digest this alternative reality I seem to have fallen into, along with my salad.

Everyone is staring as I approach. There's some whispering, too. And suddenly I'm feeling like I'm under a microscope. I kind of expect to find a cross burning in front of my door. But, nope. I let myself in and am semi-surprised to find half the room empty, without a single one of Julie's possessions remaining. I check the closet, just to be sure.

Well, the enthusiasm I was hearing in the cafeteria doesn't seem to have made its way back here. But, honestly, I don't care. I've never been popular, and I've never felt like I needed it. I'd rather I hadn't been outed to who knows how many people, most of whom will have heard false rumors. But I'm used to people talking about me in unflattering ways. No big deal.

There's a knock at my door. I've been expecting all day that one of the resident assistants would show up to write me up or something for having Hunter in here after-hours. I've never heard of anyone actually getting in trouble for that, but if anyone could, it would be me.

I steel myself for an uncomfortable conversation and open the door.

Yup. Lisa, the RA.

"Hi, Ellie — glad to see you back."

She is?

"Thanks. What can I do for you?"

"Just wanted to welcome you back and see how things were going before classes start."

"Oh! Well, it's going fine. I just got back in yesterday."

"I heard you had a visitor..."

Here it comes...

"A friend came by to see me last night. We fell asleep while he was here," I explain. "Sorry about that."

"Oh, no — not a problem. It happens. As long as it's not every night..."

So she's letting me off with a warning. I see. Well, that's a relief.

"I'll try to make sure it isn't."

She lowers her voice and leans in.

"I wouldn't really worry about it if I were you," she says. "I'm the one who files any reports, and I won't rat you out." She gives me a wink. "I'm a big fan of the band. I've been trying to get tickets for Friday, but they've been sold out for weeks."

Ah. I see now...

"I could ask Hunter if he has any more he can set aside..."

"That would be awesome! Just let me know."

She steps in a little closer.

"Hunter, eh? Lucky girl. I'm partial to Rhys myself. Love a redhead!" she adds conspiratorially. "But Hunter is definitely hot."

"We're just friends."

"I get it," she replies with a wink. "Just friends. Who fall asleep together."

"Well, yeah..."

And she clearly doesn't believe me. Never thought I'd be the one trying to get people to believe we're not together. The irony here being...

"Well, I just wanted to check in, like I said. And if you can manage to get me a ticket or two, I'd love that!"

"I'll see what I can do. I'll try to get an answer tomorrow."

"Great! Thanks so much! Tell Hunter I said hi."

And she's off down the hall, leaving me with my door, and my mouth, hanging open.

Hunter — what have you done?

CHAPTER 32

I'LL BE WAITING

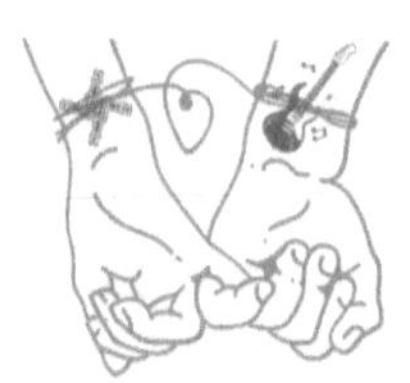

Ellie
Three months later

Ever since I got back to school, I've devoted myself to my fiber-arts class and finishing the Irish weaving.

I'm going to my other classes. I'm getting the assignments done. I'm still working part-time at Kara's shop, and I've made good on my statement to Dad that I was working with Kara to learn how to run a business.

But all my remaining time is spent on spinning and weaving, with brief breaks for meditation and devotions. And, sometimes, even sleep.

The weaving I envisioned when I first decided to do this has gone from concept to nearly complete and ready to submit for the showcase. That will leave me almost two weeks to complete the two other woven pieces I have started.

My work isn't representational. It's more abstract, suggestive of a place or a feeling or a person. Texture conveys a sense of landscape, with carefully selected shades — many of them custom-dyed — bringing it a depth and immersiveness for the viewer.

At least I hope that's what they do. If I'm successful at what I'm trying to do as an artist, people should see these works made from wool and other fibers, and feel like they're being drawn into them, like a momentary trip to a place far away or a time of distant memory.

I hope. Because my success with these three weavings could make all the difference in making everything I planned come true.

Three weeks later

Mrs. Pomeroy is one of the judges selecting works for the showcase, so I haven't let her see, or even talked about, what I've been working on. I didn't even mention my trip, though she knows some of my class projects have included Irish wool.

It's now Reveal Day, when the artists are allowed into the finished exhibit to see what works were chosen. Gathered around me are painters, potters, sculptors, glassworkers, photographers, printmakers... artists in every conceivable medium. A few freshmen, a number of sophomores and a bevy of juniors and seniors. I'm near the back of the crowd, as usual, when the doors open and we slowly make our way inside.

The exhibit is amazing. The lighting, how they've hung the pieces along walls and panels in between, it all shows off the work in an amazing way. The sculptures and pottery have been placed atop carved plinths — themselves works of art — or set up inside lighted cases, some with turntables inside that ensure every part of the work can be seen.

The exhibit also has a flow, connecting works in differing media by theme, feel, texture or color palette. The result is an artistic wonderland, drawing the viewer along on a journey to a magical place, with so much to discover along the way.

I've seen one fiber-art piece amongst the dozens on display. One. It looks like Mrs. Pomeroy had especially high standards this year, and that was before the judging group looked at the submissions. This piece is amazing. Texture and color placement are gorgeous. It's more representational than my own, less suggestive and more descriptive. But the artist is clearly talented. If there was going to be only one piece selected,

I'm glad it was one that's this exquisite. Melanie Cross. A senior. She'll be getting a solo show soon if all her work is like this.

Well, I've got one more year to try. To get better and try again. Fail up.

"Do you like Melanie's piece?" Mrs. Pomeroy asks from beside me.

"It's extraordinary. It was a wonderful selection for the showcase, if there had to be just one."

"You should still see the rest of the exhibit," she says. "I think the culmination of the works, with the flow to the end, really adds to the experience."

"It's a lovely exhibit, Mrs. Pomeroy. You all should be very proud."

"Thank you. Ellie. If you would, do me a favor and go ahead on through, and let me know how you feel about the exhibit as a whole. I think the level of talent this year is the best in a long time."

I continue working my way through the exhibit. I pick out favorites, congratulate a few artists standing by their works. There is a crowd waiting to get into the final room. I'm tempted to leave and come see it another time. But I promised Mrs. Pomeroy I'd give her my impressions of the exhibit, so I wait, giving a closeup look to the works by the doorway.

Soon, the crowd has lightened enough that I can get inside. There are three lighted cases in the middle of the room, with more works on the wall. People are clustered around them, and I have to move around a few people to see the featured work in the cases.

They're mine.

All of them.

All three.

Mine.

My primary piece is in the center, lighted in a way that picks up the texture and sheen of the yarn, the glow of pearl. Highlighted the way it is, the weaving seems like a slice of Ireland come to life. The legendary greens, the deep blue of the sea and the blue-black of the deep well, the lighter blues of the sky edged with cloudy grey that suggests rain. White stone fences, dark cliffs, thatched roofs, sandy shores, hints of golden gorse and purple heather, dots of creamy white like sheep on a hillside, and a touch of fire. Because there is always the fire... of the hearth, of creativity, of the forge, of the healing cauldron.

I've lost myself in my own weaving. In an instant I'm not just back in Ireland, I'm standing outside that cottage on the hill above the sea, Hunter's arms wrapped around me, sheep in the distance and turf smoke from the hearth fire rising into the evening sky...

"It's extraordinary, Ellie. Easily one of the best pieces I've ever seen from a student, and among the best I've ever seen, period," Mrs. Pomeroy says from behind me, releasing me back to the present place and time.

"Surely not! I'm only barely in my third year with you. I've got so much more to learn."

"The fact that your work is the culmination of the entire exhibit should tell you otherwise. The fact that, out of four fiber pieces in the entire exhibit, three of them are yours, should also tell you otherwise. It's unheard-of."

"Are you sure you didn't favor my work — unconsciously, perhaps?"

"Ellie — I had a colleague from another university review my selections. He was fully in favor of the four I picked and agreed that these three were truly extraordinary. All three, though both of us were particularly struck by the central piece. You have captured lightning in a bottle. It conveys a sense of place, and a timelessness, too, that is just astonishing, riveting."

"Wow. I don't even know what to say."

"Well, practice something, dear, because you're going to need something to say to all the admirers of your work. Look around!"

I look around me and discover people standing in clusters around the three cases, deep in discussion, some looking stunned and others enraptured, as if they, too have been carried away on a carpet of Irish wool, a soul-deep connection and a young girl's vision of a distant past.

The next night

"Oh, Hunter — you should have seen it! So many people waiting to get a closer look at the pieces. Seeming so swept away by them... I still can't believe it!"

"That's great, Elle! I'm so proud of you! You have been spending so much time on them. I know how big a deal this was."

Hunter gives me a big hug of congratulations, and I'm not sure I can remember a time when I was happier. Breakthrough success at my art, using it to explore my spiritual life and getting to share that success with Hunter.

We're sitting in the dressing room while waiting for the start of aMUSEd's third gig this week. I didn't even manage to get hold of him yesterday to tell him what happened, so he's just now hearing my news.

"So, what's next?"

"The exhibit opens to the public next week, with a big opening event. They'll select some pieces for awards, with fellowship money attached. Some of the works will be sold that night, but they'll all be on display for a month."

"Are you going to sell your pieces?"

"I don't know. They're very important to me, very personal. But I also need to be saving up for my shop. I've only got a year of college left, and then I'll need to have enough savings, or I'll have to go find somewhere where I can live and work and still manage to save up more to open the shop."

"You'll make it work, Elle — I know you will. You've believed in me all these years, and look where we are now!"

"Backstage at a really big bar, playing to a sold-out crowd."

"It's not a bar. It's a 'live music venue.'"

"That serves alcohol... from a bar..."

"OK. It's a really big bar. With a ticketed headlining performer. Which is us."

"Oh, Hunter! I'm so happy. You all have come so far, and the sky's the limit."

"For you, too, Elle."

"You're coming to the opening, aren't you? It's Friday at five."

"We've got a gig that night, as we do pretty much every night this coming week."

"Oh. Well, that's OK. You can come see it with me another day," I say, unable to keep a note of disappointment out of my voice.

"Elle — the gig isn't until nine-thirty. As long as I can be there by seven-thirty, it'll be fine. I wouldn't miss it! Can't wait to see my Ellie getting her own slice of the spotlight for a change. It's long overdue!"

He squeezes me with another hug, and I'm about as content as I can ever remember feeling.

Hunter
A week later

I cannot fucking believe it.

I had planned to get to the venue early, with Rhys, to make sure all our gear was loaded in so I'd have time to shower and change into a suit for Ellie's big night.

And then the producer called a mandatory band meeting to check where we were with the songs for the EP. At three. If we weren't all there, they were pushing back our studio time at least another month — more if they had any other bands ready to go first.

So I could not miss this meeting.

After almost two hours of wrangling over which songs were done, which needed more work, what the weak spots were in our sound, what the timetable was for getting into the studio and getting the recording done, I was finally set free.

"Don't worry, man — I'll take care of load-in for you," Rhys offered. "Go get changed and I'll drop you off. I've got to go get my kit anyway. Can't leave that girl of yours waiting on her big night!"

"She's not my girl, Rhys."

"Whatever, dude. She's important to you and she's a girl. So — 'your girl.' Own it. You already own her ass, whether you want it or not."

"Rhys!"

"Too much? I know some of the girls from the college were asking about your girlfriend. You really kiss her in front of a dorm full of girls?"

"No."

"No? Where'd they get that idea, then?"

"Elle's roommate told everybody Elle was a witch and that we had cum all over us."

"Did you?"

"No! She slammed the window on my hand..."

"That does not sound like a good girlfriend, Hunt, man."

"No — I scared her coming in the window..."

"You came in her dorm room through the window... Do you have something against doors?"

"No, Rhys. That's how I usually get in her room after hours."

"Why are you going into her room after hours if she's not your girlfriend?"

"She's just not! The point is her roommate saw us with melted ice spots on our stomachs..."

"Dude — that's kinky... Good work!"

"No, Rhys! Listen! She smashed my hand..."

"The roommate?"

"No, Elle."

"When you were coming in the window."

"Yeah. Anyway — I had ice on my hand, and we fell asleep and the ice melted between us..."

"Sounds like a hot night, melting ice between your bodies... You really sure she's not your girlfriend?"

"Rhys! Geez. Just let me finish... Anyway — the roommate walked in and thought it was something other than melted ice between us..."

"Now it sounds like a kinky networking meeting... 'melting the ice...'"

"Rhys! Anyway... the roommate —"

"Wait — is she a witch?"

"The roommate?"

"No, Elle."

"No. Well, sort of, but not really."

"If she's a witch, why didn't she just zap your ass out the window, or in it, if that's what she wanted?"

"It doesn't work that way."

"This is really interesting. Now I see why Mace wanted to spend so much time talking to her. If that's what they were really doing in his room that night... for hours... alone... together...

"'Oh, Aedan! Yes! Yes! Yes! Fuck me harder!'"

People are staring at us now.

"That did not happen!"

"How do you know? Were you listening at the door, since Declan told you you couldn't break it down that time?"

I'm starting to feel like aMUSEd having a drummer is a lot less important now than it was ten minutes ago.

Ten minutes! Fuck!

"I've got to go, Rhys! Now!"

"Yeah, yeah — keep your pants on. Unless they're covered in cum. And... even then — keep them on. I've got a reputation as a girl-magnet to maintain!"

"Let's go, Rhys!"

"You sure you don't want to explain to me why the college girls all think Elle is your girlfriend?"

"I don't have time for this! I'll change in the car, on the way! Drive!"

I jump in the back seat and grab my suit while Rhys gets behind the wheel. I've already got my shirt off before he's got the car in gear.

"Tell me while I drive."

"Fine! The roommate told everyone Elle is a witch and that she and I were having sex..."

"Which you're not, right? Otherwise, it's going to make things very awkward the next time we see Mace..."

"No! I am not having sex with Ellie! She is not my girlfriend! And she's not actually a witch. Mostly. And she's not fucking Aedan fucking Mason!"

"Were you listening at the door?"

"No!"

"Then how do you know?"

"I just know, OK?"

"You sure about that?"

"Yes! I am sure!"

"So she's still a virgin, then?"

"Yes. Maybe. I don't know."

"You going to verify that? Because inquiring minds want to know!"

"None of your business, Rhys!"

And none of mine, either, as she made very clear that night. On which she did not fuck Aedan fucking Mason!

"'That's a fine, lush ass you have there, Ellie! Can I stick my giant rockstar cock in it?'" Rhys says, pitching his voice into Barry White territory.

"'Oh! Please! You legendary cockstar you! Devirginize all of my holes! Please, Aedan!'" he continues, sounding like Mrs. Doubtfire now.

"Stop fucking around, Rhys! She did not sleep with Aedan fucking Mason! Pay attention to the road, not your pervy imagination where Elle is concerned!"

"Hey — I'm not the one who stopped changing to talk about it when they claimed to be in a hurry!"

"I *am* in a hurry, Rhys. But you keep asking me questions about Elle! Let me get changed back here!"

"Nope."

"Nope? What do you mean 'Nope'?"

"I mean I'm going to pull over and wait until you've answered my original question."

"No! Come on, Rhys! I'm already way late!"

"Answer the question."

"What question?"

"You really should try to pay attention, Hunt. Didn't anyone ever tell you it's rude not to pay attention when someone is talking to you?"

I'm too busy buttoning my dress shirt to pay attention to this insane conversation right now.

"What question do you want me to answer?"

"Not the one about paying attention. We'll discuss that later. No — I want to know if you kissed Ellie, and if you didn't, why do all the girls at the college think she's your girlfriend?"

I yank my belt free and start stripping off my jeans. This whole ride has turned into torture.

"They were gossiping about her, and it was kind of my fault, because I slept over..."

"Even though she's not your girlfriend."

"Yes! She's *not* my girlfriend! Keep up, Rhys! Geez! ...Anyway — I wanted to distract the gossip girls from spreading the rumor that Elle is a witch."

"Because she's not."

"Yeah. Mostly."

"Yeah — we're going to discuss that later, too. I'm not sure being a witch isn't like being pregnant..."

"What?"

"You know — you can't be 'a little pregnant.' I kind of feel like being a witch is a binary status. You either are or you're not."

"Well, it isn't binary for Ellie."

"So, you're saying she's non-binary..."

"Rhys!"

"Yeah. Later."

"Anyway — I wanted to replace the bad gossip with some that might actually be positive for her, so I took her out in the dorm lobby and made a big display of hugging on her and telling her how I'd missed her while she was gone and how I wasn't going to let Mace fucking Mason outdo me for her affections..."

"See — you *do* think she fucked him!"

"No, I don't! She didn't!"

"And yet you're trying to out-boyfriend him!"

"She's not my girlfriend!"

"Of course she's not! She's fucking Mace fucking Mason! That'd make her Mace fucking Mason's girlfriend!"

And I've got nothing for that. Because if I'm wrong, and she gave Mace her virginity, I'm going to have to be restrained from breaking more than a fucking door the next time I see his calmly leering "Oh, you're so interesting, Ellie! Let me borrow you from dumbass Hunter and show you how a real man treats a lady" face!

"Dude! We're here!" Rhys prompts me from up front.

I don't stop to pull on my dress pants before I throw open the door, and I'm standing next to the car, jumping up and down in my underwear getting them on, and Rhys hands me my belt, my tie and my jacket, and says, "Good luck, man. I think you're going to need it!"

CHAPTER 33

ALL STAR

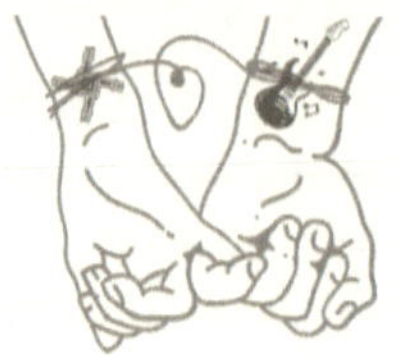

Ellie

I t's almost six, and there's no sign of Hunter. The reception is half over, and they've started presenting the awards.

There are four honorable mentions, with $250 grants each. None of them are for me. The same with third place. And second place. With three entries in the show, none of my pieces have won an award. I'm thinking Mrs. Pomeroy overestimated her lack of bias and the judges have made their disagreement known with their ribbons.

"And, now for the winner of the grand prize award for best entry in this year's Holiday Showcase..."

The dean of the entire art department is presenting the awards, and I already know he doesn't like me. He argued against Mrs. Pomeroy offering me advanced class content in the lower-level classes. But here I am, and he's going to have to eat crow — if I manage to snag this final, penultimate award.

"This was an unusual circumstance this year," he says. "We've never before had this happen. And we discussed extensively how to handle it..."

Oh, no. They decided not to give it to me because I wasn't in a high-enough level class. My determination to get the advanced level instruction has come back to bite me.

"And we were left with no other option than to..."

Disqualify one entrant because she just didn't meet the criteria...

"...double the usual grant amount, in light of the fact that we had a unanimous decision from all of our judges."

My jaw drops. Double? But there's no way it's me. I bucked the system, and they're not going to reward me for it.

"So, with the grand prize and a four-thousand-dollar grant...

Not me. Won't be me. Get used to it. Don't react. No frowning.

"Ellen Langdon, with her woven piece, titled 'Soul of Ireland.'"

What? Not possible.

Mrs. Pomeroy pushes me forward, and I'm whisked away, accepting a blue ribbon, a plaque and... what appears to be a check for four thousand dollars. Made out to me.

People are applauding, and all I can do is smile and nod and say thank you. Fortunately, it appears I'm not required to make a speech of any sort.

Dean Gregory isn't done, though.

"A number of the works in the show have already been sold at their asking price, and they're now marked on their display cards with a blue dot. The ones that are not for sale have a red dot. And ones where multiple offers have been made — they're now marked with a green dot. We'll be auctioning them off starting in ten minutes."

I'm swamped by people congratulating me, and it takes everything I have to act like a normal human and not the normal awkward Ellie.

I take a moment to go look at my work and am astonished to discover that all three pieces have green dots on them.

That's even more disturbing since I'd decided to keep one of them and not sell it.

"Mrs. Pomeroy — I had decided not to sell this one. Was there a misunderstanding?"

"Oh, my! I'll go get this sorted out right now, dear. Not to worry. You did want to sell the other two, correct?"

"'Want' isn't the right word. They all have sentimental value. But I have plans for the future and I need to fund those. So, yes, I'm selling the other two."

"I'll take care of it. Be right back with a red dot for you."

I look at the other two, smaller, weavings, and I lament having to sell any of them. But I suspected the "Soul of Ireland" would be in demand, and I can't afford to hold onto it.

"I'd love to hang that in my gallery, Miss Langdon," a well-dressed woman tells me. "Sheila Case — Case Galleries." She hands me a card, which I tuck away with that check I'm making sure not to lose.

"Thank you, Ms. Case. I'm afraid I can't loan it to you. It's going to be sold."

"Yes, dear — I'm one of the interested parties. It would be a focal piece for an upcoming exhibit. But I'd also very much like to talk to you about a solo show, whether or not I win the auction."

"That's tremendous flattering, Ms. Case."

"Sheila, please."

"Sheila. I'm not sure how many pieces I could complete in the near future. I've got another semester of classes to complete before the summer."

"Well, as much as I love them, I've got our shows booked almost a year in advance now. So you'd have some time to create additional work."

"That sounds wonderful."

"I'll be in touch after the new year," she says. "Or feel free to call me at your leisure."

"Thank you."

Mrs. Pomeroy arrives with a red dot and opens the case to apply it to the display card. I breathe a sigh of relief.

"We've got you covered, dear. But you should head back in to see the other auctions before we move back in here for yours."

I follow her suggestion, and the auctions are pretty interesting. An oil painting that had been priced at two hundred dollars sells for six. A sculpture priced at five hundred goes for nearly three thousand. A watercolor that had been set to sell for four hundred brings in four thousand. This is fine-art territory, and while I'd never thought of my weavings as being in the same league with art at these prices, I'm glad to see so many of the artists doing so well.

And, finally, it's time to auction my two works.

"Ladies and gentlemen, these are our final two auctions of the night. They've received the most offers among the works in the exhibit that were for sale. And just to clarify — the piece titled 'Soul of the Hunter' was incorrectly listed as for sale. It is not."

There's a swell of awwws.

I'm sorry they got their hopes up, but I can't sell this one. I'm not sure how I'd explain it to him if he was here, but the eponymous piece is too precious to me, as is Hunter himself.

This one is made up of all of the colors that remind me of Hunter: the deep green of his eyes, the greens of the Irish hillside, the dark blue of the sky at dusk, the tawny tones of a faithful friend who rarely leaves his master's side (except when it rains), the red-gold hues of a hearth fire and the light it casts over bare skin.... There's a thread of gold that runs through it, like his hair and his bright, shining soul...

And that's why I can't sell it. It's Hunter made tangible but abstracted. It's only when you look deeper that you start to realize just how captivating it is. And I want to spend the rest of my life looking at that, especially when I know our time together will largely have to end when he goes out on tour. This weaving will be the touchstone I keep with me when I cannot keep the man himself.

The auction of "Soul of Ireland" is next. I was surprised that it wasn't the more in-demand of the two pieces I'd agreed to sell. Sheila Case had already told me she wanted it. And it had been the grand-prize winner. But art is subjective and what one person finds valuable, another will find priceless.

Sheila Case and four other bidders battle it out for the piece. One of the bidders is apparently bidding remotely, by phone, with one of the exhibit assistants relaying the bids.

The weaving I'd priced at three hundred dollars quickly escalates in price to two thousand, then four, then six. And I think I'm going to faint. There's a hand on my back for a moment, steadying me, but when I turn to see who it is, whoever it was is no longer there.

It's down to two bidders now, Sheila Case and the phone bidder. The bidding slows at ten thousand, and Sheila tops out at twelve thousand, and I think I'm going to be sick. How could someone possibly want this one piece made by a college sophomore so badly as to pay that much?

"Twelve thousand, five hundred. Going once... twice... sold — to our bidder on the phone!"

There are more hands on my back now, patting me in congratulations. I don't like people touching me as a rule, and this is no exception. But at this moment, all I can think is that I wish Hunter was here to see this and give me his own hugs of congratulations. I don't know what happened to him, but I'm disappointed.

Then it's on to "Soul of the Deep Sea," which I'd priced at just two hundred dollars.

"This is our most bid-upon work in the show," the dean notes.

The modest starting bid is quickly eclipsed, and the bidding is at such a furious pace that I'm almost glad to lose myself in this final work.

It's deep blue upon blue, set amidst deep reddish browns traced with russet and gold, with touches of denim blue and pure white, the pale grey of a sea mist, a warm pale tan, the iridescent translucence of a shell... I'm sucked in to that deep blue the same as before — placid and bottomless, safe and warm, but with an edge of the unknown. And it makes me smile.

"Final call! Last bid is at fifteen thousand, five hundred dollars. Going once... twice..."

"Twenty thousand, from the bidder on the phone."

If there had been murmuring in the room until now, it has been traded in for gasps.

"It's an auction record, Ellie. No one has ever sold a piece in this show for that much. Ever."

"Who is this person on the phone?"

"Anonymous. Vetted by an auction house, but we won't be told who it is. Your pieces are going to someone who is clearly a very wealthy collector. You should be proud. I can almost guarantee you'll have an offer for a solo show before you leave here tonight."

"Once again — final bid, at twenty thousand dollars. Going once... twice..." Sheila Case shakes her head in the negative to show she's thrown in the towel.

"Sold! To the bidder on the phone, for twenty thousand dollars. That's an auction record, ladies and gentlemen. Miss Langdon's two pieces have eclipsed the prior record several times over. Congratulations, Ellen!"

More people patting me on the back, touching my arms, getting too close. Again, someone places a steadying hand on my back, steering me to a quiet spot in the hallway outside. I turn around to thank them, and again, no one is there. I sit down on a bench in the hallway, trying to catch my bearings.

This whole event bas been a surprise. Not the least reason that I just sold two works for a total of thirty-three thousand dollars.

Even minus the commission, which is split between the auction house and the art grants funds, it could be enough to open my shop. And if it's not, it should almost certainly be by the time I graduate.

At this point I'm just exhausted. The adrenaline of the show and the auction has sapped any remaining energy I had. I go back inside to find Mrs. Pomeroy and make my excuses for leaving early. She pats me on the arm and sends me home, just a few blocks from the art hall to the dorm. I can pick up the final checks for the auctioned items on Monday, she says.

My brain refuses to bend around the money I've just made. But I stop briefly at the display of my weavings — two of them no longer mine, sold to an owner who, it appears, will appreciate them. I take one last look at them both to bid them farewell, and a quick glance at the third, which I will bring home with me in a month. And it's that one that makes me feel warm inside. I can't wait to have it back with me.

I make it back to my room and strip out of my clothes, too tired to put on anything else, and I climb into bed, falling instantly asleep.

Hunter

I cannot believe it.

Twenty thousand dollars for a single piece.

I knew my Ellie was good. I didn't know she was *that* good. Not that I didn't think she was brilliant. But she'd made more in a night, though after months of hard work, than I'd made from a month-long tour with one of the most in-demand bands in the world.

Forget Hunter the rockstar. It's now Ellie the rockstar.

She seemed to be astonished by her accomplishment, and at one point looked like she might be getting dizzy. I started for her, but someone else got there first, steadying her before heading off in another direction. All I saw was broad shoulders in a nice suit, tailored and probably very expensive, with reddish-brown hair curling over the collar. Whoever it was was gone before I could see their face.

I'm not sure I like two apparently wealthy men — because the voice I overheard on the auction assistant's phone was decidedly male — fussing over Ellie. But I don't have time to chase the elusive suit, because I'm already running late for soundcheck.

David had offered to pick me up, since his bass rig takes a lot less time to set up than Rhys' kit or Alex's "cockpit" surrounded by his keyboards. Within five minutes of the end of the auction, I'm waiting for him outside, and we get back to the Orpheum with an hour before our first set.

Soundcheck is done except for me. David had set up my rig and done a cursory linecheck before he left to get me, so all I have to do is adjust levels, let the engineer slip my vocals and guitar into his mix, and get my in-ear monitor levels adjusted so I can hear myself and the rest of the band.

I think about texting Ellie and congratulating her, apologizing for not having gotten there in time to spend the evening by her side. But that seems like it would be better to do in person. And I have a show to do now. It will have to wait.

CHAPTER 34

AULD LANG SYNE

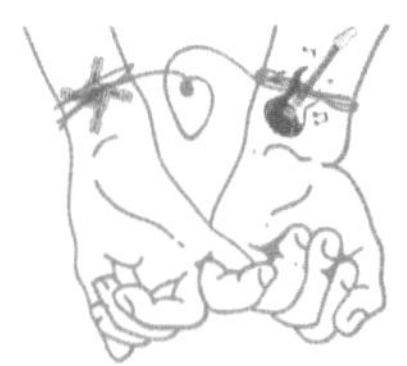

Hunter

I cannot get hold of Ellie.

Is she mad because I was late last night? Does she think I didn't go to the opening at all, since I didn't get a chance to talk to her? Does she think I forgot her?

I've left like twenty voicemails for her, asking — begging — for her to call me back.

No calls, no texts, no email — nothing.

The first thing I did when I got out of the gig last night was go over to her dorm room. I tried to let myself in through the window, like I usually do, and it wouldn't budge, apparently locked. I tossed a couple pebbles at her window. Nothing.

Well — not exactly nothing. A nice girl named Lisa opened up the window next to Elle's and did a double-take when she saw me standing there.

"Hunter Graves?"

Uh-oh. Maybe my little display a few months ago wasn't such a good idea.

"Sorry — didn't mean to wake anyone!"

"Except Ellie, presumably..."

"Yeah. That."

"I don't think she's here, actually."

Where the hell else would Ellie be this late at night? Did she even get home safely?

"Is there any way you could check? I think we've had a miscommunication, but I need to make sure that she at least got home safely after her art show tonight."

"I'm Lisa, the RA…"

Oops.

"I'm really sorry. Please don't write her up. She had no idea I'd be here or be waking people up."

"On one condition."

"Name it."

"Give Rhys my phone number."

Oh… now I get it.

"You're a fan."

"Ellie had you get me tickets for that show a couple months ago."

"Oh! Yeah. How'd you like the show?"

Someone opens another window and shushes us both. Loudly.

"Come inside. We can take care of all of this without waking people up," she urges, smiling at me.

"I'm sorry… but I'm not… not with Ellie's RA…"

She laughs.

"Ego much?"

Not *anymore*, as of right this second. Wow.

"Come meet me in the lobby."

I head back to the scene of my acting debut, which seemed to have received rave reviews.

Lisa comes down the hall to get me.

"The show was great, by the way. You all are awesome!"

"Especially Rhys?"

"Well, of course!" she confirms with a laugh.

"Here — my number," she says, stuffing a piece of paper in my hand. The girl's cute. Rhys won't mind.

"I'll give it to him tomorrow. Well, today."

"Yeah — it's late. I thought I heard Ellie go back out a while ago. But I can check."

"That would be great."

She walks back down the hall, and I follow, since she didn't tell me not to. I need to see for myself whether Elle is here.

Lisa knocks lightly on Ellie's door. When there's no answer, she fishes a set of keys out of the pocket of her robe. She opens the door and peeks inside.

"I don't..."

I don't wait for her assessment. I walk right around her. She snorts in amusement.

"She's not here," she confirms.

Her clothes she was wearing at the showcase opening are in a puddle on the floor next to her bed. And her cell phone is on her desk, still charging.

Well, now I know why she didn't answer.

The question is where she's gone.

"Hi, Hunter! Sorry I missed your calls. I left my cell phone on my desk and didn't even realize it until this morning."

She can say "this morning," because it's no longer the same day as it was when Lisa the RA (who Rhys was happy to call, by the way) let me into her room. It's been more than 24 hours.

"Where have you been?"

There's a pause. I don't like it.

"I had some things I needed to do. I just got caught up in things, and I didn't get done with things until this morning."

Things? What things? Is Ellie prevaricating? With me?

"I see..."

Silence.

"Anyway — I just wanted to apologize for the other night, for being late."

"You were late?"

"Yeah. The label called a meeting and it ran long, and I had to change in the car while Rhys kept obsessing about Mace Mason."

"Rhys has a thing for Aedan?"

"Not directly. And why are you calling him Aedan?"

"He told me to."

"When was this?"

"That night after the gig, when we were talking."

And was talking all you were doing? Hmmm?

"So you had to change in the car? With Rhys driving?"

"Yeah. I missed a big chunk of things." *But I'm guessing they weren't the same "things" you have been doing. Fucking hell, Rhys! Get out of my mind!* "I made it in time for the awards and auction, though. I just didn't get a chance to talk to you before I had to go back for soundcheck."

"Oh, that's OK. Like I said, we can go see the exhibit another time."

Who are you and what have you done with my Elle?

"Well, congratulations on the success. My jaw about dropped with that auction! Somebody really wanted those weavings a lot, didn't they?"

"It was amazing. I should have most of the money I need for my shop when things are done."

"Any idea who bought them? That guy on the phone?"

"Mrs. Pomeroy said it was an anonymous bidder. They were vetted but no one knows who it was."

"I thought I saw some guy hanging around you a couple times. Was that him, maybe? Waiting to talk to you or something?"

"Why would he have been making bids on the phone if he was there in person? Or how, even?"

"Yeah. That doesn't make any sense. So... I'm sorry I was late and then had to leave so soon."

"No biggie. You had band stuff. Thanks for making the effort, though. We can go see the show next week or something."

"You're not going home for break?"

"Dad's being a pain. If I hadn't already been staying for the showcase, I'd have stayed anyway. He's so judgmental these days."

"Giving you hell about me again?"

She's quiet.

"He is, isn't he?"

"A little. I tried to tell him I was here for the showcase and work, but he keeps implying I'm staying to go to your gigs."

"Speaking of which — are you still coming to New Year's Eve?"

"If you're sure you want me to come with you. You're free to take someone else if you want."

"You don't want to go with me?"

"No! I definitely want to go. I just don't want you to feel obligated."

"I don't. I asked you to go with me. So, come with me!"

"OK. It's not like I have other plans or anything," she adds with a laugh. "Are you all just doing regular stage clothes that night?"

"Yeah. With a little extra glitz."

"Sequined T-shirts?"

"And lamé pants. Everyone gets a different color. Signature style."

She laughs.

"Then I'll have to dig something shiny out of my closet so I don't look like your frumpy shadow."

"Elle — you've never been frumpy a day in your life."

"I do have a great retro-style dress. Kinda rockabilly. It hides all my problem areas and emphasizes the better ones."

"You'll look great in anything, Elle."

"Thanks. Am I just meeting you there, with soundcheck and everything?"

"Probably the best way to go."

"OK. I'll see you there."

"Hey, Elle... Congrats again. You deserve it."

"Thanks, Hunter. That means a lot."

New Year's Eve

They've got a nice setup backstage tonight, kind of like we had when we were on tour, only that was for Telltale Signs and this is for us. It's like we went out for a nice New Year's Eve dinner, only it's self-serve, casual dress and not nearly as many people. We're all set up, soundcheck done, with another hour before we go on.

And no sign of Elle.

After this week's little unexplained disappearing act, I'm not sure what to think. I mean, she could be getting back at me for arriving so late to her show, but (a) she's not the vengeful type, and (b) she told me it was fine and said we could go next week. And I believed her, even if she has shown a tendency in the past to feel slighted when no slight was meant.

All the guys have at least one girl with them. In fact, Rhys has brought along Lisa the RA, so apparently he didn't mind getting her number at all. Declan is doing his Declan thing, with a redhead and a blonde this time. Megan is attached to Alex's hip — I have to look closely to make sure that's not literal. David has a cute little brunette he's chatting up. No idea if she's actually his date or if he found her here, which would be his norm. And I'm here… alone.

I leave the room to go check on the crowd, peeking out along the side curtains of the stage. It's packed. You can hardly see any space between people, and they all seem to be having a great time. It's a good setup for a big New Year's gig — a sold-out crowd of happy audience members ready rock out as soon as we go out on stage.

I head back out into the hallway to grab a drink. And my jaw drops.

"Hi!"

"Elle! You're here! I was starting to get worried!"

"I told you I was coming. Just had some things to take care of…"

"And you did a great job, judging by this…" I tell her, gesturing at her from head to toe.

She didn't just go retro with the dress. She looks like a '40s pin-up girl, with her beachy blonde hair smoothed and curled in sweeping waves that run down her back, a white rose tucked above her ear. My usual no-makeup Elle now has her eyebrows arched, lashes long and full, eyeliner that's decidedly catlike and… those lips… dark red, pouty and glossy, like she's just licked them.

The deep blue dress is a far cry from her everyday bohemian style, more like her sundresses, but revved up. A full skirt that just skims her knees, some of that poufy stuff underneath, and a fitted waist that shows off her curves before hugging her chest and then offering up a beautiful view of her cleavage, cradled inside a neckline that also frames her bare shoulders. Not that I noticed.

Elle's an authentic bombshell tonight.

"Wow."

A blushing bombshell, because my response seems to have triggered her shyness again.

"Thanks," she replies. "No lamé? No sequins?"

"Nah. Declan vetoed it. Said it made us look too much like Alex clones."

She laughs. "Well, you look just fine in your regular stage clothes. I like the shirt. Geeky, yet rockstar."

I'm wearing my Stormtroopers-meets-Abbey Road T-shirt. I look like me. Elle... looks like a goddess...

"Thanks. Did you want to come get a bite to eat before the first set starts?"

"Sure. Thanks again for inviting me, Hunter."

"No one I'd rather have kick off the new year with me," I tell her with a smile. And I mean it.

We walk into the room I'd just left, where everyone is chattering loudly. Until they're not.

Because Rhys splits the air with a wolf whistle, and everyone turns to follow his gaze... To Elle.

"Whoa... Nice bombshell bit there, Ellie," Alex says, giving her a nod.

Megan glares at him and says nothing, hitting Elle with an even angrier glare when she realizes Alex didn't see her glaring at him, because he's still looking at Elle.

"You look *amazing*," Lisa tells her. "The salon did a picture-perfect job. I'm so glad!"

"Cool outfit, Ellie," David comments, his eyes glued to her cleavage. I'm tempted to step in front of her.

Declan's just standing there with his jaw dropped, speechless. For like the first time ever.

"Hi, everyone! Glad to be here. And thanks. I think it turned out pretty well."

Lisa comes over to give Elle the once-over, and they're doing the girl-chat thing when Rhys speaks up again.

"Hey, Ellie — where's Mace?"

"I'm not sure, Rhys. Why do you ask?" she replies. I notice that blush is back again. Rhys' question is probably embarrassing her. I wish he hadn't gone there.

"Just thought you might have brought him as your date tonight..."

"Hunter mentioned you were a little obsessed with Mace, Rhys... I could see if I still have his number if you'd like to ask him out..." Now she's trying to hide the grin that's sneaking its way onto her face.

The room erupts into laughter.

"Good one, Ellie!" Rhys replies, coming over to give her a fist bump and a hug. He's looking right down her cleavage when he releases her. I smack him on the back of the head.

"What?" he asks, fully aware of what. He gives me an apologetic smile and a shrug.

We get Ellie some food, and after I mention her big triumph, she spends a while talking to everyone about the awards, the grants and the record-breaking auctions.

"You sold them all?" David asks.

"No. I kept one for myself. Too much sentimental value."

Now it's me who's blushing, because even though I never asked her about it, I've assumed since that night that "Soul of the Hunter" was inspired by me. But maybe that's just my overinflated ego talking. The colors in the weaving certainly could give the impression of a hunter in a lush forest changing from green to gold and red. I've been tempted to ask, but I haven't yet. It's possible she was just using a theme, like with "Soul of the Deep Sea" and "Soul of Ireland," which had all those Irish landscape colors.

"Time to go, folks!" David points out, and we all file out of the room toward the stage.

"Are you going to watch from backstage?" I ask her. She doesn't usually like crowds and seems to like to be closer to where I'm standing on stage, which is pretty much impossible now from in front of the stage, as many people as are packed in the room.

"For a while, at least, I think. I may go out to the bar and watch from there for a bit later," she adds.

"OK — have fun! I'll see you in a bit." I press a kiss to her forehead, noting how striking her violet eyes are with the blue dress.

"Hunter!" she yells as I turn around. "I forgot the best part!"

She reaches in the pocket of the dress, and the next thing I know, the whole thing lights up like a sea of stars, pinpoints of light peeking through the deep blue.

"Wow. You look like the entire universe has been concentrated in one spot."

"I am not a supermassive black hole, Hunter!" she jokes.

"No, but you're definitely making as much impact as the Big Bang tonight," I reply with a wink.

And the sun rises over the sea of stars, with her bright smile and the rosy blush on her cheeks.

Elle is nowhere to be seen when we take a break after the first set, about ninety minutes in. I'm about to go looking for her when Alex calls us back on stage for the second set. I keep my eye out for the blonde bombshell in the Big Bang dress, but no luck. I'm wondering if she got tired and decided to go home, but it seems unlikely, as much trouble as she went to for tonight.

The next thing I know, Declan is calling a halt to our regular set, because it's nearly midnight, and we've got a special surprise for the audience. The old year drips away, second by second, and the new one approaches... Five... Four... Three... Two... One...

"Happy New Year, everyone!" Declan shouts, clinking his glass of champagne with the one the staff handed me. We both knock them back before Declan roars over the din, "Let's rock this new year!" and nods to me.

I launch into our rocked-up version of "Auld Lang Syne" with a stripped-down solo. About three bars in, I finally spot that glowing blue dress on the dance floor, Elle's face hidden behind the guy who's standing in front of her with his arms around her. It looks like they're dancing, like most of the people on the dance floor. He leans down, and I can't tell if he's kissing her, like so many others down there since the clock struck twelve, or if he's whispering in her ear. Either way...

Rhys kicks into the harder rock section of our arrangement, and I'm startled out of my focus on Elle and that guy. I don't miss a note, but it's close. Dave's giving me a raised eyebrow, while Declan is leading the audience in singing along. I look behind me, and Alex is shaking his head just a little. I may not have missed a note, but my bandmates noticed I was distracted. Not good. I throw myself into the rest of the song, and forget about everything else for a while. When we transition back into our regular set, I look for Elle amongst the crowd, but I can't see her. No sign of the guy, either.

We do our last encore song around quarter after one. And I'm off the stage in an instant, slipping my guitar onto the stand and pulling out my in-ears. The crowd isn't quite as jam-packed as it was an hour ago, but it takes me a minute to get out to the bar, where I ask the bartender if he's seen the girl in the glowing dress. He looks at me like I'm nuts. And maybe I am. I couldn't possibly have seen what I thought I saw.

"I think she went backstage," the girl next to me says.

"Huh?"

"The girl, with the blue dress that had all the lights on it, like stars? She was headed toward the backstage area a little bit ago. ...But I'm here, if you're looking for some company," she adds. "You don't have to chase *me*."

"No, sorry — thanks. But she's a friend, and I need to find her."

"Lucky girl," she says, turning to the guy on her other side, who she seems to think is a good second choice.

I head backstage again.

"Hunt — what the heck was going on there with the 'Auld Lang Syne' solo?" Alex demands as soon as I'm in the back hallway again.

"I guess the champagne just hit me funny," I reply, looking behind him down the hall in case Ellie's there.

"Hunt! Come on, man! You're running off the stage the moment we're done and almost fucking up the hallmark song for the night, and I can tell you're looking for Ellie. Frantically."

I sigh. Busted.

"You told the girl you weren't going to interfere, Hunt," he says, clapping his hand on my shoulder. "I heard you tell her that. *Mace* heard you tell her that," he says meaningfully.

"You saw her out there? With that guy? Did you see him?"

"I saw them. I couldn't see enough to tell who he was, if that's what you're going to ask."

"Yeah. I couldn't see much from where I was standing. Same angle, I guess."

"Could have just been some guy in the crowd who didn't have a date to kiss at midnight."

"Could have, yeah. Looked kind of like the guy I saw at her show the other night, though — who had his hand on her back."

"Well, good for her, then."

"What?"

"Good for her." He sighs. "Hunt, if you aren't going to give the girl what she wants, she's going to go looking somewhere else. And she should. From what I've seen, she's had the patience of a saint. And you told her you weren't the guy for her. You were pretty firm about that. You made the girl cry."

"And then she went off with Aedan fucking Mason..."

"She did."

"You think she's sleeping with him?"

"Last I heard, she was *sleeping* with *you*," he points out. "Whether she's having *sex* with *him* is another question, though you and Ellie are the only two friends I know who would have to differentiate things like that."

"That guy — you think it was Mace?"

"I have no idea, man. Could have been. The hair color is right. But then you said she had a thing for redheads, right?"

"I said she had a thing for Eric Stoltz."

"Well, maybe she bumped into Eric Stoltz," he says with a chuckle. "But odds are she just found a cute guy with red hair in the audience who decided to pay her some attention, just like Mace did. And, again, good for her."

I sigh.

"Hunt — you're acting like a jealous boyfriend, or at least her overprotective brother or dad, and she's already told you she's not putting up with that shit anymore. Moreover, if she *was* with Mace, you're *really* playing with fire, because that guy could end us with a word if he took offense to how you're dealing with even the *possibility* that she's been with him."

"I know. I'm just worried about her. We know what his life is like, on the road, at least. I don't want her to be just another random fuck for him."

"If it *was* him here with her tonight, she's not just a random fuck, Hunter."

Oh.

"I don't know, man," he continues. "Maybe they're just having another philosophical discussion." I roll my eyes at him. "Hey — it's a new year. It's a time to consider larger questions. She's a smart girl. ...And you should remember that. *She's a smart girl.* She knows what happens backstage. She was very clear about that that night. She's not walking into any situation with blinders on, except maybe where you're concerned. And she seems to like *those* blinders. About as much as you like yours."

My eyebrows shoot up in question. He gives me a raised eyebrow and shakes his head.

"Let the girl go, Hunt. Be happy for her if she's found someone who makes her happy. Now, come on back to the party."

I follow him down the hall to the hospitality room. Everyone's having a good time. There's no sign of Ellie, though.

"She said she was heading out," Lisa tells me.

I am clearly transparent.

"Was she with anyone?" I ask.

"She said she ran into a friend. I can't remember the name... Started with an M, I think..."

"Mace?"

"I really don't remember what it was. I assumed it was a girlfriend of hers."

"Ah. Thanks," I tell her with a smile. One that's mostly genuine. It must have been Maire she ran into.

I get myself a drink and start chatting up one of the numerous girls in the room, and since I'm now the only one of us here without a date (or two), that's about as easy as it's ever been. An hour or so later, I get a text notification.

Elle: *Sorry I had to leave early. You all were SO good tonight!*
Hunter: *Happy New Year, Elle! Tell Maire I said hi.*
Elle: *Happy New Year to you, too!*

CHAPTER 35

THE STRING-CHEESE INCIDENT

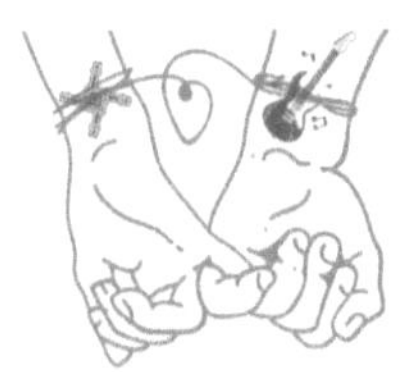

Ellie
Four months later

"So they pay you to make this fabric-string stuff?"

"Fabric-string?" I ask absently, focused on my spinning.

"You know — the string stuff you use to make fabric, like sweaters and stuff."

I stop spinning for a moment and roll my eyes.

"*Yarn*, Hunter. It's called *yarn*. Not 'fabric-string.' Have you not been listening to me talking about this for the last handful of years now?"

"I *have* been listening. Diligently. Devotedly. Raptly. With great fascination. I am your biggest fabric-string-making fan."

He makes it about two seconds with a straight face before cracking up completely.

I give him a stern, repressing look, but he reposts with an expression so delightfully goofy that I can't keep it up and crack up myself, the two of us eventually laughing so hard and so long, we're heaving in lungfuls of air, just trying to stay conscious.

He's bent over at the waist, trying to catch his breath, but keeps falling back into it. I'm so overcome with mirth that I fall out of my chair and onto the floor next to him, literally rolling with laughter.

He drops down beside me and we lay there panting, and every time one of us looks at the other — even in their general direction — we start up all over again.

It's a good 10 minutes later before we can speak again, and the amiable silence carries on as we lie next to each other, looking up at the ceiling.

"Is that one of my guitar picks sticking out of the ceiling?" he asks idly.

"Could be..." I reply vaguely.

"What's it doing up there?"

"Plotting the overthrow of the Marshall Islands..."

He looks over at me, an eyebrow raised.

"*Marshall* Islands. Get it? Like Marshall amps?" I elbow him in his ribs.

"Oof."

"Was that 'oof' for the amp joke or for my elbow?"

"Both."

"Well, that's what you get for 'fabric-string.'"

"I did earn that, didn't I?"

"Yup."

"So... what *is* my guitar pick *really* doing jutting out of the drywall in your ceiling?"

"You may have pissed me off enough at one point in the last few months that I threw it at the ceiling when I spotted it and realized it was yours."

"You threw it hard enough to wedge it into the drywall?"

"Adrenaline. Some people lift cars off their family members. I embed guitar picks in ceilings."

"That's a special talent, there."

"Yes. And I'm quite proud of it. Unfortunately, when they hold the world championship of pick-throwing, you'd have to come with me, and piss me off on purpose, just so I could stand a chance at a gold medal. And at the rate you're going, you're going to be touring Southeast Asia soon, and I can't afford the airfare to fly you back just so I can hang that gold medal on my wall."

"It *would* go nicely with the guitar pick in your ceiling."

"My interior designer told me that. She actually suggested I complement the metal of the medal and the pearloid plastic pick with some artfully arranged fuchsia fabric-string to complete the look. So, there's that..."

Hunter looks over at me with a stern expression that says I've clearly taken this too far, even for him.

And we both crack up all over again, staring up at the ceiling and the guitar pick that I'll never actually explain to him how it got there. Because, you *know* — witches be mysterious...

Hunter

Elle's not giving me any answers. And I really do want to know.

But she's developed a degree of self-confidence in the last year that sometimes means she doesn't actually give in to me. Used to be that whatever I wanted was done before I even asked for it. Sometimes when I didn't really need her to do it. And she still does that a lot. But she seems a lot more focused on her own life now. And that's good.

Except when she's being mysterious, like now, and that whole disappearing act she pulled after the art showcase. She never did tell me what "things" she'd been doing for more than twenty-four hours after leaving her dorm late that night. Well, I never directly asked her about that. But I've hinted around it a few times since then, and she's never given me a solid answer. At least the mystery of New Year's Eve was solved. No more worrying about Aedan fucking Mason.

Alex was right. I needed to stop acting like Ellie's romantic life was any of my business. And I haven't really worried about it since. I don't think she's actually dated anybody since then. Or, well, ever. But that seems to have more to do with her focus on school and her career than on me. Which, frankly, is a relief. I haven't changed my mind about not going there. Even after seeing how gorgeous she was on New Year's Eve.

Honestly, I like her better as her natural self — no makeup, no fancy hairstyle and dress. Though, that dress was pretty awesome. No heels, either. Just my barefoot beach girl in her quasi-hippie style. It reminds me how completely she's always accepted me for who I am, and I feel like I do the same. I love the girl. Even if I'm not *in* love with her.

As it stands, she's been my sounding board — appropriately — as we've prepared to go into the studio for our EP, which is set to be completed by July and released in September. It hasn't been easy going. We've had a lot of debates about which songs are ready and which ones aren't. Most of the ones we've agreed were ready were David and Declan's, about six of them. Another two were mine. One was Alex's.

We've all contributed to the arrangements we've been playing live, and they've evolved to become even better over time. But I'd still like to see more of my songs considered for the EP. We'll select from among the nine songs to get the four or five that will appear on the EP. And we're down to the wire on picking our favorites to give to the producer before we go into the studio next week.

"You're quiet again," Elle says as she lies beside me on her dorm room floor. "The EP?"

"Yeah. I just wish Dave and Declan were willing to be open to including more of my songs. Alex and Rhys agreed that they're good — really good. Dave said something's missing, but he can't tell me what. Declan's just being his usual asshole self. We can't get a consensus to try any of mine except the two."

"Which ones?" she asks.

"'Geek Out' and 'Get Some.' I also really want to get 'Makin' Somethin' Outta Nothin' on the EP, at least. I don't expect to have three of the five songs be mine. I just want to get some consideration for 'Makin' Somethin' Outta Nothin'.' It feels like it has single potential."

"Have you told the guys that? That you'd like to work on it for the EP?"

"Yeah. They're just not all on board. I mean — you've heard it enough. Is it not good?"

"All your songs are great, Hunter. And I'm glad you're standing up for yourself with them. But..."

She looks at me with an expression that tells me I'm not going to like what she says.

"I think maybe 'Makin' Somethin' Outta Nothin' still needs something, to be honest. It's great. But it feels like it could be better."

I sigh. That's disappointing.

"Listen, Hunter — you talked about it having single potential? All I'm saying is that I see the potential, but it's still just potential and not quite realized yet. I think you can get it there, so I would definitely keep pushing to try it in the studio, see if you can find the thing that will put it over the top. You owe it to yourself, and the band — and to the song, really. Make it the best it can be. Then they won't be able to refuse."

I think about that for a while, back to the silence we'd had before she'd asked me what was up. She knows me so well. She knows my music so well, even though she's not a musician herself. Sometimes, I think she gets her ideas for her weavings from the same place I get my songs — from a muse. At least it seems that way. The songs just flow into me. When they don't, I have to drag them out, and that's never good. I felt like I'd had that flow with 'Geek Out' and 'Get Some,' but I'd been halfway into 'Makin' Somethin' Outta Nothin'' when the notes seemed to start struggling to come out.

Maybe she's right. Maybe it's not there yet. Maybe if I go back to where I feel like things got hard, I can find another thread of inspiration to make it work.

"Thanks, Elle. I think I've got something to work on now."

I drop a kiss on her forehead and head out to try to get this song back on track.

CHAPTER 36

SEND IN THE FLYING MONKEYS

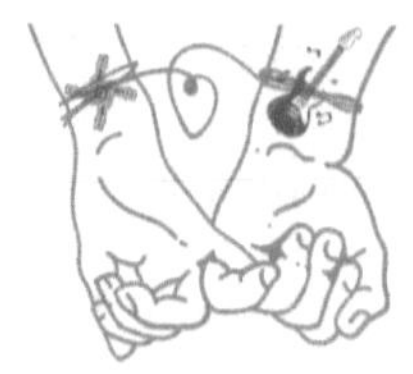

Ellie
Two months later

"You cannot possibly be serious, Ellen."

I hear the words, but I can't process them.

"Do I ask you if you're serious about your religious beliefs?" I finally reply.

"My religious beliefs don't involve witches and mythological beings and magic spells," my father counters.

I'm ping-ponging back and forth between frozen in shock and blazing with anger. How dare he!

"And that's fine for you. You can stick with prayer and symbolic wine, if that's what floats your spiritual boat. I'm not stopping you. I'm not questioning *your* sanity or *your* intelligence just because I don't happen to share your beliefs on an issue where no one can be proven right. I keep my own counsel, and my faith follows what seems right to me. I didn't invite you to snoop in my books," I point out.

"They were right there..."

"Yes, in a box, under the handful of college textbooks I opted to keep from this year and eighteen skeins of hand-spun yarn. None of which should be of any interest to you. Unless you've decided to take up weaving so we can go into business together and you just neglected to mention it to me."

"Don't be ridiculous, Ellen."

"Why not? According to you, I'm already pretty ridiculous."

"You can't possibly think this witchcraft stuff is real. You just can't."

"Dad, I have an IQ of 132, two semesters of comparative religion — which I got a 98 in, by the way, *both times* — and a minor in anthropology on top of my applied arts major. If one of us is qualified to make a call on the justification for my religious beliefs, it's me, and not the guy who hasn't stepped foot inside his church in twenty-five years except for my baptism and first communion and who has never lived anywhere except his own hometown."

"Where are you going? We're not done here."

"You may not be done with your little inquisition, but I am."

"I'm not standing for this nonsense in my house, Ellen. Your mother wouldn't have approved either. Not under our roof."

"Fine, then. But you're wrong about Mom. And to answer your other question: I'm going somewhere where I'll be treated with a modicum of respect. You have the house all to yourself now, long-term. Enjoy your nonsense-free zone."

I grab the incriminating box (Should I have painted it with a scarlet W? I wonder idly...) and my suitcase, which, thankfully, I hadn't yet unpacked, and drag them back outside to my car, which is still full of my belongings from my college dorm room, including my spinning wheel and loom. So much for a relaxing summer home from college...

I wipe away tears of anger, humiliation and frustration, mixed with a hint of terror at unhitching my future from the comfortable life my parents once provided. Everything has changed since Mom passed away a year and a half ago. Dad and I never saw eye to eye, but he's become increasingly, aggressively judgmental.

This is just the latest in a long line of confrontations we've had during the few times I've been home, over everything from the used car I bought — with my own money! — and my major and course selections to who I spend my time with. At 20 years old! He even corrects people when they call me Ellie, which is what everyone else has called me since I was 6. ("Ellen was your grandmother's name. You'll treat it with respect!")

Bottom line, without Mom, with Dad like he is now, home no longer feels safe, comfortable, or even just like… home. And it's time for me to go.

I put the car in gear, headed the one place I know I can always find refuge — with Hunter. I know he'll let me crash on the couch at his place until I can find somewhere else to stay.

I make two other phone calls first, to let Lindsey know that I won't be home this summer to work after all, and to confirm that my part-time job at Kara's shop hasn't yet been filled for the summer. Lucky for me, it's not only still open, but Kara needs more help than usual since there's been a boom in demand for crafting supplies these days.

"Honey, if you want forty hours a week, I can give it to you," she says.

"That would be perfect! And I'll keep the forty hours going into the fall. I'm done with school."

"Wait… You're dropping out? Is everything OK?"

"Unforeseen circumstances," I offer.

"Gotcha. I'm here if you want to talk about it," she says.

"Thanks."

I appreciate both the offer and the willingness not to dig into things when they're still a raw, open wound.

"Elle-belle! How's it hanging?" Hunter answers over the din of what is clearly a raging party.

"Hey, Hunt… Uh… sounds like you've got a lot going on there. You OK to talk? I need a massive favor."

He bellows for quiet, with his hand over the phone, judging from the briefly muffled sound. The din drops a few decibels.

"What's up, witchypoo? You and your broom?" Appropriately, he cackles.

"Are you drunk, Hunter?"

"A little. Maybe." He shushes loudly, and I'm not sure if he's shushing the crowd around him, me or himself. "Don't tell Dad… Oh — wait. Dad's off to parts unknown with one or more of his girlfriends. So, feel free to tell him. Or *your* dad, if you see him first."

He laughs uproariously, clearly amused at his own wit.

"That's the thing, Hunt… I just left home."

"Where are you going? Out for some dancing and drinks?" he jokes, knowing I'm too much of a homebody for that to be likely.

"No — Hunter... I've *left home*. For good. And I need somewhere to crash until I can find a place of my own..."

That sobers him up. At least a little.

"Wait... For good? What happened? Are you OK?"

I can always rely on Hunter to take care of me. Even drunk, he's sobering right up and wondering how I am.

"Not really." He's probably the only one I'd admit that to right now. "But it's been building to a head with Dad ever since the funeral, and this was just the last straw... He gave me an ultimatum... And he made fun of my religion, Hunter. He questioned my sanity and my intelligence."

"And you don't ever do that with my brilliant Elle-belle. I'm so sorry, sweetie. Sure — yeah, come crash here. You'll have to share a bed — yes, with me, don't worry — Rhys' landlord finally had enough of his 'hobbies,' so he's already claimed the sofa, and Alex's girlfriend is permanently glued to his side and sharing the other bedroom with him *and* his keyboards, lest the groupies get to him."

"Understood. It's not like we haven't shared a bed before. And I've got my own blanket, so no bed-hog threat from you, for once."

"I don't hog the blankets!" he insists, overly loudly.

"No — you hog square footage of the bed itself. But I can fend you off with extra pillows this time."

"Yeah, yeah... Don't forget I'm doing you a favor."

"A huge one. Thank you, Hunter," I add solemnly. "I'll be there in about three hours."

It's a long drive from south coastal Delaware to Northern Virginia. I crank up the stereo with a bootlegged aMUSEd CD keeping me company, listening to Hunter and his brothers-from-another-mother rock the house a couple months ago. It puts a smile on my face for the first time tonight.

He knows I'm proud of him, though he'll probably never know how much. His destiny was set the moment his mother put a guitar in his hands, and I've been tagging along on this rollercoaster ride for the last five years. Tonight's big party is to celebrate them starting to record their EP. It's a party I'm missing because Dad had insisted I come straight home once classes let out. Pretty soon, I won't be limited to the recordings Hunter cribs off the mixing board at gigs, because they'll have a real studio recording of their own. Hunter deserves every bit of the success he's had. I know exactly how hard he's worked for it. It's great to see him able to afford rent now, and even the booze for tonight's party. His star is definitely on the rise.

I know I've had it comparatively easy up until now, with my college paid for, my part-time job funding gas and maintenance on my car. Even before the art show, I'd already been tucking a little away to start my own business.

Until recently, that's been the biggest practical question-mark in my life — where and when my business would get going. But I'd had time, I had thought, with a year of college left. Even with the windfall this past winter of the fellowship and the two huge auction sales of my work, I need more startup money before I can get the shop going.

And now, I'm set adrift, with no tether keeping me in safe waters where Dad could come to the rescue, not now and not if things don't go smoothly with getting my business up and running, which I now know he'll never support. And I won't give him the satisfaction, nor the control he'd like to exert over me. Not anymore. But Hunter's days of scrambling to keep a roof over his head are coming back to me now. Vividly. And I can't afford to start dipping into my shop fund. I'm going to have to work my way out of this one. Being the person who needs safe harbor for once is unnerving. I've always been the one coming to the rescue, playing fairy godmother. Especially where Hunter is concerned. Not because he needed it more, but because doing it just gave me so much joy. Now I realize it was secondhand magic, and if I'm going to make my own dreams come true, I'm going to have to make some magic of my own.

And where better to start than with a new name? Cutting the ties that bound me too tightly for me to even breathe anymore. My father can keep "Ellen," if he's so attached to it. Out with the old, in with the new. Nowhere to go but onward and upward. Time to turn the page.

Dad may scoff at my beliefs, but I'm a certified member of the clergy now, sworn priestess and devotee of Brighid. Since it seems I've borne it before, I wonder if Herself would mind me taking Her name now as well... I ask respectfully, and I feel a sense of benediction that seems like approval.

So, Brighid... Brighid what? ...

I glance over at the passenger seat, at the box that changed my life. Skeins from my own spindle resting gently atop my books on Irish mythology and language, magical theory, anthropology, herbs and textile arts.

Weaver. Of course.

I smile to myself.

Welcome to a new chapter in your life, Brighid Weaver. May it be triply blessed, so that you can share those blessings with others, threefold.

CHAPTER 37

CRASH INTO ME

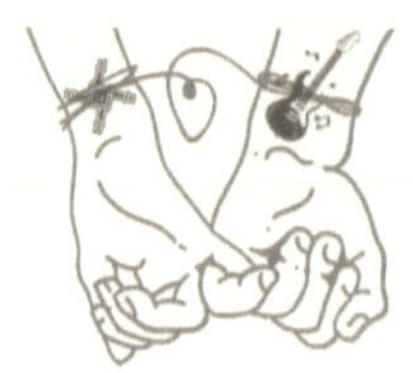

~~Ellie~~ Brighid
Nine years ago

Hunter's been awesome about homeless me crashing at his place, sharing his bed.

"I kind of owe you for all those nights I crashed in your dorm with you," he says good-naturedly.

"Yeah, you kinda do!" I tease him. "Seriously, though — I'm going to find my own place as soon as I can. I've got my savings, and I can dip into that for a deposit and first month's rent. I just need to find the right place."

"Sure. No rush. Are you thinking about a roommate?"

For half a second, I'm picturing me and Hunter living together. If he hadn't come here to stay with the Carters before I got here for college, we might already be living together... Again-ish. I don't even know if I should count "back then" as living together. But after all the time he spent sharing my bedroom at home — former home — I guess it would still be "again"...

He's looking at me, waiting for me to answer. I shake myself out of my reverie.

"I'm not sure. If I could find a nice little one-bedroom, or even a studio, that I could afford, I might do that. I want more privacy... fewer prying eyes..."

"Fewer curious questions and insulting skepticism about your religious practices?"

"Yeah," I admit. It's not easy to set up an altar with a goddess on top of it when you have a loose-tongued roommate (or a judgmental parent) who, at best, won't be able to walk past it without giving it some serious side-eye.

"I'm not even Wiccan or anything, so I'm not dealing with the misunderstandings about the pentacles and stuff like they do. But I keep things private because I want to, and quiet because it's easier that way."

There can be a lot of harassment, even threats. You have to be picky about who knows. I've been lucky that Hunter never judged me, not for a minute. But, still, just crashing here, I've kept my Brighid statue packed safely away.

"I'm also spending so much of my free time spinning and weaving now — I don't know how a roommate would deal with my loom clacking around at 4 a.m."

"I know that feeling!" Hunter admits with a laugh . "We've had to learn to keep it down or wait until we can get to Declan's and David's garage for practice. And Rhys *really* knows that feeling, since that's half the reason his landlord kicked him out."

"Half? What else did he do?"

"He... uh... He was experimenting with... uh.. some chemicals... and..."

"Chemicals? Like what? Meth?"

Hunter howls with laughter.

"No! Nothing like that! He just gets these ideas of things that don't exist or that he thinks he can make better, and he starts experimenting."

"He's an inventor!"

"Well, he'd like to think he is," Hunter admits. "He hasn't actually invented anything, except an indescribably bad smell and a new reason to get evicted."

I chuckle.

"So, what's the plan? He's crashing with you all long-term, or is he looking for another place, like I am?"

Hunter gets an odd look on his face.

"He'd make a shitty roommate for you, Ell— sorry, I mean Bridge."

"What? Oh — no, I wasn't suggesting that," I clarify, ignoring his slip with my former name. He's getting it right most of the time, even though it hasn't been that long and even though my legal name change hasn't been completed yet. "I'm really kind of wanting to try living alone, now that you mentioned it. If I can find a place."

"OK. I was just saying..." He shakes his head. "Anyway — no, he's going to find someplace else. But it's hard to find somewhere that'll let him play his drums. It's going to take a while."

"Makes sense. And Megan? She's living here, too?"

I actually haven't seen Megan leave Alex's side since I got here. I'm kind of wondering if she follows him into the bathroom, too. She's that clingy — in an aggressively possessive way.

"Not technically. I mean, she has an apartment she shares with a roommate. But she's kind of always here."

"Oh. How do you feel about that?"

"You sound like my therapist," he comments with a laugh.

"You're seeing a therapist?"

Part of me is hoping that wasn't just a joke. Hunter never talked to anyone professionally after his mother's death, at least that I know of. And I can't imagine he's been able to process things amidst the conflict with his dad, the fallout with the Carter brothers opting out of college and him moving out of their parents' house as a result.

"Uh... No. No insurance. No time. I'm only just now able to scale back to one 'day job' on top of the band. And now we're in the studio for the EP, too." He quickly changes the subject back to Megan, and I take note of that.

"She's alright, I guess. Would I rather she weren't here so much? Sure. But I can't complain about that and also ask Alex to be OK with you here. I mean, she's his girlfriend. Of course she's here a lot."

I note that he's made the distinction between Megan the girlfriend and me, not the girlfriend. It's always a stab to the heart when he does that, almost like he's ashamed of me. I know he doesn't believe in my vision, and he's made it extremely clear he's not interested in me that way. But it hurts every time.

"So, when's your next gig?"

Change of subject? Two can play that game.

"Friday night. We've got a show at one of the big clubs in D.C. — Alex has a lot of contacts, and he knows their booking person. 'aMUSEd' is already up on their marquee."

"That's awesome! How's the songwriting going?"

"We're up to about half originals and half covers for gigs. Including enough originals to be able to use the strongest four or five for the EP."

"How many of yours?"

"One, maybe two right now, as far as the EP goes. David and Declan have a bunch ready to go, and we've mostly been working on those, working them into the setlist and ironing out arrangements as we start to lay down tracks."

"Don't let them run over top of you. There are five of you now. Without you, there is no band. And your songs are great!"

"You're biased."

"Maybe. But I've been around since you started playing. We've seen how many concerts together? How many bar gigs? A ton. The answer is a ton. And you've said it yourself — my taste in music is exquisite."

"I don't think I said 'exquisite.' Maybe eccentric."

I smack him on the shoulder.

"Excellent... extraordinary... ecstatic... erotic..."

I raise an eyebrow. He's brushing up against that line he's drawn, whether he realizes it or not.

"Exceptional..."

"OK, OK, Mr. Thesaurus. I'm seeing a theme here. But the bottom line is — I have good taste. So when I tell you you're good, it's not me flattering your ego — it's your friend with excellent, erotic, exceptional taste who's giving you an honest opinion. So, don't let David and Declan just de facto become your only songwriters. You'd be shortchanging the band."

"Message received."

"Whatever happened to that melody you played for me the day you picked up your guitar again?"

"That one? I've been holding onto it. It seems... special. I want to make sure it gets the treatment it deserves. So, right now, it's still only a little melody. I think I'll know what to do with it when the time is right."

"That sounds beautiful. It is very special."

I never told him that that little melody of his carried me over between reality and vision and back again. I was afraid he'd stop playing it, like he stopped telling me he loved me. As it was, it seems to have gotten tucked away someplace close to his heart.

And I can't say that I'm not glad he seems to consider it as special as I do.

"Are you coming to the gig?"

"Did you want me to?"

"You know I do. I like having a friendly face in the audience."

"You just like hamming it up when you know someone's there who won't groan when you do."

"Also true."

I sigh and lie back on the bed. Hunter does the same, dropping a kiss on the top of my head when I put it on his shoulder.

"I'm glad you're here, Bridge. I know it's been rough, falling out with your dad. Goodness knows I've been there, if for different reasons. I'm glad we still have each other's backs."

"Always. That'll never change."

Chapter 38

Broken Record

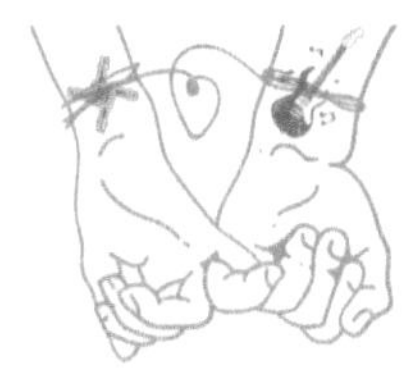

Hunter
The next day

"Well, that chord change works..."

"And?"

"And that's it."

Malcolm Fisher, the producer hired by the regional label that's supposed to release our EP in a couple months, doesn't seem to be a fan of aMUSEd. He hasn't said a single positive thing about any of the songs we had ready to record, except for that one chord change of mine he liked. We're all kind of bummed. We thought the songs were pretty good after we'd taken the better part of a year to perfect them. But then, "pretty good" isn't exactly what we want to record.

"Have you all thought about adding a lead guitar?"

"We've already got five guys in the band, dude," I point out.

"And if you need to have twelve to make your music the best it can be, you hire seven more," Malcolm says.

I'm not sure what to say. Having him point out a deficiency in the guitar-playing on the songs kind of lays the blame right at my feet. Should the guys just replace me with someone who's better?

"Hunter's tracks are excellent, and I don't like you insinuating that he's not up to par," David tells him, uncharacteristically firm and direct for David. Now I'm really glad Dave was here. He didn't have to be, since I'm the only one working on tracks today because I had to work yesterday. Malcolm's take on my work is a major downer. But at least Dave has my back.

"No — that's not at all what I'm saying..." Malcolm continues. He sighs. "Sorry — my head's in the process right now, and I keep forgetting you all are in the studio for the first time. That's a compliment, guys — you're enough like seasoned pros that I haven't done the hand-holding I usually do with a young band. I should have made it clear that I really like what you're doing with these songs.

"So let me be really clear now: Hunter's great. Hunter's guitar really carries the weight of the songs. And you've got a very strong rhythm section. Your keyboard player is one of the best I've heard in years, and I haven't heard a vocalist with Declan's versatility in even longer than that. But there's something missing. And it's not something that overdubbing more guitar parts can completely fix — not to mention you'd then be stuck when trying to replicate the album tracks live."

"So you think hiring a lead guitar player is the answer?" I ask, trying to take the criticism as the constructive effort Malcolm seems to want it to be.

"Over the longer term, yes," he says. "I've got to be honest, guys — what you have here is very good. Like breakthrough good. You could easily parlay these songs into a full record deal. But I'm feeling like they could be next-level if you had just the one additional component."

"So, what's the answer here? Do we put recording the EP on hold and then try to find somebody to help us finish it? Do we bring in hired gun for these songs and then search for a permanent lead guitarist? Do we redo the arrangements to make them better without a lead guitarist?" I really want to know what this guy thinks we should do. Even if it means I'm no longer our only guitar player.

"The label won't let you mothball the EP long enough to find a lead guitarist who's at your level and available to jump in," Malcolm says. "That's a non-starter. So we'll have to work with what we've got.

"I'm actually tempted to suggest Declan take over the rhythm parts and Hunter does lead — yes, Hunter is talented enough to do lead," he emphasizes, looking both of us directly in the eye. "But Declan's more valuable as a dedicated lead singer. Your live show would suffer with him stuck behind a guitar. He's too active on stage, too interactive with the audience, too charismatic — at least on stage — and you don't want to take that gift and mute it. At all. And Hunter's a gifted rhythm player. That's where you really shine," he tells me.

"So what I'd suggest at this point is that we make some changes to the arrangements for the recording and have Hunter do lead parts over the rhythm guitar parts he already has written. We'll use Alex's keyboard parts to help fill in some of the gaps, and I think we'll have a very bankable EP when we're done."

I heave a sigh of relief. I can do some additional guitar parts, and the songs are already getting a great reception live, so I don't think we have to worry about the live arrangements for now.

"You boys have a very bright future ahead of you. I have no doubt about that," Malcolm adds. "Let's get you over this first hump and off to a solid start in your careers. I have a feeling you're going to be doing your next album for a big label and with a producer who's got a few Grammys on his mantel. So I'm going to do everything I can to make sure that the EP we're making here and now is something you can look back on in ten or twenty years and still be proud of."

I'm happy with the new tracks I laid down today and, thankfully, Malcolm seemed to be, too.

Now it's on to tonight's gig, and I have to admit I'm looking forward to blowing off some steam. There's no feeling quite like going on stage before a crowd of 500 people and having them all dancing and applauding, and even singing along. It's a high no drug can touch, because it's all about the give and take between you and the audience. It's the one kind of relationship I have no problem committing to, because all the audience needs from me is my music, and I can give them that, happily, with no risk to either of us.

And speaking of blowing off some steam... I wouldn't mind another kind of blowing tonight, either. Living with Dad, with my sudden popularity after that talent show in high school, I'd kind of gotten in the habit of losing myself between a girl's thighs whenever my stress levels were high. Or with her between my thighs. I was happy either way. It was a momentary distraction whenever I needed it most. I'm not proud of it, but — hey, I was a horny teenage guy with a shitty home life. The shift toward actual rockstar status hasn't exactly changed my go-to form of stress relief.

And I'm definitely in the mood for some of those rockstar trappings tonight, after the stress of being in the studio all day and trying to satisfy Malcolm's high bar as both rhythm guitarist and lead guitarist. I think I managed it. We'd agreed to move on to other tracks on Monday, anyway.

So, yeah... Needing some stress relief. But I'd already asked Brighid to come tonight. Any other night, I'd love to have her here. I love seeing her bright smile and shining eyes right up front, enjoying the show more than anyone but maybe me and the guys. But there's no way I can indulge myself with a groupie backstage when Bridge is here. Maybe I can linger a little and send her home without me? Not without feeling bad about it, but desperate times call for desperate measures.

So when I get her text as we're loading in Alex's keyboards, I have to admit I'm a little relieved.

Brighid: *I'm not sure I'm going to make it tonight after all. I got an apartment viewing scheduled after work. It may take a while, depending on traffic.*

Hunter: *No — that's cool. It's an early gig anyway. We may be doing load-out by 10:30 or 11. You can miss one gig. You're not obligated to go just because you live with three-fifths of the band. LOL*

I tell her I'll see her at home when we're done.

Problem solved. No guilt and plenty of good times ahead. And, hopefully, that apartment she's looking at will be a great spot for her to settle in now that she's broken ties with her dad. Which will mean I get a bed to myself once again, and I can go back to sharing it with whoever appeals on a given night after a gig. All around, a positive turn for what was a rough day.

CHAPTER 39

A HARD DAY'S NIGHT

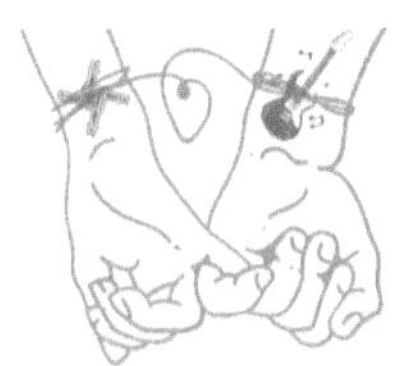

Brighid
Earlier that day

"I don't care, Alex! You need to either get a place of your own or we can get a place together — one where there's room for your keyboards somewhere *other* than our bedroom."

Megan's shrill voice is kind of hard to ignore. Especially when she's screaming at the top of her lungs — about you.

"I am not going to continue having my boyfriend shacking up with some other girl, even if she's nothing special to look at."

Yeah.

"Megan, keep it down — and be nice! Brighid is here temporarily, and she's Hunter's friend, not some groupie looking to score with the band!"

Alex's voice is considerably lower in decibels, but they're still just on the other side of a thin wall, and it's impossible not to hear.

"Have you seen the way she looks at Hunter? She's looking to score alright! As if anyone that hot would ever sleep with someone so... much less."

"Megan — I mean it! If you can't be polite, you can leave."

"Fine! I was going out dancing with Kinley tonight anyway. She said her boyfriend was bringing some of his friends. I'm sure they'll be more appreciative of me than you are."

"Are they cute?"

"Who?"

"Her boyfriend's friends."

"I don't know. He is. Very. So they probably are. You jealous?"

"Over you? Not in the least."

She screams in frustration, and I can hear her stomping out the door in her high heels.

"Good riddance."

Alex says it at normal volume, like he's just expressing relief and not trying to convey to her that he's angry with her, let alone speaking to me.

So I stay in Hunter's bedroom, scanning the online listings for apartments. It's been a month or so since I got here, and I'm having a hard time finding anything that won't start to deplete my shop fund. A lot of the listings are for apartments where I'd need two or three roommates.

But this isn't the first time since I got here that Megan has stormed out in a huff after arguing with Alex, and my name has come up in those arguments more than once.

I'm not interested in Alex, of course. I like Alex. I like Rhys, too. I like all of the guys in the band. Except Declan, sometimes. But he seems to like it that way, so I don't even worry about that. I don't think anyone likes Declan all the time, even Declan himself.

But I'm definitely not making moves on any of them. I haven't even said anything to Hunter about me and him in a long time. Based on her comment, I guess I'm a lot less subtle in my feelings about him than I thought I was at this point.

If Megan's hostility wasn't enough to light a fire under me, that observation tosses some kindling at my feet.

I make an appointment for later tonight, after work, to see a one-bedroom apartment that's just slightly outside my preferred rent range. I've got the late shift at work. Kara has let me keep my spinning wheel, loom, tools and materials in the upstairs loft where the off-season items and deep inventory are stored. I sometimes go in early when I work the late shift and spin some skeins, or stay late when I work the early shift.

We've been selling my yarns pretty steadily. They get sold at a premium, and if Kara had her way, I'd just be spinning eight hours a day. But she needs help with customers, too, since Maire is in college full-time.

Two years ago, when Maire first took me to her mom's shop, I fell in love. I instantly started thinking about having a shop of my own one day, kind of like this one, but with a more eclectic selection of things, like Maire's flower-laced paper goods, for one.

Kara saw my interest and offered me a part-time job working for her, and a spot on her merchandise shelves once she saw what I was already producing in my first classes, which had opened up a world of possibilities. I'd been basically the "teacher's pet" from Day 1 of class, getting instruction and assignments that weren't usually offered until sophomore or junior year, since I was substantially ahead of the other freshmen. Mrs. Pomeroy — Janet, as she insists I call her now — took me under her wing, telling me I was a natural. It really had felt like this was something I'd always been doing. And, maybe, if I really was wrong about my vision steering me toward a life with Hunter, it was the weaving and spinning I was actually supposed to be focusing on. That part of my vision certainly seemed to have panned out.

The landlord of the prospective apartment had gotten permission from the current tenant to let me see the place while they were out tonight, so it had lined up perfectly with my work schedule. Not so much with Hunter's schedule, since I'd been planning to go to his gig tonight. I might still be able to make it for the last part of what was an early gig for them, but I'd be pushing it.

Brighid: *I'm not sure I'm going to make it tonight after all. I got an apartment viewing scheduled after work. It may take a while, depending on traffic.*

Hunter: *No — that's cool. It's an early gig anyway. We may be doing load-out by 10:30 or 11. You can miss one gig. You're not obligated to go just because you live with three-fifths of the band. LOL*

Brighid: *Ha! You know full well that I'd have no social life if I didn't go to your gigs. Not too many people just hanging out at a yarn shop on a Friday night.*

Hunter: *We could always make an appearance, see if we can generate some hard-rock/soft-sweaters cross-interest. ;-)*

Brighid: *Kara would have a heart attack! And Maire would adhere herself to Rhys with her paper-binding glue!*

Hunter: *I'll give him a heads-up. She's cute!*

I bristle just a bit at that, but I say nothing.

Brighid: *Don't you dare! Rhys is too wild for her, and her mother would kill me!*

Hunter: *But where's the fun in that? >;-) Later, Bridge! I'll see you at home after we're done.*

I'm later closing up than I'd planned on. The rental agent said she'd wait, no problem. By the time I get there, I'm already a little concerned. The neighborhood isn't as nice as I expected. Nice meaning safe. Too many people loitering around on the streets, a police car with lights flashing and a couple arguing as the cop tries to break them apart.

My dream of a quiet little retreat for my work and spiritual pursuits is pretty much dashed even before I get out of the car, which I'm leery of parking here. When I reach the apartment and introduce myself to the agent, I have to yell to be heard over the party happening next door. Maybe that's where the current tenants were going tonight? They certainly couldn't have planned a quiet night in front of the TV with that going on.

I already know this isn't going to work. And it was the only possibility I'd found that was even close to being within my price range. I'm going to have to consider getting a roommate.

If Maire wasn't living at home, I'd ask her. I really haven't made a lot of other close friends here. I'd spent most of that time with Hunter when he wasn't working, and working on my spinning and weaving, or in meditation and devotions, when he wasn't. I'm kind of a homebody by nature.

I give the apartment a polite review and tell the agent it isn't exactly what I'm looking for. She says I'm going to have a hard time finding what I want at my maximum price but that she'll keep my info on file in case she hears of anything that might work.

I head back to my car deflated, Megan's words ringing in my ears.

Maybe I can catch the very end of aMUSEd's set. If nothing else, I can help Hunter lug equipment back to their van before we head home for the night.

The doorman isn't even taking cover charges anymore when I get to the bar. The music flowing out the door isn't live, and I know I'm too late for the show.

I head backstage to find Hunter. There's more people in the hallway than I'm used to seeing after one of their gigs. I see

Rhys right away, a beer in one hand with his other arm around a brunette who's wearing a dress smaller than my shortest skirt. I smile and nod and he smiles back, while the girl looks down her nose at me. I shrug it off and head back for the dressing room, where I expect I'll find Hunter.

Declan has a girl up against the wall, giving her a firsthand and up-close tour of his vocal cords. I don't think he even sees me, which is kind of a relief under the circumstances.

I run into Alex a moment later, with Megan once again glued to his side, giving me a glare when she catches sight of me. I guess they made up, or at least she gave in and chased after him at the gig, rather than staying out with her friend and her friend's friends.

"Hey, Bridge! I think Hunter went out to the bar. You may want to go back out and look for him there," Alex says helpfully.

"No he's not! He's in the dressing room, him and Davy!" Rhys shouts over the music and chatter from the people hanging out in the hall with the band. I don't think Rhys means that the way it sounds. David's usually the quiet one, so it makes sense that he and Hunter are hanging out in the relative quiet before they start breaking down their gear.

"Bridge—" Alex starts.

"Oh, just let her go, Alex! She's a big girl—" She cracks up at her own joke, which I've heard enough times in my life to just ignore. "She can find him by herself!"

At this point, I just want to say hi to Hunter and then head back to the apartment. The door to the dressing room is ajar, and I can hear quiet murmuring coming from inside, confirming that David and Hunter must be in there taking advantage of the relative quiet to talk.

I push open the door and freeze as I see David sitting in a chair directly in front of me, with a girl kneeling between his legs, her hands and mouth clearly occupied. His eyes are closed, and it's obvious what's happening.

I start to turn and go back out into the hallway to give them some privacy when I hear a moan from the other side of the room. My head swivels toward the sound, and I'm rendered immobile and silent as I take in a couple pressed up against the wall, her skirt pulled up around her waist and her strapless top pulled down, bare breasts being squeezed in her partner's hands as they're mashed into the wall.

The guy has his pants down around his thighs, giving me a view of his naked ass as he pounds into her from behind. Her hands are stretched up behind her, tangled in his hair, as she continues moaning in time with his thrusts. I take in the frighteningly long, sharp burgundy-painted nails where they're sliding through the dark gold strands, and my mind finally catches up with my eyeballs.

Hunter.

In an instant, two thoughts flash through my head: one, the man I love is fucking a stranger up against a wall; and, two, he's not my boyfriend, so I have no right to object.

I must make a sound, because David's eyes pop open in alarm. "Brighid!"

That alerts Hunter and his... date... who both turn their heads toward me while their bodies remain joined and pressed to the wall.

"You'll have to wait your turn!" the girl yells, giggling madly.

It takes Hunter a second to process what he's seeing, too.

"Bridge!" he breathes, startled.

That wakes me out of my frozen state, and I'm back out the dressing room door before I even notice I've turned around. Not even Hunter could outrun me tonight. I've already passed Declan, Alex and Rhys when I hear the plaintive wail from behind me.

"Hunter! You haven't finished me off! Finish me off, baby!"

"Yeah, Hunter, finish her off! Don't be a selfish bastard!" Declan adds.

"Oh, god..." Alex groans, quickly drowned out by Megan's cackling, begging the question of which of us is really a witch.

"Let her go, Alex! He's out of her league anyway!"

I make it back to the apartment in record time. Once there, I realize I have nowhere else to go. My phone pings.

Hunter: *Brighid — call me back!*

I pace around Hunter's room, around the bed we share, and all I can think is I have to get out of here. I can't be here when he gets home.

I've seen Hunter with other girls before — the parade of teenage girls in and out of his house after he moved back in with his dad didn't go unnoticed. I never said a word to him about it, but he knew I was aware that he'd gone from geeky virgin to rockstar-in-the-making/ladies' man basically overnight. Coincidentally, within weeks of the point where he'd stopped sleeping in my bed every night.

Yeah. Coincidentally.

I've had to learn to accept it. I doubt it went unnoticed that it about killed me every time I had to do it, but it killed me just a little less every time. I'd almost gotten used to it. Almost.

This is the first time, though, that I've *seen* him actually having sex with someone.

It's going to take something other than exposure therapy to get me through this one. Starting with time and space.

I pack up enough of my stuff to last me a few days, plus my personal treasures, and I carry them out to my car, along with a pillow. It isn't so cold that I can't spend one night in my car. This will be OK.

I put one of my meditation programs into the car stereo, a quiet, steady pounding of waves on sand, just to help me get to sleep, and I lay the driver's seat back as far as it goes before closing my eyes and begging for oblivion.

CHAPTER 40

SECOND TIME'S THE CHARM

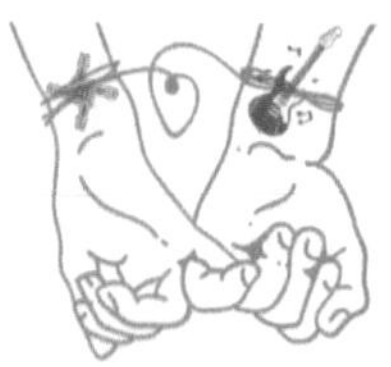

Brighid

I'm awakened by giggling, and overly loud shushing — the kind you hear when drunk people are trying to be quiet and are failing abysmally.

The next thing I notice is I'm cold. A cold front must be coming through, because it's gotten colder than I expected it to. And I didn't bring my blanket out to the car with me.

I peek up over the edge of the door, trying to remain unseen as I assess the situation. A handful of people are filing up the stairs to the second floor with a little stumbling and more laughing. It looks like the backstage party has shifted to the apartment. I suspect no one thought about where I might be after tonight's spectacle, so I doubt bringing the party back to the apartment would have seemed like something to reconsider.

Facing the scene I fully expect to find inside that apartment is an impossibility. I can't do it. It would be bad enough to have to face Hunter after that disaster. I don't see him, but he could still be up there with most or all of the guys, and a goodly number of women, judging from all the giggling I just heard. Well, some of the giggling may have been Rhys, but not all of it.

I lie back down in the reclined driver's seat and resolve to tough it out. I just have to make it through until morning, then I can figure something else out, even if I have to go with an apartment in a less safe area of town that has immediate availability.

I shape my pillow to try to make that a little more comfortable prospect. But there's only so much a pillow can do when you're sleeping in a cold car while your best friend parties with a bunch of groupies in the only other place you had to go. I refuse to even consider waking up Kara and Maire for this. That would be mortifying. Well, even more mortifying.

An hour later, my teeth are chattering, my legs are stiff and my arms have fallen asleep, though the rest of me refuses to.

I'm out of determination and I'm out of options.

With a sigh, I grab the car keys, re-lock the car and head back up to the apartment. Surely I can get in and out and snag my blanket without making a fuss. Heck — the guys are drunk enough that they may not even notice me.

It seems like I'm in luck. Alex's bedroom door is shut, and Megan is probably in there with him. One down.

Rhys is in the kitchen, a girl sitting on the kitchen counter in front of him. I'm not sure what kind of cuisine that is, but he's clearly very hungry. Two down.

Declan is on the sofa, one girl on each side of him, with the brunette facedown in his lap and the blonde pulling his head down to her bare breasts, where he seems quite happy. Three.

No sign of David. Four. And no sign of Hunter. Five. Maybe they didn't come back here after all. A sigh of relief. I may have gotten off easy. (Pun not only unintended but vastly, painfully inappropriate.)

None of these three seem to have noticed that I'm here, so I quietly cross the living room to the bedroom where I left the blanket that now seems vastly more important to my survival than it did a few hours ago.

I turn the doorknob quietly so as to avoid alerting Declan and Rhys to my presence. I push the door open quietly, keeping my eye on Declan and his... friends... So far, so good. Just need to grab the blanket and get back out to the ca—

Well, I've managed to do it twice in one night. Walked in on Hunter having sex with another woman. This time, it's a girl with purple-streaked straight black hair. No mistaking her for the curly-haired brunette from earlier tonight.

He's mixed it up with positions, too, because this girl is currently straddling him, gyrating sinuously, his hands on her hips. I close my eyes in the vague hope that when I open them, this will turn out to be even less real than my visions of our past.

Nope. Still there. Still looking pretty concrete, and...

"Ooh... yeah. Right there, Hunter. Keep doing that... Oh, god! Yeah!"

Can't scrub that out of my brain if I tried.

At this point, it occurs to me that they're splayed across the middle of Hunter's bed — the last place I saw my blanket.

Someone's fucked here, and at least one of those people is me. And not in a good way...

I purse my lips together in disbelief at how horribly wrong today has gone, from Megan's tirade to the potential apartment being a bust to missing the entire gig only to walk in on Hunter fucking someone — not once, but twice.

And the second time, on top of my blanket...

The universe is telling me to walk away. Now. Doesn't matter that I have no place to go. And also no blanket.

I've got to get out of here now. Before this day gets any worse.

"Welcome home!" Rhys shouts jubilantly at me from the middle of the living room.

I was clearly a horrible person in a past life. Probably one not spent living with Hunter on an Irish sheep farm...

Declan's now staring at me from the couch. So is his blonde. And the brunette.

"Who's that, Reesie?" Rhys' dinner inquires. "Hey — did your mama name you after the candy bar? Because you're sweet and nutty, too!"

Well, at least Megan isn't out here to witness this.

"Oh. My. God! Did you just walk in on Hunter having sex with someone who's not you for the second time today?"

That's coming from the bathroom doorway. Apparently, Megan *does* go with Alex when he goes to the bathroom.

I haven't brought myself to turn around and see if Hunter and his little cowgirl are staring at me, too. But I have to assume they are. I reach back and pull the door closed behind me.

"Brighid! God-fucking-dammit!"

"Thanks, Rhys. I'll be going now. Nice to meet you all. Sort of. As you were."

Once again, I prove that I *can* outrun Hunter. I just have to start the race while he's having sex.

I'm in my car with the engine started and the driver's seat back in place when I spot a shirtless and barefoot Hunter reaching the landing outside the apartment door. He hears the car and stops to look out over the railing.

I press my fingers to my lips and then offer them to him in salute. And I put the car in gear and drive off.

CHAPTER 41

ONCE BITTEN TWICE SHY

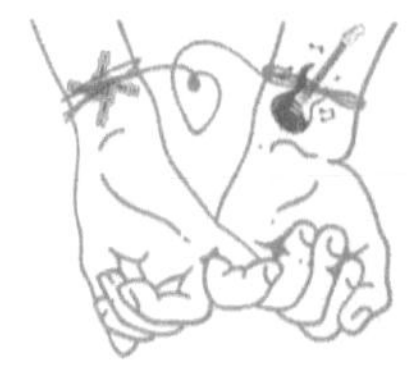

Brighid
The next morning

"Brighid, honey! Are you OK?"

I recognize the voice as Kara's, but why is she waking me up?

I get my eyes open and realize I'm sleeping on the floor in the loft storage room at the shop, the floor cushioned only by pile of my own work, with a sample quilt from the display downstairs laid over me.

Oh.

Yeah. No blanket. Because Hunter was fucking some purple-haired girl on top of it.

Right...

"Hi, Kara. Sorry about this. I had a little dwelling-unit issue last night. I didn't really have anywhere else to go. I'll pay for the quilt," I offer.

"What on earth are you talking about, Brighid? Of course you don't have to pay for the quilt. And if you need a place to stay, you're welcome to stay here, or come stay with me and Maire if you prefer. We're not going to leave you homeless or sleeping in your car."

"Yeah. I tried that. Didn't like it. It was cold. Needed a blanket."

"And you didn't have one, clearly."

"Nope. It was under Hunter, and his purple cowgirl."

"I'm not even going to ask."

"Wise choice. Nothing good can come of that."

"I'm going to go get you a nice cup of tea, and I'm going to have Maire drop off some clean towels, toiletries, a blanket and an air mattress when she heads to class this morning. You can use the little bathroom up here in the loft to clean up — the shower in there works fine. We left it ready to go in case we needed to clean up from dyeing anything. Do you have a change of clothes?"

"I do. I got everything I needed for a couple days, except towels, shampoo and conditioner... And my—"

"Your blanket. Yes. I see."

An hour later, I'm sitting in the loft on one of the folding chairs from the classroom, eating croissants from the bakery next door and drinking some of Maire's calming tea blend. She's gotten as good with herbal teas as she has with floral papers. I'm a little jealous.

Maire's gone off to class, and Kara has gone downstairs to the shop. I'm not even supposed to be working today, but I'm going to go down after I finish eating and see what I can do to repay Kara for her kindness and understanding.

I can't even face Hunter. I can't even bring myself to call him back. I'm between a rock and a hard place with this — I can't pretend last night didn't disturb me (twice) and neither can I be upset with Hunter. He doesn't owe me anything — not an explanation, not an apology, nothing.

In fact, I really owe *him* an apology. I walked in a room twice last night without knocking, and if it's anyone's fault I got an eyeful of something private — well, semi-private in the one case — then it's mine. I may have been clueless about what I'd find behind those two doors, but it's Hunter's private business, and I can't fault him for anything that he did.

That doesn't mean it wasn't tremendously embarrassing and not a little painful.

So, no — I'm dodging Hunter right now. I haven't even turned my phone on after shutting it off to save the battery last night. I've got to figure some things out before I decide what to say to him.

I hear the shop bells jingle over the door downstairs, then footsteps on the stairs headed up to the loft. As expected, it's

Kara. But rather than grabbing some yarn or crochet hooks, she pulls out another folding chair and sits down beside me.

"I put the lunch sign out a little early," she explains. "I wanted to talk to you before we got much further into the day."

"OK. I really *am* sorry for having crashed here without permission last night. I'll try to find a place today. I've been too picky finding myself a new apartment. I'll just have to lower my standards."

"No rush, dear. In fact, that's what I wanted to talk to you about." She pauses. "You are absolutely welcome to come stay with me and Maire until you find a place where you're safe and comfortable. But I have an alternative suggestion: Stay here."

"What? In the storage room?"

"It used to be a little efficiency apartment, back when the shop first opened. It was actually my apartment during college, when I was working here part-time. My mother liked the idea of having me close at hand, but I wanted some independence. So we compromised, and I moved in here. It's just the one room, but you have nearly everything you'd need, including your spinning wheel and your loom."

"I really appreciate the offer, Kara, but you can't be worrying about disturbing me just to get inventory during the day."

"Oh, I won't be. We'll move the extra stock down to the classroom. It's more convenient down there anyway, and I'm not getting any younger. All this climbing up and down the steps isn't for an old hen like me."

"You're not old!"

"I'm old enough to be your moth— Oh, dear — I'm sorry, Brighid. I wasn't thinking."

"No, it's fine. Mom would have loved that I have someone watching out for me. But this is really above and beyond. Are you sure you want to rearrange things just to give me a place to stay?"

"I do. I like the idea of another generation finding refuge and independence here. Goodness knows Maire won't be using it. She's determined to get out on her own as soon as she graduates, and she wants to run her own paper shop, not take over the yarn shop."

"I'll pay you rent — fair rate."

"Yes, you will," Kara agrees with a laugh. "But rent is cut-rate since you won't have a stove and since you'll lose some privacy to having to come in and out through the shop. But the neighborhood is safe, and you can use the parking spot in the back, so no garage costs.

"You'll want to get a bed and some other furniture. Nothing that big, since it has to go up to the loft. But I'll get a microwave, a toaster oven and a hot plate in here so you can do some basic cooking. The fridge in the classroom is yours to use, too. You'll have to make do in a few other ways, but you've got a shower, and you'll even have some shelves once we move the inventory around. And until you get a bed, you can sleep on the air mattress."

"You've really thought this out, haven't you?"

"It's a no-brainer. Especially since I just cut your commute by fifteen minutes. If you're late getting here because of traffic on the stairs, I may have to fire you, though. So don't be late."

We both laugh. And the weight that so suddenly pressed down on me yesterday lifts. The problems aren't completely gone, but enough of them are that I feel like I can maybe deal with the others pretty soon.

Just not yet.

CHAPTER 42

THREE TIMES A LADY

Hunter
A week later

I can't find Brighid.

Calls go to voicemail, texts unread. I've gone by the shop at least twice a day, but her car isn't in her usual spot out front. It's at the point where I'm wondering if she's left town and gone back to her dad's at the beach. I can't imagine she'd actually do that. It's been a month since their big blowup, and he hasn't called her and she hasn't called him. But where else would she go?

I've had Rhys run me by Maire's house, and Brighid's car isn't there either. I'm on the verge of calling her dad, just to make sure she didn't run all the way back to Delaware.

I'm a dick. I'm owning this one. Declan said I shouldn't be feeling guilty since Brighid and I are just friends and I have every right to sleep with whomever I want.

Actually, what Declan said was, "We're sex symbols now — hot and cold running blowjobs, man! Live it up!"

Yeah.

If I'm a dick, Declan is the king of dick-land.

Fuck it. I'm calling her dad.

"Hello?"

"Mr. Langdon? This is Hunter Graves. Is Ellie there?"

"Hunter. You should know quite well that *Ellen* isn't here. She ran off to live with you, didn't she?"

"She was staying with me temporarily, Mr. Langdon, after you forced her to choose between her faith and the only family she had left."

"Faith? That nonsense of hers isn't faith — it's a fantasy, a phase. She'll outgrow it, and then she's going to find that she made the wrong choice — the wrong choice in leaving and the wrong choice in running to you, with your ridiculous dreams and your hedonistic lifestyle."

I can't really argue with him on that last point. Not after the other night.

"I think you're wrong about her beliefs, Mr. Langdon. She's very devout. If you're going to continue to ridicule her over them, she's never going to come back."

"Then why are you even calling me? She's not here. I won't have her here if she's doing that nonsense. She's thrown her life away on a silly fantasy, and chased another fantasy with you and your so-called ambitions. I warned her you'd drag her down with you and then leave her to suffer the consequences of both of your decisions. The college returned my tuition check and her dorm fees for the fall. Her mail is being returned as undeliverable. She's a college dropout now, and you're the bad influence that's taken her there."

He has no idea how close that arrow lands. It's not the first time someone has blamed me for their kid dropping out...

"She can come back here when she can admit this was all a silly fantasy and agree to follow some kind of reasonable plan for her future, maybe come work at my office doing filing. Until then, she's not welcome here, and you can tell her that. Don't call me again."

But I can't tell Ellie — Brighid — anything, because I can't find her.

She promised me she'd always have my back. But I'm the one who didn't have *her* back first. I let things get out of control and I let her get hurt. Just for a quick screw with a groupie. OK — *two* quick screws with *two* groupies.

At this point, the idea turns my stomach. I can't sleep with Brighid. I won't. But screwing groupies. That's not me, either. I'm going to have to find another way.

But first, I have to find Brighid.

The next day

Screw it. I'm going to have to go the one place I've been avoiding while trying to find Brighid: inside the shop.

Her car hasn't been there once, nor at Maire's, and I have no other ideas, now that I know she's not back in Delaware.

So, I'm going to enter the dragon's den that is the bastion of old ladies, their hooks, their needles and their fabric-string.

"Are you sure about this?" Rhys asks. "I'm not sure I could go in there. My balls might shrivel up and fall off from lack of testosterone."

"No choice, if I want to be sure I've looked everywhere."

"Your funeral, man. Or at least your gonads.'"

The bells over the door ring, and it instantly feels I've got a target on my back. Three older ladies turn to look at me with a gaze that seems slightly hostile. I consider a strategic retreat but I'm too worried at this point to put self-preservation ahead of finding Brighid.

So I move farther inside.

Surreptitiously.

If I pretend like I belong here, maybe they won't attack.

I meander over to a stack of stringy stuff. I fondle it. Is that the right word? It sounds dirty. And now I feel dirty. And judging by the looks on the ladies' faces, I *should* feel dirty.

I make my way over to a rack of magazines. I pick up the one closest to my hand.

"Sweet Baby Layettes for Your Newborn."

I drop it like it's a dirty diaper.

The ladies stare at me with open hostility now.

I gingerly pick up the alarmingly titled booklet and put it back in the rack. They seem to be slightly less hostile after that, but I don't trust it.

I pick up another one and open it to the middle, raising it up to hide my face.

"Spring Afghans in the Country Home."

I'm not sure this is any better. At least this one is big enough to hide behind. String-shop camouflage.

I'm not sure I'll ever have a home where red-and-white heart blankets will be my go-to décor. If I do, please stab me. Through the heart. With one of those long needle things.

I put the big booklet back. Another catches my eye: "Irish Sweater Crochet." I wonder if Brighid would like that. She likes all this Irish stuff now. Maybe I should get it for her, in case she hasn't seen it before... In this shop. Where she's worked for years. Nevermind.

The ladies aren't paying quite as much attention now. Maybe I've managed to blend in enough to avoid being ambushed and ripped limb from limb so that my balls can be used as decorative pompoms and my hair for fringe on a fashionable ladies' sweater-vest.

"Can I help you?"

"Aaagghhh!"

Smooth, Hunter. Really smooth.

My heart is now racing faster than the beat in our latest original song, which Rhys has actually insisted should be even faster. I take a deep breath to try to calm it down.

"May-beee?" I reply to the woman who suddenly materialized behind me. Only my larynx has decided to travel back in time twenty years and produce the same kind of squeaky sound that puberty stuck me with long enough that I remember, painfully well, that this is exactly what it sounded like.

I try again.

"Um. Certainly. Yes, you can," I say. Taking care to pitch my voice lower. It's half successful. I sound like a cross between Barry White and Jon Anderson.

She looks like she's going to laugh, but she quickly stifles it.

"What are you looking for?"

"A girl."

"I think you're in the wrong shop. We sell yarn here."

Now I can see that she's making fun of me. And she's only barely holding it together as she tries to keep a straight face.

"Maybe what he needs is a dress form," one of the other ladies adds helpfully. I can see where this is going.

Rhys was wise to stay outside.

"There are some very nice ribbons just over by the counter. I could help you find one that would go nicely with those green eyes and blonde hair."

Now the other three are about to crack up and laugh openly at my expense.

It occurs to me that I may actually have earned this hazing. I'm in here because I fucked up big-time and hurt Brighid, and these are her people. I'm lucky they haven't beadazzled me where I stand.

Onward and upward.

"I'm looking for my friend Brighid."

"Ah. I see."

"Is she here? She works here. Or she did. I'm not sure at this point."

"She's not working here."

"At all? Ever again?"

"Today."

"Do you know where she is? When is she scheduled to work again?"

"I don't know, Kara — should we give him any information at all? What are your intentions toward our Brighid, young man?"

"Uh... Intentions? I'm just trying to find her. I fu—lly messed up the other day and I need to apologize."

"I'm not sure he's groveled enough yet, Kara."

"Look — I really am sorry. I need to talk to her, make sure she's OK, tell her I'm sorry. Can you tell me where she is? When she might be coming back in?"

"If she's really your friend, you should take better care of her," one of the ladies advises.

"I know that. I messed up. I'm trying to fi—"

"Kara, did that celadon green roving come in ye—"

And there she is. My Brighid. Walking down the steps near the counter.

I give the ladies an exasperated grimace.

I get a round of self-satisfied smiles in return.

"Hunter."

"Bridge — can we talk? Please? In private?"

"I'm not sure I'd trust him to be alone with her without a chaperone. He looks like a cad."

This lady gets a combination of surprised eyes and mirthless grimace from me.

A cad? Did we get transported back to 1940?

"It's fine, Dottie. He's not a cad,"   Brighid explains dispassionately. "He's just a rockstar."

"That's what I said — a cad!"

Brighid is trying very hard not to laugh. I can tell.

"We can go to my apartment and talk, Hunter."

"Your apartment?"

"I had to find someplace to live that didn't come with built-in features including a threesome on the living room sofa, cunnilingus in the kitchen, a bitchy girlfriend in the bathroom, and 'ride 'em cowboy' taking place in the bedroom I sleep in, on top of my blanket, without me actually being involved."

There's a collective gasp from behind me.

I cringe.

"Except as an accidental voyeur, that is."

"Yeah. Sorry about that. I... uh... I washed your blanket. I don't have it with me, since I didn't think you'd be here. But I washed it."

"Come on. You can see my new place."

I wait for her to come down the steps so we can go, but she stays right where she is.

"*Come on*," she repeats, gesturing up toward her.

"Oh! You're living *here*!"

She waits for me, a perfect blend of patience and annoyance. And I ascend the steps to see the new digs my Brighid has found after I chased her out of my apartment, and nearly out of my life.

Chapter 43

Forewarned Is Forearmed

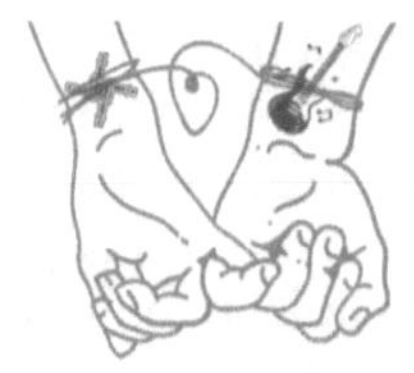

Hunter

I look around Brighid's new digs, and I'm surprised. It's pretty much exactly what she said she wanted: cozy, private, focused on her work and her faith. And it's distinctly Brighid: quirky, honest, warm, soft...

"Have a seat," she invites as she closes the door behind us. She's got a vintage tufted blue velvet chair that looks really comfortable, an old wooden rocking chair and a bench with a green velvet cushion on top that sits next to her spinning wheel. Off to the side, there's a daybed topped with a quilt and the pillow that used to sit next to mine.

"Ladies first."

Not immediately moving to sit, she gives me a small pensive smile.

"Your mom would be proud of you," she says gently.

I'm taken aback. The last thing I would have expected her to bring up today is my mother.

"After last week, I highly doubt that."

"No, Hunter — she would be. You're not perfect," she pauses almost to the point where I think she's done speaking. "But at your core, you are a kind and caring man, a gentleman, and when you figure out what you really want, what will fulfill you, you're going to be an amazing partner."

I honestly don't know what to say. She seems to have thought about this, which tells me she's been thinking about me as much in the last week as I have about her.

On impulse, I walk over to her and grab her into a hug. She seems reticent for a moment but then relaxes into my arms, just like she always has. I stand there holding her for a long time, just absorbing her presence and thankful she's OK. Even if that's no thanks to me.

Breathing in the scent of her has an instant effect on me, bringing peace and a sense of safety and belonging. The one thing I know after this week of looking over at the other side of my bed and finding it uncomfortably empty is that I can't lose her again. I've got to be more careful — both with her and with the parts of my life that affect her.

I lead her over to the daybed and pull her to sit beside me. There's silence between us, and I can tell that, regardless of the fact that she's invited me into her new home, she's not ready to throw out the welcome mat for Hunter Graves, Rockstar(TM). At least not the one I accidentally introduced to her to a week ago.

"I'm really sorry, Bridge. I can't even begin to tell you how sorry. I got caught up in the energy of the gig and just didn't think. I didn't think you'd be there to see it, or I'd never have gone down that path. And once I had, I think I just stopped thinking, period."

"It's none of my business," she says flatly. That sounds familiar.

"No — I need to explain..." I take a deep breath. "I know you've been waiting for the last five years for me to talk to you about what happened after my mom died..."

"No, I haven't. I've been waiting for you to open up to someone — *anyone* — who would be there for you, so you could get all of those emotions out and they wouldn't fester, Hunter. The sadness, the anger, the guilt, the regret, the loss, the self-punishment... The little bit you've talked to me about it has been like a relief valve opened just enough to keep you from exploding. It doesn't clear out what's creating the pressure."

I haven't really thought of it that way, but she's right. I've had her as an emergency release when things got too much to handle, but I haven't really let any of the rest of it out. Instead, I've been focusing on my career, losing myself in the little distractions that come with it, avoiding thinking about the things I never dealt with and never wanted to deal with.

"Bridge — my dad... You know how he was — couldn't restrain himself if there was sex on offer, no matter how bad of an idea it was." She nods. "When I moved back in with him after Mom died, he kept pushing me to be more like him — the big-man-on-campus bullshit with the girls and the sex and the parties.

"You know me — I'd never had that, and I'd never wanted it. I was much more comfortable with being the person my mom saw in me — geeky, creative, passionate about my music..."

"Caring, thoughtful, a gentleman..." she finishes for me. "That's who you are."

"It's who you saw in me, who you still see in me. And it is a big part of who I am. But I struggled that first year back in my dad's house. Why do you think I still spent so much of my time with you after those first couple months of putting space between us? You were the one place I could just be myself.

"But every time I walked in the door of that house, every time I walked past her room, it was like a ton of bricks fell on my back, and my dad was like an elephant stomping on top of the bricks. That stopped the day he found a girl at our front door, asking for me — a girl who wasn't you."

"Oh. I see..."

I'm not sure she does, and I'm trying to think of a way to explain how things went down that doesn't make this even worse.

"You remember the talent show that year?"

"Of course — you played 'Heart-Shaped Box.' You killed it. The entire school was talking about it for weeks. No one knew you could play like that."

"And what happened after the talent show? I mean, like, immediately after."

"You got swarmed, and I got pushed out of the way and couldn't get back near you again, and my mom was waiting, so I waved at you, and you waved back, and I went home. Beyond that, I don't know, since I left and then I hardly saw you for a while."

"That was the first time I had a girl come on to me after I played."

"Oh. OK. Well, shades of the future to come."

"In more ways than one."

She doesn't say anything.

"You remember Margot Marsden?"

"Yeah. Her fake-ass 'I made these all by myself' blinis to go with the caviar you despised. Kind of like her equally fake boobs that her mother had bought her that summer."

"I can confirm they were fake. Firsthand."

"Oh."

Stick with me, Bridge... Please... I beg her silently.

"She cornered me backstage when I went to get my guitar out of the band room. She dragged me into that single-stall bathroom they had back there for the performers, and she stuck her tongue down my throat and her hand down the front of my pants, and that was all she wrote."

"So you lost your virginity to her in a bathroom at school."

"No. She just jerked me off that time."

"And the next one?"

"She showed up at my house the next day. My dad brought her right to my bedroom, gave me a thumbs-up and a condom, and shut the door."

"And then you fucked her."

"I did. And after she left, my dad handed me a beer and told me how proud he was of me."

I'm not proud of myself, in retrospect. It was the beginning of a crazy time in my life, full of parties and beer and naked girls climbing all over me, sometimes two at a time. So, yes, shades of things to come.

"I couldn't think of a way to tell you what had happened. Not with how things had been between us since you told me about..."

"My vision."

"Yeah. All that stuff is really hard to get a handle on, Bridge, and I was not in a place where I could look at you and think about being together like that. The stuff with my dad and my mom was all too fresh. I couldn't get the look on her face when she found out what he'd done that night — I just couldn't get it out of my head. I couldn't look at you and think of being with you like that without remembering that night. And I just couldn't do it."

"I get it. So you caved to artificially-enhanced Margot a couple months later because it made your dad proud and she didn't remind you of what he'd done to your mom, because it was just casual sex."

"Pretty much," I admit. "The attention — it was all very flattering. I felt like the people who had always looked down on me—"

"On *us*."

"—had finally seen me and realized I was cool. I got invited to all the parties we'd been hearing about every Monday morning, and I was surrounded by guys handing me beers and girls sticking their tongues... well... everywhere. It felt good, and I needed to feel good."

"And I didn't make you feel good."

"It's not the same thing, Bridge. Sex was a distraction. A bit of momentary fun that took my mind off things I didn't want to think about. You wanted to talk, to have me unload all of this uncomfortable garbage on you. And I just wasn't ready to deal with any of it."

"I never pushed you to talk about it."

"You didn't. And you did. I couldn't look into your eyes when you were worrying about me and not know exactly what you were thinking."

"Because we're hardwired to each other."

"Yeah. It's not always easy, Bridge. More often than not, you read me like a fucking picture-book. We don't even need words, and you're right there in my head. There's no running away from myself with you. And sometimes I really need to run away."

"And the girls let you do that."

"For a while, yeah."

"I saw them."

"Yeah — I know. I should have locked the door to the dressing room that night, and I shouldn't even have brought anyone home with me. I'm sorry."

"No — I mean, I saw you with the girls back then. I never actually saw Margot, but I saw others, coming in and out of your house. Sometimes more than one."

Oh, no.

"And you never said a word."

"Nope."

"Why not?"

"Wasn't my business. Wasn't my business if you'd lost your virginity."

"Except I know it hurt you to see it."

"It doesn't matter. It wasn't my business that you had three or four different girls coming and going at your house every week. Not any more than it is now that you're fucking groupies up against the wall or taking them home to your bed."

"Except for your blanket."

"Well... yeah. I'm not sure that I actually even want that blanket back."

"Can't say as I blame you. But I *am* really sorry. It was insensitive of me. And, to be honest, it's forced me to rethink what I've been doing."

"How so?"

"I can't keep fucking random groupies. There's too much that can go wrong, and I don't just mean having my best friend walking in while I'm balls-deep some chick and my bare ass is hanging out."

"Yeah. I can't unsee that. Or the other thing. And the 'You didn't finish me off!' thing..."

She shudders.

"I can't promise it won't ever happen again, but I'm going to do better, Bridge. Somehow, I'm going to do better."

CHAPTER 44

GIVE ME ALL YOUR LOVIN'

Hunter

It wasn't the therapy session she still thought I needed. (See — hardwired.) But we'd said some things that had needed to be said for a long while.

I couldn't change all the things about me that caused Brighid pain, but I never really got the impression that she wanted me to change. Just to maybe think sometimes about how what I did affected her.

And I'd already promised myself, and the crochet ladies downstairs, that I'd take better care of her.

And, all in all, it seems like she's come out ahead in this week's drama. She doesn't have to deal with Megan or the guys, and while I've resolved not to bring any more groupies home, at minimum, she definitely won't have to deal with that anymore.

She's also got pretty much everything she wanted in an apartment, and it's cheap, and literally no commute to work. She should be able to save up even faster for that shop of her own that she's been dreaming of for a while now.

And we seem to be back in our comfort zone again, lying down on her bed with her head on my shoulder and my arm around her. Just lying there quietly, not even talking, or feeling like we need to. The upside of that connection.

I take in the room in more detail. There's no stove. But she's got most of a kitchenette; the bathroom, complete with shower;

the three chairs; shelves that hold her possessions, including her music; her loom and spinning wheel; an intricately-woven four-armed cross hanging over the bed; a little wooden chest with a small cast-iron cauldron, a candle and her Brighid statue on top.

My eyes fall on the statue. It's solid, warm, finished in shades of bronze, antique gold and copper that remind me of autumn leaves... or a bonfire on the beach. The goddess' face conveys gravitas, but with a softness that reminds me of my Brighid.

Her long copper hair is dressed in braids on the sides, and loose and long down her back. With a peacefulness that reminds me again of the girl in my arms, she holds a flame naked in one hand, like it's part of her, and in the other another four-armed woven cross that I also see mirrored in the silver pendant that hangs around my Brighid's neck.

Looking into her eyes, it's like staring into a bottomless well, and I feel myself pulled in. There's the sensation of a warm bath, soothing, washing away the muck and the stress and the cares of my life. Old wounds stop hurting quite so much, and there's a sense of blossoms erupting from the frozen ground — full of promise and good things to come.

I pull Brighid closer to me and press a kiss to her forehead.

"Is She talking to you?"

"Who?"

"Herself," she says, nodding at the statue. She smiles a soft Cheshire Cat smile, full of gentle knowing, and I'm reminded of the look on her face before she told me about her vision. And on the face of the goddess in front of me.

"It's a lovely statue," I reply, not answering her question.

My eyes drift over to the clock on her shelf. I groan.

"I've got to go, Bridge. We've got rehearsal tonight, and Rhys has been waiting very patiently for me in the car all this time."

It sounds odd as I say it. Rhys? Patient? And I suddenly realize that he likely took off an hour ago, and I'm going to have to call him to come back and get me if I'm going to make it to rehearsal on time.

I get up from the bed and pull her up with me.

"Can we have dinner tomorrow?" I ask her, feeling like I need to keep her close. I hug her tight to me, just to prove to us both that we're solid and together. Not knowing where she was this week, whether she was OK — it reminded me how precious she is, and I'm determined to do a better job of letting her know how important she is to me. Things are moving fast for aMUSEd, but I refuse to let it put distance between us.

"Sure — 7:30, as usual?"

"I'll be here."

I come back down the steps, expecting the ladies to be waiting for me at the bottom, ready to pounce if they find I've hurt "their Brighid."

They're not there. Instead, they're spaced around a low table, crocheting. (That is the one with the two big needles, right?) I allow myself a sigh of relief.

"Yes, dear. That's right. You've got it," one of the women says, and I'm momentarily happy that my ability to walk down stairs has been found satisfactory.

"Over here? And then around?"

I freeze.

I clearly crossed over to an alternative universe when I went through the threshold of Brighid's new apartment.

Because Rhys is sitting amidst the ladies. Crocheting.

"Rhys?!?!"

"Hey, buddy! What's up?"

"I was going to ask you the same thing."

"I'm *knitting*!" he exclaims gleefully. "Isn't this cool?"

"Sure. All kinds of cool, Rhys."

Yeah. All kinds of... cool...

"Uh — I found Brighid, Rhys. She and I talked. We can go now. We *have* to go now. We've got rehearsal. "

"But I haven't learned how to cast off yet!"

They're all looking at me expectantly now. I'm not sure what response is wise in this circumstance.

"You can come back another time, Rhys. I'll show you myself," the stealthy woman I now know is Brighid's boss says. "You can come back in whenever you like."

"Really? Awesome!" He's like a kid on Christmas morning. Rhys never ceases to amaze me. But this... I did not expect this.

"Thank you for your help, ladies. It is much appreciated," I tell them.

"Just make sure you treat our girl better in the future, eh, rockstar? We'd hate for anything ...unfortunate to happen to that pretty face. What with all the sharp implements lying around here..."

"Or to that lovely derrière..."

"Dottie!"

"Well, it's true!"

"He does have a cute butt."

That's Rhys. I close my eyes and beg whichever divine entity is handy for patience.

"You can ask Brighid! She's seen it naked now!"

Oh. My. God. Gods. Whatever.

I decide to head for the door while I retain even a shred of dignity.

"It's been a joy, ladies! I'll see you again soon!" Rhys announces as he rushes to follow me out to the car.

I say nothing until we're both inside with our seatbelts fastened.

"Really?"

Rhys is still looking like it's December 25 and he just woke up to find a brand new bike under the tree.

"That was awesome! How soon can we come back?"

CHAPTER 45

FIRE IN THE HEAD

Hunter
A month later

I'm lost in the music, ranging through the solo in the song Brighid had told me wasn't living up to its potential. I had gone back to the drawing board, begging the muses for inspiration to return.

Nothing.

We went into the studio with the same nine songs we had in January. By the time we'd gotten all the tracks recorded, Malcolm still wasn't happy with things, even with the extra guitar tracks I laid down.

"Take two weeks. Rethink everything. Decide if these five songs are what you want the people who saw you tour last summer to be buying. If they're not, bring me what you want them thinking of when they go to buy an aMUSEd album. I don't care if that's new arrangements, new songs, whatever.

"This is producer's prerogative — I'm calling in favors with the label and the studio to get you extra time to pull your shit together and to spend two more weeks in the studio. I'm cashing in my favors for you guys. Because I know you've got hits in you. And you're so close right now, I can taste it. So figure out what's going to get you over this last hill and make this EP truly special, and then make it happen."

So, Malcolm — the guy we thought hated the band and all five of us, who still wasn't happy after two months on and off in the studio, who thought we needed a lead guitar player — he was sticking his neck out for us.

And I couldn't be more grateful. Because I know this song — this falling-short-of-its-potential song — is going to be the glue that sticks the rest of the EP together and makes it great. I know it. Brighid had known it.

And that, there, was part of the problem.

She and I had mended fences, buried hatchets, gotten things back to "normal," but she'd lost the brightness and the confidence she'd had before that night things got so messed up.

I knew part of the problem was the humiliation she'd suffered under Megan's acid tongue — tearing her down, rejoicing in her pain, laughing at her expense — as well as being treated so poorly by many of the other women who were around us.

But Megan was gone — bitching all the way about Brighid having designs on Alex and me, on pretty much any male, because as far as Megan was concerned, Brighid didn't deserve to have anyone. So when she told Alex she was done with the whole mess, even after Brighid had moved out, Alex didn't try to stop her.

That wasn't to say he wanted her gone. He seemed pretty torn up about it. Not acting like his usual confident self and our built-in mommy figure in the band. Withdrawn. Kind of like Brighid, actually.

It seemed like Megan's words had struck home with Bridge in ways I couldn't fix, and I felt responsible for that, because in addition to putting Brighid in the position where Megan could treat her badly, I'd been the one who'd created the wounds that Megan's words had set into and festered.

So I did something stupid.

I called Mace. Because it seemed like talking to Mace had spurred something in Brighid last year that helped her gain that confidence and really blossom, and she needed that back. I wasn't sure he'd even answer, since Telltale Signs was now on tour in Australia. But he did answer.

I told him what had happened, and after he finished cursing at me, and the universe, for five minutes straight, he gave me some advice.

"Ask her for her help. Do you have a creative project you can ask her for help with?"

"Wow. Are you psychic, too? Brighid does this thing sometimes..."

"I'm an insightful creature, Hunter. So, you're stuck?"

"A song. One Brighid said in April wasn't living up to its potential. And I tried to strip it back to where it was coming to me easily — like, handed to me — thinking I could get it flowing again. But it hasn't worked."

"You need a spark. Brighid's the spark."

"How so?"

"The girl belongs to a goddess of poetry, Hunter. She's the next best thing to the living embodiment of a muse. Use your brain. But, more importantly, use *her*. Make her tap back into that creative source. She's not weaving, right?"

"I'd ask how you know that, but you've been scary 'insightful' already."

"You're learning. But you've got a long way to go. Get Brighid weaving, or at least spinning. She'll find her way back to herself eventually. It's work she'll have to do herself. You can't do it for her. But in the meantime, kindle that spark in her by letting her do what she's built to do..."

"Weaving. Right."

"No, Hunter. She's built to help you. You lucky fucker, you," he says with some bitterness in his voice. "Treat her like the gift she is, and ask her for her help finding your muse again. If anyone can, it's her. And in the process, maybe Brighid will start finding her way back."

I thanked him for his insight and ended the call, feeling like he was right that I hadn't been using my head in this. It was only then that I realized I'd called her Brighid during the entire conversation and never referred to her as Ellie. Not once. And he knew exactly who I was talking about.

Scary insightful.

I went straight over to the fabric-string shop. Rhys was happy to take me, since he was working on a sweater and wanted some advice from Kara and the crotchety crocheters.

And there's a sentence I never thought I would say...

I found Brighid in her apartment, lying down on her bed, listening to music with her headphones on, just staring at the ceiling.

"Is that our bootleg CD?"

"Uh... no, actually. Clannad. The 'Robin of Sherwood' soundtrack."

"From the old TV show?"

"Yeah. Irish band, Pagan-friendly show. What's not to love?"

"Whoa. I just now realized that. Herne the Hunter..."

"Well-established Celtic god. Not Irish, but still very cool. The Herne character in Sherwood Forest is a priest of Herne."

"Like you're a priestess of Brighid..."

"Yeah," she says with a sigh, looking a little sad. Yeah. There's a problem here.

"I actually need your help."

"What kind of help?"

"Getting back in touch with my muse. That song you said had potential but wasn't there yet? I've got two weeks to finish it and sell the guys on using it."

"Tall order."

"Think you can help?"

"I'm not a songwriter, Hunter."

"No. You're the sworn priestess of a goddess of poetry."

She blinks. Hard. Twice.

"I didn't think you believed in Her."

"You *do*. That's the important part. And you believe in me, which is what I really need right now. And I believe in you, because you're amazing and you're always there when I need you."

She looks torn, slightly pained and blushing all at once.

"I need your help, Bridge. You're the only one who can do it."

"Let me see what I can do," she says.

A half-hour later, I've brought back food from the bakery next door, which she said she'll need soon, but not yet. My guitar is out and tuned, because she's talked before about it putting her in a meditative frame of mind, and I don't think that would hurt.

She's in the shower, preparing for whatever her plan involves. When she comes back out, she's wearing a robe and smelling of flowers and herbs. I like the scent. It smells like Bridge.

She stops in front of her Brighid statue, where she clutches briefly at her pendant. And then she turns and looks at me.

"You comfortable being here for this?"

"What's *this*, exactly?"

"Impromptu ritual. I'm going to see if I can use the spinning wheel to connect with Her poet and fire-of-creativity aspects, maybe bring a little bit of creative spark through for you."

"That would be great," I tell her with a smile, both because she's trying to help me and because she's doing exactly what Mace suggested might help her help herself. "Do you want me to play?"

"Play what you had before the fount dried up. Go from there."

She sits down at her spinning wheel, fibers in hand, in red, green and white.

"Christmas colors?"

She smiles.

"Red, the fire of creativity. White, purity of purpose. Green, abundance, green hills and healing. I usually spin in one color. But that's for weaving and selling. This is something different, and I'm going on instinct. So, we'll have to see what happens."

"Should I start playing?"

"Yes. Let's see what we can do. Together."

I start with the core of the song. The melody and accents that came to me on their own. I play through them as she presses rhythmically on the pedals, beginning to spin the loose fibers into a thin thread — red, white and green, red, white and green, red, white and green... I lose myself in the song, as she loses herself in her work. The sound of the wheel blends with the song, becoming one, just as the colors blend together into one thread.

I lose track of how many times I've played this section through, until I look up and see her, focused and yet somehow free, and there's a glow to her that I haven't seen in months. As I watch her at her work, that glow seems to grow, consuming her in light like a flickering candle flame, and I start to see where I went astray with the song. It needed this warmth, this focus, this spark.

It feeds into me as she feeds the fibers into the wheel, becoming tangible at the touch of my fingers on my guitar, setting the song aright. It all comes together now, feeling like the most wonderful and natural flow of note to note, chord to chord, and I'm singing along to it without thinking the words. They just come to my mouth, as easy as breathing. And I'm alive with it, filled to overflowing and pouring it all into my song.

I notice the sound in the room has changed, not because of the song that's now concrete in my mind and under my fingers, but because the slow, gentle susurration of the spinning wheel has fallen away, leaving the song as the only sound left in the room. I look over at Brighid again, and she's sitting facing me now, a gentle smile on her face and pride gleaming in her eyes as she watches me play.

I bring the song to a close — its natural close, where it feels complete and whole and full of that same glowing energy I saw in Brighid at her spinning. And I set the guitar aside and jump up, giving her the biggest, happiest hug I think I've ever given anyone.

"Thank you so much, Brighid — both of you," I tell her, pressing a kiss to her temple.

"The fire in the head," she murmurs, and her smile lights up her face.

Two weeks later

The guys and I have been working our asses off getting the new song ready for Malcolm to hear. Not only that, but in the process of learning and arranging it, we found some changes we wanted to make to several of the other songs that were on the list for the EP. And the end result...

"Spectacular! Just spectacular!" Malcolm says. "What's this new one called?"

"'Fire in the Head,'" I tell him.

"Cool title. It's got an energy to it — the title and the song. Great work, guys!"

"It's Hunter's song," David points out.

"Well, Hunter's song is going on the EP. Probably the first one we'll push as a single. Now — what else do you have for me?"

By the time we've gone over all the changes to the existing top picks for tracks, Malcolm is a happy man.

"Now, *this* is what I'm talking about, boys. *This* is the EP that gets you your full-album deal, that you're still thrilled with in twenty years. Let's get these recorded and get it off to the label for release."

Brighid

Someone just sent me a twelve-thousand-dollar weaving. Anonymously.

My own weaving.

"Soul of Ireland" was delivered via messenger to me at the shop. And I have no idea who bought it or how they came to send it back to me. The only explanation was in the cryptic note that came with it.

"This artwork has been an inspiration to me these past months, and I now return that inspiration to you, so that you can draw upon it when challenges arise. Never forget the source of your creativity. Dive deep into the fire and search your depths for what gives your life meaning.

"Do not let the barbs of others' words wound you, for they are weak and you are sheathed in the armor of great passion and by Those who believe in you even when your belief in yourself fails.

"At the end of every dark road is a light. Follow the light until you emerge from the darkness, and then be the bright arrow sharing your light with those who walk in their own darkness. It is the blessing of the priest that grants insight. 'Three candles to illume the dark: Truth, Nature, Knowledge.' You possess all three in limitless amounts, if you but will see."

Well. Huh.

I guess I have a fan.

So I take the weaving back up to my apartment and hang it carefully on the wall, to one side of my Brighid's cross, with "Soul of the Hunter" on the other side.

Whoever bought this one, and "Soul of the Deep Sea," somehow knew I had need of it now. And they placed so much value on me that they returned the thing they'd paid twelve thousand dollars to have as their own. I hope I can return it to them someday when I no longer feel the need for it. And I hope they have enough inspiration now to hold them until that time comes.

CHAPTER 46

LOVE'S LIGHT

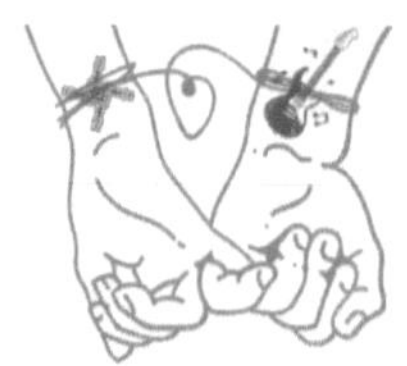

Hunter
Three months later

"Come on, Bridge! You need to come out for New Year's Eve, at least! We've been sold out since the end of September, but I reserved you a ticket, and I can get you another one if you want to bring someone with you instead of being my plus-one."

"I don't think so, Hunter, but thank you for offering."

"Why not?"

She's quiet for a minute.

"I'm just not feeling much like going out these days. I've been working on a bunch of projects, plus work. Case Galleries are still interested in me doing a solo show, but I've got to get enough gallery-quality pieces together before they'll schedule it."

"That sounds great. But you still need to take a break and get out to enjoy yourself sometimes."

"I get plenty of enjoyment out of my weaving, Hunt."

"Brighid..." I look at her, equal parts concerned and exasperated. "It's not good that you're staying home so much these days. I want you to start coming to our shows again. I miss seeing you there." Normally, I'd be invoking my best puppy-dog eyes for a plea like this, because I know she can't resist it, but this means more to me than that.

"I know, Hunter. I'm just not comfortable going out right now. It's nothing personal. I'm thrilled that things have been going so well for you and the band. You've more than earned the success. I'm always going to be your biggest fan…" she flinches at her own words. "I'm just not feeling like it's a good place for me to be these days. And I really do have a lot of things to do. I'd like to start looking for a spot for my own shop within the next year."

"Wow! Thats great news! Have you decided where you want to have it? Are you thinking of buying out Kara? Finding a spot somewhere else in NoVa?"

"I was actually thinking about going back to Mystic Beach…"

"Whoa. I never thought I'd hear you say that."

"Why not? I loved it there. Just because my dad and I aren't speaking anymore doesn't mean I don't want to go back. Just because your life is here doesn't mean I don't want to go back."

Now I'm the one who's silent. We both know that she came here for college because I was already here. We'd been planning on coming here together before I'd decided not to do college at all. I look at her, trying to read her expression, which is carefully neutral. But her eyes are shiny with tears she's trying not to let loose.

"What's going on, Bridge? This is about more than just your work or whether you're comfortable going to gigs after the shit you went through this summer."

She flinches again, and I'm instantly sorry I had to be so blunt, but it needed to be said, even if she won't admit it. A tear trickles out of one of her eyes, and she rushes to wipe it away. I lean over and hug her, pulling her into my chest.

"Talk to me, bestie."

She heaves a small sob before she swallows it back down again.

"I'm losing you, Hunter, and I know it."

"You're not losing me!" I tell her, pulling back to look her square in the eyes. "I'm right here. I'm asking you to come out to our gigs, come do New Year's Eve with me!"

"I just don't belong there, Hunt. It's not my world."

"What does that mean? Not your world? You're my friend. Of course you belong there."

She frowns.

"I've seen what it's like backstage, Hunt. It's not a place I fit in. I'm not comfortable there. I don't feel like I'm welcome there, let alone wanted."

"Why would you say that? I want you there! You're welcome to be there."

"I see how the other guys look at me. I'm an annoyance. A hanger-on. In the way. Ruiner of the good time, especially when that means they're restraining themselves around the groupies just for my benefit. And the girls are *worse*, all those girls hanging out in the hallways, the dressing rooms, the hospitality rooms... It's like being in high school all over again, shunted aside after the talent show, and walking down the halls with people talking about me, making jokes, only now the girls are overtly there to compete to sleep with you all, and they really don't like me being there, no matter why I'm there or who I am to you."

I hadn't even thought of it that way, but she's right. It's the scrum that is the high-school hallway, but after the talent show, when the guys wanted to hang out with me and the girls wanted to make me their boyfriend, and Ellie — Brighid — was, at best, left behind.

"I'm sorry it's been like that for you. I hadn't fully realized, hadn't realized at all how it would remind you of unpleasant times in the past. I wish I had an answer for you. I do think you're wrong about the guys. I haven't had any of them complain about you being around. I mean, Dave wasn't thrilled at being walked in on by someone he knows. And Declan... well, Declan's a dick to everyone. You know that. You can't pay him any attention. Rhys *loves* you, even if he's a little more interested in your sex life than he should be."

She blushes.

"And Alex, he's actually kind of fond of you."

"Even after Megan dumped him over me..."

"He's better off without her, and we both know it. Ten years from now, he'll be thanking you for giving her an excuse to get out of his life."

She chuckles. "She was horrible, wasn't she?"

"The worst," I confirm. "You're not losing me, Bridge. I'm still here."

"But you won't be."

"I'm not going anywhere. I already told you that. You need to believe me, trust me."

"I do trust you, Hunter, but you've forgotten one thing: You're going on tour for two months. You're going to be gone for a long time. Not just a few weeks with a stop back here in the middle. And I'm going to have to get used to that, because this isn't going to be your last tour, not by a long shot. And that's a good thing!" she assures me with a smile. "I always knew you were going to be a star. I just don't think I fully realized what that was going to mean for me, for us."

And I don't have an answer for that, because she's right. I don't have a wife or kids that I'm leaving behind to go on tour, so it hadn't occurred to me that my being gone for two months next year would be impacting anyone. What would it be like for her when I was on tour for five months, or eight months? Why should she keep building a life here if she wanted to be back at the beach, when I wasn't going to be here most of the time anyway?

"I'm not going to let touring get between us, Bridge. We'll talk on the phone, email, text, just like we do now. We don't have to be in the same room, or even the same state, to stay close."

"I know it sounds silly, Hunter. But I can already feel the space growing between us, and it makes me sad. I miss 'us time.' I miss hanging out and falling asleep together and eating together and watching movies together. Those are things we're already doing less of, and you're not even on tour."

I sigh.

"We Are aMUSEd," our EP, and "Fire in the Head," our first single, have been a huge success since they were released in October. The CDs we have for sale at our gigs are usually gone before beginning of the second set, and we're getting some traction on the online sales charts for digital downloads. Our gigs are packed, every time. If there are tickets, they're sold out soon after going on sale. If it's open-admission, the venue is packed to capacity well before we're scheduled to start our first set.

We could be gigging five or six days a week and probably still pack the house at the local venues we've been playing. And we've already warned the fans that they're going to have to be patient for a little while, get used to seeing us a little less often, because we'll be going on tour in March and April. We're on the cusp of breaking out on a national level. We're hoping this second opening stint for Telltale Signs will put us over the top, maybe with a full album deal and headlining our own tour.

Our own tour. As headliners. We could easily be gone four to six months, at minimum. We'd be gone as often as we're home. And is it really home if you spend more time away than you do there? I love touring. I love doing a live show in front of a huge crowd. I love going places and meeting new people. And that's going to be my life going forward. And Brighid won't be there with me.

Now *I'm* the one who's sad. I pull her in close again.

"I'm not going to let it happen, Bridge. I'm going to make time. I'm going to make it a priority for us to stay in touch. I'll come visit whenever I can, whether you're in Virginia or in Delaware. I promise."

She gives me a wan smile.

"Thanks for wanting to do that," she says. And I know the subtext of that statement is that, no matter how much I want to do it, it won't happen. She's given up hope of us staying close friends, maybe even friends at all. I'm going to have to prove her wrong.

Brighid
Three months later

"Yes, Ms. Case — Sheila," I correct myself. I'm so use to thinking of everyone of a professional age as being an "adult" and myself as still a college kid. "I can have at least eight pieces ready by the end of May. Maybe nine or more. I have six that are essentially complete. And I can certainly do at least two more by then."

"Excellent, Ellie— sorry, Brighid. I like the name change, by the way. It's distinctive, and people will have no problem remembering who this hot new textile artist is. We'll play it up in the PR for the show and try to bring in some of our international clients with deep pockets. Hopefully, we'll be able to bring in the same kinds of prices that you got for the two pieces from the showcase a year ago."

"Do you think that's likely? I know the bids that night were much higher than usual for that show, let alone textile works."

"I think there's a very good chance, Brighid, or we wouldn't be planning a solo show for your work. Even if they don't bring in that twenty-thousand-dollar price tag, I think we can very reasonably expect even some of your smaller works should net in the thousands of dollars.

"Beyond that, it's all what the market will bear. And you seem to have at least one well-heeled collector who is very fond of your work. That will all but guarantee a solid price point, especially when other collectors see how much people are willing to pay for your work. And I can tell you right now that I expect to buy at least one or two of your pieces for the gallery's permanent collection."

"That's wonderful, Sheila. I hope you'll find something you really like amongst these pieces."

"I'm sure I will. You'll be attending the opening and assisting with the promotion, correct? We can't have you being a shrinking violet if we're going to get the maximum exposure and prices for the show."

I hesitate. I'm not fond of being the center of attention. One-on-one, I'm good. But even at the showcase, all that attention, all the drama of the auction... I was feeling faint. If someone hadn't gotten me out of there, I'm not sure I wouldn't have fainted. And it's only gotten worse since...

"Brighid?"

"Oh — I'm sorry, Sheila. I had a thought about one of the new pieces. I was just making note of it so I don't forget." Yeah. That's a lie. Hopefully, a good one. "Yes, certainly, I'll be there for the opening. I can make some of the completed pieces available for promotional photography in the next month or so if you need the lead time. And if you want me to do an interview or something, I can do that. Just let me know."

"Great. I'll be in touch over the next couple months so we can keep this all on track for our June show slot. Are you interested in doing another one later in the year or next year?"

"Well, Sheila — I'm giving some thought to relocating."

"Oh? To where?"

"Back to Delaware, where I grew up."

"Oh, well, that's no problem. You're still in doable driving distance if we need to meet about future shows, and you can drop off individual pieces to sell between shows."

"You'd want individual pieces?"

"Oh, certainly. Once we do your solo show, the gallery will be associated with your work. It helps us build our clientèle if we continue to have pieces by our more in-demand artists. If they come in to see your latest work, they may find something else they like, too. Anything you'd like us to show for you, we'd be glad to do it. Would you mind if I asked why you're thinking of moving?"

"Honestly, I miss the beach. And there's a lot less holding me here than had been. It feels like it's time to start something new, so I'm looking at opening my own shop — just yarn, handmade paper and such, so no gallery competition for you, if you want to keep displaying and selling my work."

"That sounds delightful. What a great way to invest your earnings so far! Just make sure you don't give up your art. Running a business is challenging, I can tell you firsthand. But once you get things up and running, make sure you find that life balance. That's what will keep you enjoying your life even when challenges arise."

"When challenges arise..." Where had I heard that recently? I scan the room, trying to job my memory, and when my eyes land on "Soul of Ireland," I remember — that note the buyer had included when they'd sent it back.

"Thanks for the advice, Sheila. I'll be in touch as things move forward."

I hang up and go to the shelf where my little keepsakes box sits. I pull that note from inside and look at it again.

"I now return that inspiration to you, so that you can draw upon it when challenges arise. Never forget the source of your creativity. Dive deep into the fire and search your depths for what gives your life meaning."

I'd been drawing upon that inspiration for months now. The result was six new weavings that had been generated with the same kind of spiritual underpinnings as the three that had been so successful in the showcase.

Well, seven new pieces, actually. I'd created one inspired by Herself, called "Soul of Inspiration," which included the yarn I'd spun with Hunter, when he pulled "Fire in the Head" from the ethers, where it had been stuck. This piece was never intended to be sold, nor even shown to anyone. It has been a touchstone for me through troubled times. Even when I'm not feeling comfortable in my own skin, I draw strength and comfort from it, and from my weaving and spinning.

"Soul of Inspiration" is now displayed alongside my other touchstone, "Soul of the Hunter," which I've been looking to so often these days, while Hunter is gone, and knowing that the days Hunter and I have together are numbered, drifting away like grains of sand in an hourglass.

Now, stacked carefully on my shelves are "Soul of the Tide," "Soul of the Dragon," "Soul of the Bright Arrow," "Soul of Sound," "Soul Food" and "Soul of the Siren." All complete in their basic construction, still awaiting little touches like the stones, shells and metal bits I'm using as accents, much as I had with the prior three.

And then, all that remained was a blessing, for each of the weavings I had created, from "Soul of Ireland" onward, had been blessed, with blessings requested from Herself and my personal blessings as Her priestess. Based on how they'd been received, and the deep meaning they still held for me, and for others, it very much seemed that blessing had been successful. Now, six more works were nearly ready to go out into the world.

As, frankly, am I. And I'm very much hoping that, come June's show, I can take that big step into my future.

CHAPTER 47

ON TOP OF THE WORLD

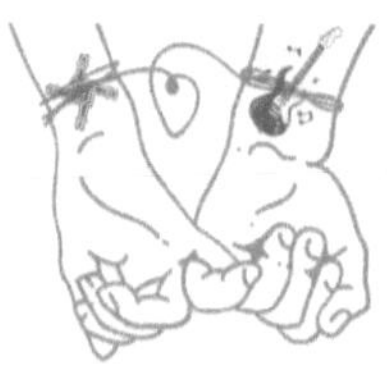

Hunter
Three months later

Six years ago, I was living with the Langdons, still mourning the loss of my mother and unsure when, if ever, I'd pick up my guitar again. Today, I am sitting in a New York City office building, a member of a band signed to a three-album deal with Siren's Song Records.

In the last six years, I've left home; slept on floors, cots and couches; worked two and three jobs, sixty, eighty hours a week; dragged equipment in and out of dozens of venues; slept on a tour bus for months, twice; spent countless hours writing, rehearsing and recording original songs; and entertained tens of thousands of people, both those there to see us and those brought along for the ride.

And it's all led me here. My four band brothers and I are about to be national recording and touring artists. And get a big enough chunk of change to not have to worry about rent or other basics for years to come.

David and Declans' parents brought in a family friend to act as our lawyer. He's done this kind of work before and has said everything in the contract is pretty standard, even a little generous. We're getting an above-average advance, good royalty terms, the rights to the bulk of tour and merchandise profits, and keeping our publishing rights (which I insisted on), and on our end, all we have to do is produce three albums over the next seven years and tour in support of them, including making music videos and doing other promotional work.

It's a done deal.

The label has recommended we hire a manager, because we're going to be too busy for Declan and Alex to handle everything that needs to be handled. We've got a meeting set up this afternoon with a guy Mace Mason recommended we talk to.

We've got PR people at the label, and we've requested to keep Malcolm on as our producer for at least the first of the three albums. They're approaching him with that offer, and we're hoping he'll sign on. He stuck his neck out for us, and it paid off handsomely. We'd not only like to reward him, we want to keep that kind of success moving forward.

Next comes the hard work — writing and recording and touring, and then doing it all over again, and again. But David, Declan and I have songs banked to start with, and Alex says he's got one in the works, too. Rhys said he has one that's ready to record, but it's all drums. Literally. He wants a six-minute drum solo. On an album. We said we'd talk to Malcolm about it.

I've got only one person I want to share this news with. The record deal. Not Rhys' idea on revolutionizing the hard-rock genre with six-minute drum solos.

"Bridge! You're never going to guess where I am!"

"Hi, Hunter — can I call you back? I'm kind of in the middle of something here."

"Sure — but I just need to tell you: We got our record deal. Three albums and tours and everything. Siren's Song Records out of NYC. We're up here right now and just signed the paperwork!"

"Oh, wow, Hunter! That's awesome! I'm really happy for you! And proud! So proud. I want to hear all about it. I just can't..." her volume level drops, like she's put her hand over the phone. "I'll be right there, Sheila. ... Yes. ... Yes, I did do the interview prep. I'll be right there. ... Thanks! —Sorry, Hunter. Like I said, I'm in the middle of something. Tell me all about the deal the next time we talk, OK?"

"What's going on, Bridge? Did you have a job interview? Why..."

"Television interview, Hunter. Joy," she says with sarcasm. "I've got an opening tonight... in like... five hours? Sorry — I really have to go. They're turning this around for the afternoon news. Again, congrats! Love you!"

Opening? TV interview? Brighid on the news?

Well, (a) she's going to hate being on TV. She'll probably never watch the interview herself anyway. And (b) how is she having an opening, with TV PR, and I knew nothing about this?

I run back into the conference room.

"Guys — I need to get home. Like now."

"What? I don't think so, man," Declan declares. "We've got that meeting with Billy Neal in two hours. And we're going out tonight to celebrate! Party-time in NYC, with a hot-off-the-printer recording contract and all the girls the VIP section can handle! The label's already set it up for us!"

"Why do you need to get home, Hunt?" Alex asks. "What's so urgent?"

"Brighid has an art opening tonight, at like five. A big-deal one, with TV coverage and everything. I didn't know, but I can't miss it!"

"No can do, man," David says. "Even if you got on the next flight out to Dulles that you could get through security and make before takeoff, you'd be lucky to get there and in a cab by six. And I don't know where the opening is, but it's unlikely to be within a half-hour of Dulles."

I sink down in my chair, deflated.

"You can't miss this meeting, Hunt," Declan says. "We've got to be in full agreement if we decide to hire this guy. We're going to be relying on him for damn near everything for a long time to come. I don't want to have you deciding you hate the guy a month in when we've got a five year-contract with him."

"You just can't do it, Hunter. Call her," Alex suggests. "Tell her you've got a meeting you can't get out of, and you can't make it back in time. Congratulate her. Congratulate her for us. Catch up with her when you get back. Go see the exhibit with her. She'll understand. She never stays mad at you — you've said it yourself."

"Guys, this isn't about trying not to make her mad. This is about being there for her like she deserves, like she's been there for me, for us, every step of the way. Getting through the bad stuff and celebrating the good stuff. And she's had so much bad stuff in this last year. We need to celebrate this — *I* need to celebrate this with her. When it's happening, not a day or a week or a month later."

"Reality of rockstar life, man," David says. "You're going to have times you can't be where you want to be, even for the people you love. Telephone calls and emails and rainchecks are going to be the rule going forward, for a lot of things. It's the big downside to what we've chosen to do with our lives."

"That and paparazzi and gossip rags," Rhys adds.

"We're a long way off from paparazzi and tabloids, Rhys," Alex tells him.

"I'm kind of looking forward to having cameras following me around, actually," Declan puts in. The rest of us roll our eyes but say nothing.

"Send her some flowers. They can get them there in a couple hours," Alex suggests. "Ask her for a raincheck for next week. Take her out to dinner. You can afford it now."

"You can afford to give her a llama now, if you want," Rhys points out.

"A llama? Why would I give her a llama?"

"They use them to make yarn, don't they?"

"I think that's usually alpacas. Llamas are kind of mean. They spit. Besides which, where would she put it? She lives in an apartment above the shop!"

"So, buy her an apartment with a yard."

"How much money do you think we got in our advance, Rhys?" Alex asks.

"A fuck-ton."

"Not so much. Don't go planning on buying apartments and llamas and private jets," Alex explains. "You can't afford it."

"Yet," Declan adds with a big smile.

"How about KITT?"

"You want a new kit? You can afford that," I agree.

"No, K-I-T-T. KITT. The Knight Industries Two Thousand."

"What the fuck is that, Rhys? Some kind of robot?" Declan asks.

"It's a car, man. The coolest, most amazing, talking car ever. Didn't you watch 'Knight Rider' when you were little?"

"I think Mom might have watched it when *she* was little," David says.

"So, you're wanting a 1980s-era sports car. A talking sports car. More than a decade into the two-thousands... Gotcha. Yes, you can probably afford to buy the car. The talking part, probably not."

"Awww, man!" Rhys whines.

"Make it up to her when you get back, Hunter," Alex says. "Take her out to a nice restaurant. It'll be fine. She loves you."

I hope so. Because I'm afraid this is only going to cement for her that I won't be there for her now that my career is really taking off.

CHAPTER 48

WE ARE FAMILY

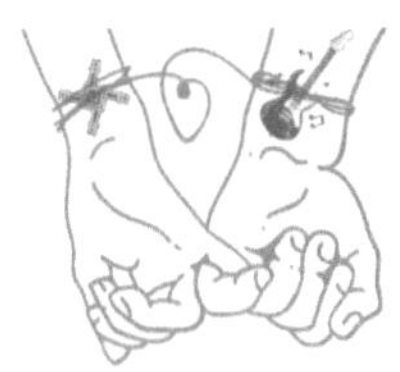

Brighid
The next day

This is it.

With the opening-night sales of my work at Case Galleries, I have enough money to get my shop up and running in Mystic Beach. With enough left over to maybe afford the downpayment on a house. The gallery is holding the payments for the weavings until the scheduled close of the show in a month. So, I've got a month to decide for sure if I want to go back to Mystic Beach and start my life there.

I'm considering it a new start, not a return, because it's Brighid Weaver — fiber artist and entrepreneur, with certificates in holistic healing and clinical herbalism — who's going to Mystic Beach, not the girl who grew up there.

I've contacted Lindsey to see if she's interested in selling her shop. She's reached retirement age, and it would be an easy transition. If she's willing, I could take over ownership this summer and transition to the new name, product range and look over the fall and winter, when things are quieter.

Every single one of the weavings in the show sold last night. Case Galleries purchased the last two I made, "Soul of Summer" and "Soul of Autumn." The prior six all had anonymous buyers. Sheila said her finance guy had handled the vetting, as per usual, and she had no idea if it was the same buyer for all six or if there was more than one, let alone whether it was the same buyer who'd bought "Soul of Ireland" (and returned it to me) and "Soul of the Deep Sea." She respected her clients' privacy and would never ask, she said.

I respected her ethics and didn't inquire further, as much as the mystery was nagging at me. I really did want to return "Soul of Ireland" to its buyer. I felt duty-bound to do it. And one day I would, I promised myself.

Hunter sent me flowers. A beautiful arrangement of white roses that now sits upstairs, next to my Brighid statue. It was sweet of him. I think it's the first time anyone has ever sent me flowers. I'm not sure why there was a llama on the card, but I suspect Rhys was involved.

I actually don't know where Hunter is right now, so I can't return the favor to congratulate him and the guys on their even larger-scale success. Though I'd probably send them a basket full of meat, cheese and chocolate instead. I suspect they'd prefer that.

And now the next thing on my list...

"Kara, do you have a minute to talk?"

"Uh-oh. That's a phrase that never starts a conversation the person wants to have."

"Yeah. I don't know how you're going to feel about it, but I've got some news. I just spoke with Sheila at the gallery. She said all of the weavings in the show were sold. They're paid for, pending the close of the exhibit."

"And you have enough money for your own shop..."

I nod grimly.

"That's amazing news! I'm so happy for you!"

"You are? I mean, of course you are. I just don't like leaving you with one less employee and no one to take over the shop someday."

"Well, Maire could yet change her mind," she hedges. "But I didn't really expect you'd be here forever. You've got something pulling you on to new adventures, and I think now is the time. But I want you to know if you ever need anything, you can call, email, whatever. You're family, and we won't be strangers, even with a little distance between us."

She gives me a quick hug, but notes what I suspect is a brittle smile.

"What's wrong, Brighid? You seem troubled."

"Hunter's band signed a three-album record deal yesterday. Three albums, three tours, over seven years."

"Well, they've worked very hard for it, with no small amount of help from you, and they're a talented bunch of boys. No one is more deserving of that success. But I know that's difficult for you, knowing he'll be gone so much."

"Yeah. I've felt like this separation was coming. I always knew it would come one day. I am just having a harder time dealing with the loss than I expected to."

"Well, I just said it — you're family, and a little distance won't change that. You and he — you're both the closest thing the other has to a real family. You've been there for each other through some very challenging times, and the bond you share can't easily be broken."

"There's that word again, 'challenging.' It keeps coming up lately."

"That's usually meaningful, especially when you notice it."

"Yeah. I don't know what it's telling me, though. Is there a challenge coming? Have I had my challenge already and I should learn from it?"

"Have you tried a tarot reading to get some guidance?"

"I haven't. It been so busy. I haven't read any oracles in a long time."

"You should, then. I could do a reading for you, but when I've seen you do them, you did a better job than I usually do. You have tremendously keen insight, bordering on claircognizence. Maybe you should add tarot to your services at the shop," she suggests. "You've done your reiki training and certification, and now your herbal course. You can round it out with tarot readings. Maybe some spiritual counseling? Put that priestess aspect of yourself to work, even if it's not as clergy for a group."

"It's something to consider. Thanks. I wish I was as good at reading for myself as you seem to think I am at reading for others."

"You're too close. Too invested. It's entirely natural that it's more of a challenge. But you're also highly intuitive, and you can put that to work for yourself, if you can find the frame of mind to do so with clarity. Meanwhile, what are your plans as things stand now. How soon are you leaving?"

"It's still up in the air. I haven't even decided for sure. I know I have the money. But I need to decide if I really want to go back to Mystic Beach, and before I do that, I need to know if Lindsey is ready to retire. She's got the perfect spot, established clientèle for the usual yarn-shop stuff and a full inventory. Some additions will make it my own. I haven't talked to her in a while, but she had been talking about retiring. I think she might take me up on the offer."

"Sounds like kismet!"

"It feels that way, too. I kind of feel like life is telling me it's time to move on, to establish myself on my own terms."

"You have the talents and now the resources to do that. It's up to you to decide how you want to do that, what you want in your life."

"I know what I want. I also know I can't have all of what I want. So now I need to figure out how to make the rest of it happen."

"Why do you think you can't have all of what you want?"

I sigh, unable to put it into words.

"Brighid, you need to keep in mind that the Silver Wheel does not reveal our fate all at once. Nor do all of the things we're fated to have come on a single, simple timetable. Sometimes, fate steps in to lead us in the direction we're meant to go, gathering bits and pieces of our future selves along the way. And it's often not until that last piece is in our hands that it all falls into place. Patience is a virtue. But it's also a necessary component of a full and happy life. I know you've already had to exercise great patience, but you need to learn to be patient with yourself more than anyone. And you need to understand that there is no specific point at which one has been sufficiently patient. Sometimes it's a moment, and sometimes it's a lifetime. The things coming to you will come in their own time, never on a schedule you set. And there is a reason for that."

"What reason?"

"No — it's not that there's one reason why things don't arrive in your life when you want them. It's that there's always a reason why a given thing doesn't. Sometimes it's a little thing, and sometimes it's because if it arrived any earlier, it wouldn't be at all the thing it is supposed to be. So, my dear: Patience."

"There's a reason you're high priestess. You just demonstrated it."

"And you've demonstrated much of the same, Brighid. I think you'll find that, wherever you end up, people will come to you for guidance. And they will be lucky you are there to give it."

Kara gives me a hug, and I feel like one of those little pieces along the road has just fallen into place. Maybe the others will, too.

Hunter

"You are on the cusp of a long and prosperous career. The question is whether you have a roadmap to get yourselves there or whether you're going to hire a guide. How are your map-reading skills?" Billy Neal asks us.

"What's a map?" Rhys asks him.

Alex smacks him on the back of the head.

"Ignore him. He knows what a map is, even if he needs a GPS to find common sense."

"I can already see the dynamics you all have in the band..."

I raise an eyebrow.

"Rhys is the annoying but cute little brother..."

"I'm actually the second oldest, even in dog years."

"My point stands. Alex is the mom — don't take offense, it's a managing-the-kids function that includes seeing to the practical matters with a degree of care."

"No offense taken. It's not the first time it's been said."

"Declan is the cranky dad, who's convinced nothing happens in the family unless he's there to control it."

"Now, I *do* take offense at that."

"My point stands."

Alex and I exchange a grin.

"David's the serious older brother, shut up in his room with his guitar and his books."

"Not untrue," David says.

"And Hunter is the classic middle child: often feeling overlooked, often actually being overlooked, a mediator, an easygoing innovator, good under pressure and forming solid long-term relationships."

"He nailed you, dude," Rhys enthuses. "Except the long-term relationships part. So much pussy, so little time!"

I roll my eyes. But neither Rhys nor Billy are wrong. I have formed solid long-term relationship with these guys, and I've had one with Brighid for most of our lives, even if it's a platonic one. At least I think I still have that... even though I didn't get back to see her like I wanted. We've already stayed overnight to have a longer talk with Billy after coming to a consensus yesterday that we liked him as a potential manager.

"And you're the guy with the map who can tell us how to get where we want to be?"

"I am. As we discussed, I've managed two other bands who were at this stage in their careers when I took them on, though I usually come on board before the record deal is signed... You all have your obligations to Siren's Song over the next seven years, and it's going to require a lot of logistics, PR, coordination with venues and media... You need someone who's going to handle all of that for you so you can focus on the music and performing. Chances are, you're going to also want personal assistants and security at some point, but we've got a ways to go before that.

"And speaking of a ways to go, and roadmaps... Guys, before we even sign a deal with each other, I'm going to tell you something you may not want to hear. But I feel like full disclosure is needed going into a relationship like this."

We all look at each other, concerned about whatever he's going to say.

"I talked to Malcolm Fisher last night after we met. I wanted to get his take on where the band is and where it needs to go for you all to have the kind of success you should have."

"And?" I prompt.

"The good news is I think you'll find he's happy to come on board for your first album, and maybe more."

"And the bad news?"

"He says you need a lead guitar player."

"Oh, come on, man — we already dealt with this when we were recording the EP!" David says, once again stepping up to support me, even though it's out of character for him to express objections to anything. "We took another swing at things and pulled it out just fine in the end. Better than fine — we're here, signed to a three-album deal with two stints opening for Telltale Signs under our belts. If we were lacking anything as substantial as an extra member, we'd never have gotten here."

"I know what happened with the EP recording," Billy replies. "And I have to tell you, you lucked out with Malcolm on your side. I've seen promising bands dropped by labels because they couldn't get it together when they got into the studio. Even an extra day or two can scuttle an album, and a band. Malcolm pulled your bacon out of the fire..."

"Mmmm... bacon..." Rhys intones. Alex visibly restrains himself from enforcing his mom-style discipline.

At precisely that moment one of the label staff comes in with a big gift basket full of food.

"This just arrived for you, care of the label. We normally vet any unexpected deliveries, especially with food, but the card seemed to indicate you knew the sender."

I pluck the card from the basket.

"Congratulations, guys! I knew you'd get here. You've earned it! Enjoy the success. Blessings on your careers going forward. Love, your biggest fan, and your in-house witch, Brighid."

"See, Hunter — I told you she was a witch!" Rhys exclaims. "And Oh. My. God. Bacon jerky! It's fucking food magic! She *is* a witch!"

I drop the card on the table.

"And there's a llama on the card! See — I told you to buy the girl a llama!"

"I should have at least sent her flowers..." I hang my head. I've messed this up so badly.

"You did," Alex says. "'Mom' took care of it for you."

"You did? Really?"

"A big arrangement of white roses. She likes those, right? She had one in her hair that last New Year's Eve..."

"She did. And she does. And I should have been the one who sent them. Thanks, man. You really saved—"

"Your bacon!" Rhys jumps in.

"Have some chocolate. It'll make you feel better," Alex says, tossing a bar of my favorite dark chocolate at me. Brighid even had them include my favorite chocolate. I'm really going to have to make things up to her.

"OK, guys, now that you've got your snack..."

A bottle of water sails past Billy's head, snatched out of the air by Declan in a wordless demonstration of brotherly coordination.

"Now that you've got your snack, let's get back to Malcolm and the assessment he gave me last night...

"I don't say this lightly. This is not a suggestion. This is a warning from your, I hope, soon-to-be manager that I don't think you'll make it past a single album, if that far, without a lead guitar player. Hunter's colossally talented. His songwriting is the other thing that made the EP a success. But you need someone who can add that extra umph to your sound, and your live performance."

"We've already got five members, Billy. Most bands have four, tops," David points out.

"You have a keyboard player, which most bands don't have these days, so you're automatically going to be one member heavier. And, as I know Malcolm said to you, Declan's more useful to you if he's free to roam on stage — no guitar to distract him or the fans. So, that's one more member you need. That takes you to six."

"Telltale Signs works fine as a four-piece, even with Mace spending most of his time behind a guitar," David says. "We should be able to pull this off with five members."

"I'm going to be blunt again, guys. You are not Telltale Signs. Their sound is complete with four members, and Mace is stronger on guitar than Declan is, by all reports."

"I want to take offense to that, but, honestly, I'd rather not have to take over rhythm guitar," Declan admits.

Now we're all silent, thinking about that. If Declan doesn't want to do anything but lead vocals, Malcolm and Billy could have a point.

"And — full disclosure — I also talked to Mace last night. He and Telltale Signs played a huge part in you all getting this deal, from requesting — demanding, really — aMUSEd as fill-in openers to recommending to the label's CEO, Marina Matthews, that she bring you on board and be generous with terms."

Whoa. That's a bombshell... though that word makes me think again of Brighid and that New Year's Eve, which then makes me think about the mysterious red-haired guy she'd been dancing with and/or kissing... Could it have been?

"OK. That's new information," David says. "No one ever told us Telltale Signs had requested us. We got the impression that it was someone at the label who'd spotted us and wanted to give us a try with the short notice."

"It was Mace. I can tell you that for a fact," Billy says. "He saw you all one night in D.C. after you brought Rhys on board and had kept an eye on you ever since. Don't get me wrong — you all are talented enough to have gotten here on your own. I don't want you to think for a minute that you aren't. But this business runs on luck and who you know, and you got lucky enough to get a guy who can make or break a band in your corner from almost Day One."

"Wow." I have no other words. I guess it's a good thing I didn't break down his dressing room door that night he was talking to Brighid... "I guess we owe him some thanks."

"You do, but he won't take it. He'd probably rather you didn't even know. But I think you deserve to, and he deserves the respect for having had the insight to see the potential in you. But that's the key word here — potential. Because Mace is in full agreement with Malcolm. You need a lead guitar player."

"Ugh..." That comes from several of us.

"Well, then I'm going to ask you the same thing I asked Malcolm. Do we start auditioning new members? Hire a session musician to help with the album and then see who we can get for the tour? Put the word out and see who comes knocking on our door?"

"Actually, I may have a solution for you."

"Oh?"

"I know a guy. Actually, Mace recommended him. But I would have done it myself if Mace hadn't thought of it first."

"So, he's good?"

"A true virtuoso."

"And he's not already in a band or working as a solo artist?"

"He's not."

"Then what's the problem? Because I'm sensing there's a problem."

"He hates the spotlight. He won't tour and he doesn't want to be a public face of a band."

"So, what, we use him in the studio and find someone else for touring?"

"No. You're going to persuade him to change his life. For himself and for aMUSEd."

Chapter 49

Battle of Evermore

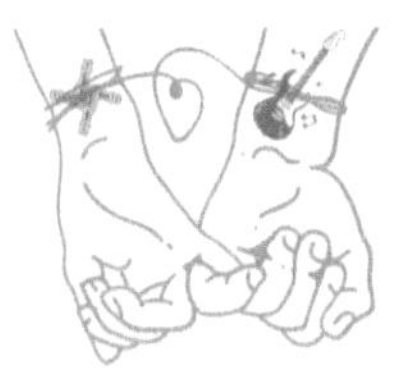

Hunter
Later that night

"**I**f this guy doesn't perform live and he hates the spotlight, what are we doing here?" Declan asks Billy.

"You're going to sit quietly and watch what happens, to start."

Billy's allowed to order Declan around like that now. After today's revelations and Billy's take on them, we've hired him as our manager. Which is only reinforced as a good decision when Declan doesn't argue.

We're seated at a table in a very small New York City bar. Not quite a hole in the wall, but not much more than that. The stage is set for a three-piece band — drums, bass and guitar.

By the time we've gotten our drinks, the bass player and drummer are in place. There's some quiet conversation back and forth between them, and some shrugging. This isn't looking good.

"Give it a minute," Billy urges.

A few minutes later, a guy walks in with a guitar case, sets it down on the stage beside him, opens it up, plugs in and proceeds to blow everyone in the room away. Including the professional guitar player in the room, which would be me.

Even in the dark club, with the stage lights pretty low, he's wearing sunglasses. His hair is long, falling down around his face, disguising him even further from the audience. It's a distinctive reddish-gold, rather than strawberry. If he's aiming to hide behind the sunglasses and hairstyle, he's lost some anonymity with that hair color.

Not that he could avoid notice for a moment when he makes a guitar sing like that. He's playing a custom left-handed Fender Strat — clearly custom, because its dark natural-wood finish is carved and inlaid intricately with Celtic knotwork that I know would have Brighid drooling.

And as he turns in the little bit of light on the stage, I can see that he's decorated to match — ink marking his skin in shades of blue and green from his left wrist to the bottom of the sleeve of his vintage Sinéad O'Connor T-shirt, and probably beyond. I'm going to make a guess and say the guy is Irish, or at least Irish American.

That's as much as I can take in before he launches into a solo that careens across the top of the solid rhythm section, and my jaw drops. This guy is good. Really, really good. As in Billy wasn't exaggerating when he called him a virtuoso. He's got a style that reminds me of Steve Vai, with a bluesy hint of Stevie Ray Vaughn or Kenny Wayne Shepherd.

And he's got that feel of a man who is one with his instrument, like it's part of him and he doesn't even have to think for it to do his will. And his will appears to be for it to pull the guts from every person in the room, because the guitar is crying, screaming, soaring through space and time, and just generally killing us all with the emotion he's pulling from it. Just wow.

The next two songs are just as impressive. In any other room, the bass player and drummer are stars. Here, this guy owns the room. And, frankly, I'm a little frightened. Because he's better than me. Different style, different aesthetic, but inarguably better than me. And my career flashes before my eyes, over before it really started.

After the third song, just as quickly and quietly as he got on stage, he unplugs and packs up, not a word spoken. He's making his way toward the door when Billy intercepts him, pulling him aside and speaking too quietly for me to hear what he says.

The guy shakes his head fervently no and he's headed out again, until Billy puts his hand on his arm and says something. The guy puts a hand up to his face and slides his shades down just enough to peek over at us. Billy speaks while the guy looks at us, and Rhys waves enthusiastically, which makes Alex yank Rhys' hand back down onto the table.

The guy hasn't spoken a word since he walked in the door. Not even to Billy. But whatever Billy's telling him seems to have piqued his interest, and he visibly relents, following an excited Billy back to the table. He grabs a chair from the next table over and turns it around, sitting on it backwards.

"Guys, this is Kieran O'Connor. Before you ask — no relation. He works as a session musician here in town. Kier, these guys are aMUSEd, signed with Siren's Song yesterday, for a three-album deal. That's David, bass; his brother Declan, lead singer; Alex, on keys; Hunter, guitar; and the very enthusiast Rhys, probably predictably, their drummer.

"They need a lead guitar player."

Kieran pulls his sunglasses down and gives us the once-over, and says softly, "I don't play out."

"But you just did!" Rhys interjects.

"I did favor for a mate," Kieran explains, a gentle lilt in his voice confirming that I was right about his origins. "He asked me to show up and play a few songs. I did as he asked. Favor repaid. But if you're looking for a full-time lead guitarist, I'm not your man. I don't like crowds, spotlights, cameras, the press, or anything else that comes part and parcel with touring or being part of a band. And when I say I don't like it, I mean I won't do it. Period."

"Why?" That's Alex, always digging into everyone else's emotions.

Kieran pauses for a moment before finally sliding off his sunglasses, revealing intensely blue-green eyes just as striking as his hair.

"I've seen what it does to people, to their lives, to bands, to the music. And I won't let it happen again... not to me."

Wow. There's a story there.

"Man — I hate to admit it, but we need you," I tell him. "Full props — you're one of the best guitar players I've ever heard. Anybody would be lucky to have you playing on their album. But we need someone who can tour with us, and ideally someone who wants to be part of building this band into what we know it can be."

"Fellas — I'm sittin' here now for one reason and one reason only... the same guy who asked me to come play today had Billy ask me to hear you out. I've got a lot of respect for the man, or I wouldn't have done that much. If you want a session player for your album, I'll consider it. But I pick my projects, and I will not tour."

"We can't work with this asshole," Declan suddenly declares. "He's happy in his nice little box, playing prima donna of the studio. Probably has stage fright or something, can't man up and get up in front of a crowd of more than twelve people."

"Dec..." David starts.

"Declan, is it?" Kieran asks.

"Yeah."

"You're a dick. And I'm not getting into a pissing contest with a guy who measures his worth by how much of an arse he can be to other people. I've got my reasons for what I do. I don't require your approval. I don't have to work another day in my life, so when I choose to spend my time on something, it's because I've decided it's worthwhile. And even if I was starving, you couldn't pay me enough to spend my time with someone whose ego casts such a large shadow over everyone around them."

He slides his shades back on.

"Gents, Dick... it's been a pleasure. Best of luck to you."

And he gets up, picks up his guitar case and walks straight out the door.

"Smooth move, Dick," I tell Declan. "Where are we going to find anyone even vaguely in that guy's league? The point of coming here wasn't to insult him and convince him we're a bunch of assholes. We were supposed to be persuading him to join the band."

"Don't care. Don't want him. Don't need him. I'll play rhythm before I work with that guy."

"You may have to."

"Not so fast, guys — Malcolm, Mace and I have all been very clear that Declan on rhythm isn't a real option," Billy reminds us. "You need a lead guitar player. And, frankly, Kier's the best you could hope to get. You need to try to make this work, for all of you. Because this is your shot at superstardom. And I know that's what you want — especially you, Declan."

Declan frowns deeply but says nothing.

"How do we walk this back?" I ask. "Can we even get him to discuss things again? Maybe ask him to do the studio work and see if he likes what we do well enough to consider joining us?"

"I think that would be a start," Billy says. "I'll give Mace a call and see if he can help mend fences. You're going to owe that man your firstborn if you keep this up, Declan. Don't make me regret signing that contract. Learn to play well with others, like the rest of the adults do, OK?"

"Hey, man, if..."

"Declan — shut it," I say, putting my foot down. "You've dug us a big enough hole. I'm not letting you bury us. If I've got to suck it up and try to get us a second guitar player — one who's better than I am — then you can find enough humility to admit we need him and do whatever you need to do to make this work. Including apologizing to the guy. Because if you can't, this ride could well be over for us."

There's an uncomfortable silence. In the space of a single day, we've gone from being on top of the world to hoping we're not going to end up six feet under.

Later that night

It's 4:30 a.m., and my phone is ringing. This is either an emergency or it's someone whose working hours aren't the norm. Either way, I need to answer it.

"Hello?"

"Get Declan's ass straightened out, Hunter."

"Good morning to you, too, Mace."

"No patience for pleasantries right now, man. I've spent the last two hours trying to get Kieran O'Connor sufficiently drunk on twelve-year Redbreast that he's even willing to entertain being in the same building with Dick-lan, let alone work with him."

"Did it work?"

"I'm not just intuitive. I'm persuasive. What do you think?"

"When and where?"

"Tomorrow — correction, *today*, at 5. Billy knows where the studio is."

"OK. I'll make it happen."

"You'd better, Hunter. You all need him. And he needs you. This needs to happen."

"I'll make it work if I have to gag Declan between takes. And, Mace..."

"Yeah?"

"Thanks."

"I want this collaboration to happen."

"No — I mean for that, and everything. Including Brighid. I never thanked you properly for that suggestion."

"It worked?"

"Kind of. She got me unstuck. The song turned the whole EP around."

"'Fire in the Head'?"

"Yeah. How'd you know?"

"It's Brighid. Of course it was 'Fire in the Head.' She started spinning and weaving again?"

"She has. She just had a solo show that opened the other day. We were up here. I missed it. Actually, I didn't even know about it until hours beforehand."

"That's not good, Hunter."

"I know. She's still not herself, Mace. She's better, but she's not going to gigs, not going out much at all."

"Do you know why?"

"I think I do. Part of it, at least. She said she doesn't feel like she fits in this world, this lifestyle. That she thinks she's losing me."

"Is she?"

"Instinct says, 'Fuck no,' but if I'm being honest, this week was a good example of her stepping up for me and me failing her. I don't like myself for having let it happen."

"Then do better. That's it, Hunter. Do better. She deserves better."

"Mace..."

"What? Spit it out. I need some fucking sleep."

"You called her Brighid before I told you she'd changed her name. She calls you Aedan, not Mace. And sometimes you seem to understand her in ways I don't, and I've known her almost our entire lives. What is going on here? With you two?"

"None of your fucking business, Hunter. She made that very clear. You want the right to know? Earn it. Wake the fuck up, pull your head out of your ass, and treat that girl like the goddess she is. I can't clean up all of your messes for you, especially that one. And if you're not careful, you'll lose what you have before you even realize what that is."

There's a click, and I realize Mace has hung up. It's a punctuation mark on his warning, and I find myself hoping that I'll manage to clean up that mess and not just make it worse.

CHAPTER 50

PUSHIN FORWARD BACK

Hunter
Later that night

"**D**eclan... so help me..."

Declan makes a zipping gesture over his mouth. It's likely the first time he's ever done that in his life. So I'm marginally hopeful.

We walk into the studio, the five of us and Billy, and Kieran O'Connor is on the other side of the glass from the control room, headphones on, playing what looks to be the first few bars of Steve Vai's "For the Love of God" — which isn't Vai's most technically challenging work, but is probably his most beautiful and emotive one. I say "looks to be," because the engineer at the mixing board has his headphones on, too, so there's no sound to be heard. Billy nudges the guy in the shoulder and nods toward Kieran, and the engineer takes off his headphones and cuts the studio monitors on.

"He's just warming up," he explains. "Charlie," he says, shaking hands with Billy. "I'm going to grab a drink. I'll be back in ten or so, if he asks. Which he probably won't."

"Is he that difficult to work with?" I ask.

"Nah, man. He's a prince, except when things aren't working, which is basically never. But he's so focused when he's in there that he'll forget there's anyone else on the planet, let alone in the control room."

Charlie ducks out, and we all just stand, staring at the guy who is going to be joining our band. As soon as we can persuade him that he actually wants to.

And I've got an idea how to do that...

I unpack my beloved PRS, slide the strap over my head and walk straight into the live room, closing the door behind me. If Kieran notices me, he's not showing it. So I plug in to an amp and dive in with the rhythm guitar part of the song. Billy's at the board, tapping a few buttons and sliding a fader or two. He smiles and nods, and I assume that means he's added me to the mix they're hearing over the monitors in the control room.

But after I've been playing about thirty seconds, Kieran's head raises up, and he sees me, acknowledging me only with a nod. He doesn't lose a beat, and instantly focuses back on his guitar. The next thing I know, Rhys is up on the studio kit behind us, and then Dave has plugged in his bass. By the time we're at the fast-soaring midpoint of the song, Alex has commandeered the studio keyboards and joined in, too.

Declan and Billy remain in the control room, Billy smiling from ear to ear and Declan leaning back with his arms folded over his chest, with an expression somewhere between disapproval and grudging respect.

Kieran's improvising an additional solo section that doesn't exist in the original composition. The rest of us just go with it, and it becomes more than a bunch of musicians playing a beautiful song together for the first time — it transcends that and becomes revelational.

It's so compelling that when the song finally draws to an end some ten minutes later, I immediately dive in to "Fire in the Head," with my band brothers coming along for the ride. Kieran listens for just a moment or two and starts adding his own lead parts in place of the ones the song has on the EP, which I have to simplify for our live shows. All we're missing now is...

And there it is, Declan's growling, emotional vocal, piped in from the iso booth off to the side of the live room, by Charlie, who's sitting back at the desk while Billy stands next to him, now grinning like he's won the lottery. Declan immerses himself in the lyrics whenever we perform this song, which is all about the creative spirit, the need to make something that doesn't yet exist and the siren song of the muse who leads you to it.

At the end, it's all but an ode to my own personal muse, though I've never told anyone — including her — that. Lyrics just handed to me in those moments when the song was finally let loose through my fingers and my mind. The song's last peak speaks to the passion of creativity, rising up like a man walking forever to the sea and finally reaching the crest of the dune, seeing before him a limitless expanse of water and all the world laid out at his feet.

When the last notes from Kieran's guitar fade away, we're all standing there, in silence, looking at each other like we're coming down from the best, most epiphany-inducing orgasm ever experienced by man. Kieran raises his head up, shakes his hair out of his face, and smiles.

"You've got yourselves a session player if you want me," he says.

"I d—" is all I hear before Declan's mic cuts off, and I see Billy's fingers on the board as he tries to smother an amused smile.

I look around at the others, seeing reflected on their faces the same thing I'm feeling.

"Done."

Three hours later

"I don't care what your objections are, Declan. You're going to make this work," Billy tells him. "Whether you want to admit it or not, you need Kier, and what I just saw is concrete proof of that. You have all but instantly gone from amazing to stellar! This is Telltale Signs-level greatness, Declan. Don't tell me that's not something you want, because I've known you three days, and I can feel you hungering for exactly that kind of fame. If you want it, this is your shot. You won't get another one."

Declan is, for once — at least without intervention via mixing board — silent.

A full minute later, he finally speaks.

"We still need a lead guitarist for the tour," he points out.

"We do," I say. "But we'll cross that bridge when we come to it."

There are nods of agreement from everyone in the room, which doesn't included Kieran, who's tinkering with a riff while we talk about him in here.

Cross that bridge...

Oh, crap! I forgot to call Bridge again. Even after Mace's warning.

"If we're in agreement on that... Billy, can you work out the details with the label and Kieran, and figure out a schedule for getting into the studio? I need to make a very important phone call."

"More important than this?" Billy asks.

"At this moment, yes. But lucky for me, we have a top-notch manager to handle logistics," I add with a smirk.

I head out into the hallway to make my overdue call, and she picks up straight away. I love seeing her face light up when she gets my video calls.

"Hey, Hunt! How are things going in rockstar-land?"

"Amazing, Bridge! We've got the deal locked in, and we hired a manager, and we've even got a lead guitarist joining us for the album who is one of the best I've ever heard!"

"Is that good news? That last bit? You're not worried..."

"That he'll replace me? No. First off, we've just had an amazing couple of hours just jamming and running through our originals, and this is definitely a tremendous *addition* to the band, not me being shunted off to the side. I'm imagining some great new work ahead of us."

"That's great! What's the second thing?"

"What?"

"You said the session was the first thing about why you weren't worried. What was the second? Or was there a second?"

"Yeah. And it's a mixed bag... He also can't replace me because he won't tour. Refuses to perform live or officially join the band. I'm not sure what the deal is, but I'm hoping we can change his mind."

"You won't. Not happening."

The voice behind me has that Irish lilt to it, and I cringe, because if we were playing our cards close to the vest on this plan, I just blew it.

"Sorry, man — didn't realize you were there... I—"

"Wait — is that him? He's Irish?"

"I am, sweetheart," he says to Bridge with a smile, and I try not to cringe. "Though I've been in New York for a good while now."

"Sorry — Kieran, this is my lifelong best friend, Brighid Weaver. Bridge, this is Kieran O'Connor, who's going to help us out with the next album and such."

"Dia dhuit, a Chiaráin!" Brighid says to him. His eyes go wide.

"A Gaeilgeoir? Where'd you find yourself an Irish-speaking American girl, Hunter?"

"Níl ach cúpla focal agam," Brighid replies.

"Ah, well... A couple of words or more, it's a sound for sore ears."

"Dublin?" she asks.

"Thereabouts," he replies vaguely.

"I thought that was the accent I was hearing."

"You didn't answer my question — how did you come to be speaking *any* Irish at all, darlin'?"

Again, I cringe at the term of endearment.

"Is giolla leis an Bhandia Bríd mé, a Chiaráin," she says demurely, showing him her pendant over the phone screen.

"Ah. Well, that explains it."

"What does?" I ask, totally lost. "Non-Irish speaker here."

"She said she serves the goddess Brighid... which I take it you were aware of." I nod. "Ah... and hence the name. You don't happen to be an actual weaver, do you, Brighid?"

"She's a very noted fiber artist, actually. She just had her first solo show!"

"Oh, Hunt — that's *my* big news! All of the weavings from the show sold. I've got enough money to open my shop!"

I'm smiling at her, but part of me is gutted, because I know this means she'll be moving back to Delaware. And I'm going to miss her.

"That's wonderful news, Bridge. You've been wanting this for a long time." Something flickers in her face, but I'm not sure what.

"Well, comhghairdeas, Brighid Weaver," Kieran says. "Best of luck to you."

"Go raibh maith agat, a Chiaráin! Agus beannactaí ort agus ar do chuid ceoil."

"Go hiontach! Maith thú, a Bhríd! And now I'm after talking to Billy about the recording schedule. So, if you'll both excuse me, I'll leave you to your call. Slán, a Bhríd!"

"Slán, a Chiaráin! Le do thoil, tabhair aire mhaith do mo chara. Tá mo chroí istigh ann."

"Tuigim," he replies with a nod at her and then a glance and a nod at me, before heading back into the control room.

"What was all that about? Sounds like your Irish is better than you implied."

"I'm still a beginner, Hunter. I just wished him well with the recording and such. Pleasantries."

Brighid
Ten minutes later

I have no idea what possessed me to tell a perfect stranger that I'm madly in love with Hunter. I just felt like Ciarán? Or does he use the anglicized version with a K? I just felt like he was someone I could confide in. Kara always says to trust my instincts, and knowing that I'm likely to be moving in a month or so, and that Hunter is likely to be spending a lot more time in the future with Kieran? than he is with me, it seemed natural to ask him to take care of the man I love.

I wonder why he won't agree to join the band and tour with them. They seem like a good fit. I hope he's as good a guitarist as Hunter suggested he is, especially if they're going to try to get him to join them. I wonder if Ciarán has any videos online so I can see him in action.

No guitar-players with the name Ciarán and that amazing red-gold hair I saw on the video call. I try again with the other spelling. Nothing. The guy must be pretty new or something. He said he'd been working in New York for a while, but maybe he's better known in Ireland? Maybe search for music rather than just guitar? Nothing with the K spelling. How about the traditional spelling? Or the traditional spelling of his surname?

Oh. It can't... But it *has* to be...

I pick up my phone again.

"Hey, Hunt — sorry to bother you again, but I had a question — is it Ciarán with a C or Kieran with a K?"

"A K, I think. Is that all you needed? We're getting ready to sit down and discuss some details."

"No — I mean I had a question for Kieran. Could you get him for me? You can just hand him the phone. This should be quick."

"O...K..."

I'm glad he doesn't ask any more questions.

"Hello again, lovely Gaeilgeoir. Hunter said you had a question?"

"Are you alone? Out of earshot?

"Yes. I'm out in the hall again. I won't mention your little confession there at the end, if that's what you wanted to be sure of. You seemed to be telling me that in Irish so he couldn't understand."

"Yes, and thank you for not mentioning it to him. But I called back for another reason..."

"Which is...?"

"Do you have any secrets of your own that I should be careful not to mention to Hunter and the guys should a cursory internet search turn up information related to another spelling of your name?"

Dead silence on the other end of the phone.

"I'm going to take that as a yes."

"What do you want?" His voice is dark, almost menacing. Batman would be proud.

"Want? Oh, mother of twelve gods — you don't think I'm blackmailing you, do you? I would never. Wow. Is it that much of a secret? I just didn't want to let it slip if you didn't want them to know."

"Oh. Sorry. No, I don't want them to know, Brighid. No one knows, except one friend and a label exec who've kept it a secret for years now. And it's not in her interest for my secrets to get out, nor is it in Mace's... Oh, bollocks. You've got me so off-kilter with this that I said something I shouldn't have. Forget that name. I never said it. Please?"

"Mace? Mace Mason. Aedan Mason?"

"I said 'please.' Can't you just..."

"No, Kieran — I'm asking because I'm well familiar with Mace — Aedan."

"I should have known. They've toured with them…"

"Yes. But the reason I mention it is that if you have any concerns about my intentions, or my ability to keep a secret, Aedan can vouch for me."

"Oh?"

"Yes, and that's all I'll say. If you're worried, ask Aedan. That should set your mind at ease. … There is no such thing as coincidence, only fate."

"How so?"

"Kieran — aMUSEd is going to press you to join them. You need to do that."

"Not a chance. You now know why. I've already told them I've seen the spotlight destroy lives, souls. And I like mine just as intact as it is currently, thank you very much."

"Kieran, I'm not saying this as Hunter's friend. I'm not saying it as a supporter of the band. The spotlight can destroy. But light can also lead you out of the darkness and illuminate the things you have been blind to. You've been hiding in the dark, and it's time to come out and let the sun burn away the cobwebs and reflect off that talent, and that hair of yours. Which is astonishing, I must say."

"Thanks. I should have dyed it black years ago…"

"Don't you dare! That would be a crime against nature. And that's beside the point. I'm telling you this with everything in my being, Kieran. You need to join aMUSEd. For their sake, but especially for yours."

"Did your goddess tell you that?" he asks, sounding skeptical.

"No. Not directly. But Hunter will tell you I'm very intuitive. And Mace can confirm that. So, ask him, ask them. They'll tell you you should trust me in this, I think. I know Mace will."

"I see…"

"Kieran — I'm going to keep your secret, which is truly the *only* reason I called, to confirm whether it *was* a secret. You don't have to take my advice. But you should at least talk to Mace, since you trust him, and see what he has to say about what I've told you."

"I already know what he'll say. He's already pushing me to join the band."

"Has he ever done that before?"

"Actually, no."

"Then there's a reason it's now and with these guys. Trust him. Trust me. Just do it."

He's silent. I'm afraid I'm losing my case.

"Kieran, have you listened to 'Fire in the Head' yet?"

"I hadn't, but we played it together tonight."

"And how did that go?"

"Incredible. Literally. So good it's hard to believe it was real. It's a great song, but this was... more... Why?"

"Hunter got stuck on that song. It was going to be scrapped from the EP. He asked me to help him find some inspiration to finish it. I did that. It helps when you serve a goddess of poetry and creativity. Where do you think it got its name?"

"Oh. Oh! She... 'Fire in the Head.' Yeats. That was you."

"Or more likely Her. Or both. Or some amazing manifestation of the creative spirit. Regardless, there is more import to all of this than just whether a band hires a new guitar player. I'm not sure what yet. But it's there, screaming at me to make sure this happens. Please. Trust me. Ask Mace. But trust me. You have to become part of aMUSEd."

He's quiet, but I wait.

"I'll talk to Mace, and I'll think things through. I've got to get back in there. Thanks. I think."

He hangs up.

I can only hope he listens. The more I think on it, the more important it seems that Kieran O'Connor, however he spells it, becomes the sixth member of aMUSEd.

Chapter 51

Already Gone

Brighid
One month later

"Brighid, dear, you don't have to rearrange everything overnight. I thought that's what you'd planned to do over the winter."

Lindsey is entirely correct. But I'm having a hard time keeping my mind busy, so I've already started transitioning the store from Mystic Needle Arts, which is full of yarn and pattern books, hooks and needles, to Dream Weaver, which will feature all of that — heavy on the yarn — and more.

The new shop will also offer Maire's handmade paper goods, herbs and herbal teas that she and I will produce, incenses and oils, ethically-sourced crystals, and a small selection of esoterica, including tarot decks, rune sets, candles... And I'll be offering consultations on homeopathic and other forms of healing, and, as Kara suggested, tarot readings.

I'm even looking into becoming a certified pastoral counselor, which will enable me to be clergy-of-record for hospital patients, as well as, I hope, offer me some background in spiritual counseling I could offer at the shop.

The closing on the store is next week, but Lindsey said I could come early and start getting things organized. And, honestly, I needed to get out of Virginia.

Hunter's moving, too. To New York. The whole band is. Their manager and the label, and maybe even Kieran, persuaded them to make the move, since they're going to be recording in NYC. And then off on tour for a year or even two, depending on how the album and ticket sales go. He won't be gone for just two months. It'll be more like gone for six, back for a few weeks, maybe a month, and then out on the road again, for another four or six months.

Then there are the music-video shoots, promotional appearances, charity events... Most of which will be done out of New York. I guess I should be grateful they didn't want them to move to L.A.

With my business just getting started, I can't take off to go to New York for any length of time. Probably not for years to come. If I want to see Hunter, he's going to have to come to me. Which I'm not counting on. I knew this was the way things were headed. It's just hitting me really hard that he won't be around.

"I know, Lindsey. I've just got all these ideas on how I want things to be, and it feels weird to be here and not be working on that."

"Have you had a chance to look for a place to live yet?"

"I've got an appointment this afternoon. I haven't decided on renting versus buying. I've got a downpayment, but I want to make sure I have the perfect place picked out."

"Very responsible of you. You've grown up so much since you last worked for me."

"I've had a lot of things happen in my life in a very short time."

"Yes, your poor mother... Such a shock. And your father... Can't say I blame you for changing your name and moving on. He's not... He's not the same man he was, and, to be honest, he was never an easy man to begin with."

"Have you seen him?"

"Oh, not in... well, it's probably been since the funeral. He seems to keep to himself. I've had a few customers who've mentioned they don't see him anymore when they used to run into him regularly. But not anymore. I don't think you'll run into him at the grocery store, if that's a concern."

"I honestly hadn't thought that far, but I'd rather avoid him knowing I was back at all. I don't want to be little Ellie all grown up and come home. I'm Brighid Weaver, entrepreneur and artist, newly arrived in Mystic Beach and looking to make it home."

"Well, we're lucky to have you, Brighid Weaver. I read about your showcase and the sale. Are you going to keep showing your work?"

"In D.C. I may keep a few sample pieces on display here to show off my handspun. But I'm going to let Case Galleries handle the shows and sales. All that's left for me there is Kara and Maire, and they've promised to come visit, take a beach vacation, whenever Kara has enough help to take the time off."

"You're missing Hunter, aren't you?"

"I am."

"You two have been like two peas in a pod since you were little. I imagine it's difficult for you, being away from him, especially when things are changing so much for you both. Hopefully, he can come visit, too."

"I'm not sure he's going to have time, Lindsey. I've resigned myself to that, even though he keeps saying he'll make it work. He's got so much going on for him now. I can't even imagine all the balls he's having to juggle, and that's before they decided to move up there. It's going to be a while before I see him again, I'm sure."

"You'll manage, dear. Friends as close as you have been are never apart for long."

"I hope you're right... I really hope you're right."

Hunter

I never thought we'd end up living in New York City. Not even short-term.

But Billy has a friend who has a friend who wasn't using their home until April. Who has a five-bedroom home in New York and doesn't use it for the better part of a year? I guess somebody who's got an eight-bedroom home in London and only likes the New York weather for three months of the year.

So we've got a place to stay while we write and record, and when we go on tour, I'm not sure we'll need anything more than a place to store what few possessions we have, other than our equipment. What I had to bring with me wasn't much more than what I'd packed for the couple of days we'd come up to sign the deal with Siren's Song. Beyond clothes and my gear, I basically had a couple photos — of Mom and of Brighid and me — and a handful of favorite books, my songwriting notebook, a few trinkets... not much else.

The other guys had more stuff, since they'd never been essentially homeless. Alex said he's going to sublet the apartment and just bring his personal stuff. I'd never realized how many clothes and boxes of jewelry Alex had until we packed it all up. No wonder Megan complained about there being no space once his keyboards were in the bedroom.

Dave and Declan's parents weren't thrilled with them heading off to an even bigger city. But they were very happy how successful they were becoming. Not quite enough to forgive me, but enough that there was a lot less tension between the brothers and their parents. That was nice to see. They'd been good to me, for a while.

We canceled all our remaining performances. The fans were disappointed, but they were also very excited that we'd be putting out a full album and coming back through for at least a few dates on the tour. We'll always be a hometown band for them, wherever we are.

I quit my job, with thanks to Jerry. He'd been a good boss, especially when I'd needed a spot to crash.

And last, but nowhere near least... Brighid.

This has been killing me. It didn't help much that she was leaving, too. I still had to say goodbye to my best friend, knowing I probably wouldn't see her for at least a few months, maybe longer. We hadn't been apart that long since I'd first moved in with the Carters. And it was very hard to watch her struggle with it, too.

She's been better, more herself, since she had her show and arranged to buy the shop and move back to Mystic Beach. But still not the bright Brighid she'd been a year or so ago. Stronger, but... brittle, maybe? It's fascinating to hear her practice her Irish with Kieran. It was all unintelligible to me, like someone had sneezed and the whole room had erupted in a chorus of "Gesundheit."

I don't know what made Kieran change his mind — playing some more with us, talking to Mace, Billy's persuasiveness or the terms of the contract Siren's Song offered him to join the band — but he'd jumped in with both feet. Or, at least one foot and a toe. His pinkie toe.

"I am *not* doing interviews."

"I'm not sure how we have six guys in a band and we only let them interview five of us," I told him.

"Oh, it can be done — believe me."

"Alright. Talk to Billy. Talk to the label. I'm not getting in the middle."

"And no photos."

"I'm pretty sure that's in your contract, and I didn't even see it."

"They can put a blurry spot over my face."

"I don't think that's how that works, Kier."

"They can do it anyway."

"What about the videos? Live performances? Are you going to wear a bag over your head? One of those leprechaun masks they have for St. Patrick's Day?"

He heaves a heavy sigh.

"I really can't get out of this, can I?"

"No, I don't think so."

"Is it too late to change my mind?"

"I'm pretty sure that ship sailed when you signed on the dotted line there, buddy."

"Speaking of which — I need more ink."

"(A) Do you have any room left to put any more in? And (B) Are you really getting tattooed just because you feel like getting tattooed?"

"(A) Yes. I've still got most of my back and most of my chest, an arm and at least one leg left."

"At least? Are you not sure how much is covered?"

"I haven't looked at the back of my calves recently."

"I see."

"And (B) Fuck yes. How did you manage to make it this long as a musician and not have any tattoos? They're addictive! Endorphins, my man."

"Until a few weeks ago, I was a starving artist. I couldn't afford to pay anyone to turn me into a permanent canvas. So I never really thought about it."

"Well, it's time to think about it, Hunt! I've got a great artist who'll fit me in whenever I give her a call. She'll get us both in. Come on — let's go!"

"Wait! I have no idea what I'd even get."

"What's the most important thing to you in this whole world?"

"Music."

"What symbolizes that for you? If you had to put it into a visual medium, what would that be?"

"Hmm... My guitar? Music notes? The new band logo is pretty cool..."

"There you go! We'll give her some ideas and let her come up with something custom-designed just for you. But you really should consider getting a Fender tat, not a PRS. Way cooler," he teases.

"My mom gave me that guitar. It's the last birthday present she ever gave me, when I turned 15, not long before she died."

"Wow. Then one green PRS tattoo coming up. Take a photo with your phone, and let's go!"

And suddenly, getting a tattoo seems like a brilliant idea. It's one more way to keep Mom with me, even when I'm not playing my guitar.

Six hours later

"Sick, man! Now we all have to get one!"

As usual, Rhys is very enthusiastic.

"Not me!" Declan pipes up. "I'm keeping this body pristine."

David rolls his eyes.

"What he means is Mom would kill him."

"I am a grown man."

"Says the guy who brought his teddy bear with him to New York City."

"It's a plush grizzly bear, and it has sentimental value."

"Then why is it hiding in a drawer and not in a place of honor?"

"Because it has private sentimental value."

"Ahh... I see."

"So, are you getting one, Davey-boy? Or is Mom's horrified expression chasing all possible designs out of your head?"

"I'm thinking about it. I've been thinking about getting one for a while."

"What? Reserved, retiring David?"

Dave shrugs. Whatever he's thinking, he's not spilling it now.

"I'm up for it," announces Alex, who already has a handful of smaller tattoos on his arms and back. "Give me your artist's number and I'll set something up."

"Sure thing," Kier replies.

"Now, *that* says commitment!" Declan says, giving my ink a closer look.

"Don't touch it! It's gotta heal!" I tell him when he tries to touch, shoving his hand away.

"I like how she incorporated the guitar with the logo."

My right upper arm now bears the new aMUSEd logo of a woman's face, with a traditional comedy mask held up along one side, with my green PRS held in her other hand and extending down my arm, like she's offering it up as an invitation to join with her and make music.

The woman's face is kind of indistinct, veiled, like she's shrouded in mist, or maybe mystery. This version of the logo, which was designed as album art, has her long hair streaming out behind her, full of music notes, quill pen, scroll, lyre, panpipes, grapes, a sword and a compass — traditional symbols of the nine Greek muses.

Kier's artist, Olivia, suggested we leave the piece mostly uncolored for now. She said everyone's idea of a muse would be different and could even change over time, so waiting to add details and color would allow each of us to have a piece that would evolve with us while still maintaining the cohesiveness of a single originating design. It sounded like a great idea to me. My green PRS stands out against the mostly black-and-gray design, and it feels like a fresh spring day, full of promise.

CHAPTER 52

HEY, LADY GODIVA

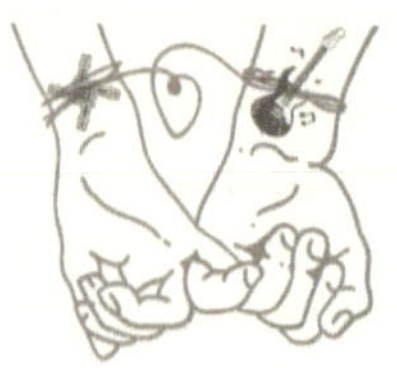

Brighid
Five months later

"**M**rs. Lowell! How nice to see you! Is there anything specific I can help you with today?"

Mrs. Lowell is now a regular customer. She occasionally came into the shop when Lindsey owned it, but she seems to like the additions I've made.

"I need some more of that wonderful tea of yours."

"The Yuletide Yoga blend?"

"That's it! I'm going to browse your handspun, too. I've got a project I'm working on, and it would be absolutely perfect for that."

"Well, let me know if you don't find exactly what you need. I can do a custom order for a specific color, or I can work up some silk if you find a color you like but prefer that to wool."

"That might be just what I need, Brighid. Let me look at what you have."

"Take your time, dear. It's a quiet Tuesday at the beach. I'll bag up your tea while you look."

Mrs. Lowell reminds me of my maternal grandmother — energetic, beyond spry, even though she has to be more than 70, with a streak of shrewd curiosity. She's still eager to experience life, and she's not letting her age hold her back — not one bit.

Just as I finish getting her tea packaged up, my phone rings. I hesitate to answer it while I have a customer in the shop. But it's Hunter, and he calls rarely enough these days that I don't want to miss a chance to talk to him. Especially when this is the first time he's video-called me since he moved to New York.

"Greetings from the beach, big-city rockstar! Whoa — you're getting kinda fuzzy there!"

"Hey, Bridge. Yeah, I'm growing a little serious-musician scruff, make sure people take me seriously," he says, making a totally ridiculous face. I chuckle. At least that hasn't changed. "How's it going there?"

"Very well, all things considered. My weekends are crazy, and the weekdays quiet, so the shop is doing pretty well overall. Knock on wood," I say, knocking on my head, an old joke between us, but also tapping the wood of the counter, just in case. "How's it going in the Big Apple?"

"Peachy!" he replies with a grin.

"Cute! But you know you have to come back to Delaware for the best peaches!"

Hunter's expression falters.

"I know it's not peach season, Hunter, but you can still come visit."

"I can't come back yet, Bridge. We've got studio time starting tomorrow."

"Oh! Well, that's good news, right? You've got songs ready to start recording!"

"We've got a couple dozen that are in varying stages from lyrics and riffs to ready to go and already tested out with an audience!"

"You're playing out? I thought you wouldn't be performing again until the tour, once the album's done." Now it's my smile that's faltered.

"Billy suggested we do a few impromptu weeknight gigs at local clubs, see how the new material is received by a non-D.C. audience. We only gave them a couple days' notice."

"So you had a couple days' notice that you'd have a weeknight gig..." I observe tightly.

"Yeah. They loved all of the new material, too... ...Oh, Bridge — I'm sorry. I should have thought to call and see if you wanted to come up. It's just been so crazy, and with getting the new songs ready... it just didn't occur to me. I'll let you know next time. I promise."

"It's OK, Hunter. I'm not sure I could have gotten away anyway."

This is patently false. On a weekday, I could have closed the shop for a day or two and have made up any lost revenue on the weekend. Especially in the shoulder season. But what else do you say when you've been forgotten? And that's on top of my offering to come visit several times since July and always being told that it'd be better to do it in a couple weeks. And again a couple weeks after that... Rinse. Repeat.

Hunter can see that I'm disappointed. He does that nervous thing where he runs his hand through his hair. And as he does, he turns the phone just enough that I spot it.

"Hunter? Is that a tattoo?"

"I didn't mention getting a tattoo?"

"No. You did not. When did this happen?"

"Back in July, I think?"

And the hits just keep coming. How did something major like that happen and I didn't know a thing about it? It's not like he was already covered in ink and this was just one more.

"What did you get done?"

He turns the phone camera to focus on his upper arm.

"It's the new band logo, with my guitar incorporated in it," he says, moving the camera around to show it off in detail. "Mom's with me all the time now."

And my heart jumps and breaks all at the same. I'm happy he's found a way to remember his mom. After all those weeks when he wouldn't even take his guitar out of the case because it reminded him of her, being reminded is now a good thing for him. It's an outward sign of the very slow process of him healing from the loss and finally putting that guilt to rest. And he did it five months ago and never even mentioned it to me.

"That's an amazing design, Hunter. I love the logo — I assume that's a muse?"

"Yeah — she's got the comedy mask because we're 'amused,' and then she's got all these symbols in her hair, with the music notes and the lyre and stuff."

"Representing the nine muses."

"Exactly."

"Like I said — very cool design!"

"Kier got one, too. His artist is the one who did them. And then Alex and Rhys. And we left them a little unfinished — no real color or anything — because she suggested we could each make them our own as life inspires us."

"That's a great idea. I like that she's kind of ambiguous. You never know what form inspiration will take."

"Yup."

There's an awkward silence, which I'm not sure Hunter and I have ever had. But his life is so focused on his work and what's going on up there that I can't think of anything else to ask him. I don't know what *to* ask. And I suspect he's feeling the same way.

"I've been looking at houses again," I volunteer. "With the off-season here, people are finally putting their houses on the market."

"Find anything you like?"

"There have been a couple. There's one older house I really liked. It's just a block or so from the beach. It needs a little updating, but it's got plenty of room for me and my loom and wheel — even this great little alcove off the bedroom that has amazing light during the day. And — oh, my gods — you've got to see the bathtub in the upstairs bathroom!"

"Jacuzzi? Seats eight?" I can't tell if he's joking or hopeful that's what it actually is.

"No — it's an old Victorian-era enameled cast-iron tub. It's super-deep — not big enough for eight people, but it'll fit even me comfortably. I'd have bubbles up to my neck and enough hot water to soak for an hour without getting cold."

"That sounds great!"

"And the wallpaper in there..." I nearly crack up trying to think of how to explain it.

"What? What about the wallpaper?"

"Well, it's not original or even period to the house. But I guess someone in the last fifty or so years thought that a neoclassical-style pattern of women depicted as if they were going bathing would be an appropriate wall covering in a bathroom with an old tub like that."

"'As if they were going bathing'?"

"What do you usually wear when you take a bath, Hunter?"

"Well, I haven't had a bath since I was about eight... or, rather, when *we* were about eight," he says, his tone mischievous. I blush — that would be the last time we had a bath together, before the parents decided we were too old for that to be appropriate. "But usually one wouldn't wear... Oh! So they have naked-lady wallpaper in the bathroom?"

"Yup! It's not pornographic or anything. Nothing you wouldn't see in a neoclassical statue or something like Botticelli's 'Birth of Venus,' but — yeah, boobies galore!"

"OK, now you *have* to buy that house. For the naked-lady wallpaper alone."

"Hunter! I can't buy a house just because you want to see breasts in my bathroom..."

Well, now that just got awkward...

His eyebrow quirks up.

"I mean — you surely have enough naked breasts to look at up there..."

No, that didn't make it any better.

Both of his eyebrows are now up near his hairline.

"Umm... Yeah. Well, since you insist, I guess I'm buying a house..." I'm joking, but as I say it, I realize that I actually mean it. I'm buying a house! With naked-lady wallpaper in the bathroom. Even if Hunter's fascination with boobs on the wall isn't the only reason I've decided to buy it.

"Of course, you'll have to actually come to Delaware to see it..."

His face gets serious once again.

"I will. As soon as I can, Bridge. I promise."

"I miss you."

"I miss you, too. Really. I'm going to try. I will."

"Brighid, dear — do you have any silk in this celadon green color?"

I startle. Because I'd forgotten Mrs. Lowell was even here. And all that talk about naked ladies in the bathroom...

"Let me come see exactly which shade you're wanting, Mrs. Lowell!" I call back.

"I've got to go, Hunter. Love you. Miss you. Come see me soon!" I blow him a kiss through the phone and hang up.

At least this time I didn't have to hear him reply to my "I love you" with "I know." After all this time, that still smarts.

CHAPTER 53

THE PROMISE

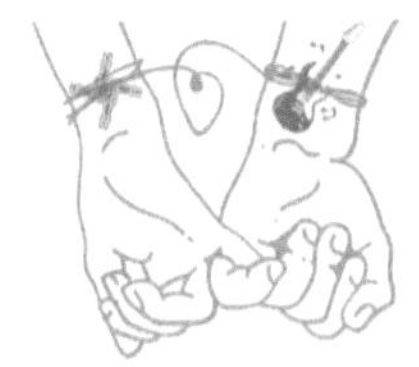

Brighid
A year later

It's my first time in New York City. I couldn't tell you where I am or how to get anywhere from here, including home. I'm used to D.C., but this is a city on a scale I've never seen before. Dublin felt intimate compared to this.

Hunter sent a limo for me at the airport, and it brought me straight here, to this fancy club, where velvet ropes keep a big crowd away from the front entrance. Someone opens the limo door for me, and I step out, instantly regretting Hunter's suggestion that I just get dressed up for their album release party like I would for a Friday night out. After more than a year, Hunter seems to have forgotten that I don't go out on Friday nights except to see aMUSEd, and I haven't seen them since I went back to Delaware and he moved to New York.

In fact, I haven't laid eyes on *Hunter* in all that time. Except via video call. And a lot of photos on the gossip sites: Hunter going into a club with a fashion model. Hunter spotted walking out of a model's apartment in the morning — different model, same clothes. Hunter eating dinner with a woman labeled "an influencer," whatever that means. Hunter dancing very intimately with a model/actress I think I saw in a one-line roll on TV last week. (Hunter does not dance. I am not sure how this happened. But considering I've desperately wanted to dance with him since we were 13 or so, and didn't even do that at the one homecoming dance we went to, I find myself resenting this turn of events.)

That homecoming dance was the first — and last — time I wore actual heels. My normally catlike reflexes seem to be allergic to my head being any higher than my natural five-nine or so with flats on. I ended up barefoot within twenty minutes. And then Kevin Ferguson stomped on my foot as he walked by with his buddies from the football team. Maybe on purpose. OK — it was definitely on purpose, but Hunter was off getting us a drink, so...

So when Hunter said to wear what I would for a Friday night out, I pulled my nicest sandals out of the closet. Flat-heeled sandals. The rest of my outfit is reminiscent of that amazing retro dress I wore several New Year's Eves ago. No light-up skirt, but it's figure-hugging where that's a good thing and flowing where it's not. (Hello, thighs! There you are! As if I could have forgotten you...) I thought I looked nice when I left the house for the airport earlier today.

And then I arrive here, and I realize just how out-of-place I feel. The bouncers are wearing tuxes. The woman posing for photos on the sidewalk in front of the door sparkles in a slinky sequined dress that looks painted on, and when she turns, there's not much back to it at all. I see a hint of butt crack just above the skirt, and there's nothing between there and her neck. There has to be adhesive involved in this minor miracle of costuming.

The TV reporter who's interviewing a man off to the side — I think he might be one of the members of Nickelback — *she's* wearing a dress that looks like it belongs on the red carpet at one of the big movie awards events, and she's just here to work.

I look down at myself and sigh. I'm not sure what I would have done differently if Hunter had given me a better take on the dress code for this thing, but it's too late now anyway.

I walk up to the door, past a lot of screaming people and cameras flashing wildly. Here goes nothing.

"Are you on the list?"

One of the bouncers is standing in front of me. He stepped out so fast that I'm looking at his shirt buttons from about two inches away.

"Uh... I should be. Brighid Weaver?"

He steps back just far enough to scrutinize his clipboard. "Seaver?"

"No. Weaver — like someone who makes cloth."

"I'm not seeing it."

"I'm Hunter Graves' guest. The band's rhythm guitarist?"

"I know who he is, ma'am. I don't have your name on the list, though."

"Can you get someone to check with him? I came all the way from Delaware. I'm supposed to be on the list."

"Dela—where?"

"Delaware — little state south of Philadelphia. Hunter's from there."

"If you say so, ma'am."

I wait for a response. In vain.

"Can you please get someone to check with Hunter, since I'm apparently not on the list?"

"Step over here, ma'am." I swear — if he ma'ams me one more time... He gestures off to the side of the doorway. My thighs and I are impeding traffic, apparently.

He whispers in one of the other bouncers' ears, and that guy goes inside — hopefully, to clear up this snafu.

The first bouncer nods at a couple walking up behind me, and they walk in without a word.

"Were they on the list?"

"They belong here."

And there you have it, folks.

I try to call Hunter directly, but the call goes to voicemail. So does the second call. And the third.

The longer I wait, the more anxious I get. Are people staring? Am I causing a scene? I consider fleeing, hailing a cab off the street and going straight back to the airport to wait on my early morning flight out. (Hunter said he'd have promos to do all day tomorrow, so he'd show me around the city another time. I hadn't even packed a change of clothes. I figured we might be out until early morning anyway, knowing how hard these guys party.)

The bouncer guy is looking at me with pity on his face. That doesn't mean he's letting me in, though.

Finally, a much smaller man, also in a tux, comes striding down the hall and straight up to me.

"Miss Weaver?"

"Yes. Brighid Weaver."

"Yes — I'm Billy Neal." He offers me his hand, and I shake it reflexively. "I'm aMUSEd's manager."

"Oh! Yes! Hunter's talked a lot about you. Thank you so much for looking out for him and the guys."

"They're superstars in the making, Miss Weaver. I'm just helping them navigate things."

"Well, it's very much appreciated."

"I apologize for the miscommunication. I got the limo arranged, but I thought Hunter had already put you on the list."

"Oh. I thought Hunter had arranged for the limo..."

"That's what he's got management for now."

Of course. Completely to be expected.

Billy glances at my outfit.

"Am I underdressed? I don't think Hunter gave me a good frame of reference for the dress code."

"No, no — not at all," Billy assures me. "They're just used to a different kind of style here. You stand out."

I'm not sure how to take that, so I just nod.

"If you'll come with me, I'll take you in to the party. The band's due to go on for a brief performance before they come out to greet their guests."

"I can't go backstage? I wanted to say hi to Hunter, at least."

"Not right now. We're keeping things very controlled to keep the guys focused on their performance."

"How's that working out? Is Rhys jumping off his drum riser yet?" I chuckle. Because I've seen "The Madman" do that — over and over, until my legs hurt just watching. He said it burns off his nervous energy before a show. Hey — whatever works.

Billy gives me a look of surprise.

"How did you know?"

I laugh.

"I've known these guys since they joined the band. I know that the same way I know Rhys had something to do with that llama card they sent me after they got signed."

Billy gives me an appraising look and then nods his respect.

"Did you know Rhys knits?" I ask.

"Can't say that I did. The boys haven't had a lot of downtime."

"The gossip sites suggest otherwise..."

"Yes... Well..." He looks a little embarrassed. "It's all part of the package. They're going to spend a lot of time schmoozing with people who can help them become even bigger than they already are."

"Yes... schmoozing... one-on-one... at 5 a.m." Sorry — did I say that out loud?

"What can I say? They're rockstars..."

Apparently I did.

Billy directs me into a large ballroom that has a stage at one end, with curtains concealing the sides. Presumably, Hunter's back there somewhere.

"Can I get you a drink?" Billy nods toward the bar on one side of the room, which is crowned with an ice sculpture of the band's comedy mask logo.

"Not right now. But thank you."

"If you'll excuse me, then, I've got to go check on the boys. Enjoy!" He waves and jogs off toward the stage.

The room is packed, people clustered in little groups and jamming onto the dance floor in front of the stage, which already seems to be at full capacity as a DJ plays club music from the side of the stage.

This is why I hesitated when Hunter invited me for their release party. Awkward Brighid is now stuck at a party where she doesn't know anyone. After standing uncomfortably off to the side for a few minutes, I decide to get a drink.

"Do you have oran..."

"I'll have a scotch. Neat." The man walking up next to me talks straight over me, and the bartender goes straight for the scotch bottle. I wait patiently for an opening to put in my request for a soda.

"Appletini, please," a woman asks from my other side.

"White wine."

"I'd like a cosmo."

By the time I catch the bartender's eye, I think I've heard half the drinks in the bartender's guide ordered and delivered.

"Do you have orange soda?" I ask wearily.

"Sorry. Sprite?"

"That's fine."

He hands me my drink, and I take a sip, which nearly empties the cup since there's so much ice in it. I consider asking for a refill, but people have already closed in around me. I drop a few dollars on the bar for a tip and take my cup of ice and find an empty spot next to a potted palm. I check my phone. No return call or text from Hunter. I check my email, browse the internet, play a trivia game — and kick butt, I'll note — and still nothing from Hunter. A half-hour later, the dance music stops, and there's a commotion near the stage. It must be time for the band to go on.

"Welcome, everyone!" Billy says from the mic at the front of the stage. "We're here to celebrate the release of the first full-length album by one of the hottest new acts in the country. You may have seen them opening for Telltale Signs on their last two tours, but from here on, they're headliners! Please give it up for aMUSEd!"

The curtain rises, and it's a mini version of a classic aMUSEd gig, just with better lighting and some fog. But you wouldn't know that by the audience response, which nearly drowns out the band. All these VIPs, the glitterati, the other musicians invited to join in tonight's celebration — they're all caught up in Declan's thrall from the moment he utters a single note. And their eyes follow Hunter around the stage as he hams it up with Alex and David, Kier in his little self-contained guitar-god zone, where a spotlight literally shines on him during his intricate solos.

I've heard every single song aMUSEd has ever written or recorded. I was there when a lot of them were being written. But these new songs blow even me away. The guys seem to have come into their own here in New York, and I find myself a little sad that I wasn't here to see it all happen.

"Aren't they amazing?" a woman asks me. She doesn't wait for a reply. "I've seen every show they've done in the last eight months. They just get better and better. Don't you just want to eat them up?"

I nod politely. Because that's true, but only for one of them, and I can't put my mouth anywhere near him without causing some degree of implosion. So best not to think about it.

"I managed to get backstage twice last month," she confides. "And that Hunter — I'm telling you — ravenous! Can't get enough! It's like the man was born to eat pussy..."

I instantly turn a deep shade of red. And then green. Because I'm now feeling a little nauseated. I smile politely again and excuse myself, making my way back out of the room and into the hallway.

I head straight for the nearest restroom, which is blissfully empty, and I lean over the sink, catching sight of myself in the mirror, pale but with burning spots of red on my cheeks. I run some cold water on a paper towel and pat my face with it, hoping it'll make me feel better. It doesn't. I need to sit down. In private. Pull myself together.

I head into one of the restroom stalls and sit carefully, my head down between my legs, hoping the nausea will go away. But the woman's words keep repeating in my head, like some sort of sick dance track spun by a sadistic DJ.

"Ravenous…" "Born to eat pussy…" "Eat them up!"

I moan. And not in a good way.

There's a clatter and the door swings open, with the voices of several women coming closer before they come to a stop in front of the mirror.

"That was the best thing ever!" one woman enthuses.

"I know, right? I'm so glad I got back in town in time for this. The flight from Milan was delayed. I thought I'd have to stand him up!" the second one says.

"I'd have been happy to have stood in for you," a third woman volunteers.

"Not on your life. He's mine. You go find your own guitar player." This must be Kier's date. I peek out at her through the slit in the stall door. Tall, thin, pretty, long jet-black hair trailing down yet another barely covered back.

"Maybe. I mean, the Irish guy is cute, but I think you hit the lottery with Hunter. His date at the premier party! Hanging out backstage before they go on?"

I suppress the urge to pass out and/or throw up. I don't want to end up in a puddle of my own vomit at a New York social event.

"Lucky you!" she continues. "You'll be on all the gossip sites. Make sure you play that up."

"Oh, I will be, believe me. But the real payoff is when the cameras are long gone. The man is an animal in bed. Insatiable. I'll be lucky if I can walk tomorrow. Well, tomorrow night — because we'll still be fucking each other's brains out at noon, based on past experience."

I groan. Loudly.

"Uh... You OK in there? Should I get someone for you?" one of them asks.

"No! I'm fine. Thanks." That's all I've got.

My presence seems to chill their conversation, and a few moments later they're back out the door.

I sit and stare at the inside of the stall door for a while. I'm not entirely sure how long. I know it's been a while and the show is undoubtedly over. Will Hunter be out there yet? Will he be waiting to see me, or will he have that brunette on his arm, just waiting to drag him behind the stage and...

Nope. Not going there.

Once again, I'm consumed with what I know is unreasonable jealousy. And it's not just that he's dating and sleeping with other women. I remind myself he has every right to do that. It's that he finally asked me to come here, to see him in the first time in more than a year, and he not only didn't make an effort to actually see me yet, he brought a date and told me he was too busy tomorrow to hang out, when clearly what he meant was he had plans with someone else.

Tears well in my eyes, and I do my best to calm myself. Maybe I'm overreacting. Maybe the Milan girl was just hoping for his time, and he didn't really promise her anything, since he was busy with promos. That makes sense, right?

I take a deep breath and open the door. I don't look any better than I did when I went in there. If anything, I'm even paler, with my eyes now big and glassy. I sigh and force myself back into the event room.

There's a huge cluster of people up near the stage, and I make my feet take me over there, where the band is certain to be. I can see the top of Rhys' head, his height and bright red hair making him stand out even in that crowd. He looks up and spots me, his eyes showing recognition.

"Bridge!" he bellows enthusiastically, forcing the crowd to part around him as he makes his way to me and wraps me in a bear hug. "You made it! You look awesome!" He actually grabs me tight enough to lift me off my feet and spins me 360 degrees.

"Rhys! Put me down! You're going to hurt yourself!" As nice as it sounds, I don't trust anyone to pick me up without damaging a disc. And I probably weigh as much as Rhys does...

"Nah! I've been lifting weights now that we have a gym in my apartment building. It's fine."

I stand back to look at him, and his lean figure of several years ago has definitely filled out. His arms and shoulders were always muscular. He's a drummer, after all. But he's added bulk everywhere else. Not musclebound, but definitely athletic-looking now.

"Have you been rock-climbing?" I ask.

"How'd you know? I go to a climbing gym twice a week, at least. Helps me..."

"Burn off extra energy," I finish for him.

"I missed my favorite witch!" he enthuses, and I cringe a little.

"Not really that witchy, Rhys. Just Pagan."

"But you knew about the llama and bacon jerky, and that I was climbing!"

"Just educated guesses and intuition, Rhys. No magic involved."

"Yeah, right..." he elbows me and winks conspiratorially.

"Where's Hunter?"

"Oh, he's right over there." He points to the other side of the scrum of people, which reminds me uncomfortably of the fans who crowded around him after that talent show, leaving me on the outside for what turned out to be far longer than just that night.

If he's right next to where Rhys was, why didn't he come over with him? I frown.

"Come on!" Rhys says. "Let's go get you a hug... Hey — maybe Hunter can pick you up, too! He's been working out with me sometimes."

I smile at that, just because it reminds me how much Rhys is like a big kid sometimes. I wouldn't have him any other way.

As we get around the crowd and walk up behind Hunter, I see that he does indeed have the brunette clinging to him proprietarily. Declan's on his other side.

"Hunt was busy with Audrey, so Billy had to go out and get her. The bouncer wouldn't let her in!" he says loudly, chuckling. "All the models and actresses coming through that door... it was like that Sesame Street bit... what was it?"

"'One of these things is not like the other,'" David supplies neutrally from next to Declan. "'One of these things...'"

"'Just doesn't belong.'" Hunter finishes. Everyone in the group chuckles, except Alex, who clears his throat. Loudly.

Hunter, Declan and David all turn around, embarrassment plain on their faces. Even Declan.

"Bridge! There you are!" Hunter exclaims, unsuccessfully trying to free himself from the girl's — Audrey's? — clutches.

Rhys wraps his arms around me from behind and hugs me again, this time protectively. As often as he sticks his foot in his mouth, he's not the one I expected to have comforting me after a social faux pas. He sets his chin on top of my head, our height difference making it a perfect fit if he ever gets tired of holding his head up.

"Is this Rhys' girlfriend?" the girl asks with another chuckle.

"Sure is!" he says before kissing my temple. Then he grabs my hand and leads me away, backstage.

I'm in a fog as Rhys sits me down in a chair, kneeling in front of me.

"You OK, Bridge? That was not cool. Even I know that."

"Not really, Rhys. But thank you for caring. I wish Hunter did."

"Hunt's kinda stupid sometimes. But you know that better than anyone."

"Yeah, I do. Though I'm starting to suspect that I don't know him as well as I used to."

"Things have changed a lot up here. But you're still my favorite witch," he adds with a smile, this time kissing my forehead. It's sweet, and I appreciate the gesture, but despite my love of redheads, having Rhys' lips on me doesn't comfort me nearly as much as Hunter would.

"Bridge!" Hunter comes racing through the doorway, out of breath. Maybe he needs to add some cardio to his weight training. But then he seems to have other things he does for cardio...

He glares at Rhys.

"You didn't have to do that."

"Well, one of us did. Even if it wasn't the person it should have been." He shakes his head at Hunter and walks out the door, giving me a grim smile on his way out.

There's silence now. Just me and Hunter in the room. Me trying not to look at him and him clearly trying to think of the right thing to say.

"You made a couple very dramatic entries here tonight, Bridge. You sure you don't want to be on Broadway instead of backstage at a gig?" He chuckles nervously.

I just look at him, my expression blank.

"Too soon?" he asks.

Silence.

"Come on, Bridge — it was all in fun. Don't be so uptight! We were just joking..."

"This isn't a joke to me, Hunter." I think back to all time times I've felt like I didn't belong. Backstage. At rehearsals. In the school cafeteria every day after the talent show... the list goes on and on. I try not to think about the night I walked in on him in flagrant delicto, twice, and Megan's cackle as she laughed mercilessly at my expense.

"I know you and your friends seem to get a kick out of making fun of the silly little hanger-on, but it's not a joke to me, at all. And treating it like one treats me like a joke, too. And I thought you were better than that."

Silence again. Only this time the conversational ball is in his court. And nothing. Not even an "I'm sorry."

"'I'm not sure I'm rich enough to be your friend,'" I finally tell him.

He knows the line I'm referencing. He winces. He knows where that line comes from. We've watched that scene so many times together. Two friends with something between them... He knows I don't mean it literally. It's an "if this is how you treat your friends..." thing.

"Bridge..." He runs out of steam after that. His face is stricken, but he's saying nothing.

"Congratulations on the album. The new material sounds great, and I wish you the best of luck," I tell him, meaning every word. "And now I'm going to go."

"Bridge — no! Stay! I just got carried away... I'll make this up to you. I promise!"

"You say that a lot, Hunt, but when it comes down to it, you don't usually follow through. And I've got to start looking out for myself, because no one else — except maybe Alex and Rhys, of all people — seems to care about doing it. And that's fine. Maybe it's time I started getting used to being on my own."

"Bridge... Don't. Please! You know things have been crazy..."

"I do. I've been driving you crazy, and you've been driving me crazy. Neither one us needs any extra crazy in our lives right now. And I don't want to see what we have turn from friendship into hate and resentment." I take a deep breath, preparing to paraphrase something I know will hit home with him, maybe finally get the message to sink in.

"I'd rather not see you and have you think fondly of me, rather than deal with this life that seems to have already changed you and have you hate me because you feel pressured or obligated. I can't bear the thought of you coming to hate me, after all we've been through. You mean more to me than anything else in this world, and I couldn't survive that. So I think it's best that I don't make you try to keep doing this. Us."

"Bridge... what are you saying here? You're not shutting me out, are you? Over a bad joke?"

"That's not all it is, and you know that. Deep down, you know it." I frown at him. "We both know I can't stay mad at you." I give him as much of a smile as I can manage. He smiles back, hesitantly. "But I think this time it's me who needs the space, and Delaware's far enough away to give me, us, that. We need to take a break for a while, let things settle down, get used to our new lives. Our separate lives. We haven't really had that since the day we met. Not really. It's past time. And you've got so much ahead of you — so many wonderful things!"

I stand up and walk to him where he stands against the door frame.

"You really do." I run my fingers down his cheek, savoring the feel of that short growth of beard he's been sporting up here. "I know it. I've always known it. So you go and be a rockstar. And I'll go home and spin some yarn and take some walks on the beach."

"I miss the beach."

"You should come back more often, then."

"Maybe I will..."

He pulls me into his chest, kissing the top of my head. A drop of liquid hits my scalp. I want to give him that masculine distance and pretend I don't know he's crying. But I'm crying, too, and I think we both need to see how much this is impacting the other.

I haven't seen him cry since his mother died, though he's too often seen my tears, dried them, and sometimes, yes, caused them. But you don't feel this sad unless you care about someone just as strongly.

I wipe the tears off his cheek, sticking my finger in my mouth to wash off the salt. His eyes are glued to my mouth, and for just a moment, I wonder...

He swipes his thumb along my cheek and imitates the gesture, and my breath catches.

"I love you, Bridge."

"I know." It's the best I can do right now. Partly because my mind is numb and that's the thing I hear in my head now when those words are uttered. Partly because I can't bring myself repeat his works back to him, knowing it might be the last time I say them to his face, if at all.

"You sure about this? You don't have to leave."

"I really do. And we both know it."

He puts his arm over my shoulder, and we walk back out into the room together. The band, now including Kieran, is standing gathered in a solemn group — no girlfriends, no groupies, no fans, no Billy. I get another grim smile from Rhys and a sympathetic one from Alex.

"Bridge is going to head home," Hunter tells everyone.

"No!" Rhys objects. "You just got here!"

"I was going home in the morning anyway, Rhys."

He nods solemnly.

"I just want you all to know that I love you dearly, and I think you've made an amazing new album and you're headed to the stratosphere after this."

"Is that a Brighid prediction?" Alex asks.

I nod. "Trust me."

Alex walks up and, in an uncharacteristic physical expression, hugs me.

"It'll be OK. You'll see," he whispers in my ear.

I nod. "Is that an Alex prediction?"

He nods sharply back.

"I'll call you a car," Kieran says. "Slán, a Bhríd."

"Slán, a Chiarán," I reply, and he leaves the room.

Hunter pulls me into a hug, brushing my hair back from my forehead.

"Be good to Brighid — you hear me?" he admonishes me. "She's my best friend and she deserves the best. Treat her that way."

"And you make sure Mama Alex is taking care of you when you can't do it for yourself," I reply with a chuckle.

"I will," Alex swears.

Hunter and I look each other in the eyes, and there's so much there this time, even more than usual. So much behind us and in us... it's overwhelming. But it's also home.

And now it's time for me to head back to my other home. Kier gestures from the doorway, and Hunter follows me out, his hand on my back.

He silently ushers me into the waiting car out front, one last kiss on my forehead. And I can't help myself. I throw my arms around his neck and kiss him gently on the cheek. Tears are welling in my eyes again as he steps back and closes the door. The car pulls away as I watch him stand there, looking miserable, the band arrayed out behind him. His band of brothers. They'll take care of him for me. I know they will. Kieran and Alex have both promised me they would.

And now it's time for me to take care of me. Maybe once I've learned how to do that, to put myself first, at least in some things, Hunter and I can find a peace with each other that we haven't fully had since the day I had that vision. It's been a rough path, but it's taken us both to some amazing places we probably never would have gotten to if I hadn't seen what I'd seen.

My visions have always shown me the past, not the future. I can still see where we've already walked, but with this earthquake having dramatically changed the landscape of our lives, I no longer have sight of a path laid out before me, before us. Today begins an adventure into uncharted territory, where we'll each have to forge our own path. Only time will tell where it takes us from here.

EPILOGUE

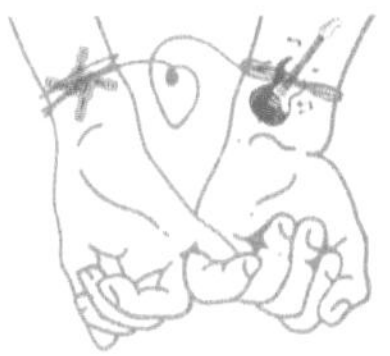

A couple weeks later

I'm staring at my phone. It's not ringing. I don't expect it to ring. But the fact that it's not ringing still bothers me. Even though it was my idea.

My first trip to New York City was a bust. Beyond a bust. It was an epic disaster worthy of a B-grade TV movie. It cemented everything I'd ever feared about how I would end up cast off once Hunter's career really took off. I wasn't thin or pretty, or talented at glamorous things like music or modeling. I don't even deal well with people half the time. OK — more than half the time. But out of loyalty and nostalgia, and maybe pity, too, Hunter had coddled me, let me hang around him and his band when I didn't have any business being there. Until that glamorous life became his whole world, and then there was no room left for me. The man I saw that night wasn't a Hunter I recognized. And the miserable creature he'd kicked the legs out from under wasn't a Brighid that I recognized or wanted to be.

So, I took a page out of his book from years ago and asked for space. And time — time to get myself to a place where I could stand on my own two feet. No more relying on Hunter for my social life. No more falling back on his support when things go awry. No more letting my world settle into an orbit where Hunter is the sun. I have a business to run, a house to bring a little further into the 21st century, a home to settle into, a beach to enjoy, a faith to practice, maybe a book or twelve to read. But no movies. I can't take the reminders of Hunter right now.

And that, of course, is why I'm staring at my phone. Because I can't allow myself to pick it up. If I do, it'll be dialing Hunter's number in a heartbeat. And I can't do that.

I never thought Hunter would be a habit I'd have to try to break. I knew the day was coming when he wouldn't be in my life much, if at all. I just never thought that I'd be the one who'd made that happen. But it was necessary. A line had to be drawn. A life — and our relationship — had to be reshaped, rebalanced and, maybe, someday, rebuilt. On a healthier, less codependent model. And if that's going to happen, I cannot call Hunter.

I leave the phone sitting on the coffee table, where it has the grace, in its inanimate way, to look a little guilty, though I'm not sure if it's feeling guilty because it's taunting me to call Hunter or because it's not already ringing with him on the other end of the line. But it can stay there, like a child in a time-out, because I'm not having anything to do with it right now, either way. So there. I stick my tongue out at it. Yes, literally.

I give a longing glance at my shoes by the back door. I'm going to want them, but I'm not going to need them where I'm going. Better I don't even take them. I bundle up in my oversized cardigan made of Irish wool, undyed, a classic creamy Aran color, spun by me and knitted by my own hand. (It's amazing how productive a knitter I can be when I'm trying to keep my hands from picking up my phone.) And I head out the door, down to the beach.

No one's down there. It's late afternoon two days before the winter solstice. It's cold, overcast and a little blustery, the wind sweeping the old year out the door and making way for a new one. I can't decide whether that's a symbolic plus or a terrifying thematic overlay to my current life dilemma.

I need answers. I've found them on the beach before. I've found certainty there, even when I didn't like the things it made me certain of. And I need that now. I need some sense of resolution when my soul is crying out for things it can't have and maybe shouldn't even want.

My bare feet ache as soon as they hit the sand, the cold biting into them, straight to the bone. It's a momentary distraction from the ache in my heart. And I sit my butt straight down on the sand, watching the winter sea churning lightly a dozen yards away. The wind kicks up, and I close my eyes against it, tuning my senses to the sounds of the water.

As much as I've always been a beach girl, Herself isn't a sea goddess. But still She comes to me sometimes when I sit here, usually when I'm most in need of Her. And today I sit here, waiting, hoping for anything — a sign, an omen, silent guidance, a warm touch to let me know there's a way forward from this moment where my path seems so utterly blocked. And... nothing.

My eyes open again, the sea looking much the same as it did when I closed them. The rush of water in my ears. An empty beach. Half-frozen toes. I reach for the hood of my sweater and pull it forward to shield my cheeks from the wind. And then I see it — a massive flock of gulls. Herring gulls. In summer, they'd be menacing tourists and stealing fries, whether plain, doused in vinegar or sprinkled with Old Bay. In winter... they land ten feet in front of me and start scouting for any unsuspecting creature, or remnants of one, left on the sand as the tide creeps back out.

Hardly the omen I was hoping for. A ubiquitous bird, scavenging for whatever sustenance they can find. Making do until a more bounteous time. One they can't ever know for certain is coming, being dependent on wind and tide. It's the nature of their life, untethered, unsure. I sympathize, especially these days. I've finally found a spot to call home, and the one anchor I've had for the last twenty years proves to be something — someone — I can't fully rely upon.

And it seems the gulls can't rely on the sea to provide right now either. They're gone in a flash. No — correction. All but one. She's still at it, searching, determined. And... there. She's found something, downs it whole. If a bird could smile... She can't, but she calls out, triumphant, and then takes flight. Amazing how the other birds in her flock had to fly off somewhere else before she found what she needed...

If Herself was human, She'd smack me on the back of the head. As it stands, there's a solid grasp on my shoulder that as good as says, "Wake up, kiddo — there's your answer."

I told Hunter I needed time on my own. I told myself I needed to find a way to stand on my own two feet, without him. I knew that. I know that. I may not want to listen to that advice, but I've not only already said it — I've now been reminded of the value of it, of letting go and standing alone.

I ignore the phone when I get back inside, warming my toes in front of the fireplace, plugging in the lights on the tree that sits in the bay window of the front porch. It's the first time I've let myself do it since I got back. Symbolic — the return of the light, the evergreen's promise of life continuing through a harsh winter. I settle in on the sofa, perusing the patterns in the new crochet book that came in yesterday. I take a deep breath and let it out in a sigh, the tension that had gripped my heart slowly loosening.

And the phone rings.

I lay down the book and peer over at it.

Hunter.

It rings again. And once more.

I can do this. I have to do this.

I pick it up and answer the call.

But darned if I can think of anything to say. Even "Hello" seems like too much of a challenge.

"Bridge?"

I inhale and exhale.

That voice I so love to hear... It would be so easy to just let it go. To just pretend that day never happened. But then were would I be? Where would we be? Exactly where we were a few weeks ago, or a few years ago. And that's not a place I can go back to. Not until things change.

"Hunter."

"Bridge! Thank god. I was starting to wonder if you were still speaking to me. I know you asked for some time, some space, but... Listen — I know I messed up. Really, really messed up. I'm owning that. And I'm sorry. I got caught up in everything that's been going on here, and I just wasn't thinking. I owed you way better than that, and... I'm sorry. I'm indescribably sorry. I want to make it up to you, but you said you wanted space, and I kind of thought maybe you'd have called by now, but you haven't called, and I was starting to worry you weren't ever going to. And I... I can't lose you, Bridge. Maybe I deserve to. Maybe this was the last straw for you. But I need to fix this. Somehow. I can't have all of this great stuff happening for me and then lose you.

I'll blow off the promotional appearances. I can be down there tomorrow. We can have Yule together. ... Bridge? Brighid?"

I take a deep breath and let it out.

"I'm here, Hunter."

"I'll get on the next plane out to Ocean City."

"No."

"No?"

"No. I know you haven't heard that word from me very often, but... No."

"No, I shouldn't get on the next plane out?"

"Yes — no, you shouldn't get on the next plane out. No, you shouldn't come down here. No, you can't come for Yule. And no, you can't fix this. Not like this. Not now."

My voice is steady, but I can feel the tears coming on. I have to do this. I know I have to do this. I just have to.

"Bridge... Please. I'm so sorry. I need to fix this. Tell me what to do. Tell me what I can do to fix things between us."

"Grow up."

"What?"

"Grow up, Hunter. That's what you can do. It's what I've had to do. I have a house, a mortgage, a business and a responsibility to the people around me, including you. And myself. And my responsibility to you, and to me, means, right now, that I have to tell you to grow up. And to stay away. Don't come here. Don't call me. Don't text me. Don't email me. Focus on your career, and on what you want in your life, who you want to be. If that's the asshole rockstar I saw in New York, then go do that, but don't expect to be welcome here or anywhere in my life. And if that person you decide you want to be... if he's my best friend — one who can truly act like my friend — then maybe, someday, I'll be ready for you to come back. But that day's not today, and I can't honestly tell you when that day will be."

"Bridge... Please don't do this."

"I have to, Hunter. For both of our sakes. If you come back now, if I let myself just forgive you like this was just another stupid mistake, I'd be doing a disservice to both of us. This had to happen, Hunt. It was meant to happen. Because you have needed to wake up for so very long, and I have needed to realize that I can't have a healthy relationship with you — a healthy friendship with you — until I know down to my bones that I can live my life without you in it and still be content. Don't think for a moment this isn't killing me. Because it is. And that's exactly why I have to do it. For both of us. I want us to be more than just the rockstar and his shadow. I need us on equal footing in our relationship, or at least a lot more equal.

"I'm not going to pretend that we can get there overnight. And I'm not going to pretend that just wanting it to be so will make it that way. So, yeah — I have to do this. I have to stand on my own two feet. And you've got to grow up, wake up, and realize you owe me better. You owe both of us better. I wouldn't be your best friend if I didn't tell you that. I've let it go for too long, for both of us. I can't stay this doormat I've become. And you've got to learn to get out of your own way, stop punishing yourself for things that happened when you were just a kid and be the person I know you really are inside. That's the guy I'll welcome back in my home. And in my heart. Find him, Hunt. For both our sakes."

And I hang up the phone. And I block Hunter's number.

To be continued in "Dream Weaver"...

FROM THE AUTHOR

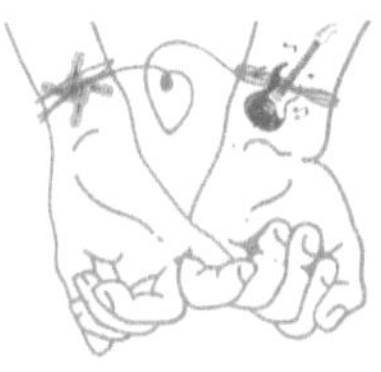

Thank you so much for reading "Once Upon a Dream"! I'm so excited to have you join us in Mystic Beach, and I can't wait to tell you the rest of Hunter and Brighid's story, and introduce you to the other members of aMUSEd one-on-one, as well as some really awesome women and other friends you'll be meeting soon.

Please consider taking a few moments to leave a rating and/or a short review on Amazon and/or Goodreads. Even a few words can help tremendously. Authors (especially independent authors) rely on reviews to sell books, and they're doubly important for a new author. Good reviews mean more readers, which means I can feed the voracious teenage boy who occasionally emerges from his bedroom to eat us out of house and home, and that I can provide sustenance for all the plot-bunnies in my head that are busy creating new novels in this series and at least one other. (Note: I am knee-deep in plot-bunnies. Send help. Preferably a professional editor.) Thank you once again for reading. I hope to see you in Mystic Beach again very soon!

Aislinn

Dream Weaver
July 14, 2022

It's time for some beachside R&R&R&R — rest, relaxation, recording and romance!

Hunter is back in his coastal hometown after years on the road with his band, aMUSEd. The band will be working on their fourth album, while Hunter also gets some quality time with his lifelong friend Brighid. It's a perfect working vacation. Until his label throws another R at him — a reality dating show!

Brighid has loved Hunter since the day they met, at age 6. She's been *in love* with him nearly that long. But her unrequited feelings and visions of a past life together have made things complicated. So why not add four girlfriends, TV cameras and social media to the mix?

Can even the intervention of a goddess keep these two "just friends" besties from being torn apart forever?

Down to the Sea
June 17, 2022

Are you wondering what actually happened between Brighid and Aedan Mason? "Down to the Sea" reveals the secret story of Brighid's brush with a rock superstar before Hunter had even made his first album. (Warning: Ireland is cool, but Mace is hot. Pack for summer heat! — and if you want to remain blissfully in the dark, skip this one. You won't miss a bit of the Mystic Beach arc for aMUSEd. Just pick up with the next in the series, "Dream Weaver." Or, read "Dream Weaver" first and then come back for the secrets!)

What's Next

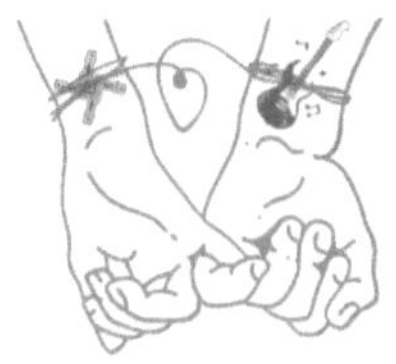

W hat's next? Well, a lot more romance, plenty of laughs, a few tears, a bunch of secrets, a vacation in Ireland and another at the beach, plentiful music and magic... *so* much more magic! "Once Upon a Dream," the kickoff novel for the series, is just the tip of the iceberg on the fantasy element of the series, so if you're hungry for more magic and myth, get ready for some real fun ahead! (And if you're wanting more "divine inspiration," you'll get that, too!)

Originally set to be next up in this series was the official series kickoff, "Dream Weaver," the first of the series set in the present day and entirely in Mystic Beach. But the series train (or is a boat?) got a little hijacked by everyone's favorite Sexiest Guy on the Planet and Telltale Signs frontman, Mace Mason, who demanded a novella that he then revealed was actually a full novel.

Thus "Down to the Sea" was born. It's officially Book 1.5 in the series, since it's an interstitial that takes place between "Once Upon a Dream" and "Dream Weaver." It tells the story known by only two of the characters in "Once Upon a Dream" and "Dream Weaver." The story is told from Brighid's point-of-view and reveals things Hunter, and the reader, were kept in the dark about during the course of events in "Once Upon a Dream" and "Dream Weaver."

"Down to the Sea" can be read before or after "Dream Weaver," but should be read *after* "Once Upon a Dream." Or you can opt out entirely — you won't miss any of the main story arc for Brighid and Hunter or aMUSEd. "Down to the Sea" should not be read as a standalone and should be avoided by anyone not wanting spoilers for "Once," as well as those who'd prefer to remain in the dark about what actually happened "off-the-page."

"Dream Weaver" continues where Brighid and Hunter's story leaves off in "Once," as we arrive in the present day and see how these two best friends have dealt with the impacts of a musical career on a trajectory to the stars, as well as their divergent takes on visions, fate, love, sex and friendship. Just to make things even more challenging, aMUSEd's label has decided to throw a reality dating series in Hunter's path, and since reality TV is an agent of chaos, it could unravel everything.

After Hunter and Brighid's story wraps up (for now) in "Dream Weaver," we'll get to know quiet, intellectual aMUSEd bassist David Carter in a way no one ever has before, when he stumbles onto a secret that defies belief, let alone his understanding of science. Lives depend on how he handles what he discovers, and we'll see whether it's his legendary levelheaded response that wins out or the kind of passion that he usually reserves for his music.

His brother, and aMUSEd's resident diva, Declan, will take center stage after that, with a story that'll make you reconsider first impressions and assumptions made. That will be followed by an otherworldly Rhys Madigan drum break, and a mysterious Irishman's guitar solo that just might turn into a thrilling duet. Last (for now) will be our band-mom Alex's story, where we'll finally find out why our keyboard virtuoso is such a secondhand romantic and whether a shot at firsthand romance is finally in the cards for him.

If you're ready to continue the journey with aMUSEd, your next stops are "Down to the Sea" (June 2022) and/or "Dream Weaver" (July 2022). (And if you want to dip back into the past, sign up for my newsletter, the Mystic Beacon, and you'll be able to download the series prequel novella, "Good Golly Miss Molly," Molly and Logan's story, and the pre-prequel short story "Here Comes the Sun," which tells the story of that day Brighid and Hunter first met, at age 6.) Thanks so much for reading, and welcome aboard! I'm looking forward to having you along for this amazing ride!

The aMUSEd Series Roadmap

• Here Comes the Sun (Mystic Beach Fantasy Rockstar Romance series No. 0.25) — Brighid & Hunter, sweet pre-romance pre-prequel short story (newsletter subscriber exclusive, February 2022)

• Good Golly Miss Molly (Mystic Beach Fantasy Rockstar Romance series No. 0.50) — Molly & Logan, steamy series prequel novella (newsletter subscriber exclusive, March 2022)

• Once Upon a Dream (Mystic Beach Fantasy Rockstar Romance series No. 1) — Brighid & Hunter, series opening act and part one of the Brighid & Hunter duo (May 13, 2022)

• Down to the Sea (Mystic Beach Fantasy Rockstar Romance series No. 1.5) — Brighid point-of-view interstitial novel (June 17, 2022) (spoiler warning for "Once" and those preferring to remain in the dark about some secrets)

• Dream Weaver (Mystic Beach Fantasy Rockstar Romance series No. 2) — Brighid & Hunter, part two of the Brighid & Hunter duo (July 14, 2022)

• Smoke on the Water (Mystic Beach Fantasy Rockstar Romance series No. 3) — David (summer/fall 2022)

• Remind Me (Mystic Beach Fantasy Rockstar Romance series No. 4) — Declan

• Mad World (Mystic Beach Fantasy Rockstar Romance series No. 5) — Rhys

• Drawn to the Rhythm (Mystic Beach Fantasy Rockstar Romance series No. 6) — Kieran

• Carry Fire (Mystic Beach Fantasy Rockstar Romance series No. 7) — Alex

And much more to come...

PLAYLIST

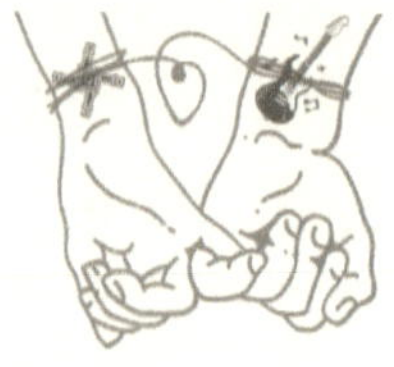

Many books these days have their own playlists, especially rockstar romances, because what is a book about amazing musicians without amazing music to go with it?

You'll find this playlist informed by my own... eclectic ... tastes in music. There's only a couple genres I don't listen to, and everything else runs the gamut from classic rock to world music to metal to folk and beyond. And maybe you'll even discover a new favorite in here amongst the many 1980s "new classics." I've even included an original instrumental, "Changes," from Al Cook, who was a big part of the inspiration for Hunter.

An important note: When I set out to make a playlist for this book, I had two separate lists to pull from: (1) the song-title-based chapter titles that I'd decided on a whim to try to use, which I was selecting to at least nominally match the content and, ideally, the feel of each chapter; and (2) songs for reading (or writing) the book.

But a strange thing happened when I started pulling songs to fit those criteria — songs I hadn't even known existed turned out to, nearly perfectly, fit the chapter with those tentative chapter titles; and songs I pulled for listening, or to give me a mental musical image/feel of a performance or songwriting scene, they just magically (spookily at times) fit perfectly thematically or lyrically with the chapter I was writing.

There's a lot of synchronicity (seemingly related things happening by actual inexplicable coincidence) in this book, to the point where it is openly declared that there is no coincidence, only fate. But in the writing of the book there has been exactly that — coincidence that defies the odds of being explainable. An inexplicable amount of it.

So, while not every song on this playlist fits perfectly with the chapter that bears its title (and some chapter titles aren't songs at all), in listening to the playlist and in reading the book, know that much of what you're reading, and hearing, came straight out of the ethers, as if it was being handed to me by a muse... or perhaps by a goddess of poets and the creative spark — the "fire in the head."

"Once Upon a Dream" Playlist

Once Upon a Dream — from Walt Disney's "Sleeping Beauty"
Father Figure — Tori Amos (cover), or Father Figure — George Michael
Motherlode — King Swamp
Break On Through — The Doors
Waiting For A Star to Fall — Boy Meets Girl
Here Comes the Sun — The Beatles
Into The Fire — Sarah Mclachlan
In For A Penny — Slade
Home Is Where the Heart Is — Lynyrd Skynyrd
Heart-Shaped Box — Nirvana (credit to Dan Debuque, whose amazing solo slide-guitar cover of the grunge classic inspired Hunter's take)
Mama, I'm Coming Home — Ozzy Osbourne
Home Sweet Home — Mötley Crüe
Changes — Al Cook (hear it at https://soundcloud.com/amcook1971/changes)
Little Lies — Fleetwood Mac
Cliffs of Dover — Eric Johnson
Mad World — Tears for Fears
Spoonman — Soundgarden
We Will Rock You — Queen
Oran Sniomh (Spinning Song) — Mary Jane Lamond
Mothers Talk — Tears for Fears

Breathe (2 AM) — Anna Nalick
Hundreds Of Tears — Sheryl Crow
Fell On Black Days — Soundgarden
Spinning — Benjamin Orr
Cherry Pie — Warrant
Fame — Duran Duran (my favorite cover of the David Bowie original, done by Class of 2022 Rock & Roll Hall of Fame inductees Duran Duran, otherwise known as "The Fab Five")
The Muse — The Wood Brothers
Witchy Woman — The Eagles
The Cantina Band — John Williams, Star Wars Trilogy
My Girl — The Temptations
Go Insane (Live, 1997) — Fleetwood Mac (Lindsey Buckingham)
Óró (feat. Darkin) — Seo Linn
Moves Like Jagger — Maroon 5
I'll Be Waiting — Michael Franti & Spearhead
All Star — Smash Mouth
Auld Lang Syne — Red Hot Chilli Pipers (read that name twice)
Ramble On — The String Cheese Incident
Gimme Shelter — The Rolling Stones
Crash Into Me — Dave Matthews Band
You Spin Me Round (Like a Record) — Dead or Alive
A Hard Day's Night — The Beatles
Second Hand News — Fleetwood Mac
Once Bitten Twice Shy — Great White
Three Times a Lady — The Commodores
Early Warning — Baby Animals
Give Me All Your Lovin' — ZZ Top
Fire In the Head — The Tea Party (Note: I did not know this song existed until after I named the chapter. The common thread is "The Song of Wandering Aengus" by William Butler Yeats.) or Fire in the Head by Sharon Knight (a more on-theme acoustic song from Celtic folk artist Sharon Knight, whose work is well-known in among Pagans worldwide)
Love's Light — Vertical Horizon (If this book has an overall theme song, it's probably this bittersweet gem.)
If I Ever Lose My Faith in You — Sting
Everybody Wants to Rule the World — Tears for Fears
We Are Family — Sister Sledge

The Battle Of Evermore — Heart, or The Battle Of Evermore — Jimmy Page & Robert Plant

For the Love of God — Steve Vai

Pushin Forward Back — Temple of the Dog

Already Gone — The Eagles

Hey, Lady Godiva — Dr. Hook & the Medicine Show

The Promise — Arcadia, or The Promise — When in Rome (You can pick your option here. Feeling optimistic? Go with When in Rome and the promise of a happily-ever-after. It's coming. I promise. More pessimistic? Wanting to feel Brighid's angst? The Duran Duran side-project Arcadia is a slice of wistful trepidation. Plus, it's got Sting, David Gilmour and Herbie Hancock.)

GLOSSARY & TRANSLATIONS

Author's note: I have had the Irish in my books reviewed by a fluent speaker, but if there are any errors, they are my own. I am only an advanced-beginner Irish speaker, which is why Brighid has that level of knowledge. If you'd like to learn Irish, check out Dublin City University's (DCU's) online classes via FutureLearn. Or, if you live in an area where in-person classes are offered, sign up and give it a try! (By the point when we get to spend some quality time with Kieran, you could understand what he's saying!)

Note: Irish uses a different word order than English. It's a verb-subject-object (VSO) language, as opposed to English's subject-verb-object (SVO) structure.

If you want to hear words pronounced, check out one of the definitive online Irish dictionaries, at Teanglann.ie.

Dia dhuit, a Chiaráin — Hello, Ciarán
    Gaeilge — the Irish word for the Irish language
    As Gaeilge — in Irish
    Gaeilgeoir — an Irish-language speaker

Gaelscoil — a school that teaches in the Irish language, predominately or exclusively. (Irish is compulsory in Irish schools, but many Irish people learn only enough to get by for school and then use it rarely if ever. There is considerable controversy about compulsory Irish language learning and whether it has helped or harmed the effort to restore the Irish language to its predominance in the country. One of the alternatives is the gaelscoil, which has been part of a national effort since the 1970s to help more Irish people once again become native, daily speakers of their own language. I'm throwing this in here now to provide some context for Kieran's Irish language skills and his delight that an American girl can speak even a little of it. We'll find out more about his Irish language background as we get to his story.)

Níl ach cúpla focal agam — literally, "I only have a few words," meaning the person only knows a little Irish (a few words or an early beginner)

Is giolla leis an Bhandia Bríd mé — I am a servant of the goddess Brighid

Comhghairdeas — Congratulations

Go raibh maith agat — Thank you

Agus beannachtaí ort féin agus ar do chuid ceoil. — And blessings on yourself and on your music

Go hiontach — wonderful

Maith thú, a Bhríd — Good for you, Brighid

Slán — Goodbye

Le do thoil — Please

Tabhair aire mhaith do mo chara — Take care of my friend

Tá mo chroí istigh ann — literally, "My heart is inside him," meaning "I'm madly in love with him."

Tuigim — I understand

A note on the many names of Herself: There are literally entire videos devoted to the many variations of the names for the goddess (and saint) Brighid. Some are regional or more common to a period of time, others used as they seem appropriate to whoever is using them. Except to differentiate between the saint (Naomh Bríd) and the goddess, they're largely interchangeable. In Irish, Brighid and Bríd are pronounced pretty much the same — that H aspirates the G, leaving the I the only sound in the middle of the word that is pronounced — like "Breed." Brigid, on the other hand, is an Anglicized form and is pronounced like most English speakers pronounce the name. But, as you may have noticed, Hunter calls our Brighid "Bridge" for short. Brighid didn't start learning Irish until after she started exploring the legends around Herself, so she uses the Anglicized pronunciation, and that's what Hunter and everyone else use thereafter. Now that she knows some Irish, she uses the Irish pronunciation when speaking Irish and the Anglicized version when speaking English.

A note on Herself herself: The veneration of Brighid, as both goddess and saint, is on the rise, both inside and outside of Ireland. As a recent New York Times article ("As Ireland's Church Retreats, the Cult of a Female Saint Thrives," March 11, 2022) notes, even while the influence of the Catholic Church has waned in Ireland, veneration of Brighid — as both goddess and saint — has only increased. That's affirmed by the 2022 addition of an official government holiday honoring Brighid, observed on or around Feb. 1 each year, on the saint's feast day, which was itself aligned with the older spring holiday of Imbolc, or Brighnassadh, as I prefer to call it. The Brighidine sisters in Kildare seem to have greeted this phenomenon with open arms, welcoming Christians and non-Christians alike. It has seemed to me to be a hallmark of Brighid's devotees that they generally accept each other very freely. She has a pragmatic reputation in both her forms, so this is not unexpected. You do what needs to get done, with the tools at hand. If you're curious, there are numerous groups and websites online that offer further insight into Brighid in both her forms.

ACKNOWLEDGMENTS

There are so many people to acknowledge for their impact on the creation of this book. First, despite the apparent resemblance to a number of real-life people, it is a work of fiction, and the situations and characters herein are fictional and any resemblance is purely coincidental. Yes, indeed.

That said, the biggest chunk of credit for this book goes to my best friend, Al, who was the inspiration for the best aspects of Hunter's personality, as well as aspects of several of the other characters in this series. A full-time professional musician and sound engineer himself, Al taught me enough a decade ago that I could work as a live sound engineer, and he believed in me in that respect almost as much as our Brighid believed in her Hunter. He even got me a job and insisted I get paid for it once I got good enough.

In this prequel (the official Book 1 of this series), what carries across most is Al's sense of humor, which has kept everyone who knows him cracking up, rolling their eyes and/or grinning from ear to ear so often that they haven't yet gotten around to throwing him so hard at the ceiling that he gets embedded in it. As tempting as that may sometimes be. Snippets of real-life have been pulled as inspiration for some of the elements of this story, though the outcomes are different, and the names have been changed and the credit dispersed to protect the guilty and confuse the innocent.

Al's wife — yes, ladies, (and you, too, fellas), he's taken — gets the credit for my incorporating into the book the real-life "string-cheese incident," in which the term "fabric-string" was coined. I took it to a whole other level as fiction. But the creative and accidentally hilarious brain-fart belongs to Al, who approved of me borrowing liberally from real life (he's married to a writer, so he knows how it works), and he gets the credit for the inspiration.

But please don't draw any conclusions about Al from the content of this book, or about Hunter from... well, Al... (Al actually stole my Eagles tour T-shirt, not my Fleetwood Mac shirt. He keeps promising to return it. Usually when it's soaked with sweat from load-in.) Hunter's had a much different life, and he's got a lot more challenges to deal with as a result. But give him time. He'll get himself sorted out and (eventually) get out of his own way.

I also have to acknowledge Al's real-life bandmates, the legendary Ocean City, Md., classic rock band Tranzfusion, heading toward 40 years of rocking peoples' socks off, and for which Al has been around for nearly a decade of that. My personal "guitar hero," Hank, offered some insight on his beloved PRS guitars that helped me properly equip Hunter (Al helped there, too), and there may be a few conversations and scenarios herein that were inspired by real-life interactions with the band members, their families and fans. All of whom are wonderful. I promise. Come out and see them sometime. Tell Al he's extra-famous now!

I want to again thank all my friends who supported me in adding professional fiction writer to my professional journalist identity. From serving as beta readers and editors to just plain encouraging me to keep at it — 12 years after an app glitch ate most of my notes for the first Aurora Carmichael/Mystic Beach novel — you made things a lot easier, and I appreciate it. That particularly includes IT and graphics guru extraordinaire Shaun Lambert, who wrangled into submission the cover image for the paperback edition of this book, as well as my spawn, who offered up his own graphics assistance. I also want to thank Audrey Nickel — among other things, author of "The Irish Gaelic Tattoo Handbook: Authentic Words and Phrases in the Celtic Language of Ireland" — for checking my Irish for me. She confirmed I know about as much Irish as I thought I did and fixed the bits I got wrong. If there's anything remaining that isn't correct, that's entirely on me. And thanks to my UF Masterminds writer's group, the members of which have been very tolerant of the fact that I delved in to the rockstar romance portion of my fantasy world of Mystic Beach before I got around to the mostly-fantasy part, and in some cases helped me stop second-guessing myself (mostly) on this project.

Last, but definitely not least, I have to thank my family, both by blood and otherwise, for getting me where I am today, that I could start writing about these characters with whom I've fallen totally in love.

Don't take some of my characters' dysfunctional relationships with their families as indicative of my own. All in all, I had a pretty normal childhood that gave me the leeway to do things I'm good at and enjoy, and I'm grateful for that. We lost my dad in early 2021 to COVID-19, and as I write this I'm still grappling with that loss and its impacts on me and my family. I know we are not alone, and I hope you all have someone to support you through your losses as beautifully as Hunter did in Brighid and vice-versa.

Hunter's mom's illness and her fate also hit close to home for me, as I have struggled with clinical depression for most of my life and know very well how challenging it can be just to get out of bed in the morning and make dinner at night. I haven't always managed it, though I've done the best I could at any given time. And I want to express my deepest love for those among "my people" who have had to help take up the slack or deal with the impact of that slack on their lives, and who have done so so gracefully and lovingly. None of us are perfect, but you make it a lot easier to keep trying.

And, finally, for anyone who's feeling like just one more thing going wrong, one more harsh word or slight, will be too much to bear, I ask you, please, to talk to someone — especially a professional. You have no idea how many people value your presence in this world nor how many of them would happily give you a hand to hold you above water until you can swim on your own again. Give them the chance to do that for you and give yourself the grace to let them.

As I write this, I'm reminded of how many times Chris Cornell's voice served as inspiration while I wrote this book (if you want to know what aMUSEd sounds like in my head, Temple of the Dog and Soundgarden are in the neighborhood), and I continue to lament that he's not still with us today, writing incredible music and letting us enjoy one of the greatest voices ever in rock.

As actor, author and geek extraordinaire Wil Wheaton has often noted, "Depression lies." No matter who you are, there's somebody who would desperately want you back if you were gone. Never think otherwise. Give people the chance to help. If you or someone you know is in an emergency, call the National Suicide Prevention Lifeline at 1-800-273-TALK (8255) or call 911 immediately. If you're uncomfortable talking on the phone, you can also text NAMI to 741-741 to be connected to a free, trained crisis counselor on the Crisis Text Line.

About the Author

Aislinn Archer

Aislinn Archer is an award-winning journalist, columnist and photographer, music and tech journalist, and editor, as well as a semi-retired live sound engineer.

She is in the process of writing two interconnected series spanning the urban fantasy and rockstar romance genres, set in her personal stomping grounds in Coastal Delaware. She is a member of Mensa and the Order of Bards, Ovates & Druids.

In her free time, Aislinn is an Irish language learner, persistent advanced-beginner guitar and bass guitar player, photographer, foodie, gadget guru, jewelrymaker and lampwork glass artist. She is a voracious reader of the urban fantasy, fantasy and rockstar romance genres, and dedicated music fan across many genres. Aislinn also loves visiting Disney World with her teenage son and her best friend, attending concerts and spending time on the beach.

For release updates, freebies, sneak peeks and inside details, sign up here and follow Aislinn Archer on social media, at https://www.facebook.com/AislinnArcher; on Twitter @AislinnArcher; and on Instagram and TikTok @aislinnarcher. Visit her website at AislinnArcher.com and MysticBeachRocks.com.